"*Hollow* charms with a lovable cast, witty humor, and beautiful artwork and colors. I'd be willing to go back to high school if it meant going on spooky adventures with Izzy, Vicky, and Croc."

—NATALIE NOURIGAT,
WRITER/DIRECTOR, DISNEY'S FAR FROM THE TREE

"A fun and magical play on a classic! *Hollow* has such a charming cast of characters who lead the reader into the story; an addictive, twisting mystery of a plot, with lovely art to boot!"

—SAS MILLEDGE, *MAMO*

"As Halloween should be, *Hollow* is a little bit spooky and an awful lot of fun. Izzy, Vicky, and Croc are perfect companions for a visit to a town where the bitter is always chased down with something sweet."

—JOHN ALLISON, *GIANT DAYS*

"*Hollow* combines queer teen angst and New England horror in one perfect package. It's hilarious and charming and it never pulls its punches."

—JOSH TRUJILLO,
THE UNITED STATES OF CAPTAIN AMERICA

"*Hollow* fills readers' hearts with characters to love in a world that brings delicious new twists to a classic legend. I dare you to not love this charmingly spooky book!"

—SINA GRACE, *ICEMAN, GHOSTED IN L.A.*

HOL

Written by
SHANNON WATTERS &
BRANDEN BOYER-WHITE

Illustrated by
BERENICE NELLE

LOW ™

Colored by
**KAITLYN MUSTO,
KIERAN QUIGLEY, GONÇALO LOPES**

Lettered by
JIM CAMPBELL

Cover illustrated by
NAOMI FRANQUIZ

Designer **MARIE KRUPINA**
Associate Editor **ALLYSON GRONOWITZ**
Editor **SOPHIE PHILIPS-ROBERTS**
Executive Editor **SIERRA HAHN**

Special thanks to Salt & Sage Books, and our other
readers, whose input strengthened our characters
and story immeasurably.

Pages 1-69 colored by **KAITLYN MUSTO**
Pages 70-117 colored by **KIERAN QUIGLEY**
Pages 118-168 colored by **GONÇALO LOPES**

BOOM! BOX

HOLLOW, September 2022. Published by BOOM! Box, a
division of Boom Entertainment, Inc. Hollow is ™ & © 2022
Shannon Watters & Branden Boyer-White. All rights reserved.
BOOM! Box™ and the BOOM! Box logo are trademarks of Boom
Entertainment, Inc., registered in various countries and categories. All characters, events, and
institutions depicted herein are fictional. Any similarity between any of the names, characters,
persons, events, and/or institutions in this publication to actual names, characters, and persons,
whether living or dead, events, and/or institutions is unintended and purely coincidental.
BOOM! Box does not read or accept unsolicited submissions of ideas, stories, or artwork.

BOOM! Studios, 5670 Wilshire Boulevard, Suite 400, Los Angeles, CA 90036-5679.
Printed in China. First Printing.

Hardcover Edition ISBN: 978-1-68415-851-5, eISBN: 978-1-64668-598-1
Softcover Edition ISBN: 978-1-68415-852-2, eISBN: 978-1-64668-599-8

To Branden's Gramma,
who has always encouraged her love of reading
and spooky stories.

To Shannon's Grandma,
who loved her comics. May she read and adore
this one from the other side of the veil.

To Berenice's family and friends,
for all of their encouragement and enthusiasm.

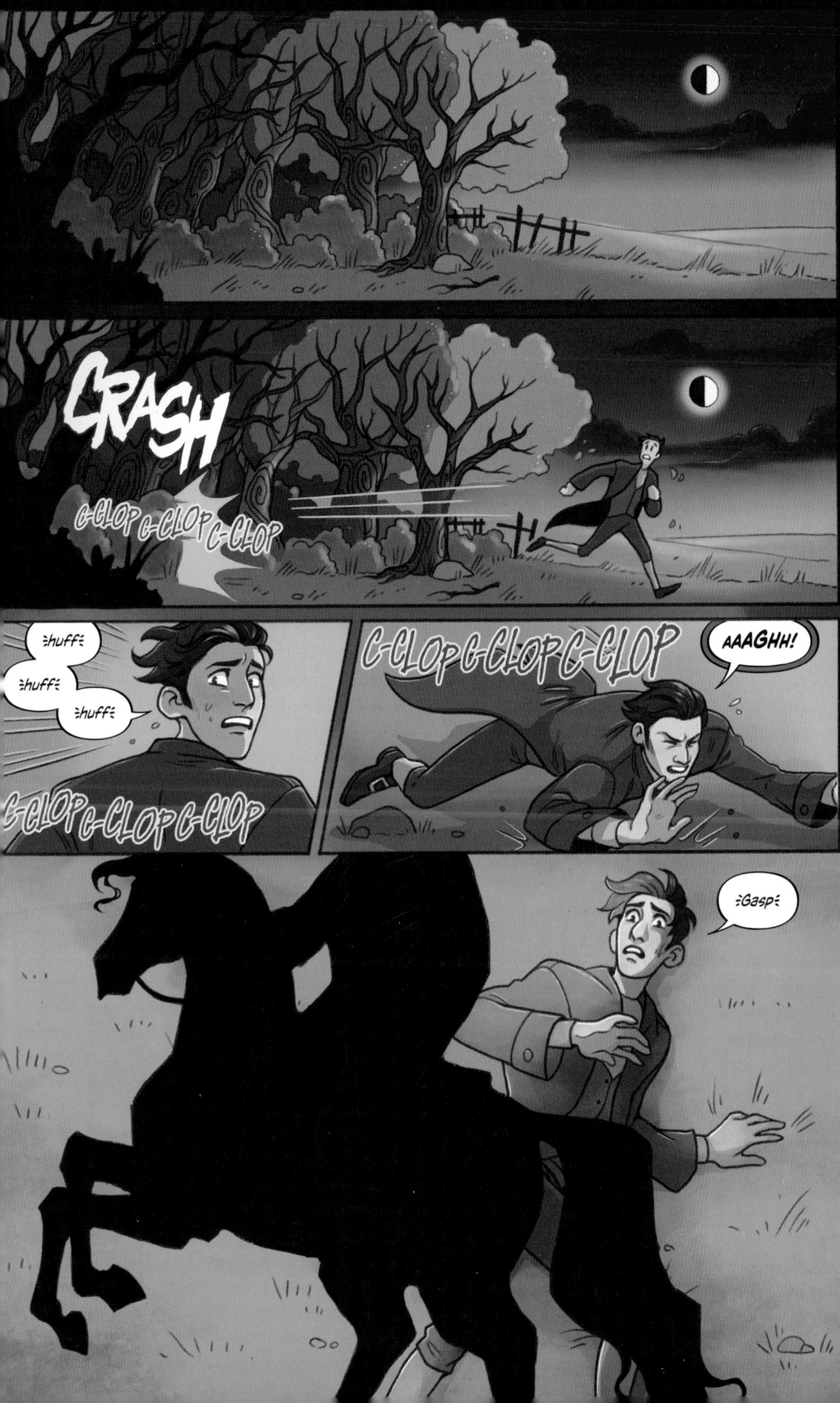
CRASH
C-CLOP C-CLOP C-CLOP
huff
huff
huff
C-CLOP C-CLOP C-CLOP
C-CLOP C-CLOP C-CLOP
AAAGHH!
Gasp

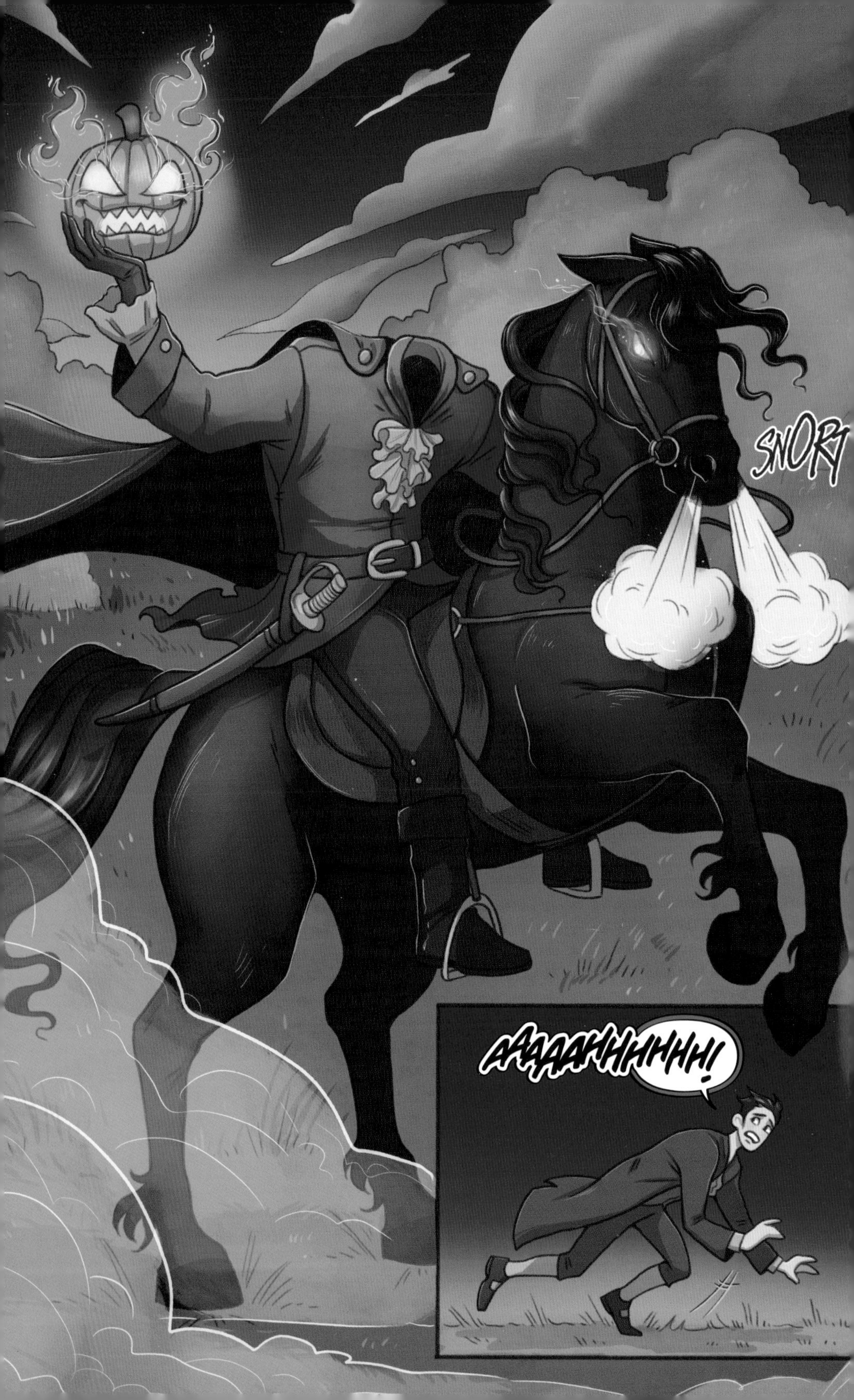
SNORT
AAAAAHHHHHH!

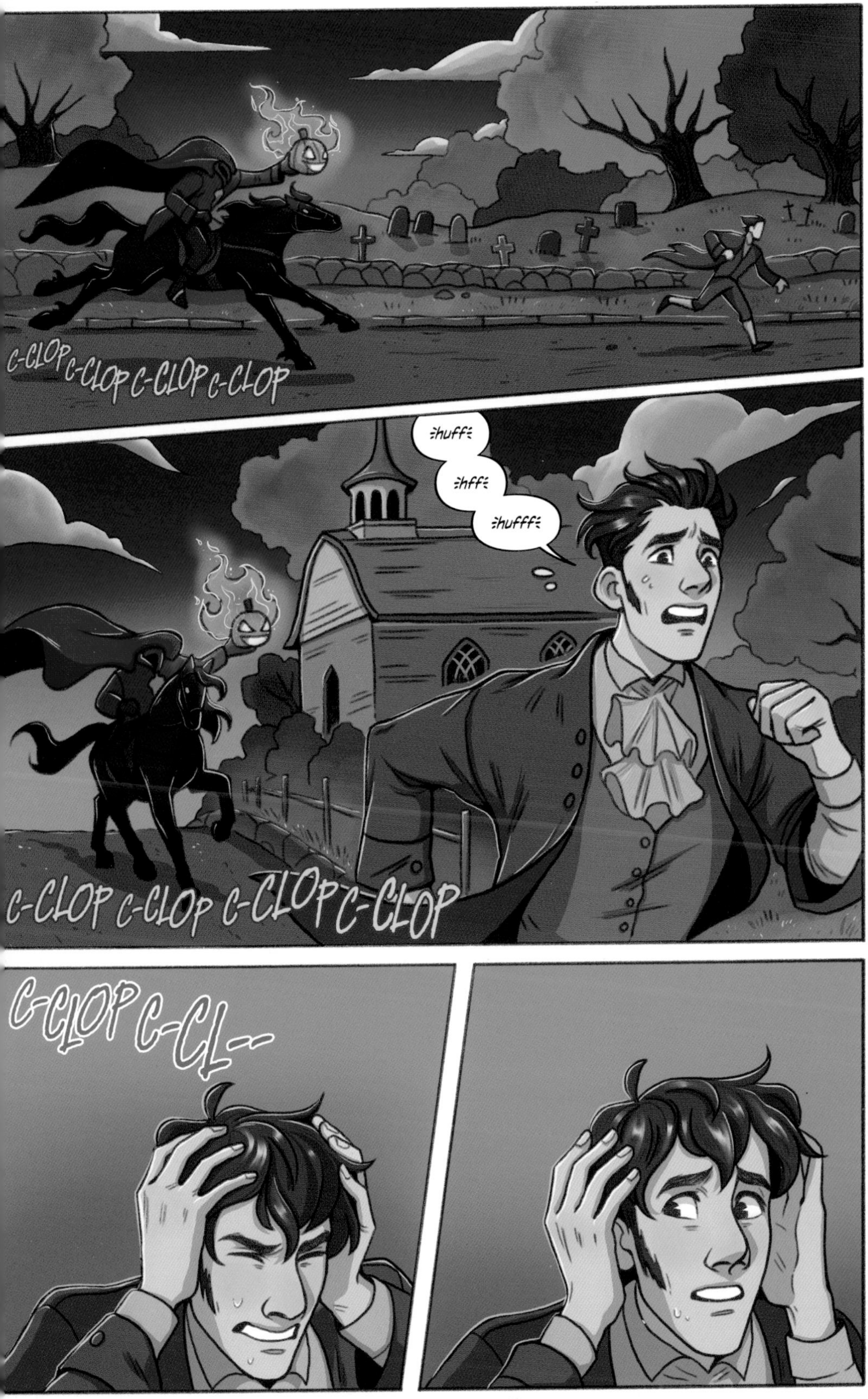
C-CLOP C-CLOP C-CLOP C-CLOP
huff
hff
hufff
C-CLOP C-CLOP C-CLOP C-CLOP
C-CLOP C-CL--

CRICKET CRICKET CRICKET

GAS

SNACKS | ATM

Babe, you will not **BELIEVE** what just happened to me...

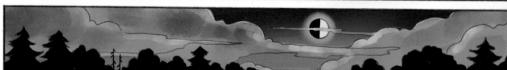

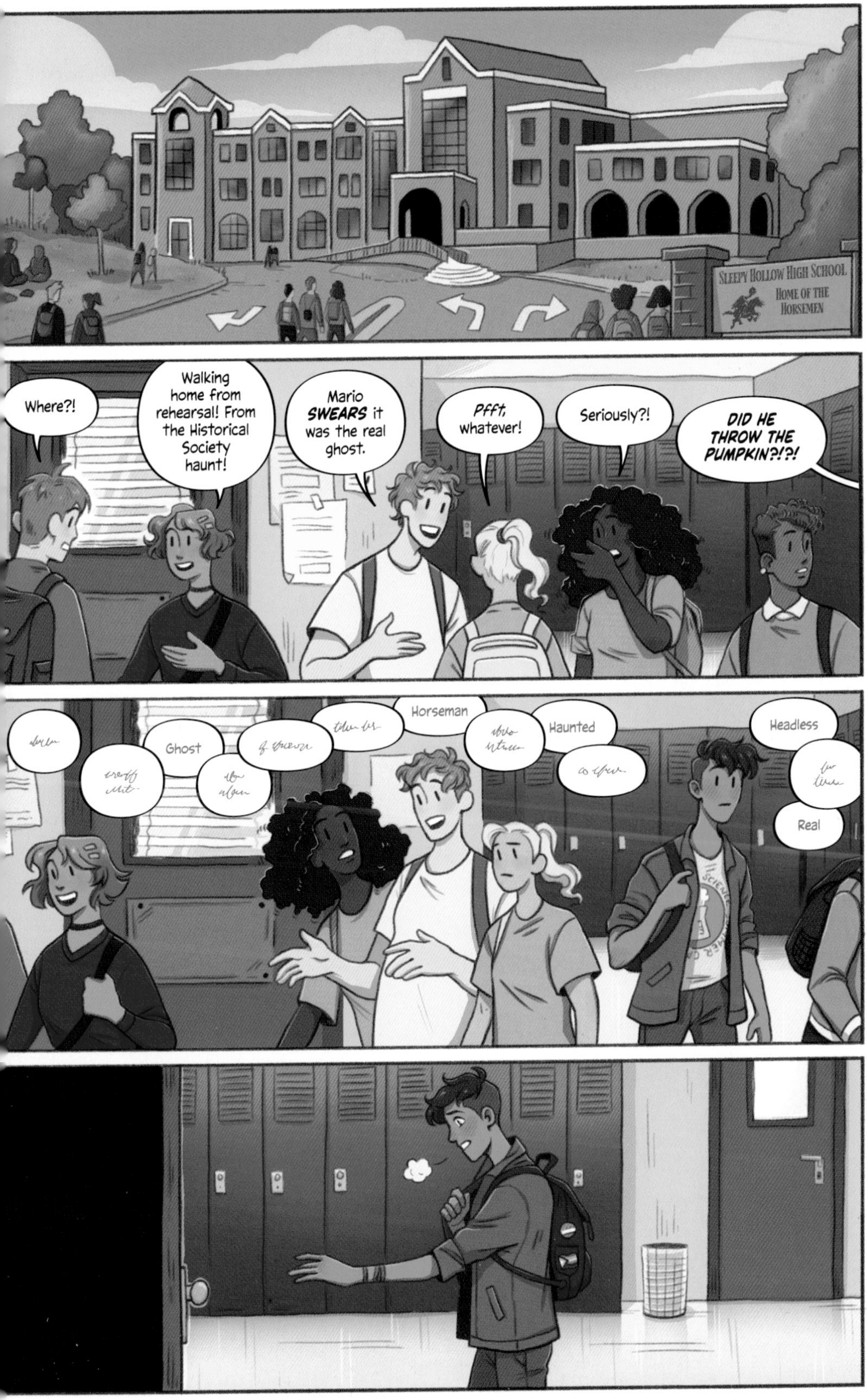
SLEEPY HOLLOW HIGH SCHOOL
HOME OF THE HORSEMEN
Where?!
Walking home from rehearsal! From the Historical Society haunt!
Mario **SWEARS** it was the real ghost.
Pfft, whatever!
Seriously?!
DID HE THROW THE PUMPKIN?!?!
Ghost
Horseman
Haunted
Headless
Real

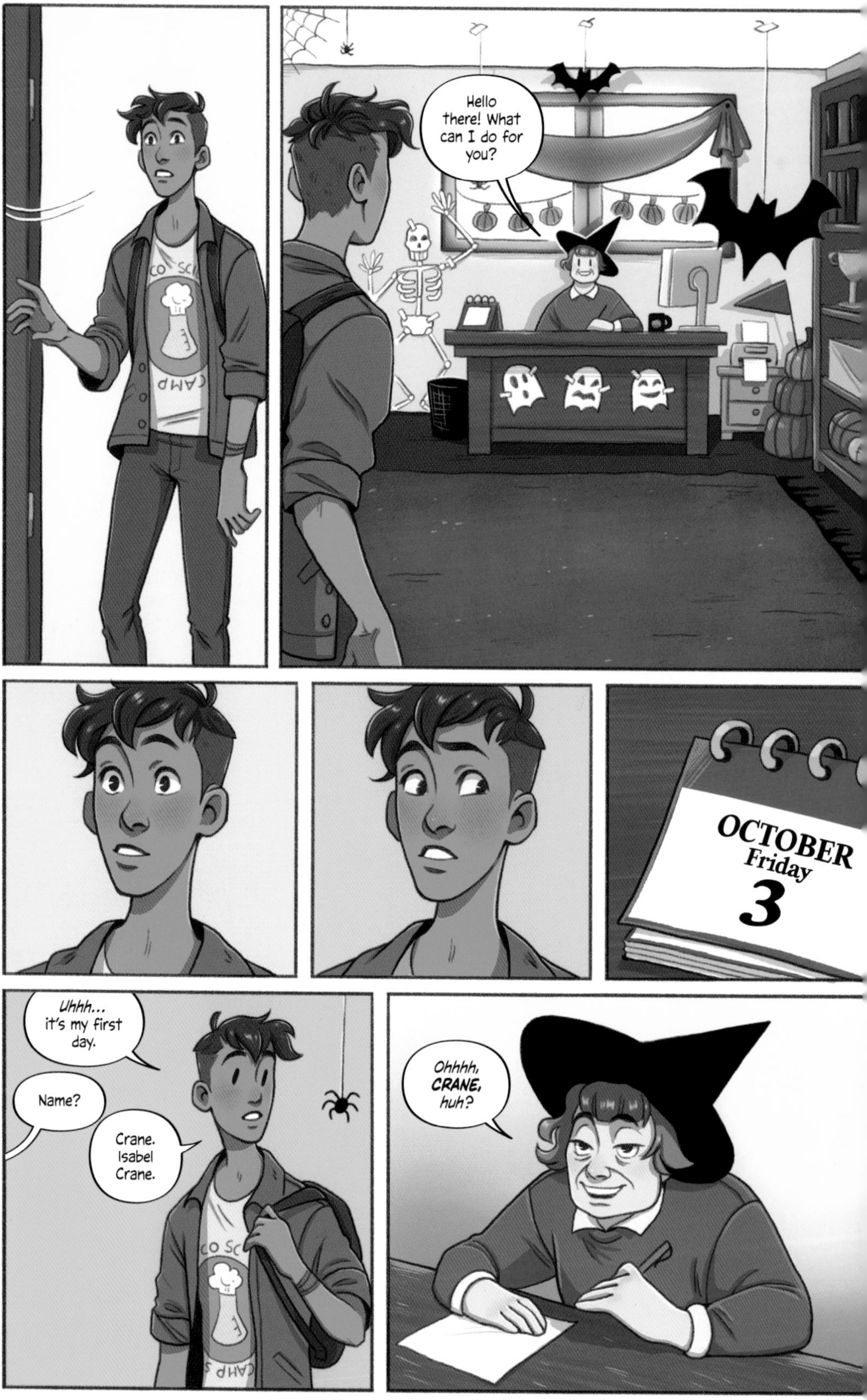
Hello there! What can I do for you?
CO SCI CAMP
OCTOBER
Friday
3
Uhhh... it's my first day.
Name?
Crane. Isabel Crane.
Ohhhh, CRANE, huh?

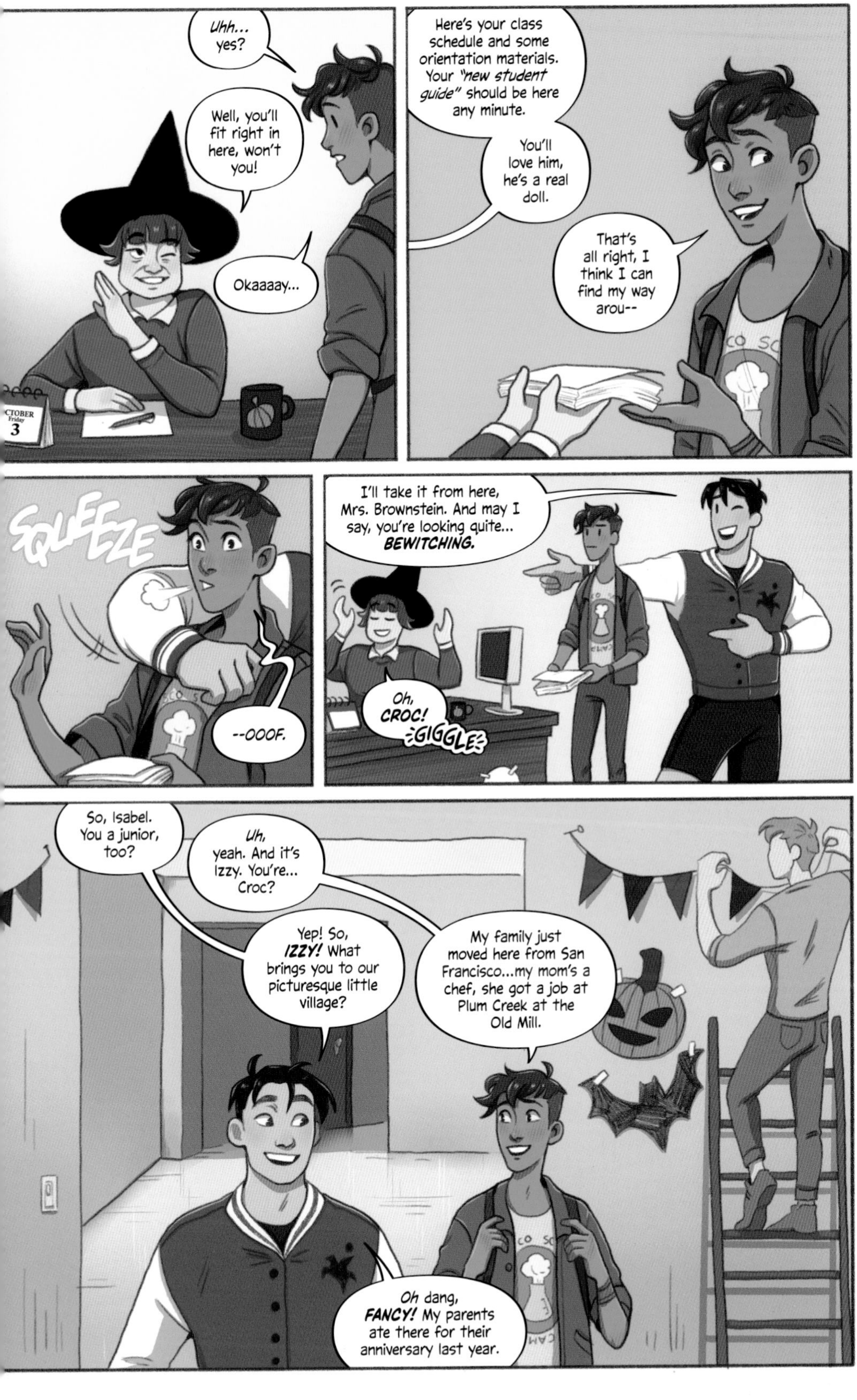
Uhh... yes?
Well, you'll fit right in here, won't you!
Okaaaay...
OCTOBER Friday 3
Here's your class schedule and some orientation materials. Your "new student guide" should be here any minute.
You'll love him, he's a real doll.
That's all right, I think I can find my way arou--
SQUEEZE
--OOOF.
I'll take it from here, Mrs. Brownstein. And may I say, you're looking quite... BEWITCHING.
Oh, CROC!
GIGGLE
So, Isabel. You a junior, too?
Uh, yeah. And it's Izzy. You're... Croc?
Yep! So, IZZY! What brings you to our picturesque little village?
My family just moved here from San Francisco...my mom's a chef, she got a job at Plum Creek at the Old Mill.
Oh dang, FANCY! My parents ate there for their anniversary last year.

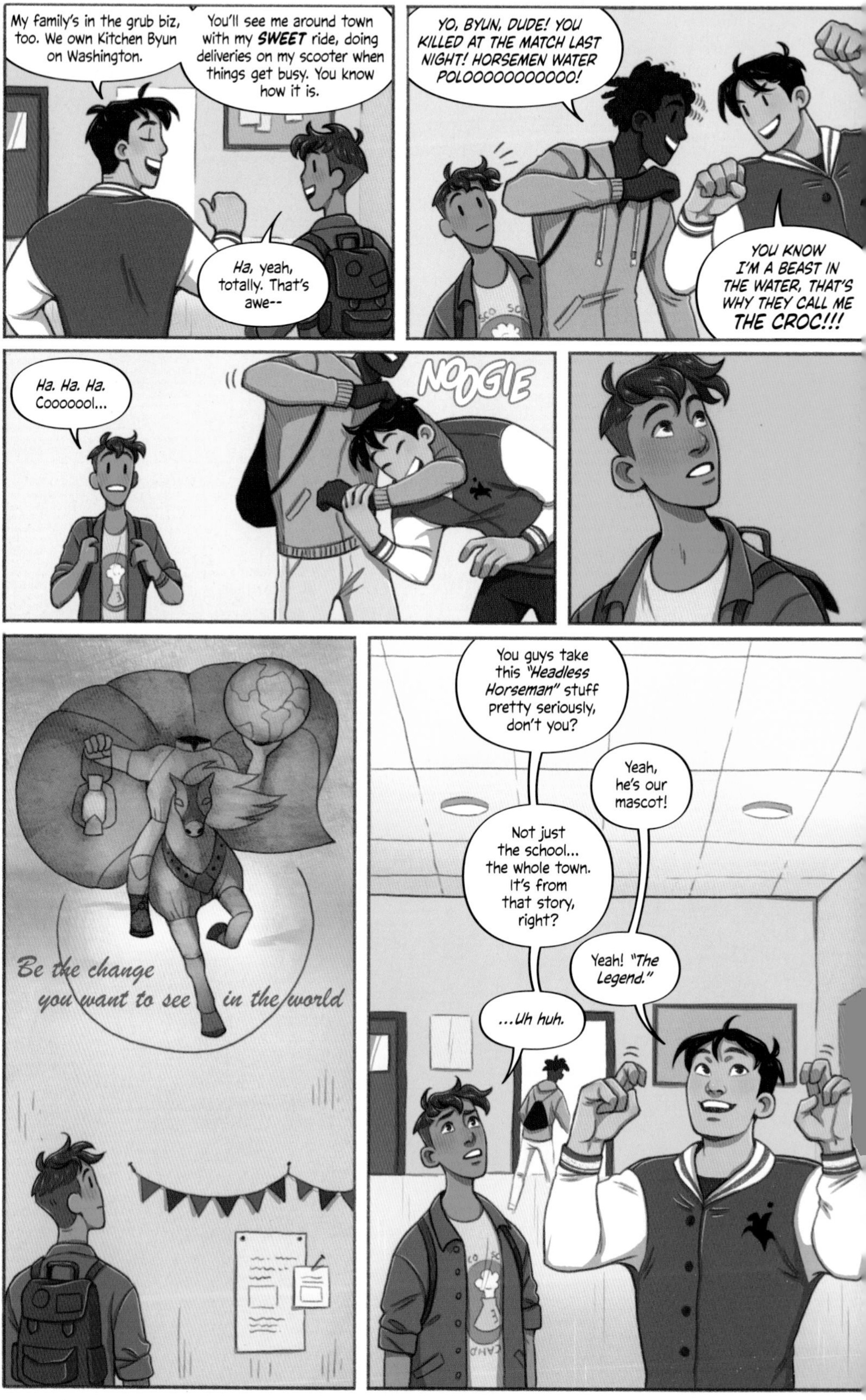
My family's in the grub biz, too. We own Kitchen Byun on Washington.
You'll see me around town with my **SWEET** ride, doing deliveries on my scooter when things get busy. You know how it is.
Ha, yeah, totally. That's awe--
YO, BYUN, DUDE! YOU KILLED AT THE MATCH LAST NIGHT! HORSEMEN WATER POLOOOOOOOOOOO!
YOU KNOW I'M A BEAST IN THE WATER, THAT'S WHY THEY CALL ME **THE CROC!!!**
Ha. Ha. Ha. Coooooool...
NOOGIE
Be the change you want to see in the world
You guys take this *"Headless Horseman"* stuff pretty seriously, don't you?
Yeah, he's our mascot!
Not just the school... the whole town. It's from that story, right?
Yeah! *"The Legend."*
...Uh huh.

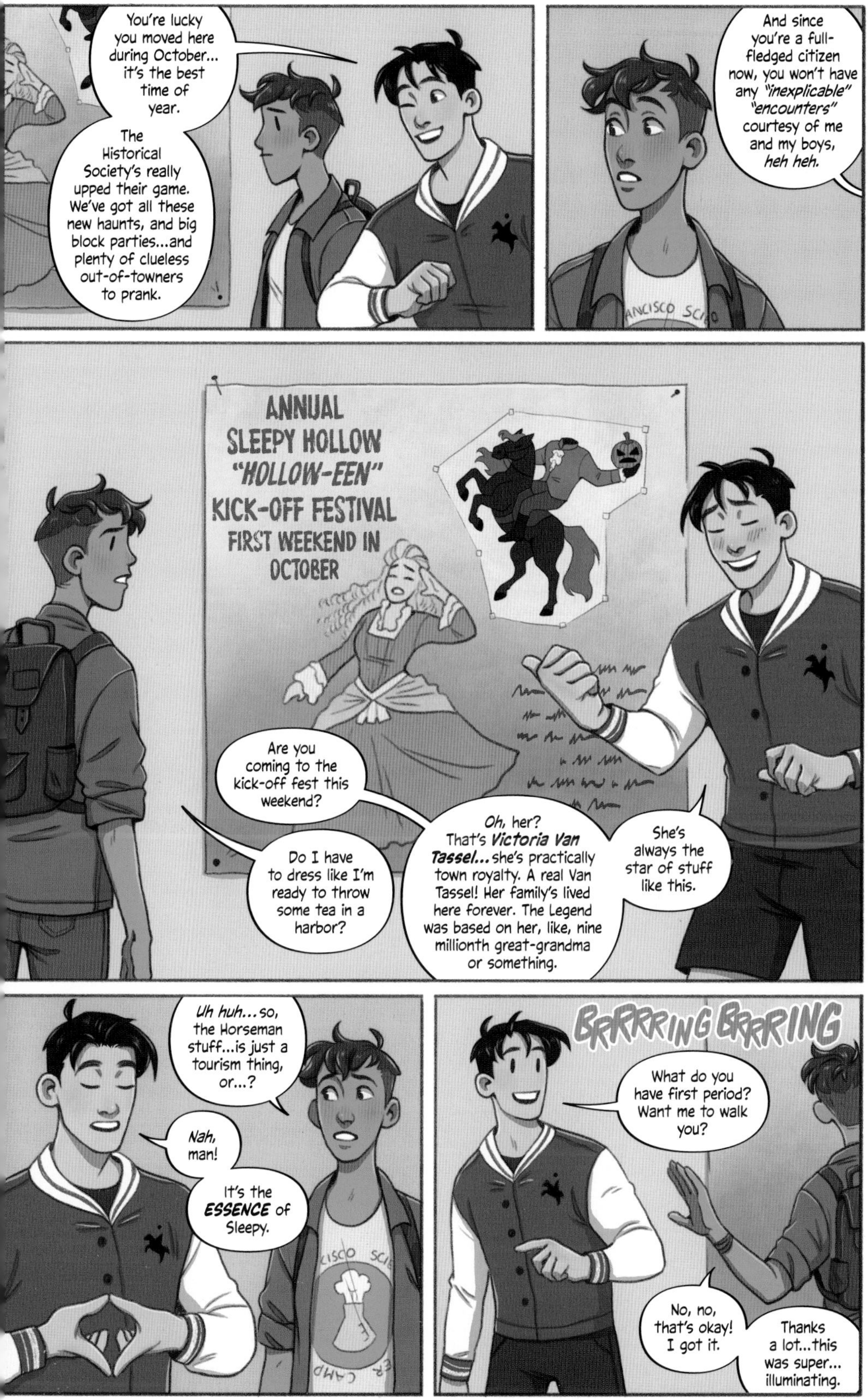
You're lucky you moved here during October... it's the best time of year.
The Historical Society's really upped their game. We've got all these new haunts, and big block parties...and plenty of clueless out-of-towners to prank.
And since you're a full-fledged citizen now, you won't have any *"inexplicable" "encounters"* courtesy of me and my boys, *heh heh.*
ANCISCO SCI
ANNUAL SLEEPY HOLLOW "HOLLOW-EEN" KICK-OFF FESTIVAL FIRST WEEKEND IN OCTOBER
Are you coming to the kick-off fest this weekend?
Do I have to dress like I'm ready to throw some tea in a harbor?
Oh, her? That's ***Victoria Van Tassel...*** she's practically town royalty. A real Van Tassel! Her family's lived here forever. The Legend was based on her, like, nine millionth great-grandma or something.
She's always the star of stuff like this.
Uh huh... so, the Horseman stuff...is just a tourism thing, or...?
Nah, man!
It's the ***ESSENCE*** of Sleepy.
BRRRRING BRRRING
What do you have first period? Want me to walk you?
No, no, that's okay! I got it.
Thanks a lot...this was super... illuminating.

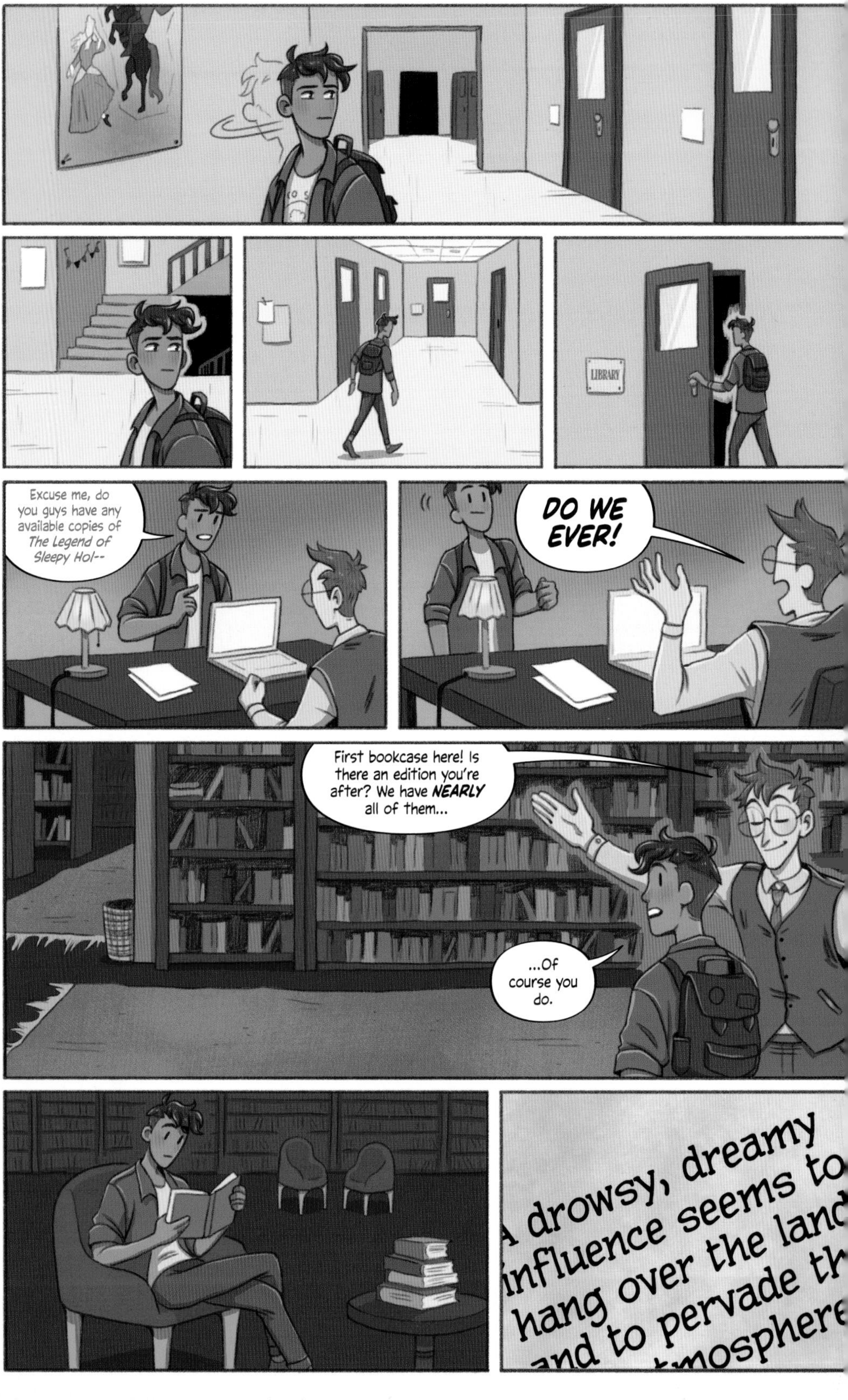
LIBRARY
Excuse me, do you guys have any available copies of The Legend of Sleepy Hol--
DO WE EVER!
First bookcase here! Is there an edition you're after? We have NEARLY all of them...
...Of course you do.
A drowsy, dreamy influence seems to hang over the land and to pervade th

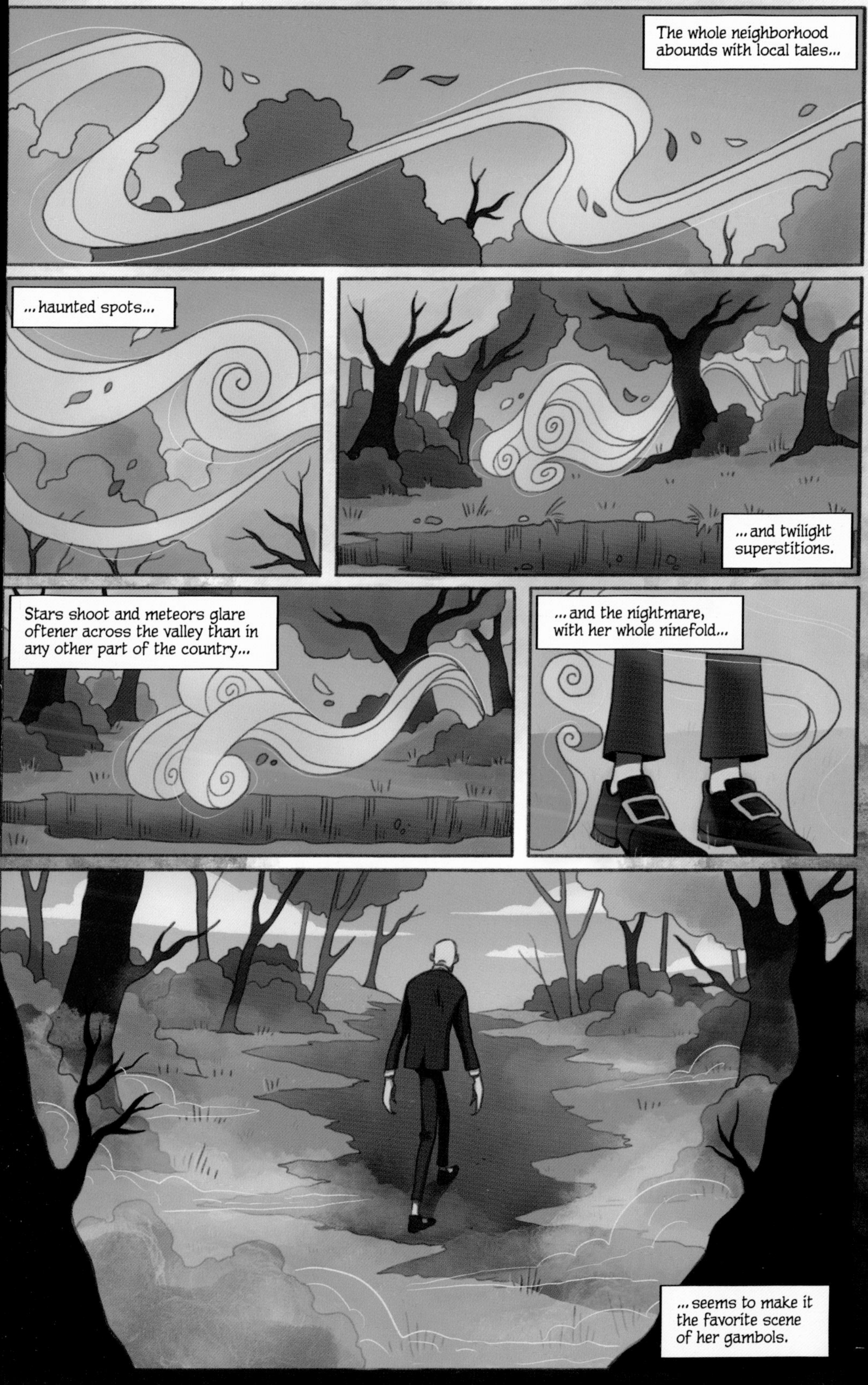

The whole neighborhood abounds with local tales...
...haunted spots...
...and twilight superstitions.
Stars shoot and meteors glare oftener across the valley than in any other part of the country...
...and the nightmare, with her whole ninefold...
...seems to make it the favorite scene of her gambols.

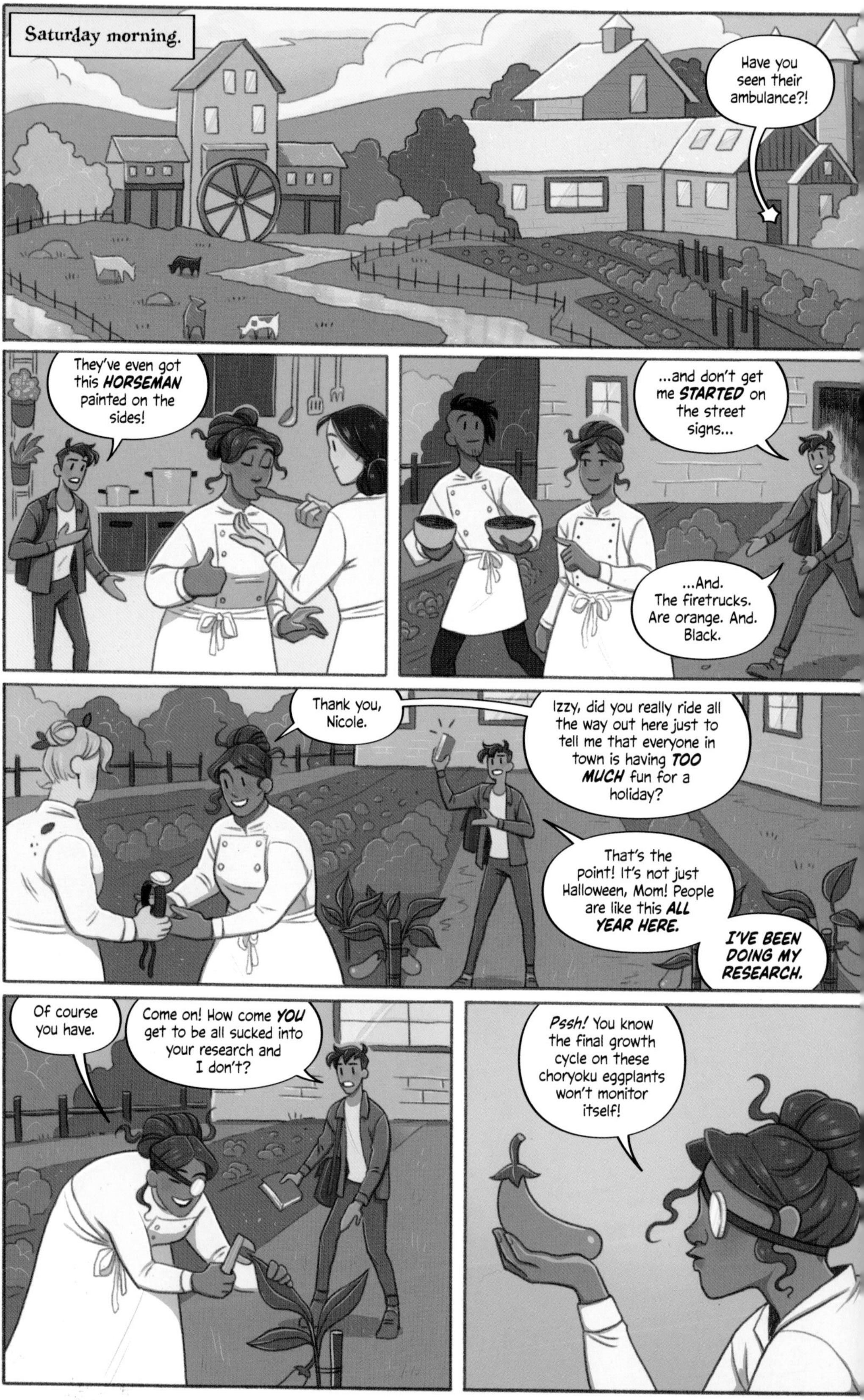

Saturday morning.
Have you seen their ambulance?!
They've even got this HORSEMAN painted on the sides!
...and don't get me STARTED on the street signs...
...And. The firetrucks. Are orange. And. Black.
Thank you, Nicole.
Izzy, did you really ride all the way out here just to tell me that everyone in town is having TOO MUCH fun for a holiday?
That's the point! It's not just Halloween, Mom! People are like this ALL YEAR HERE.
I'VE BEEN DOING MY RESEARCH.
Of course you have.
Come on! How come YOU get to be all sucked into your research and I don't?
Pssh! You know the final growth cycle on these choryoku eggplants won't monitor itself!

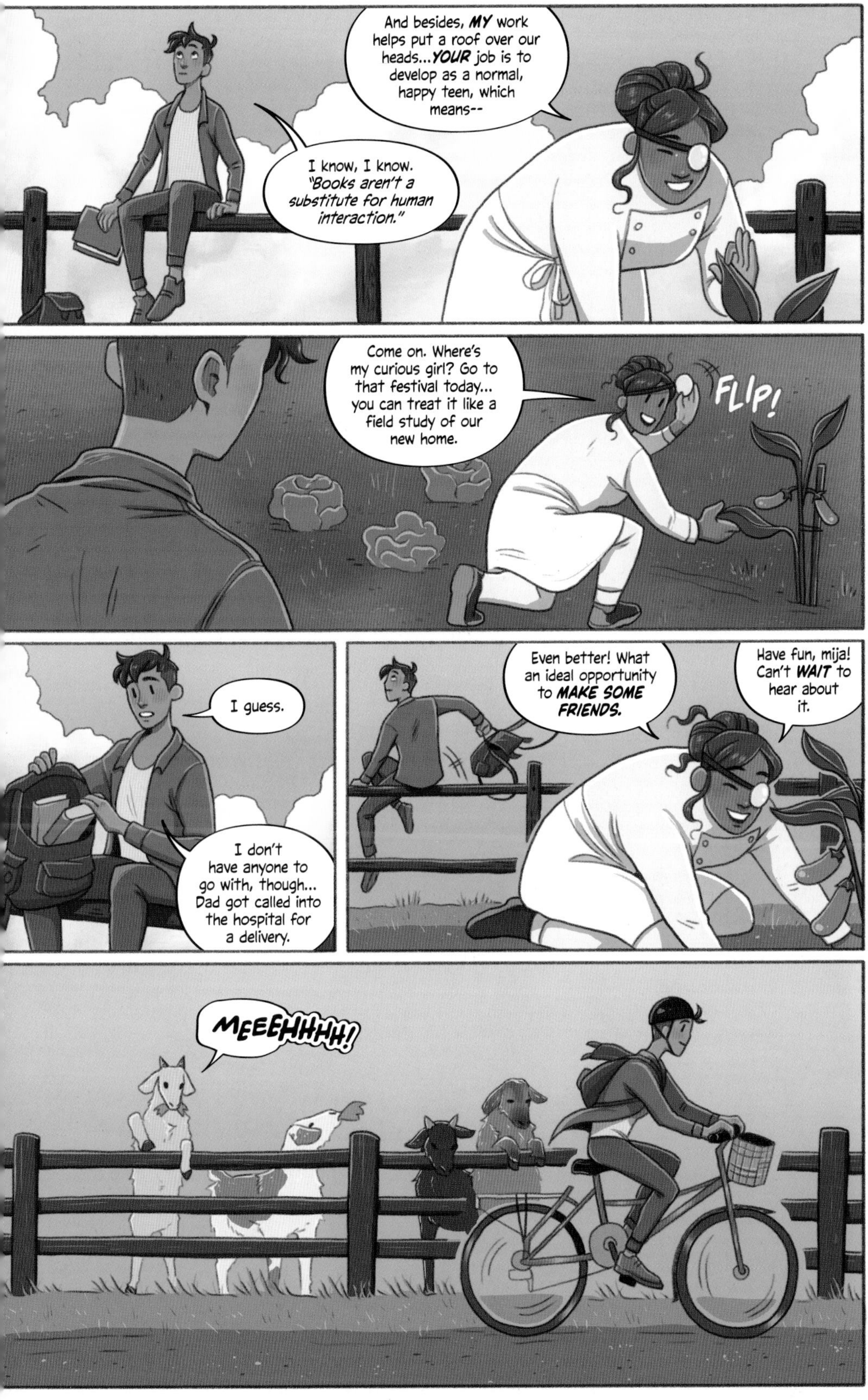
And besides, MY work helps put a roof over our heads...YOUR job is to develop as a normal, happy teen, which means--
I know, I know. "Books aren't a substitute for human interaction."
Come on. Where's my curious girl? Go to that festival today... you can treat it like a field study of our new home.
FLIP!
I guess.
I don't have anyone to go with, though... Dad got called into the hospital for a delivery.
Even better! What an ideal opportunity to MAKE SOME FRIENDS.
Have fun, mija! Can't WAIT to hear about it.
MEEEHHHH!

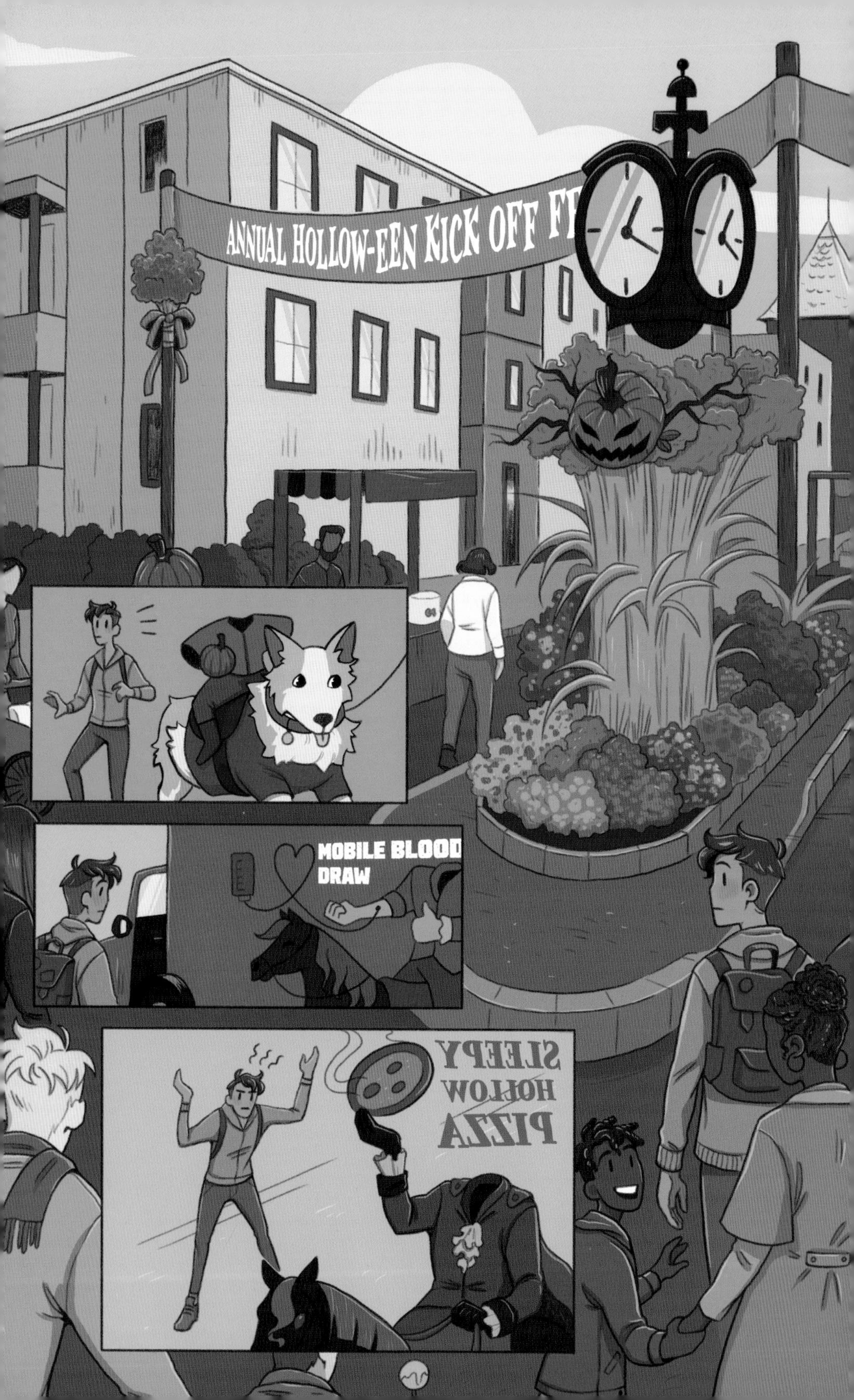
ANNUAL HOLLOW-EEN KICK OFF FE
MOBILE BLOOD DRAW
SLEEPY HOLLOW PIZZA

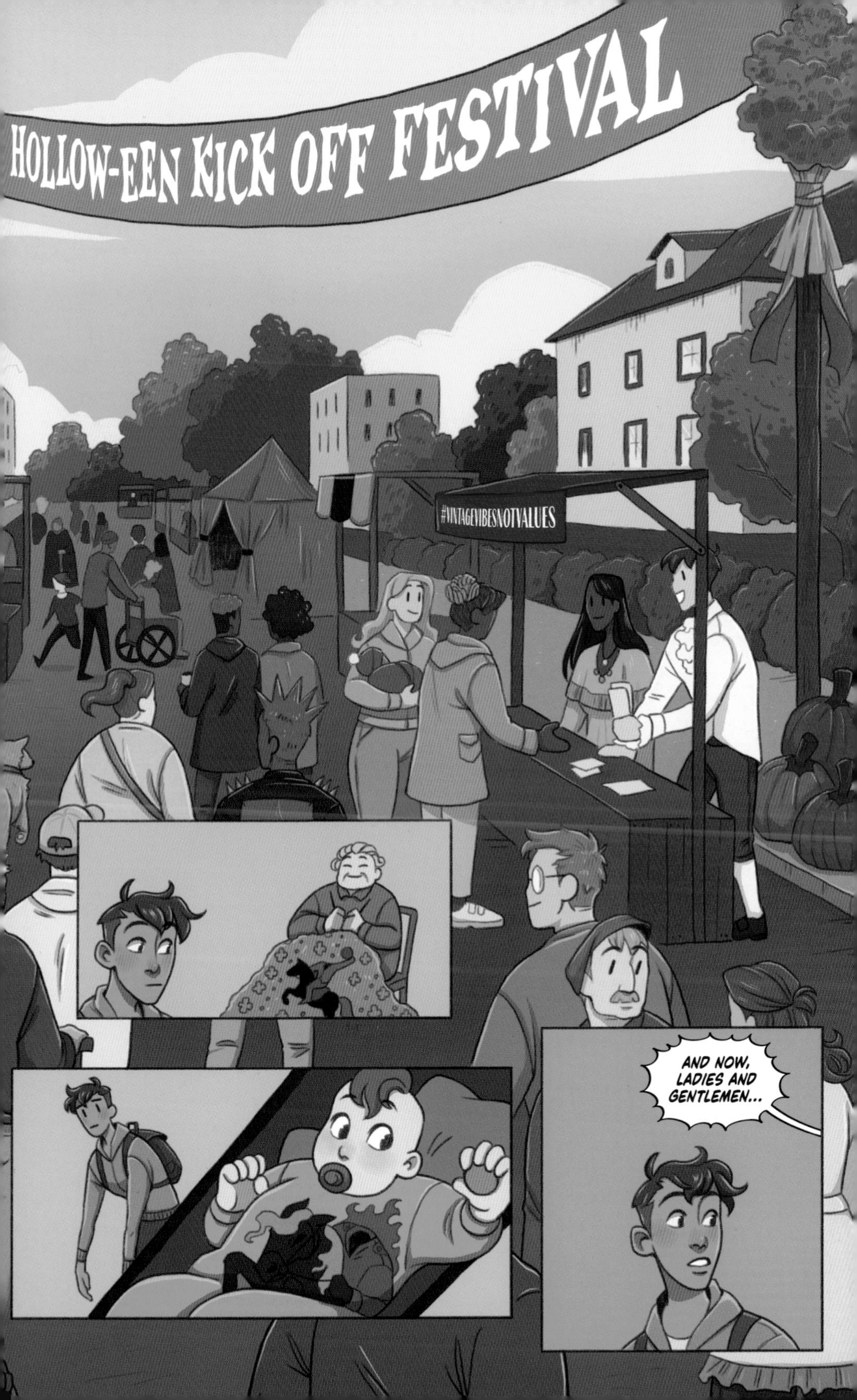
HOLLOW-EEN KICK OFF FESTIVAL
#VINTAGEVIBESNOTVALUES
AND NOW, LADIES AND GENTLEMEN...

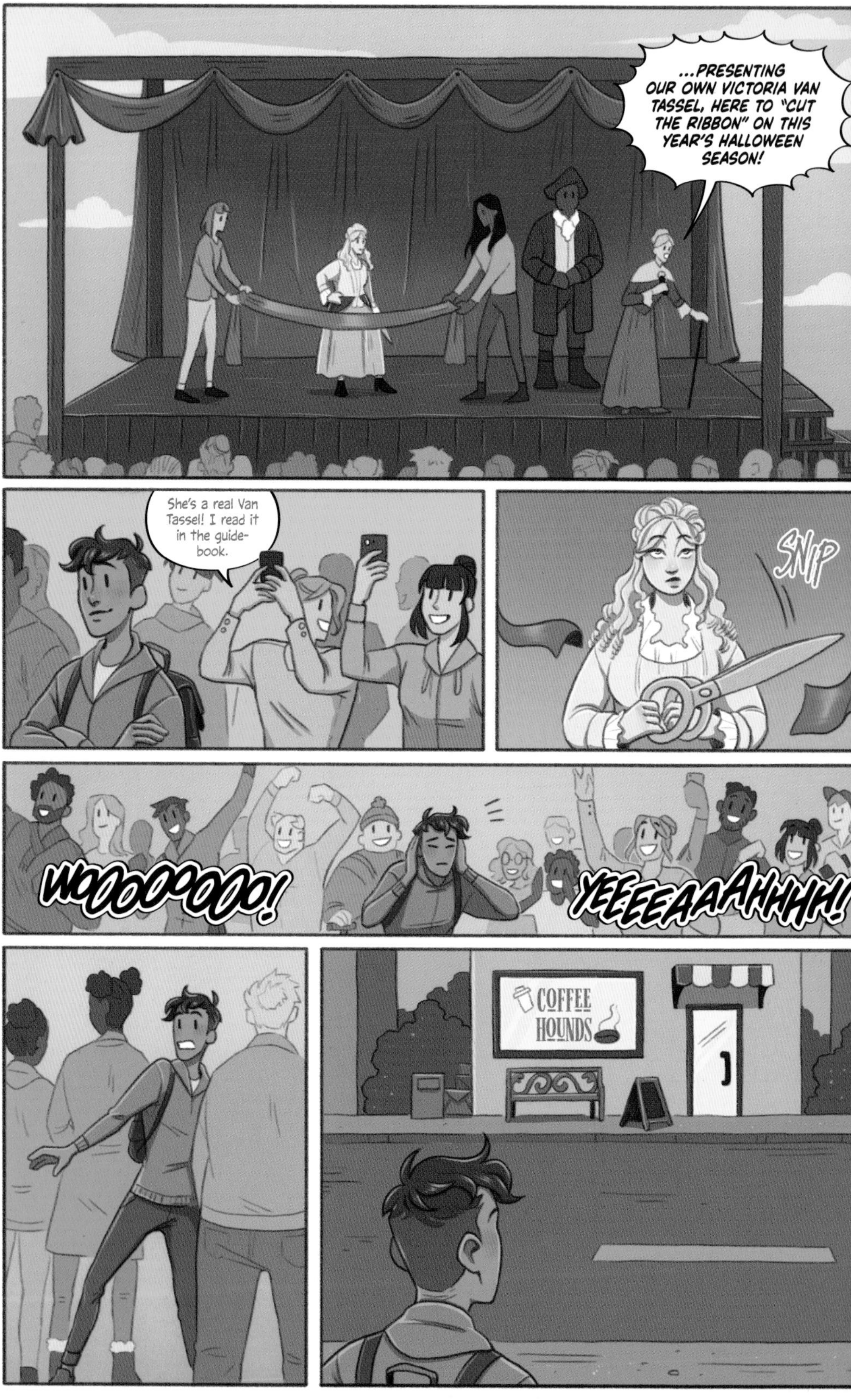
...PRESENTING OUR OWN VICTORIA VAN TASSEL, HERE TO "CUT THE RIBBON" ON THIS YEAR'S HALLOWEEN SEASON!
She's a real Van Tassel! I read it in the guide-book.
SNIP
WOOOOOOOOO!
YEEEEAAAHHHH!
COFFEE HOUNDS

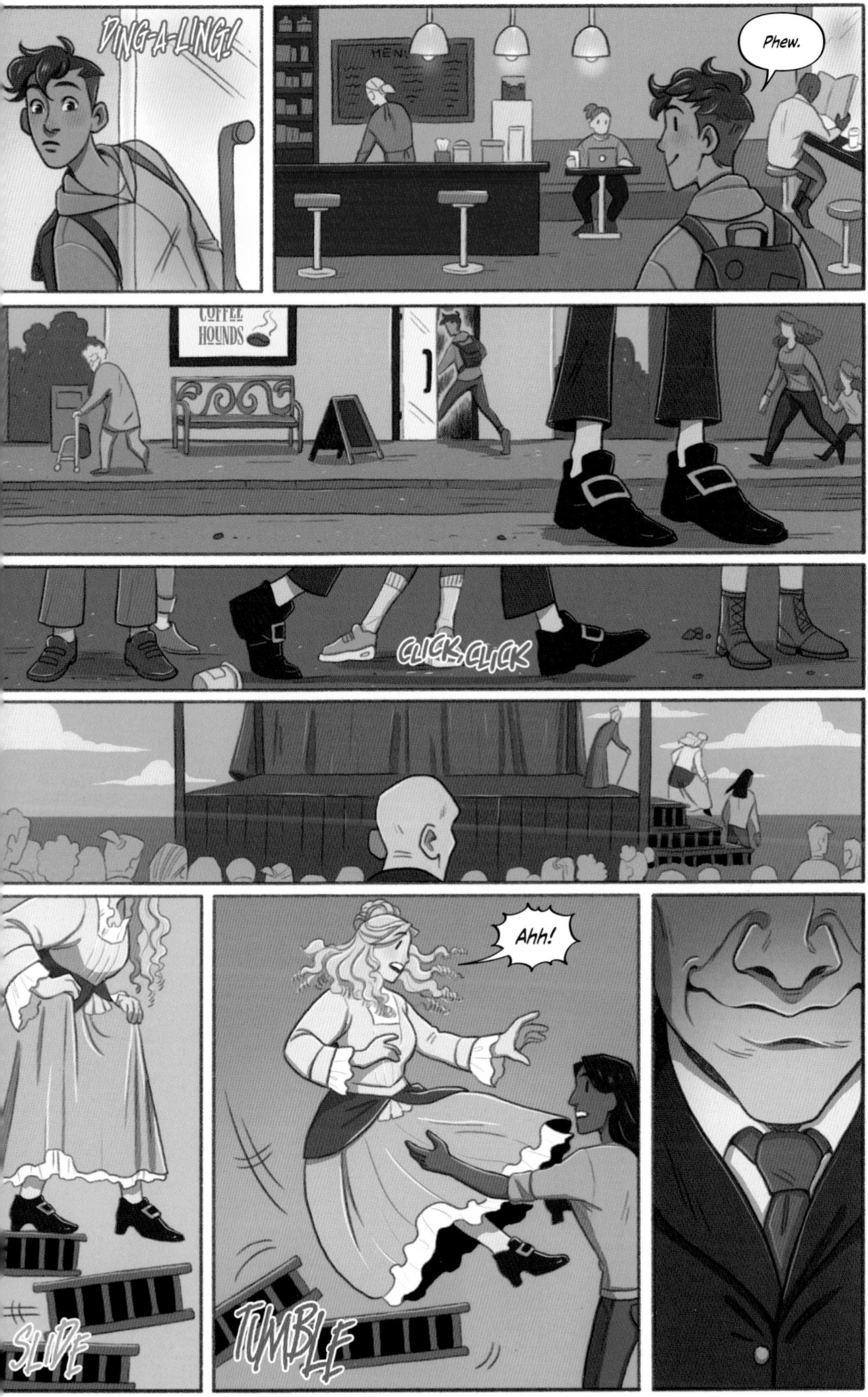
DING-A-LING!
Phew.
COFFEE HOUNDS
MENU
CLICK, CLICK
Ahh!
SLIDE
TUMBLE

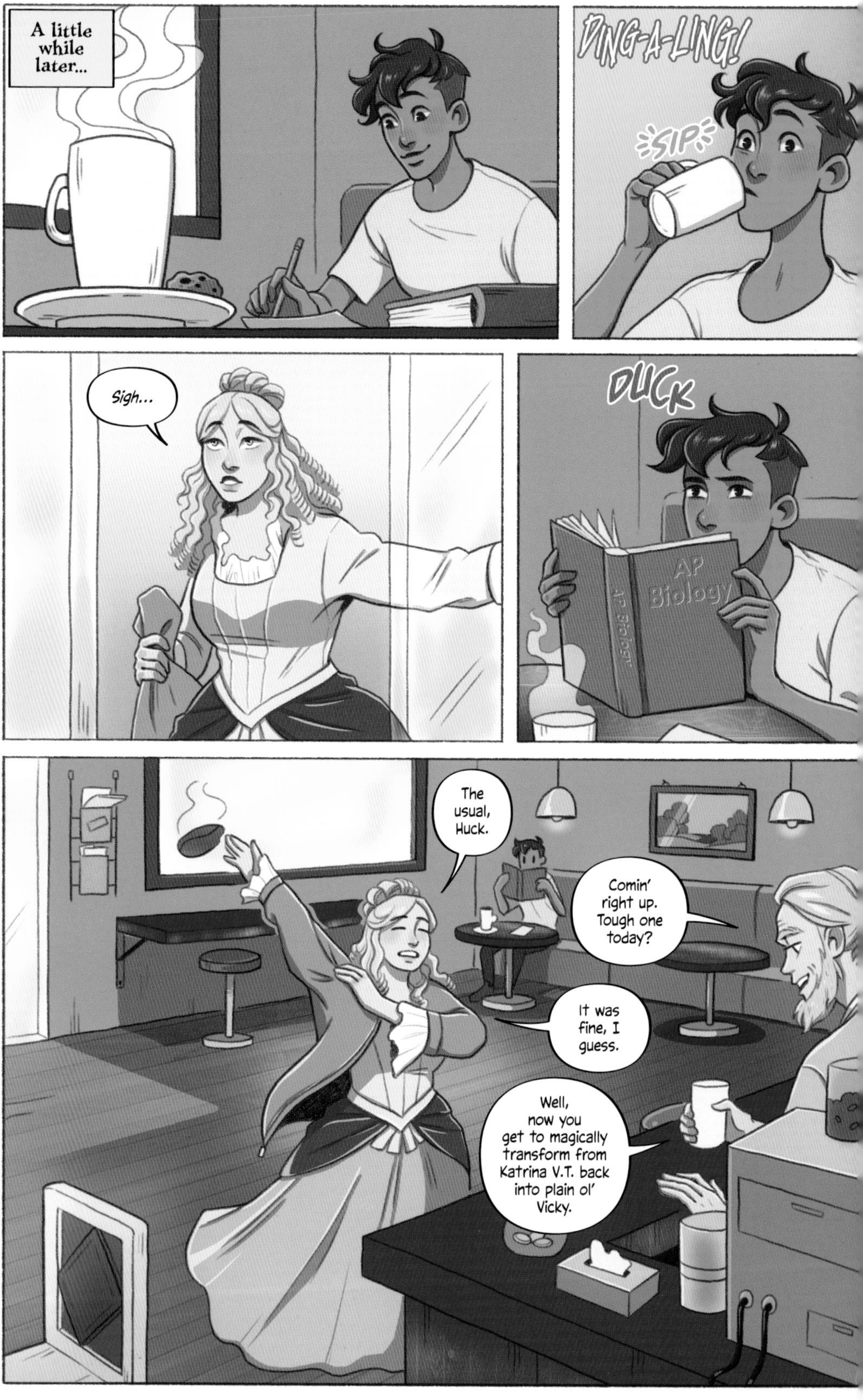
A little while later...
DING-A-LING!
SIP
Sigh...
DUCK
AP Biology
AP Biology
The usual, Huck.
Comin' right up. Tough one today?
It was fine, I guess.
Well, now you get to magically transform from Katrina V.T. back into plain ol' Vicky.

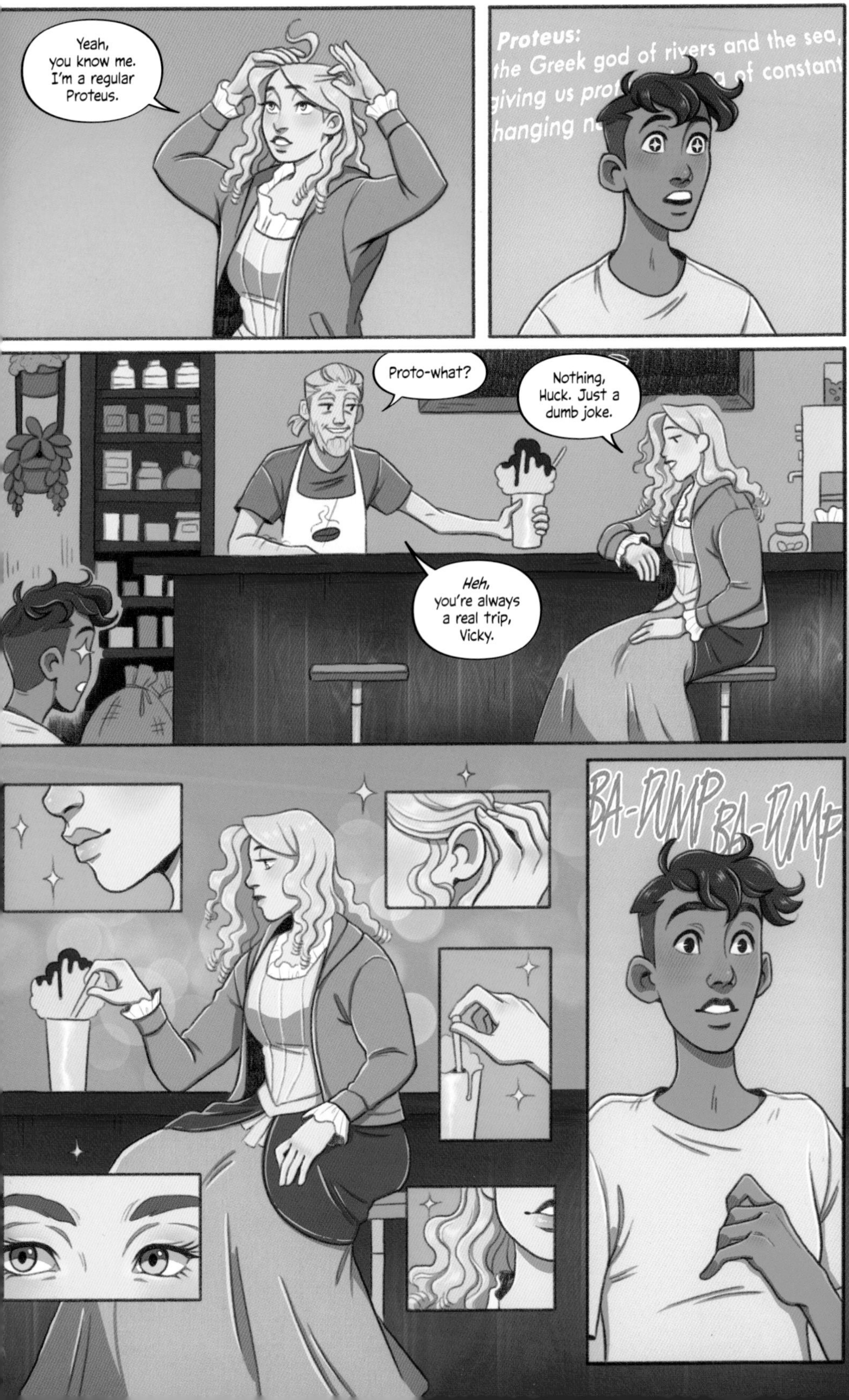
Yeah, you know me. I'm a regular Proteus.
Proteus:
the Greek god of rivers and the sea,
giving us pro of constant
hanging n
Proto-what?
Nothing, Huck. Just a dumb joke.
Heh, you're always a real trip, Vicky.
BA-DUMP BA-DUMP

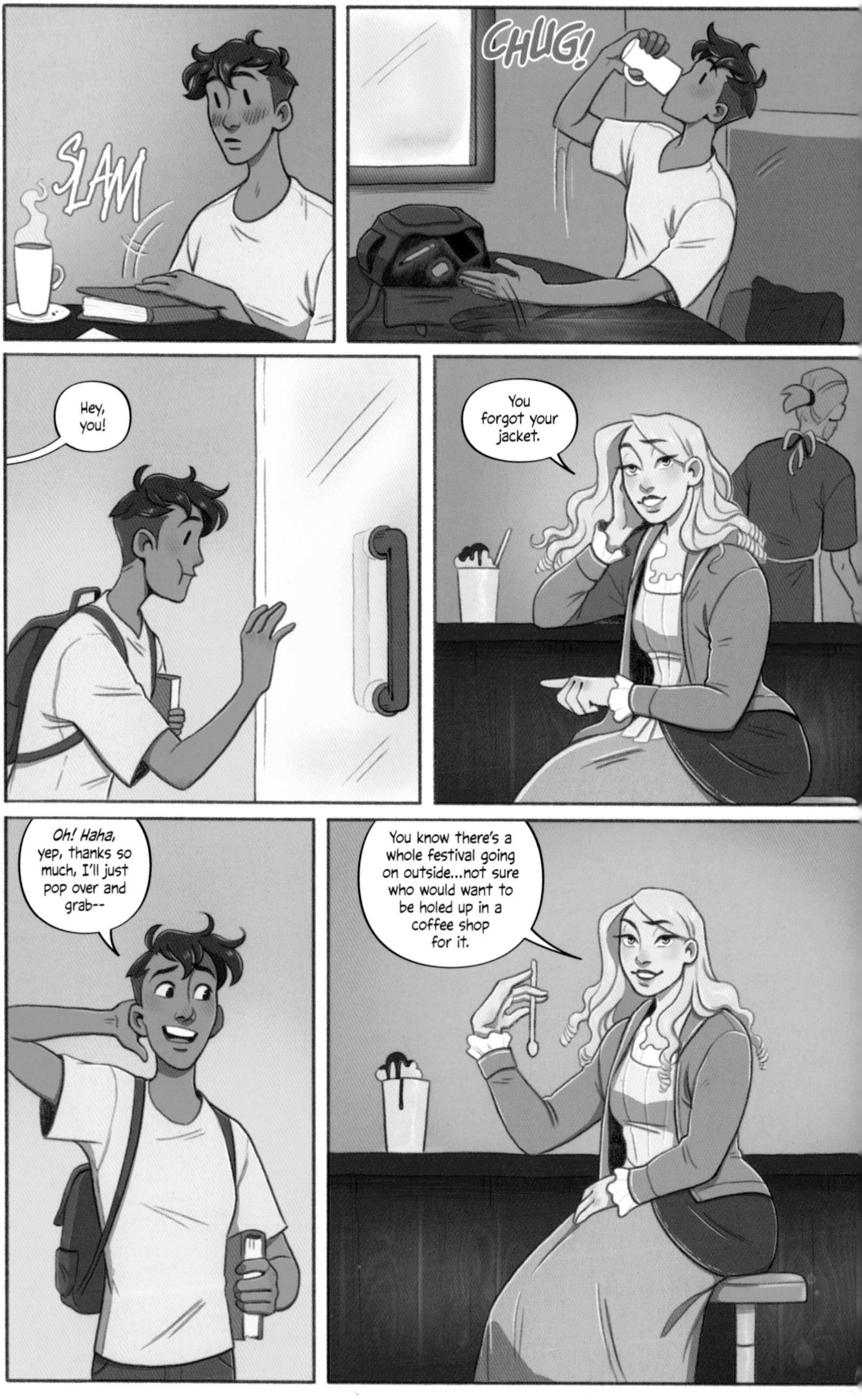
SLAM
CHUG!
Hey, you!
You forgot your jacket.
Oh! Haha, yep, thanks so much, I'll just pop over and grab--
You know there's a whole festival going on outside...not sure who would want to be holed up in a coffee shop for it.

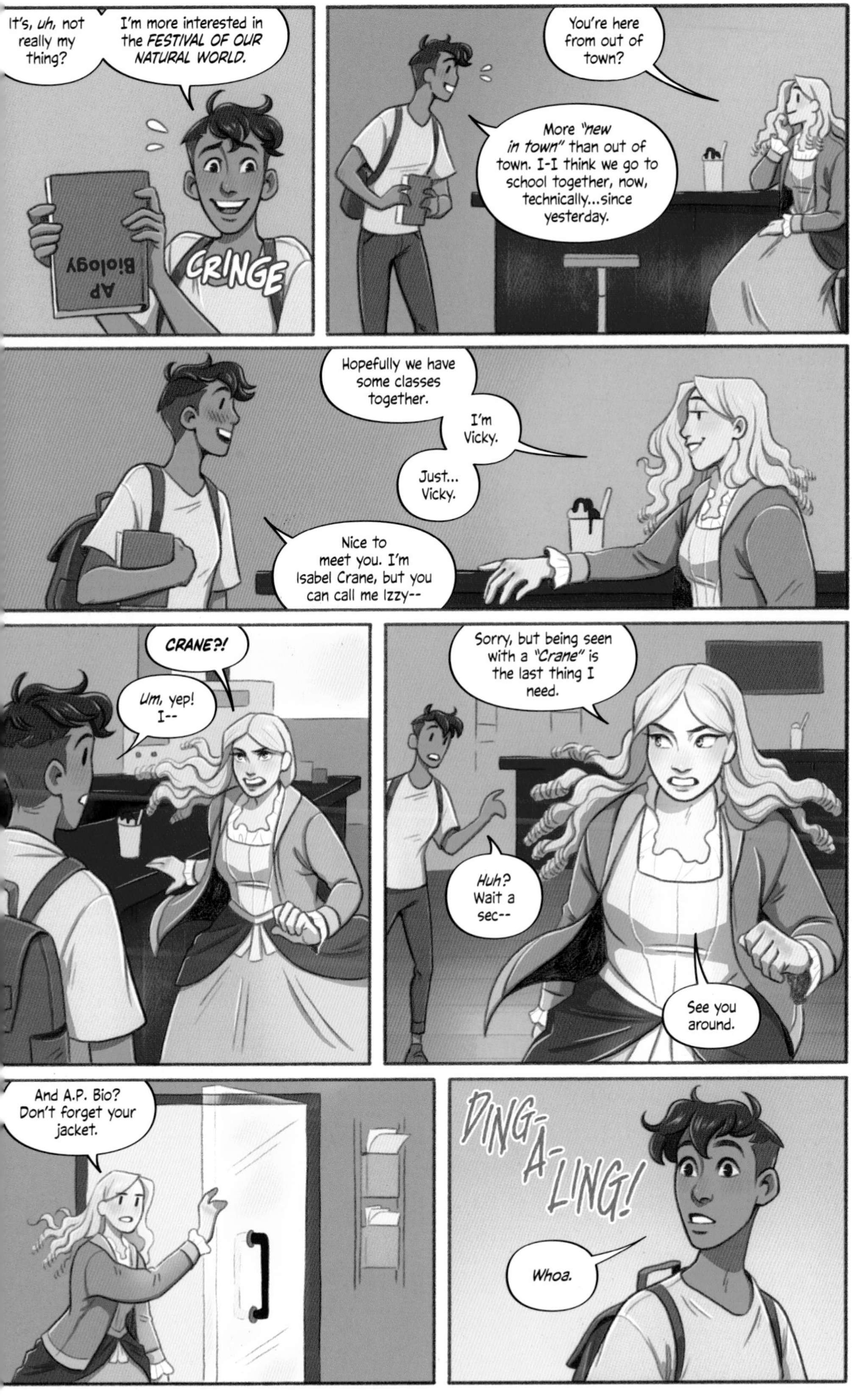
It's, *uh,* not really my thing?
I'm more interested in the *FESTIVAL OF OUR NATURAL WORLD.*
AP Biology
CRINGE
You're here from out of town?
More *"new in town"* than out of town. I-I think we go to school together, now, technically...since yesterday.
Hopefully we have some classes together.
I'm Vicky.
Just... Vicky.
Nice to meet you. I'm Isabel Crane, but you can call me Izzy--
CRANE?!
Um, yep! I--
Sorry, but being seen with a *"Crane"* is the last thing I need.
Huh? Wait a sec--
See you around.
And A.P. Bio? Don't forget your jacket.
DING-A-LING!
Whoa.

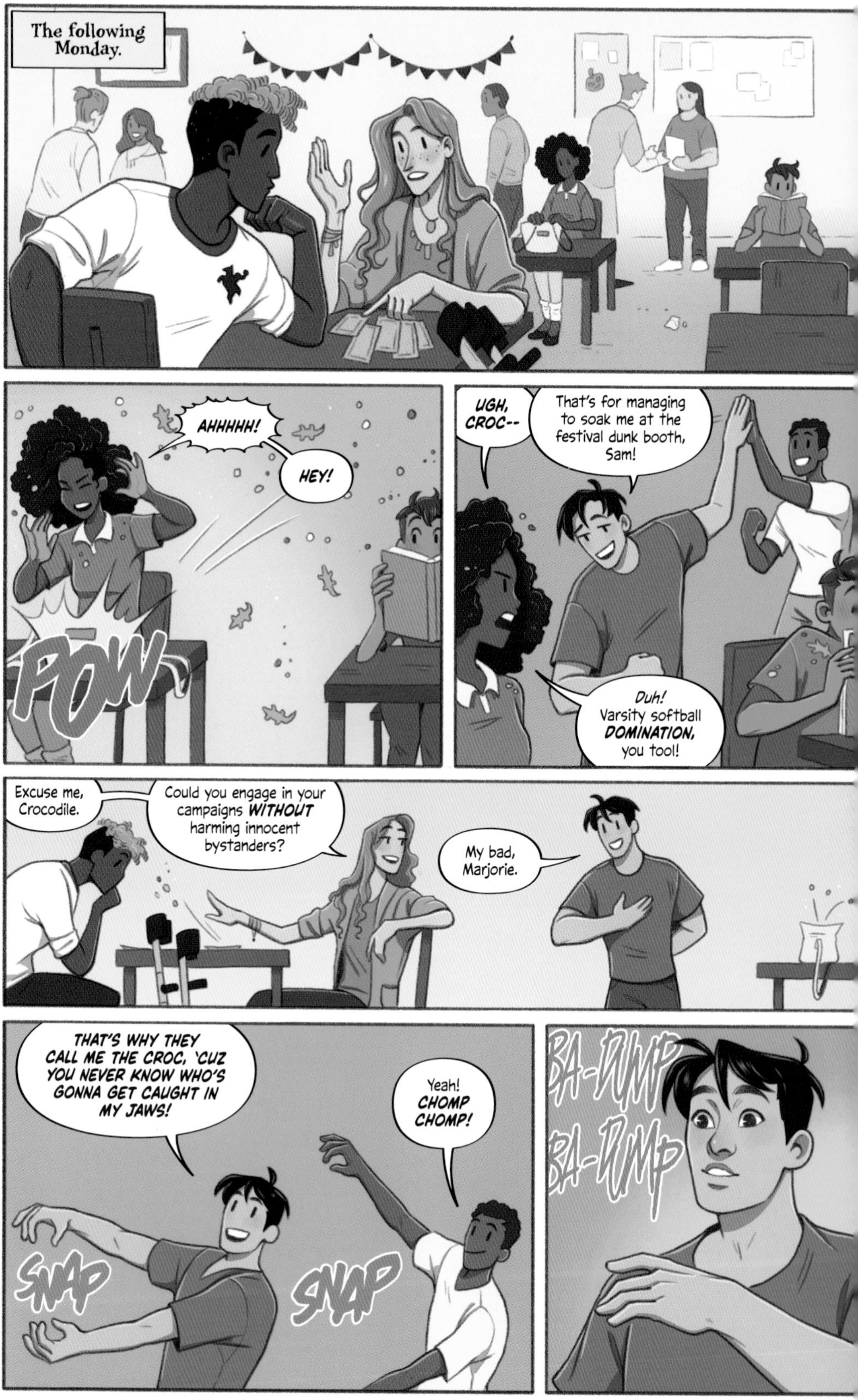

The following Monday.
AHHHHH!
HEY!
POW
UGH, CROC--
That's for managing to soak me at the festival dunk booth, Sam!
Duh! Varsity softball DOMINATION, you tool!
Excuse me, Crocodile.
Could you engage in your campaigns WITHOUT harming innocent bystanders?
My bad, Marjorie.
THAT'S WHY THEY CALL ME THE CROC, 'CUZ YOU NEVER KNOW WHO'S GONNA GET CAUGHT IN MY JAWS!
Yeah! CHOMP CHOMP!
SNAP
SNAP
BA-DUMP
BA-DUMP

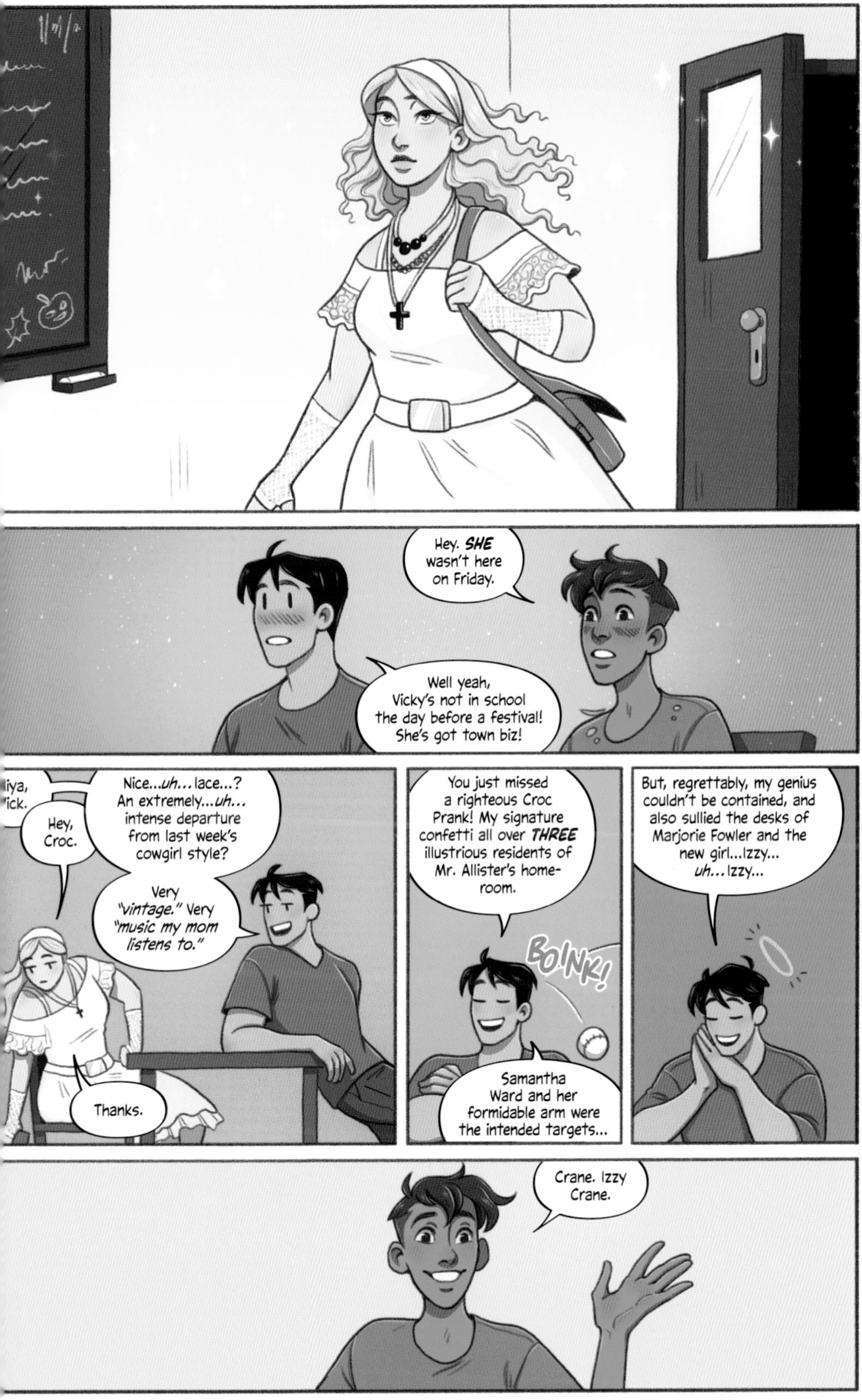
Hey. SHE wasn't here on Friday.
Well yeah, Vicky's not in school the day before a festival! She's got town biz!
Hey, Croc.
Nice...*uh*...lace...? An extremely...*uh*... intense departure from last week's cowgirl style?
Very *"vintage."* Very *"music my mom listens to."*
Thanks.
You just missed a righteous Croc Prank! My signature confetti all over THREE illustrious residents of Mr. Allister's home-room.
BOINK!
Samantha Ward and her formidable arm were the intended targets...
But, regrettably, my genius couldn't be contained, and also sullied the desks of Marjorie Fowler and the new girl...Izzy... *uh*...Izzy...
Crane. Izzy Crane.

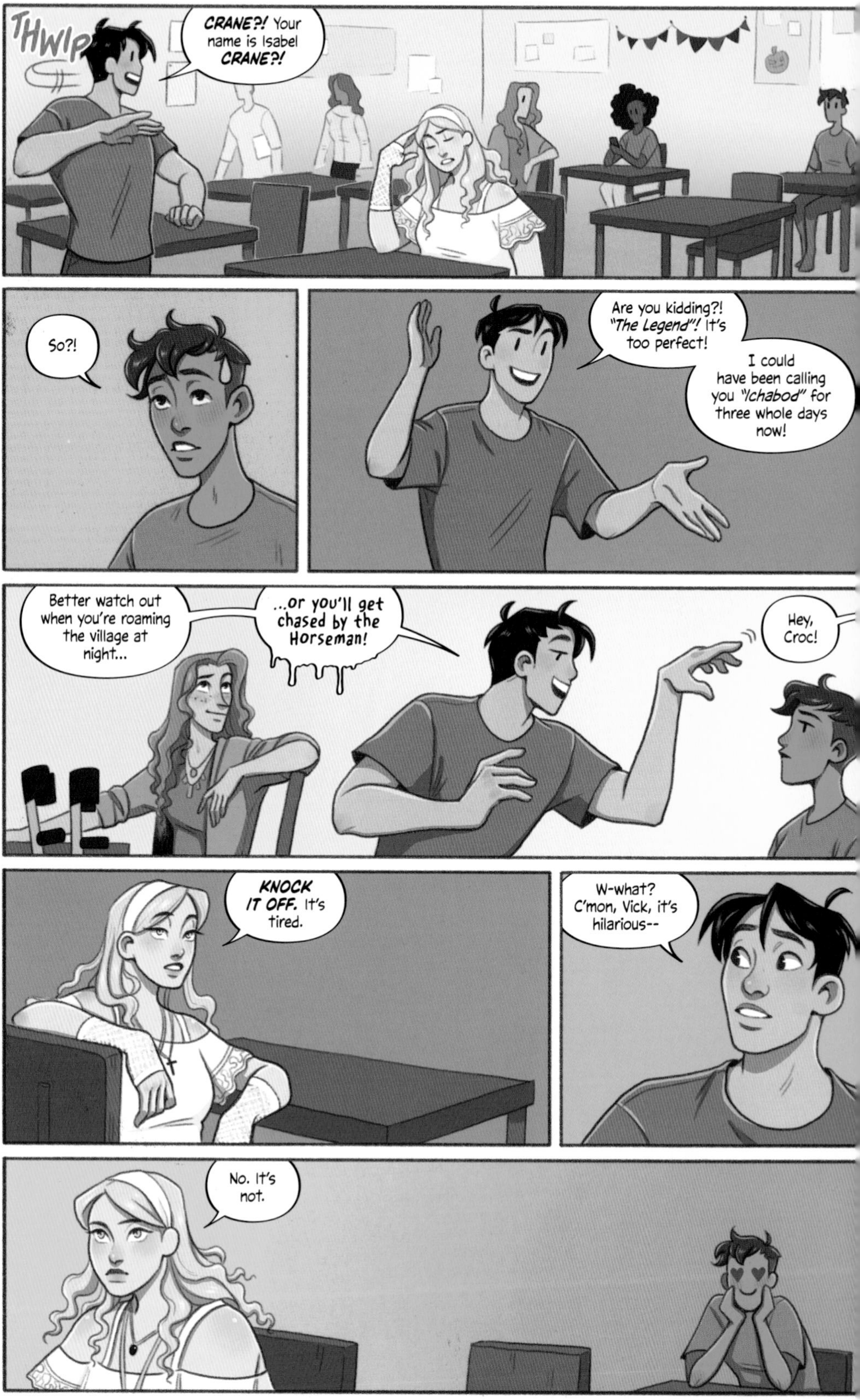
THWIP
CRANE?! Your name is Isabel CRANE?!
So?!
Are you kidding?! "The Legend"! It's too perfect!
I could have been calling you "Ichabod" for three whole days now!
Better watch out when you're roaming the village at night...
...or you'll get chased by the Horseman!
Hey, Croc!
KNOCK IT OFF. It's tired.
W-what? C'mon, Vick, it's hilarious--
No. It's not.

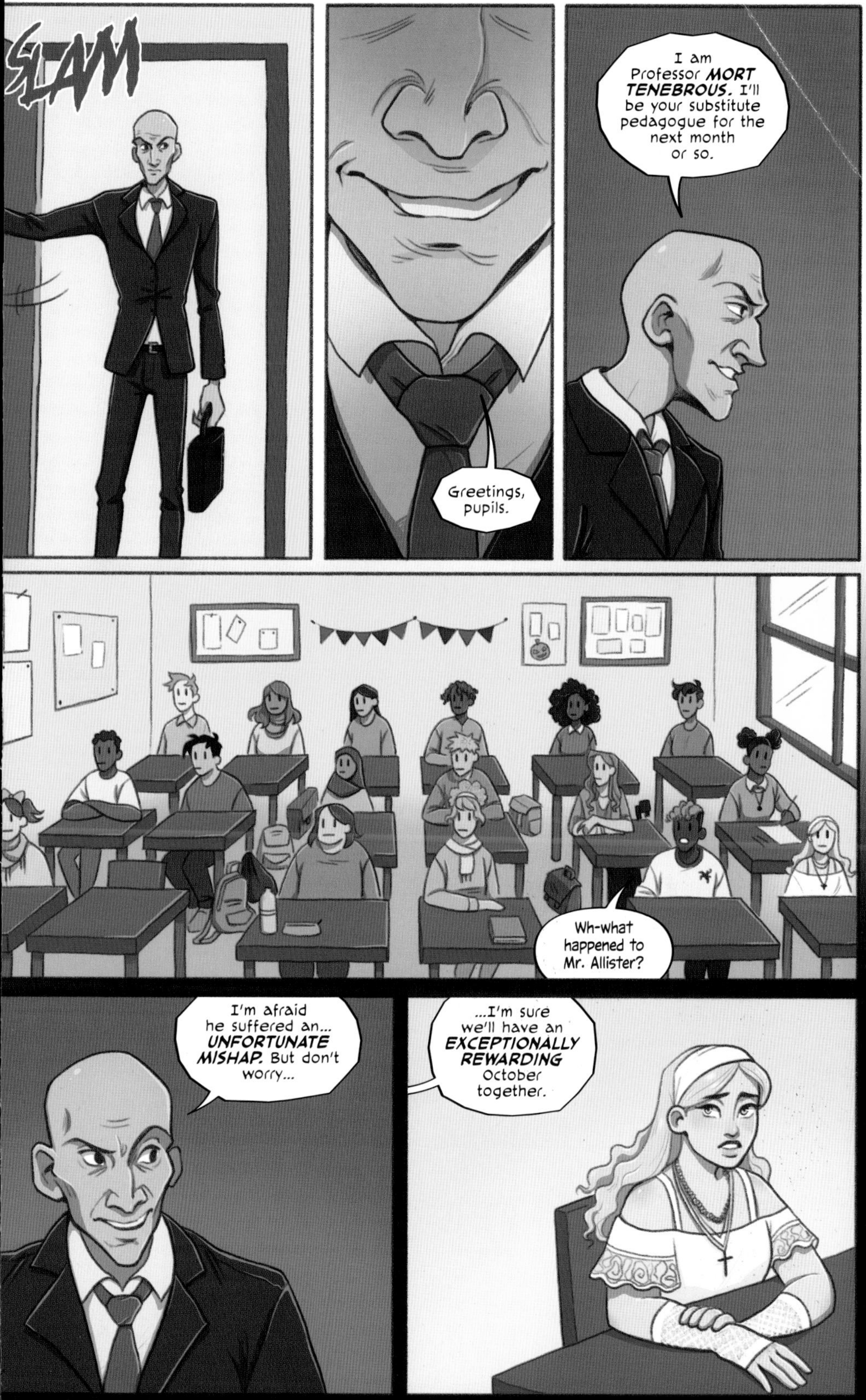
SLAM
Greetings, pupils.
I am Professor MORT TENEBROUS. I'll be your substitute pedagogue for the next month or so.
Wh-what happened to Mr. Allister?
I'm afraid he suffered an... UNFORTUNATE MISHAP. But don't worry...
...I'm sure we'll have an EXCEPTIONALLY REWARDING October together.

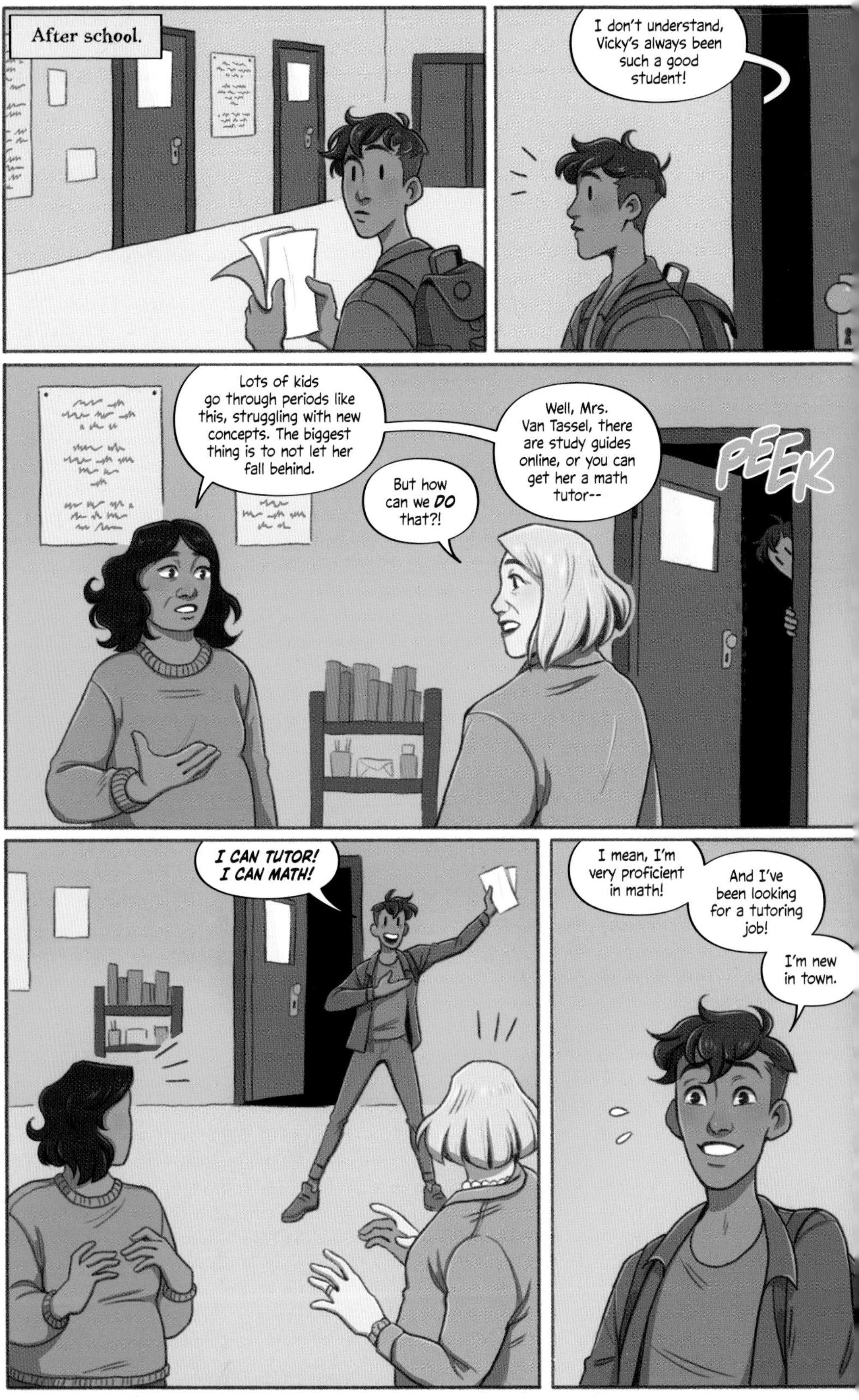
After school.
I don't understand, Vicky's always been such a good student!
Lots of kids go through periods like this, struggling with new concepts. The biggest thing is to not let her fall behind.
But how can we *DO* that?!
Well, Mrs. Van Tassel, there are study guides online, or you can get her a math tutor--
PEEK
I CAN TUTOR! I CAN MATH!
I mean, I'm very proficient in math!
And I've been looking for a tutoring job!
I'm new in town.

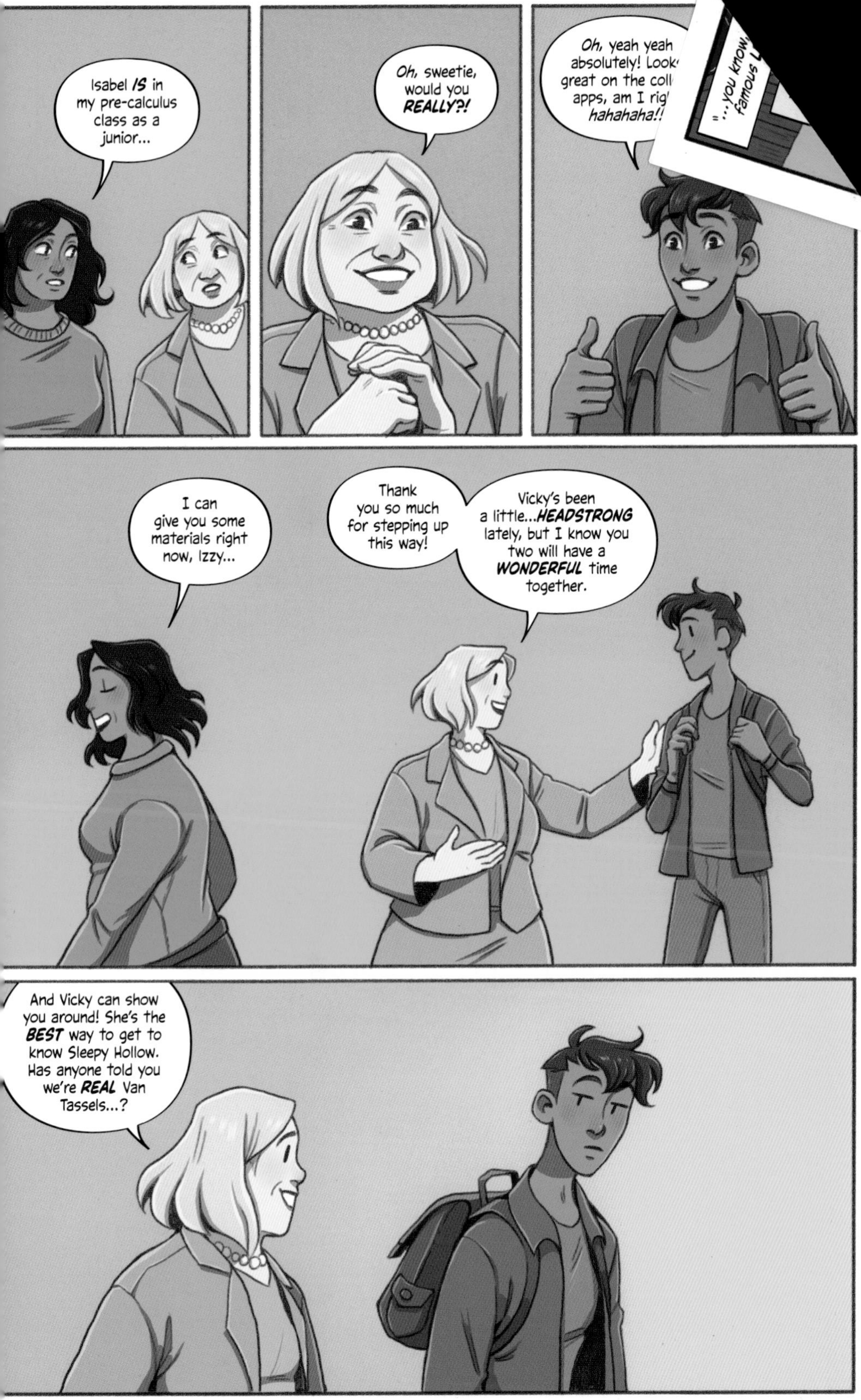
Isabel *IS* in my pre-calculus class as a junior...
Oh, sweetie, would you ***REALLY?!***
Oh, yeah yeah absolutely! Looks great on the coll apps, am I rig *hahahaha!!*
I can give you some materials right now, Izzy...
Thank you so much for stepping up this way!
Vicky's been a little...***HEADSTRONG*** lately, but I know you two will have a ***WONDERFUL*** time together.
And Vicky can show you around! She's the ***BEST*** way to get to know Sleepy Hollow. Has anyone told you we're ***REAL*** Van Tassels...?

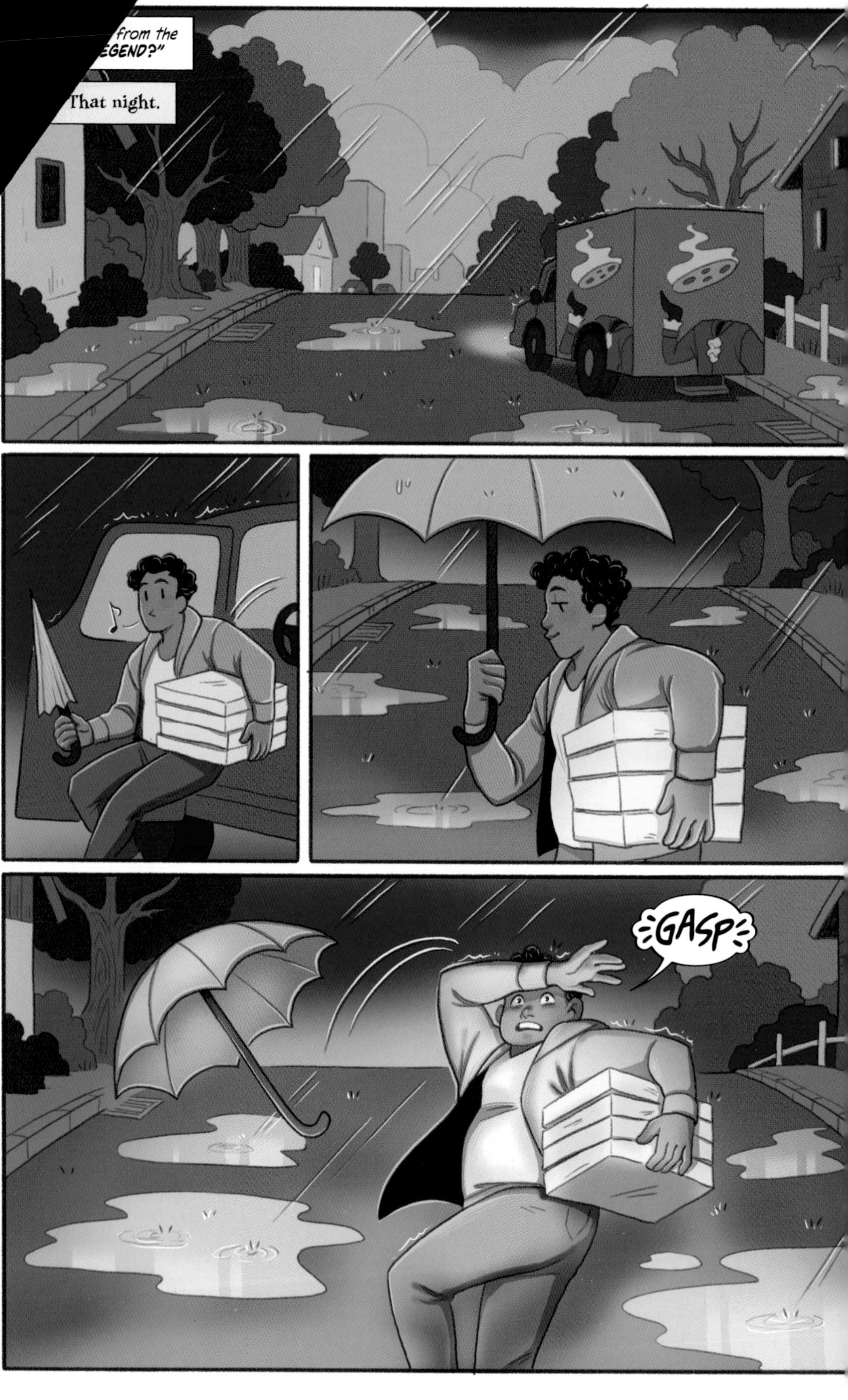
from the
EGEND?"
That night.
GASP

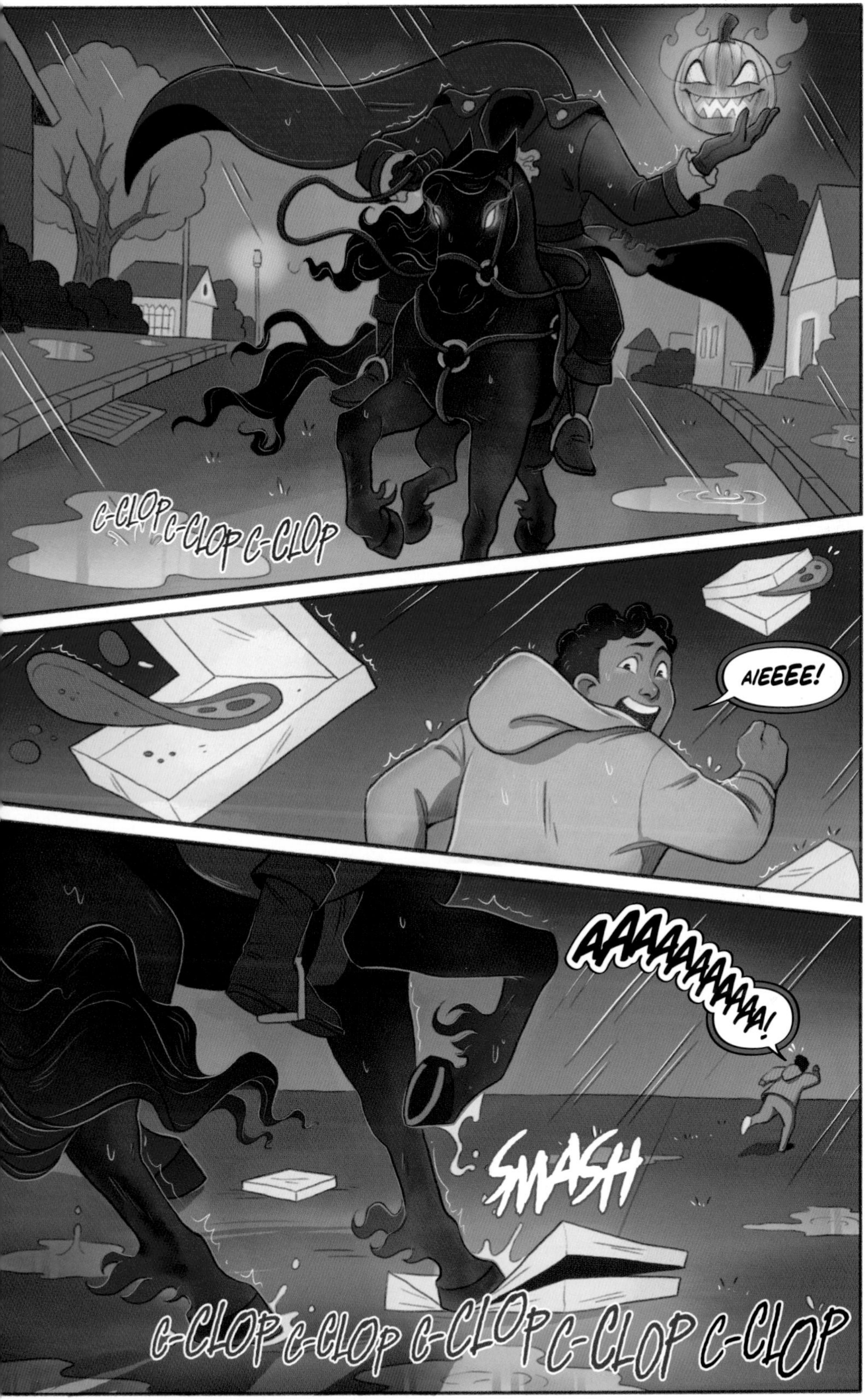
C-CLOP C-CLOP C-CLOP
AIEEEE!
AAAAAAAAAAAA!
SMASH
C-CLOP C-CLOP C-CLOP C-CLOP C-CLOP

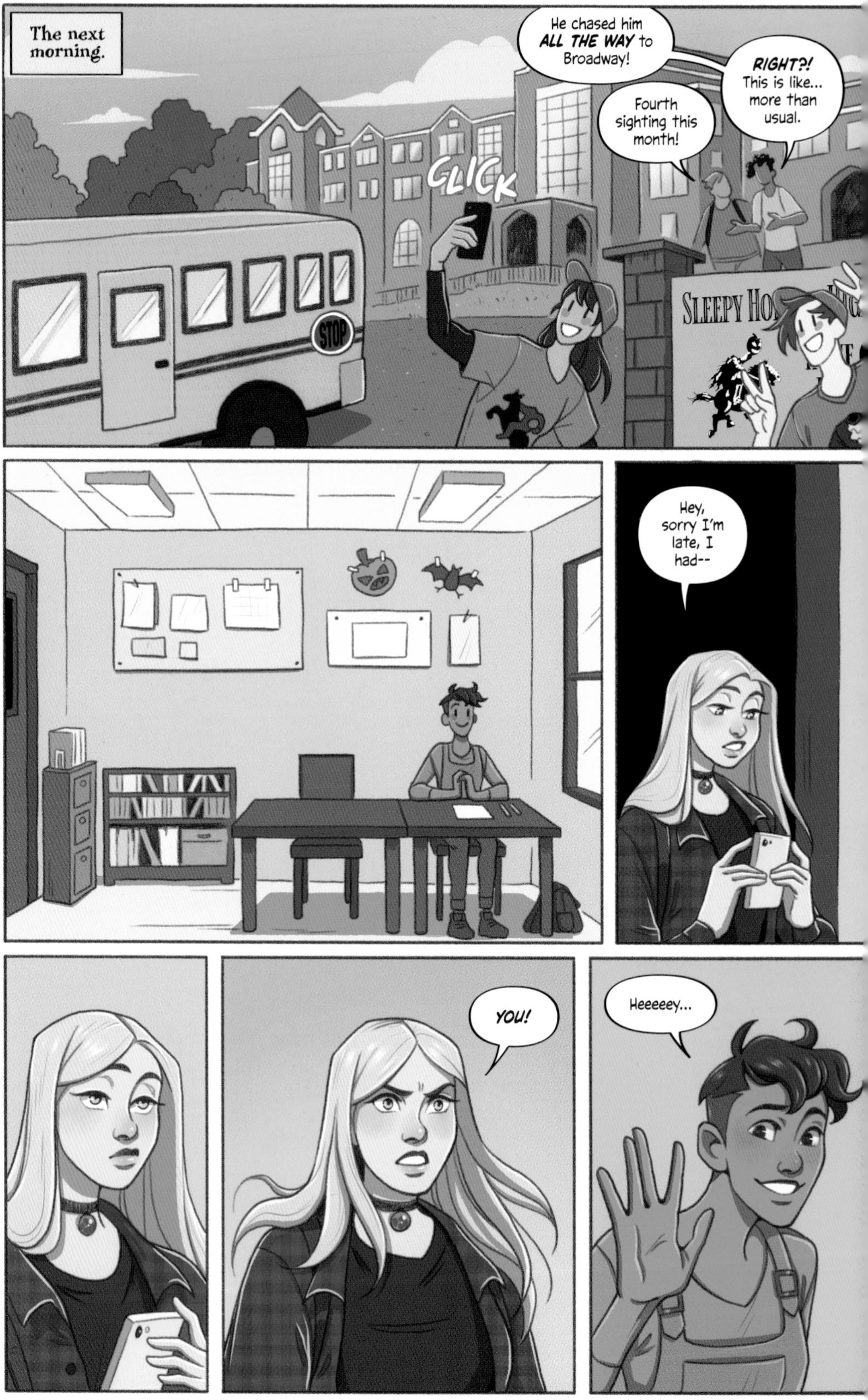
The next morning.
He chased him ALL THE WAY to Broadway!
Fourth sighting this month!
RIGHT?! This is like... more than usual.
CLICK
STOP
SLEEPY HO
Hey, sorry I'm late, I had--
YOU!
Heeeeey...

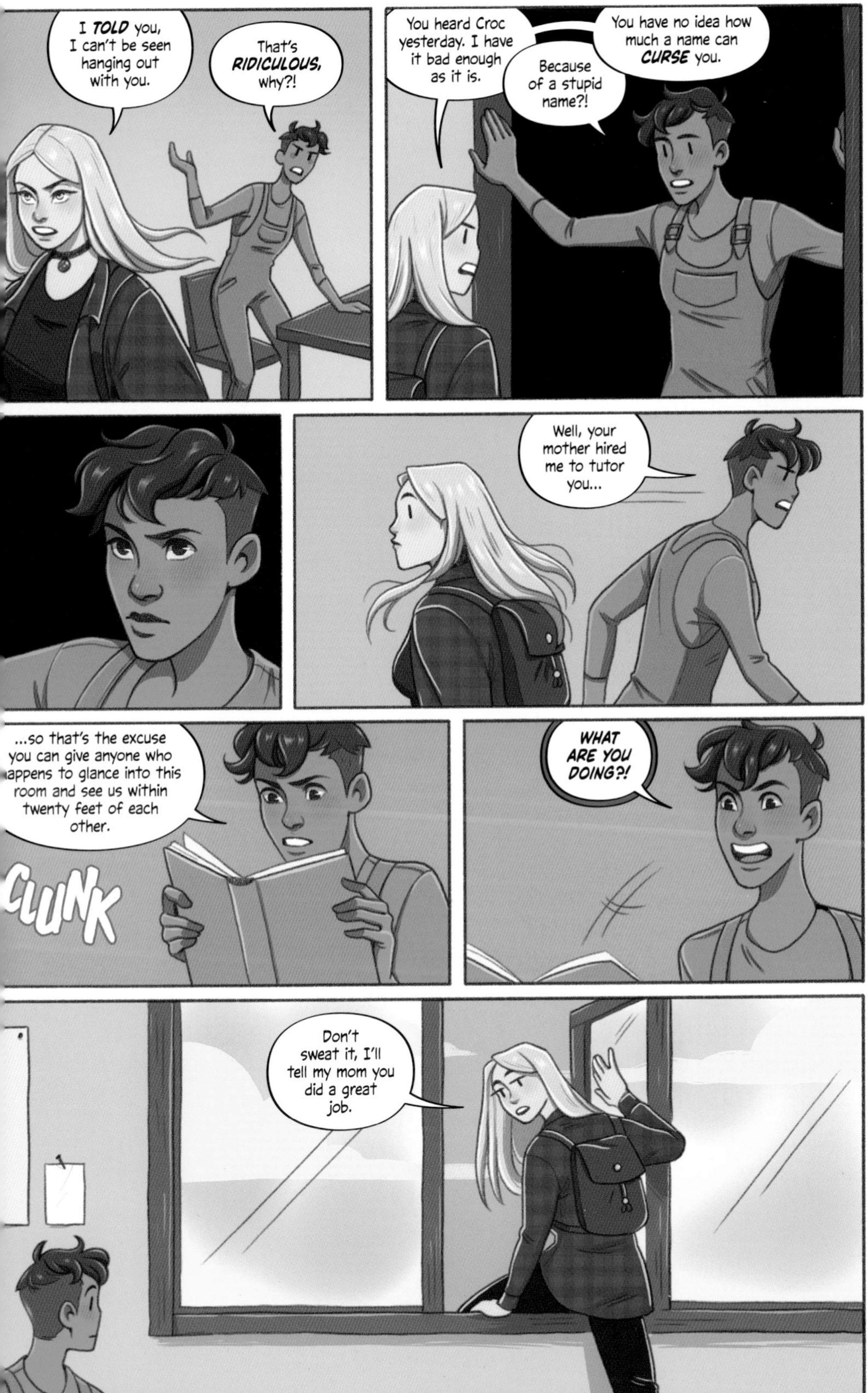

I TOLD you, I can't be seen hanging out with you.
That's RIDICULOUS, why?!
You heard Croc yesterday. I have it bad enough as it is.
Because of a stupid name?!
You have no idea how much a name can CURSE you.
Well, your mother hired me to tutor you...
...so that's the excuse you can give anyone who appens to glance into this room and see us within twenty feet of each other.
CLUNK
WHAT ARE YOU DOING?!
Don't sweat it, I'll tell my mom you did a great job.

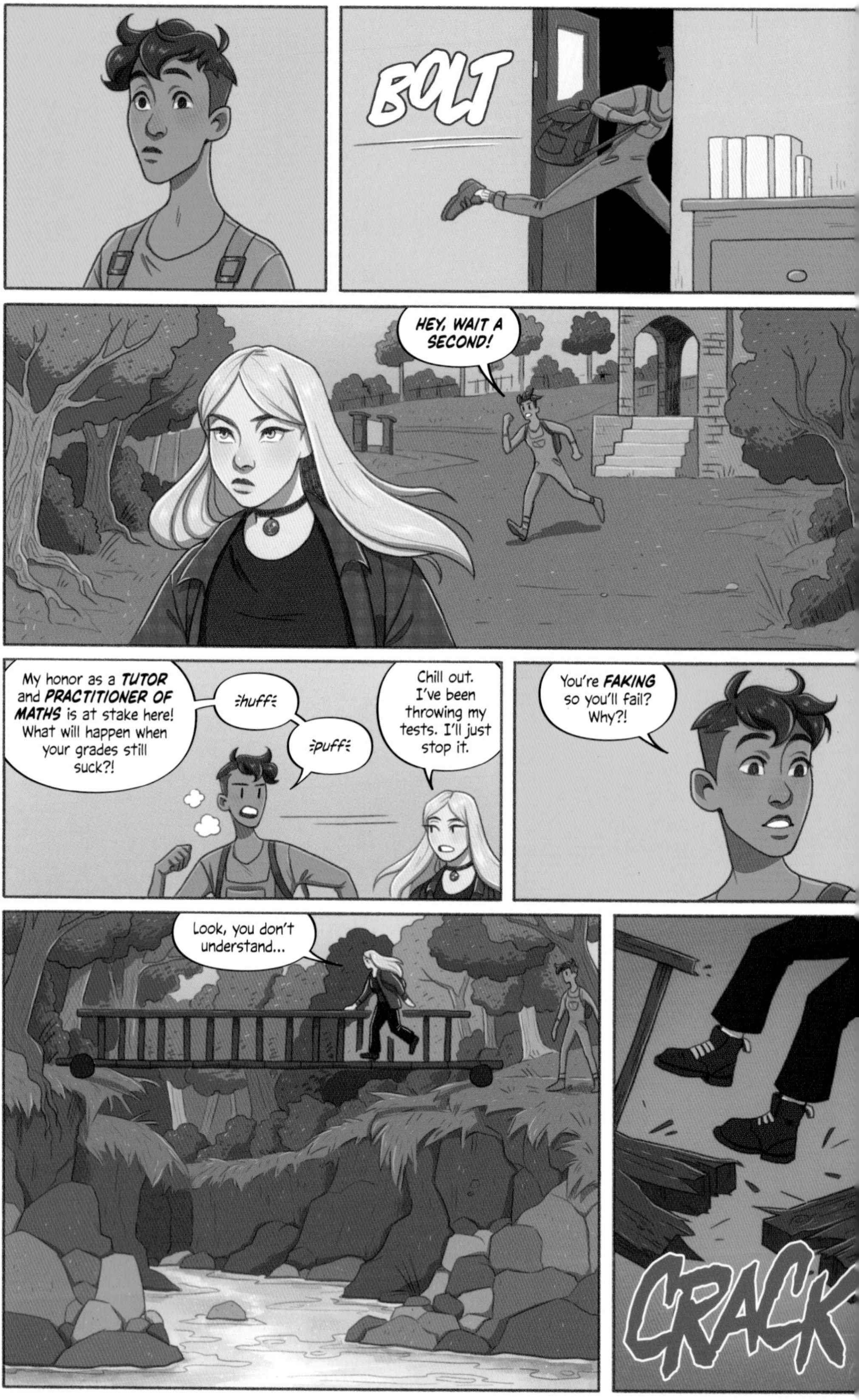

BOLT
HEY, WAIT A SECOND!
My honor as a **TUTOR** and **PRACTITIONER OF MATHS** is at stake here! What will happen when your grades still suck?!
huff
puff
Chill out. I've been throwing my tests. I'll just stop it.
You're **FAKING** so you'll fail? Why?!
Look, you don't understand...
CRACK

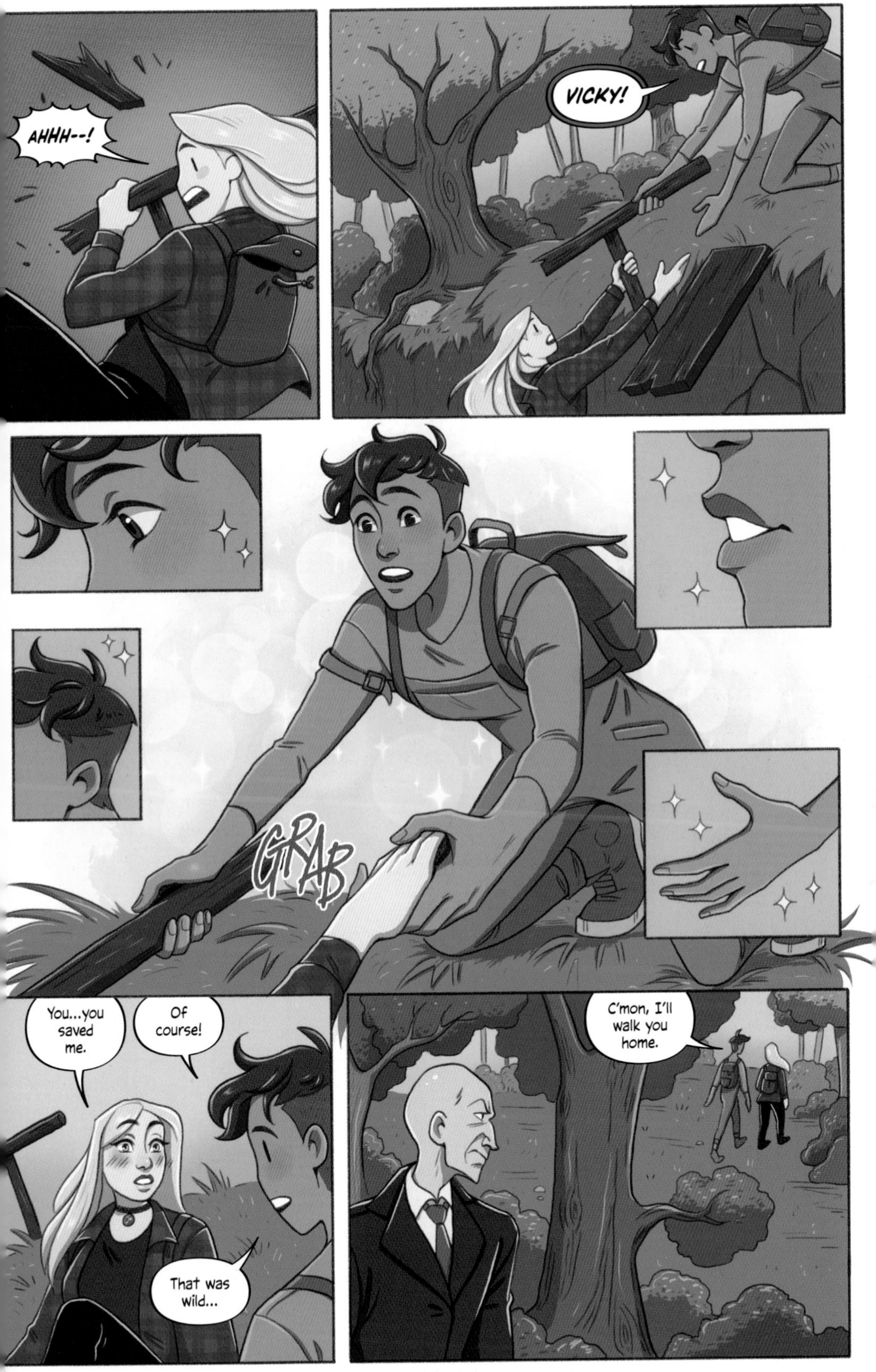
AHHH--!
VICKY!
GRAB
You...you saved me.
Of course!
That was wild...
C'mon, I'll walk you home.

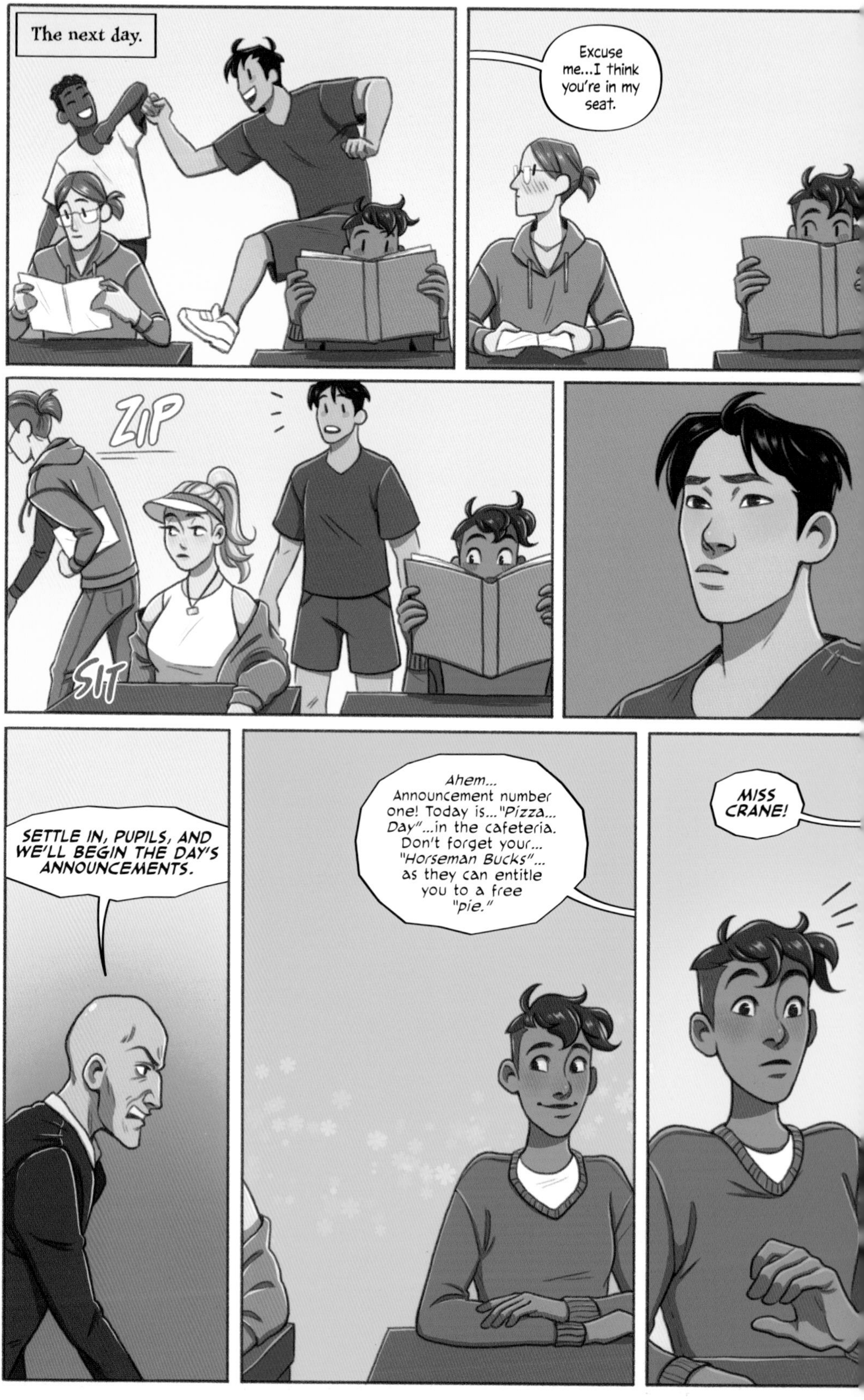
The next day.
Excuse me...I think you're in my seat.
ZIP
SIT
SETTLE IN, PUPILS, AND WE'LL BEGIN THE DAY'S ANNOUNCEMENTS.
Ahem... Announcement number one! Today is..."*Pizza... Day*"...in the cafeteria. Don't forget your... "*Horseman Bucks*"... as they can entitle you to a free "*pie.*"
MISS CRANE!

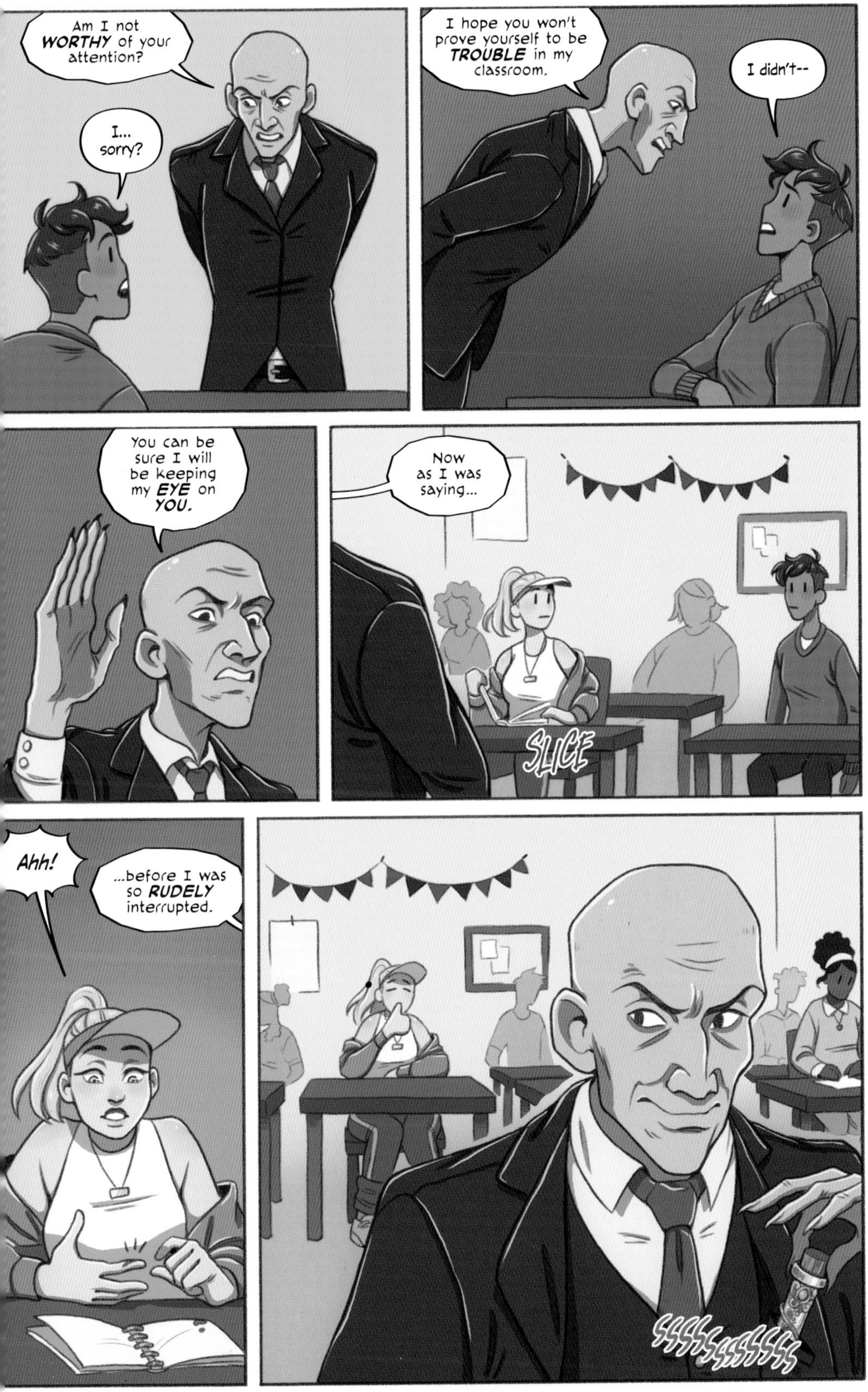
Am I not WORTHY of your attention?
I... sorry?
I hope you won't prove yourself to be TROUBLE in my classroom.
I didn't--
You can be sure I will be keeping my EYE on YOU.
Now as I was saying...
SLICE
Ahh!
...before I was so RUDELY interrupted.
SSSSSSSSSSSSS

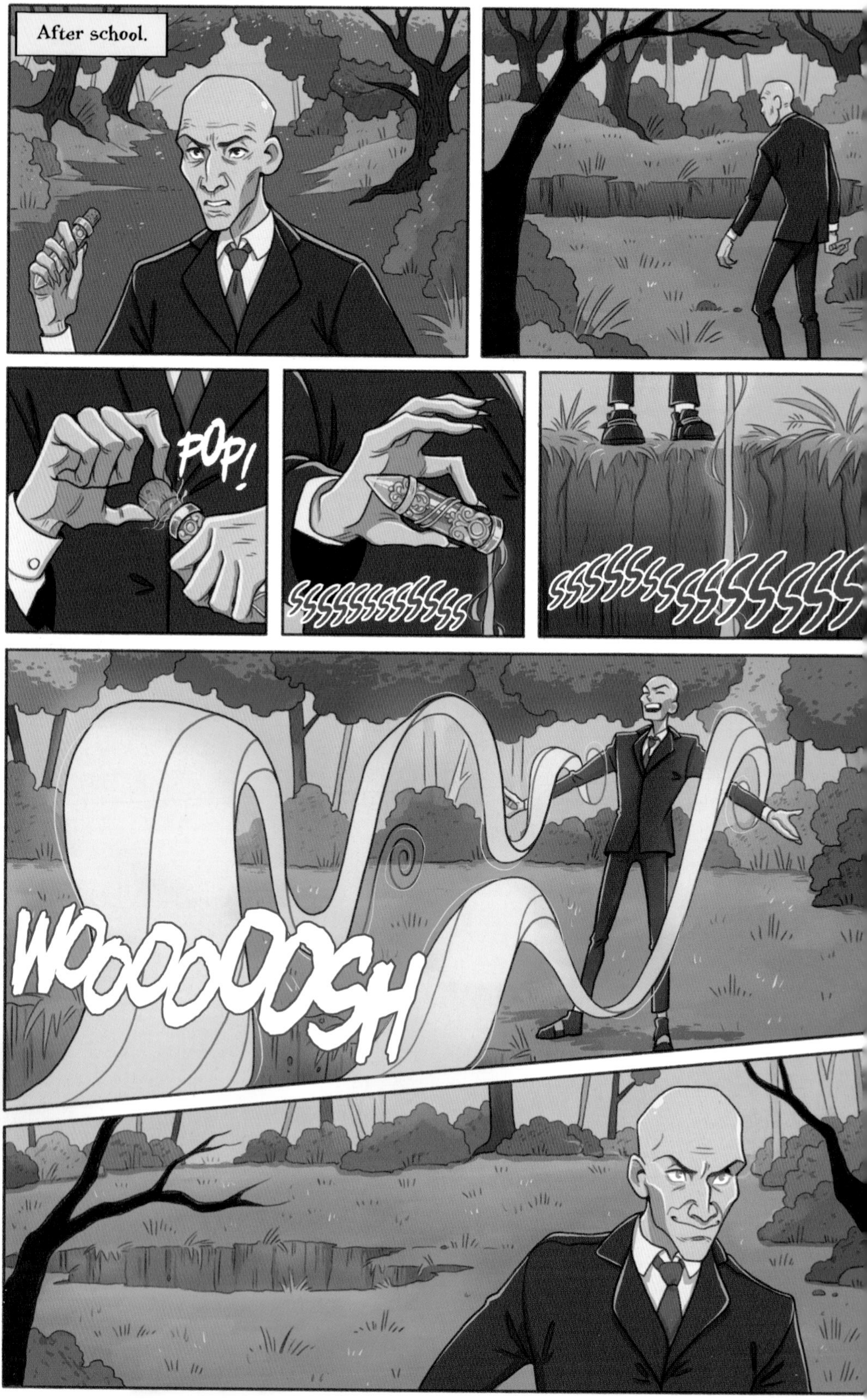
After school.
POP!
SSSSSSSSSSSSS
SSSSSSSSSSSSSSSSS
WOOOOOOOSH

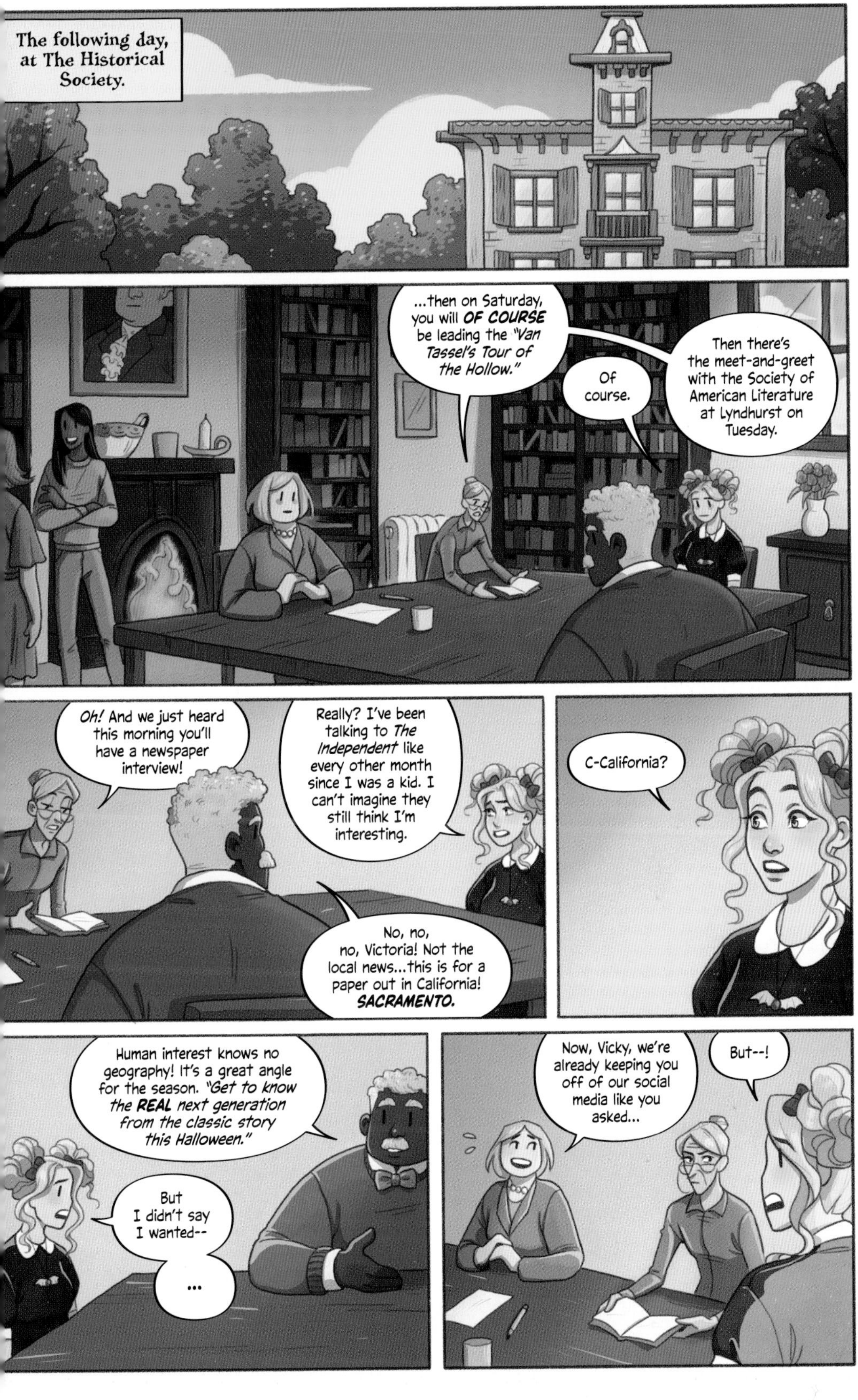
The following day, at The Historical Society.
...then on Saturday, you will OF COURSE be leading the "Van Tassel's Tour of the Hollow."
Of course.
Then there's the meet-and-greet with the Society of American Literature at Lyndhurst on Tuesday.
Oh! And we just heard this morning you'll have a newspaper interview!
Really? I've been talking to The Independent like every other month since I was a kid. I can't imagine they still think I'm interesting.
No, no, no, Victoria! Not the local news...this is for a paper out in California! SACRAMENTO.
C-California?
Human interest knows no geography! It's a great angle for the season. "Get to know the REAL next generation from the classic story this Halloween."
But I didn't say I wanted--
...
Now, Vicky, we're already keeping you off of our social media like you asked...
But--!

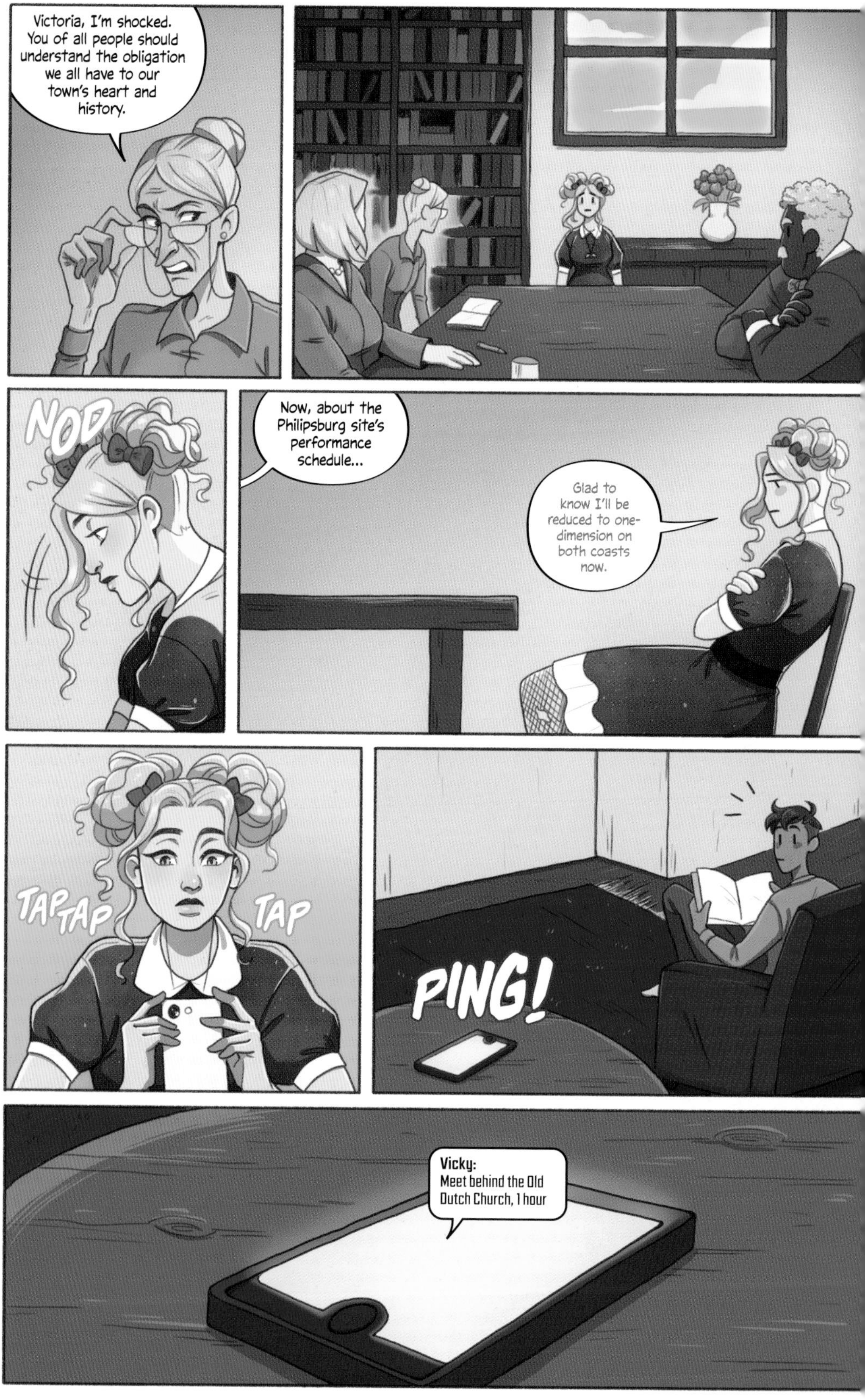

Victoria, I'm shocked. You of all people should understand the obligation we all have to our town's heart and history.
NOD
Now, about the Philipsburg site's performance schedule...
Glad to know I'll be reduced to one-dimension on both coasts now.
TAP TAP TAP
PING!
Vicky:
Meet behind the Old Dutch Church, 1 hour

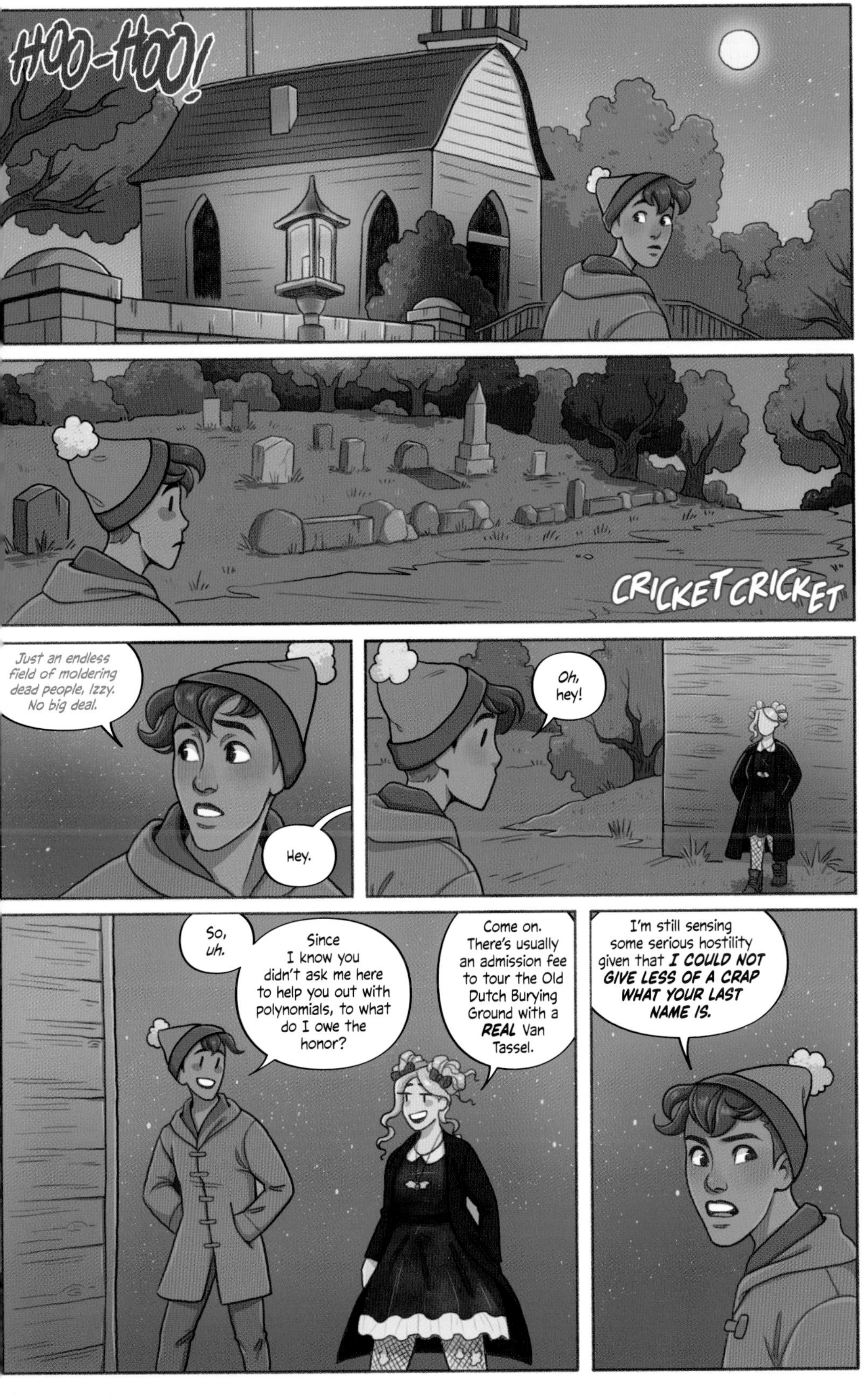
HOO-HOO!
CRICKET CRICKET
Just an endless field of moldering dead people, Izzy. No big deal.
Hey.
Oh, hey!
So, uh.
Since I know you didn't ask me here to help you out with polynomials, to what do I owe the honor?
Come on. There's usually an admission fee to tour the Old Dutch Burying Ground with a **REAL** Van Tassel.
I'm still sensing some serious hostility given that **I COULD NOT GIVE LESS OF A CRAP WHAT YOUR LAST NAME IS.**

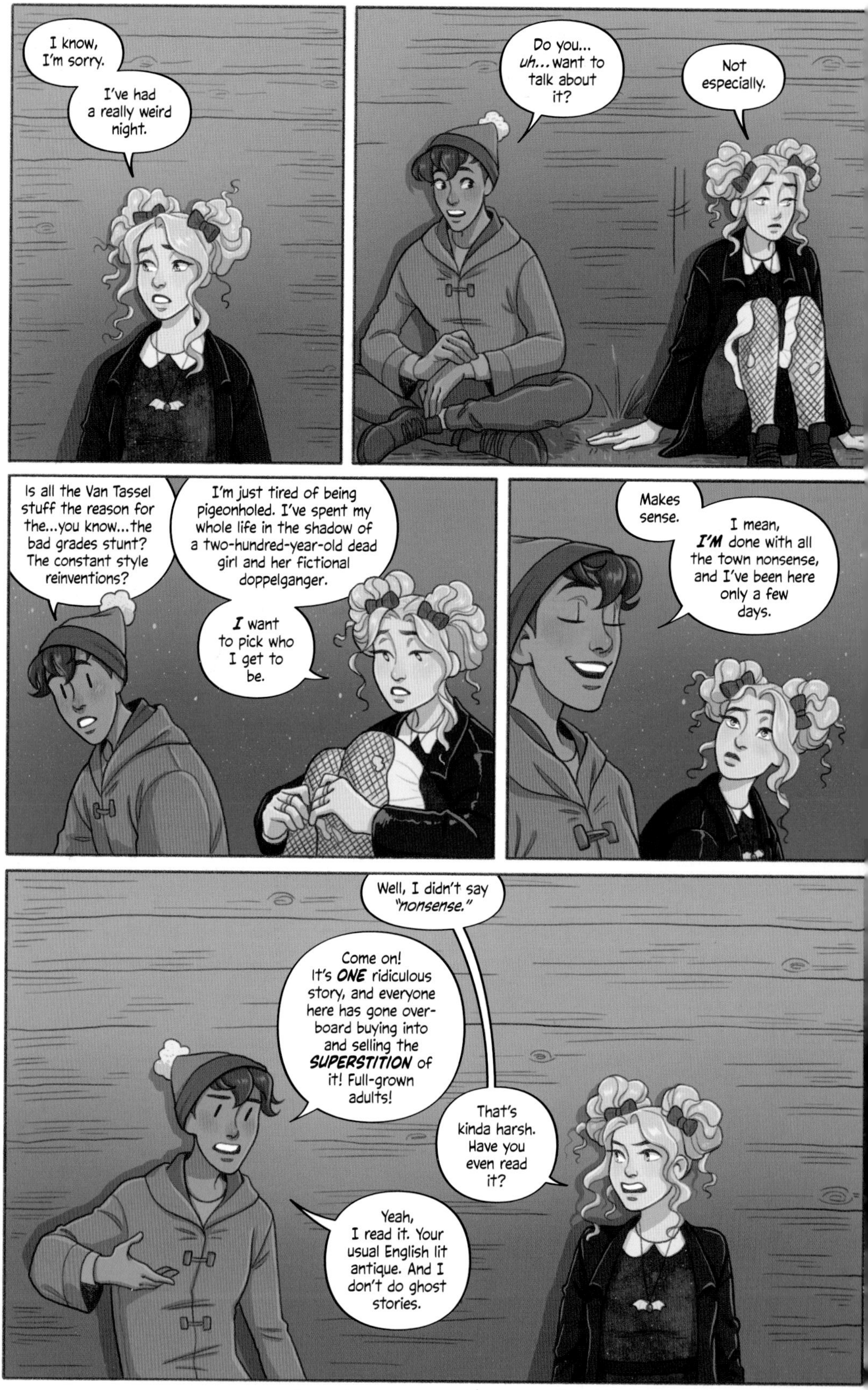

I know, I'm sorry.
I've had a really weird night.
Do you... *uh...* want to talk about it?
Not especially.
Is all the Van Tassel stuff the reason for the...you know...the bad grades stunt? The constant style reinventions?
I'm just tired of being pigeonholed. I've spent my whole life in the shadow of a two-hundred-year-old dead girl and her fictional doppelganger.
I want to pick who I get to be.
Makes sense.
I mean, *I'M* done with all the town nonsense, and I've been here only a few days.
Well, I didn't say *"nonsense."*
Come on! It's *ONE* ridiculous story, and everyone here has gone over-board buying into and selling the *SUPERSTITION* of it! Full-grown adults!
That's kinda harsh. Have you even read it?
Yeah, I read it. Your usual English lit antique. And I don't do ghost stories.

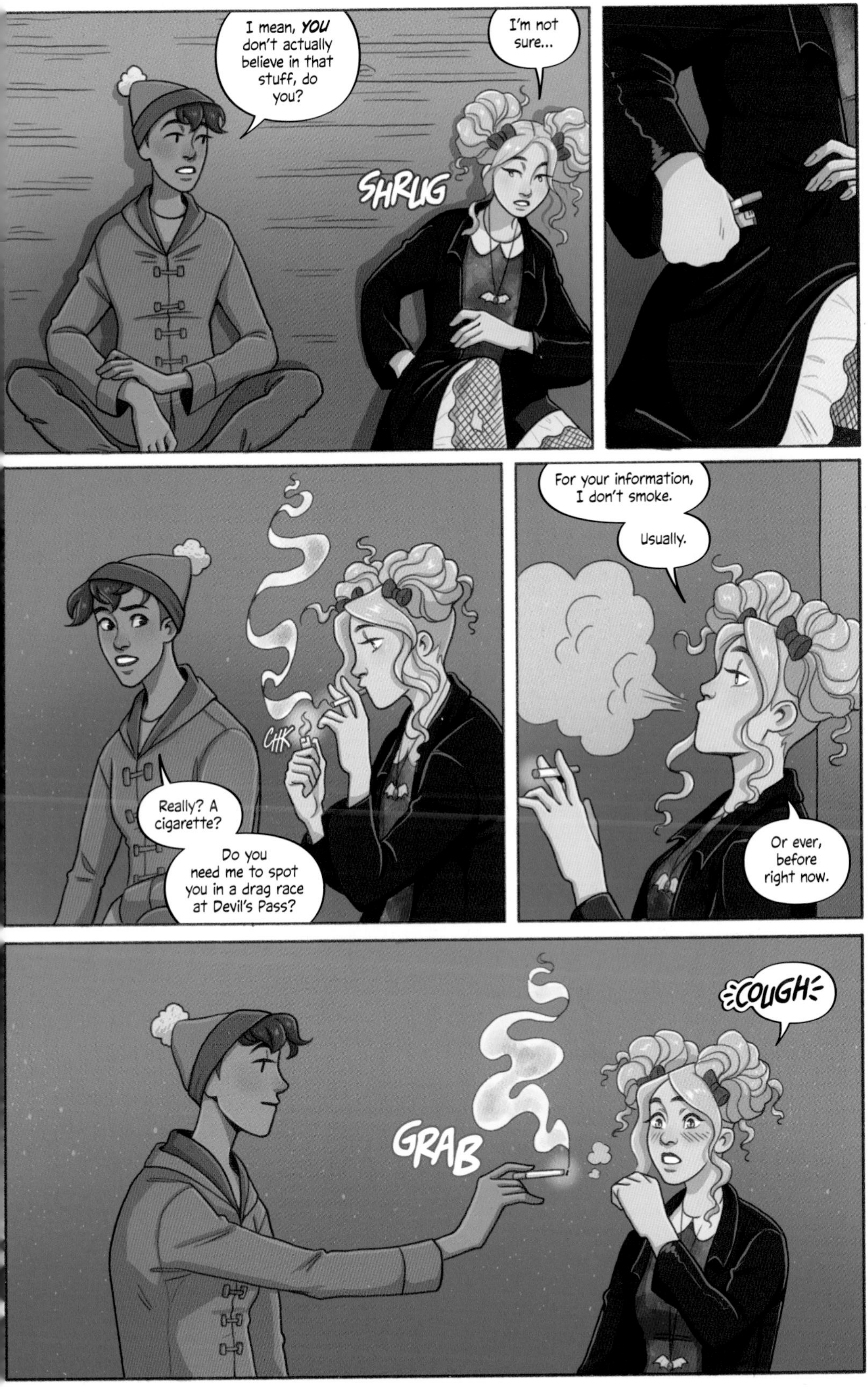

I mean, YOU don't actually believe in that stuff, do you?
I'm not sure...
SHRUG
CHK
Really? A cigarette?
Do you need me to spot you in a drag race at Devil's Pass?
For your information, I don't smoke.
Usually.
Or ever, before right now.
COUGH
GRAB

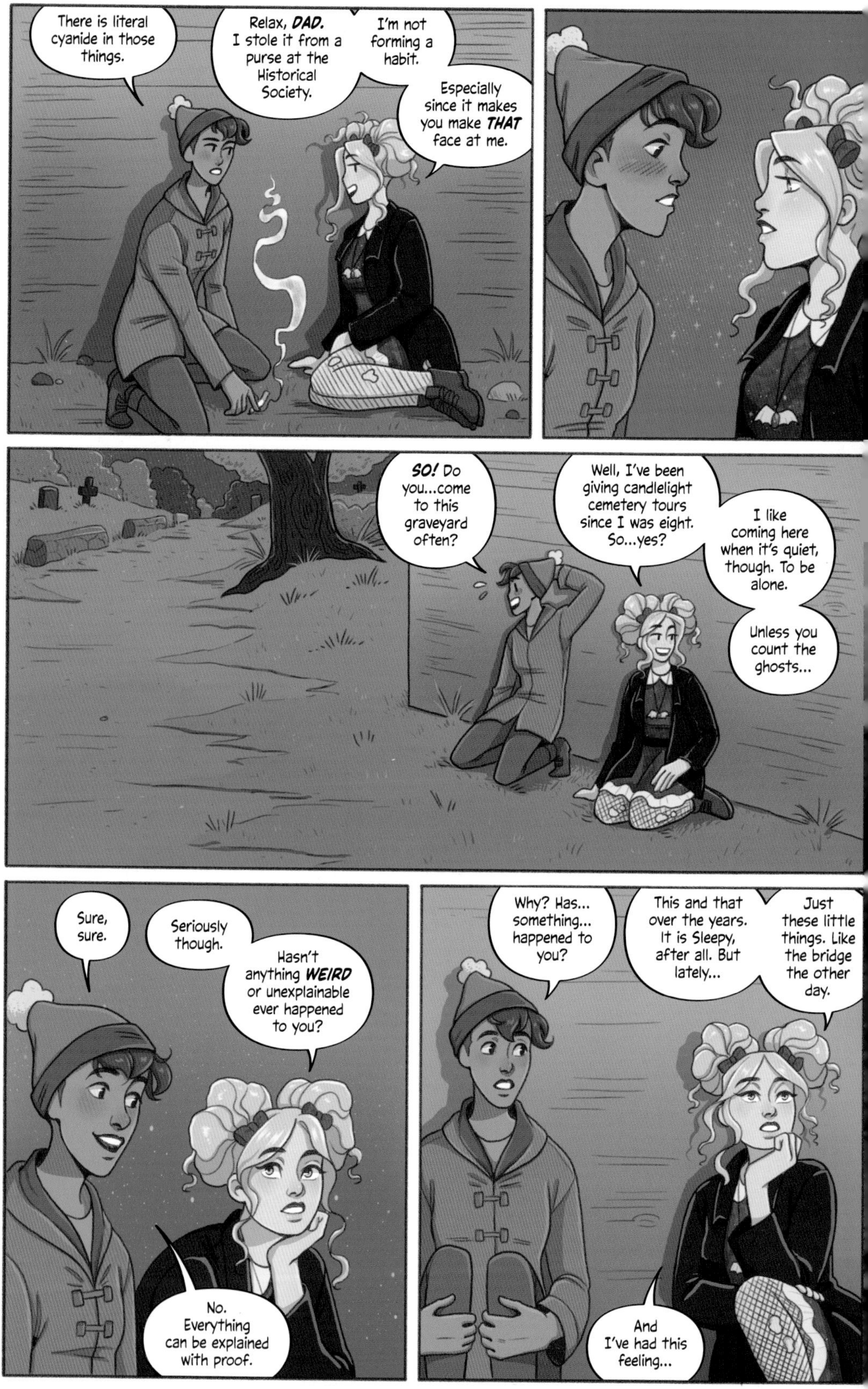
There is literal cyanide in those things.
Relax, DAD. I stole it from a purse at the Historical Society.
I'm not forming a habit.
Especially since it makes you make THAT face at me.
SO! Do you...come to this graveyard often?
Well, I've been giving candlelight cemetery tours since I was eight. So...yes?
I like coming here when it's quiet, though. To be alone.
Unless you count the ghosts...
Sure, sure.
Seriously though.
Hasn't anything WEIRD or unexplainable ever happened to you?
No. Everything can be explained with proof.
Why? Has... something... happened to you?
This and that over the years. It is Sleepy, after all. But lately...
Just these little things. Like the bridge the other day.
And I've had this feeling...

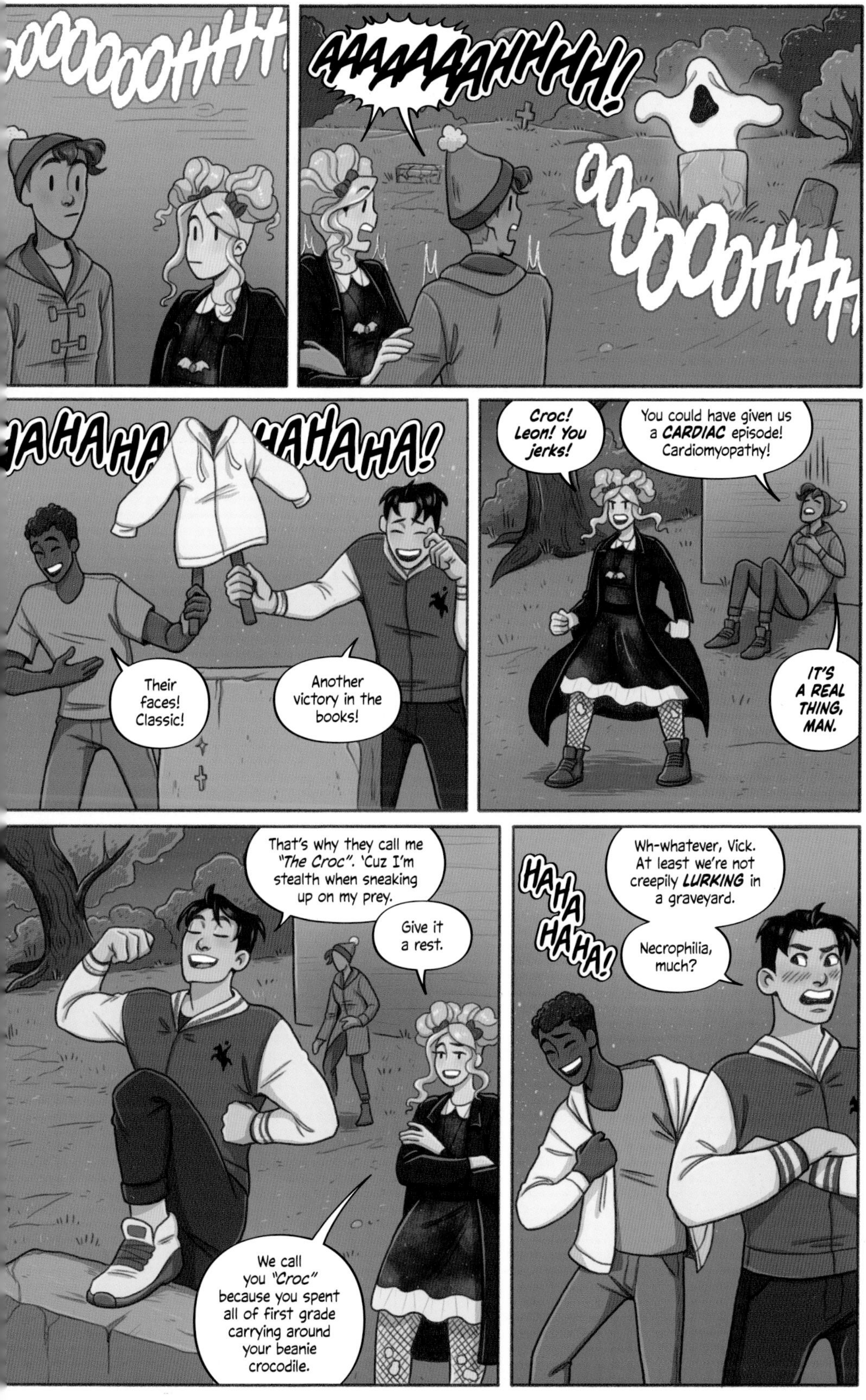
OOOOOOOHHHH
AAAAAAAAHHHHH!
OOOOOOHHHH
HAHAHA HAHAHA!
Their faces! Classic!
Another victory in the books!
Croc! Leon! You jerks!
You could have given us a CARDIAC episode! Cardiomyopathy!
IT'S A REAL THING, MAN.
That's why they call me "The Croc". 'Cuz I'm stealth when sneaking up on my prey.
Give it a rest.
We call you "Croc" because you spent all of first grade carrying around your beanie crocodile.
HAHA HAHA!
Wh-whatever, Vick. At least we're not creepily LURKING in a graveyard.
Necrophilia, much?

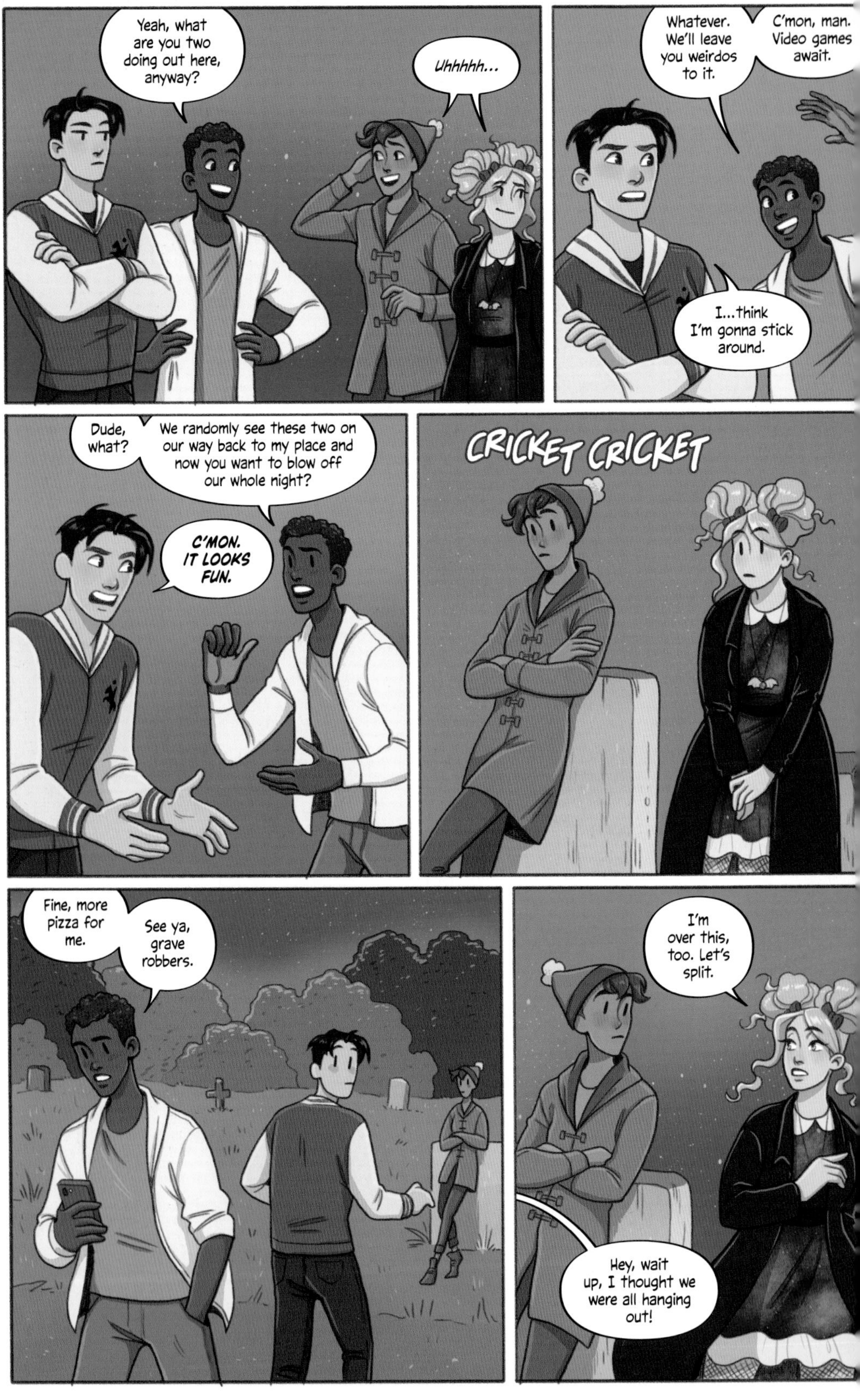
Yeah, what are you two doing out here, anyway?
Uhhhhh...
Whatever. We'll leave you weirdos to it.
C'mon, man. Video games await.
I...think I'm gonna stick around.
Dude, what?
We randomly see these two on our way back to my place and now you want to blow off our whole night?
C'MON. IT LOOKS FUN.
CRICKET CRICKET
Fine, more pizza for me.
See ya, grave robbers.
I'm over this, too. Let's split.
Hey, wait up, I thought we were all hanging out!

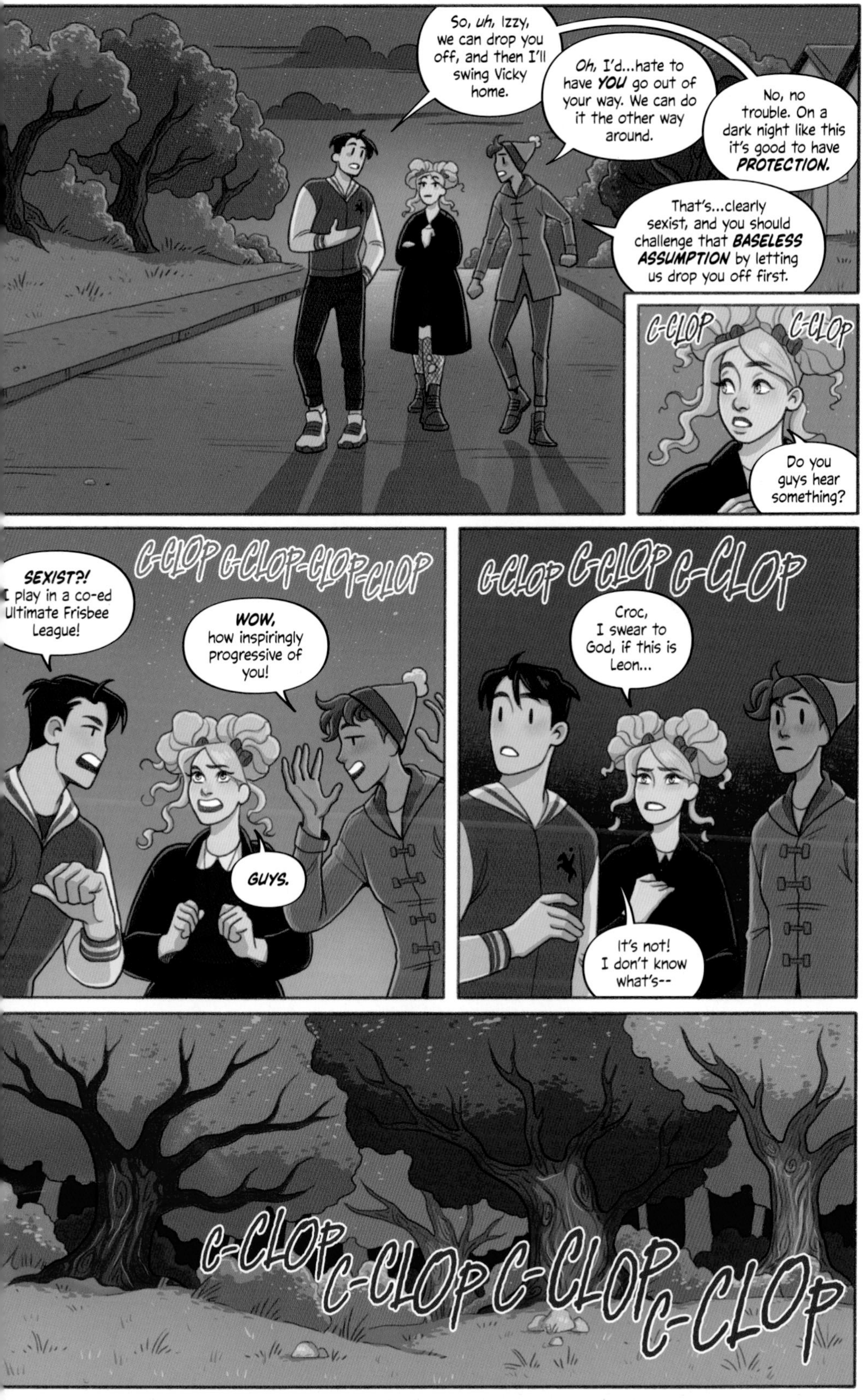
So, *uh,* Izzy, we can drop you off, and then I'll swing Vicky home.
Oh, I'd...hate to have **YOU** go out of your way. We can do it the other way around.
No, no trouble. On a dark night like this it's good to have **PROTECTION.**
That's...clearly sexist, and you should challenge that **BASELESS ASSUMPTION** by letting us drop you off first.
C-CLOP C-CLOP
Do you guys hear something?
C-CLOP C-CLOP-CLOP-CLOP
SEXIST?! I play in a co-ed Ultimate Frisbee League!
WOW, how inspiringly progressive of you!
GUYS.
C-CLOP C-CLOP C-CLOP
Croc, I swear to God, if this is Leon...
It's not! I don't know what's--
C-CLOP C-CLOP C-CLOP C-CLOP

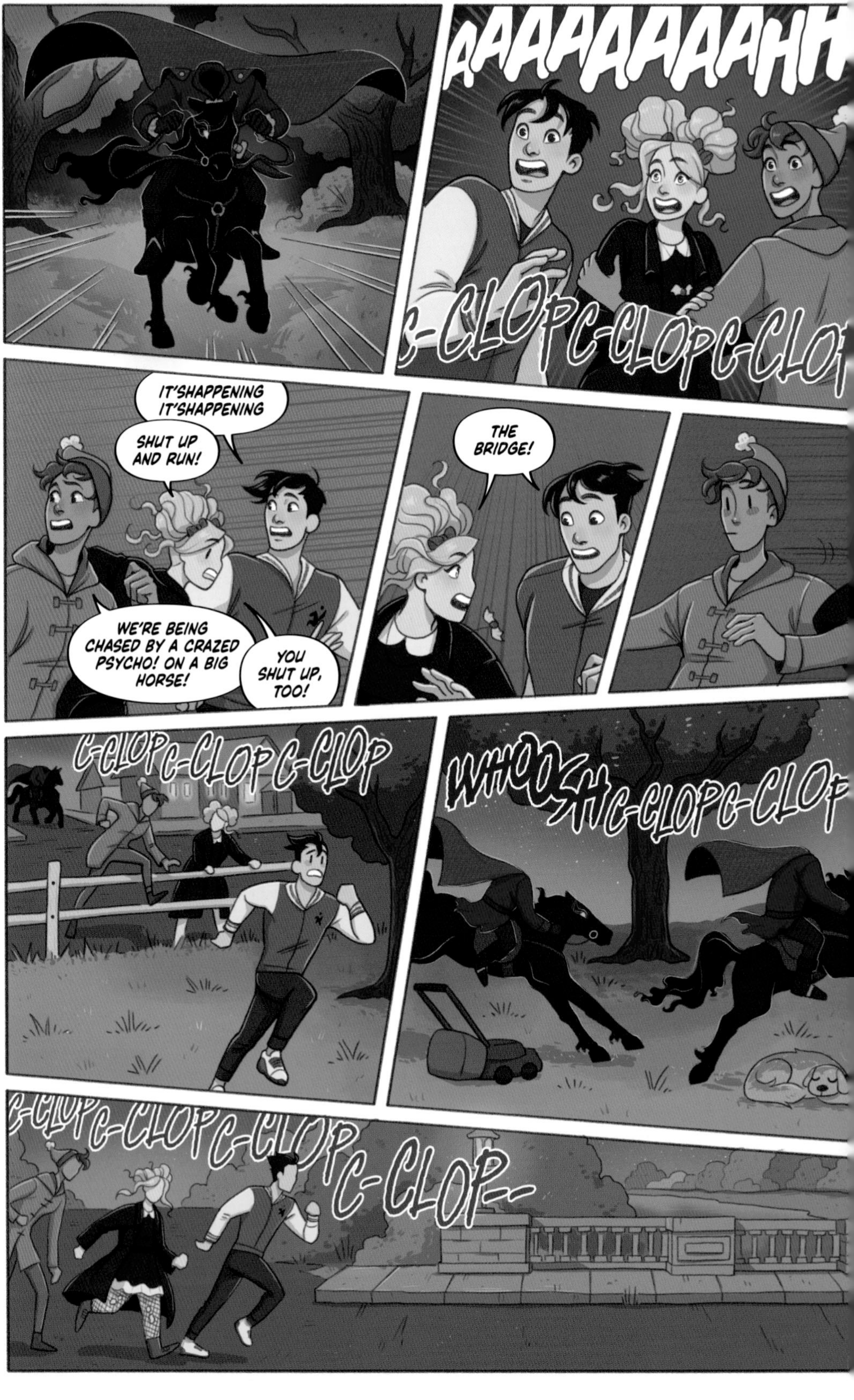
AAAAAAAAAAHH
C-CLOP C-CLOP C-CLOP
IT'SHAPPENING IT'SHAPPENING
SHUT UP AND RUN!
WE'RE BEING CHASED BY A CRAZED PSYCHO! ON A BIG HORSE!
YOU SHUT UP, TOO!
THE BRIDGE!
C-CLOP C-CLOP C-CLOP
WHOOSH C-CLOP C-CLOP
C-CLOP C-CLOP C-CLOP C-CLOP--

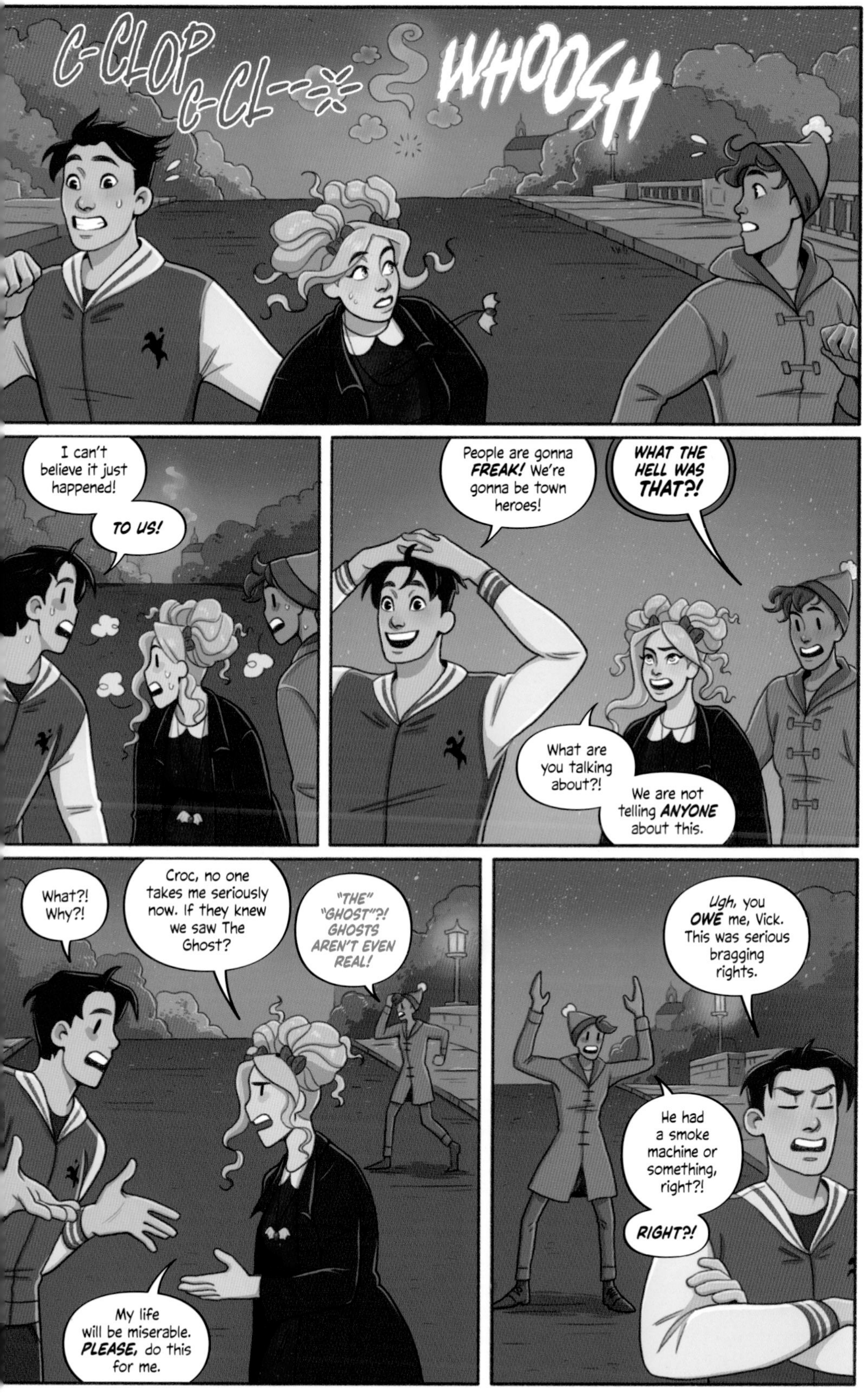
C-CLOP C-CL--
WHOOSH
I can't believe it just happened!
TO US!
People are gonna FREAK! We're gonna be town heroes!
WHAT THE HELL WAS THAT?!
What are you talking about?!
We are not telling ANYONE about this.
What?! Why?!
Croc, no one takes me seriously now. If they knew we saw The Ghost?
My life will be miserable. PLEASE, do this for me.
"THE" "GHOST"?! GHOSTS AREN'T EVEN REAL!
Ugh, you OWE me, Vick. This was serious bragging rights.
He had a smoke machine or something, right?!
RIGHT?!

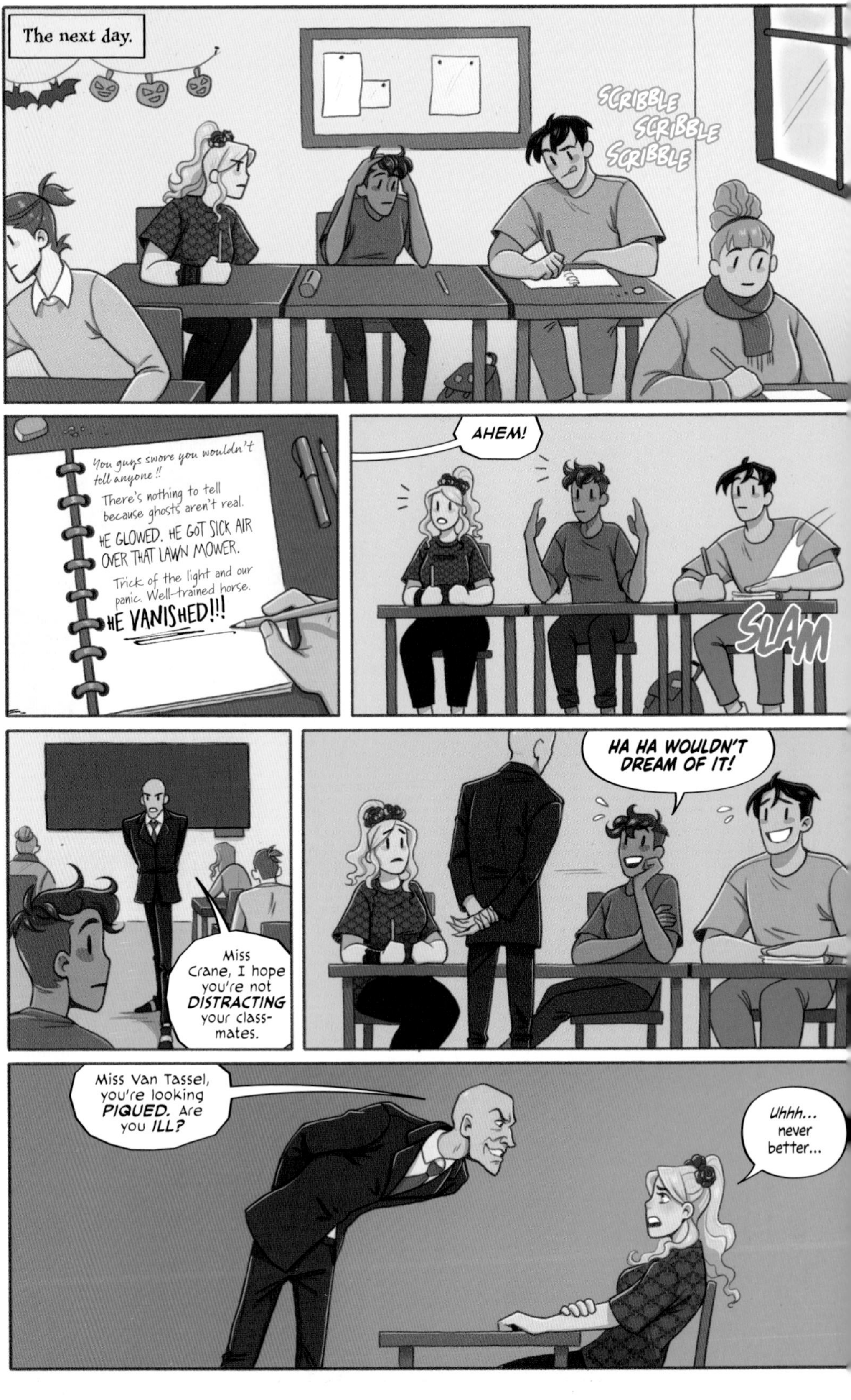

The next day.
SCRIBBLE
SCRIBBLE
SCRIBBLE
You guys swore you wouldn't tell anyone!!
There's nothing to tell because ghosts aren't real.
HE GLOWED. HE GOT SICK AIR OVER THAT LAWN MOWER.
Trick of the light and our panic. Well-trained horse.
HE VANISHED!!!
AHEM!
SLAM
Miss Crane, I hope you're not DISTRACTING your class-mates.
HA HA WOULDN'T DREAM OF IT!
Miss Van Tassel, you're looking PIQUED. Are you ILL?
Uhhh... never better...

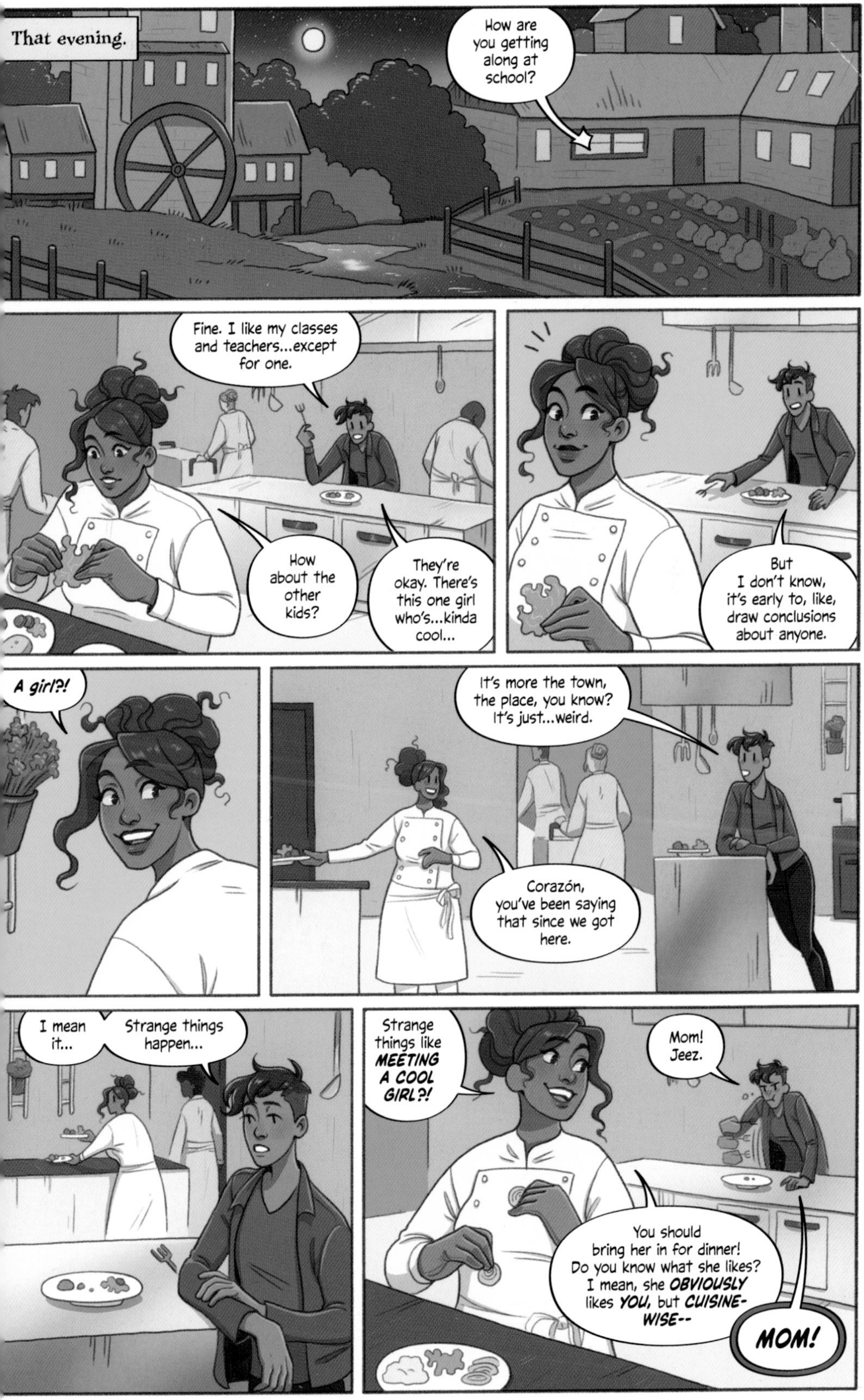
That evening.
How are you getting along at school?
Fine. I like my classes and teachers...except for one.
How about the other kids?
They're okay. There's this one girl who's...kinda cool...
But I don't know, it's early to, like, draw conclusions about anyone.
A girl?!
It's more the town, the place, you know? It's just...weird.
Corazón, you've been saying that since we got here.
I mean it...
Strange things happen...
Strange things like MEETING A COOL GIRL?!
Mom! Jeez.
You should bring her in for dinner! Do you know what she likes? I mean, she OBVIOUSLY likes YOU, but CUISINE-WISE--
MOM!

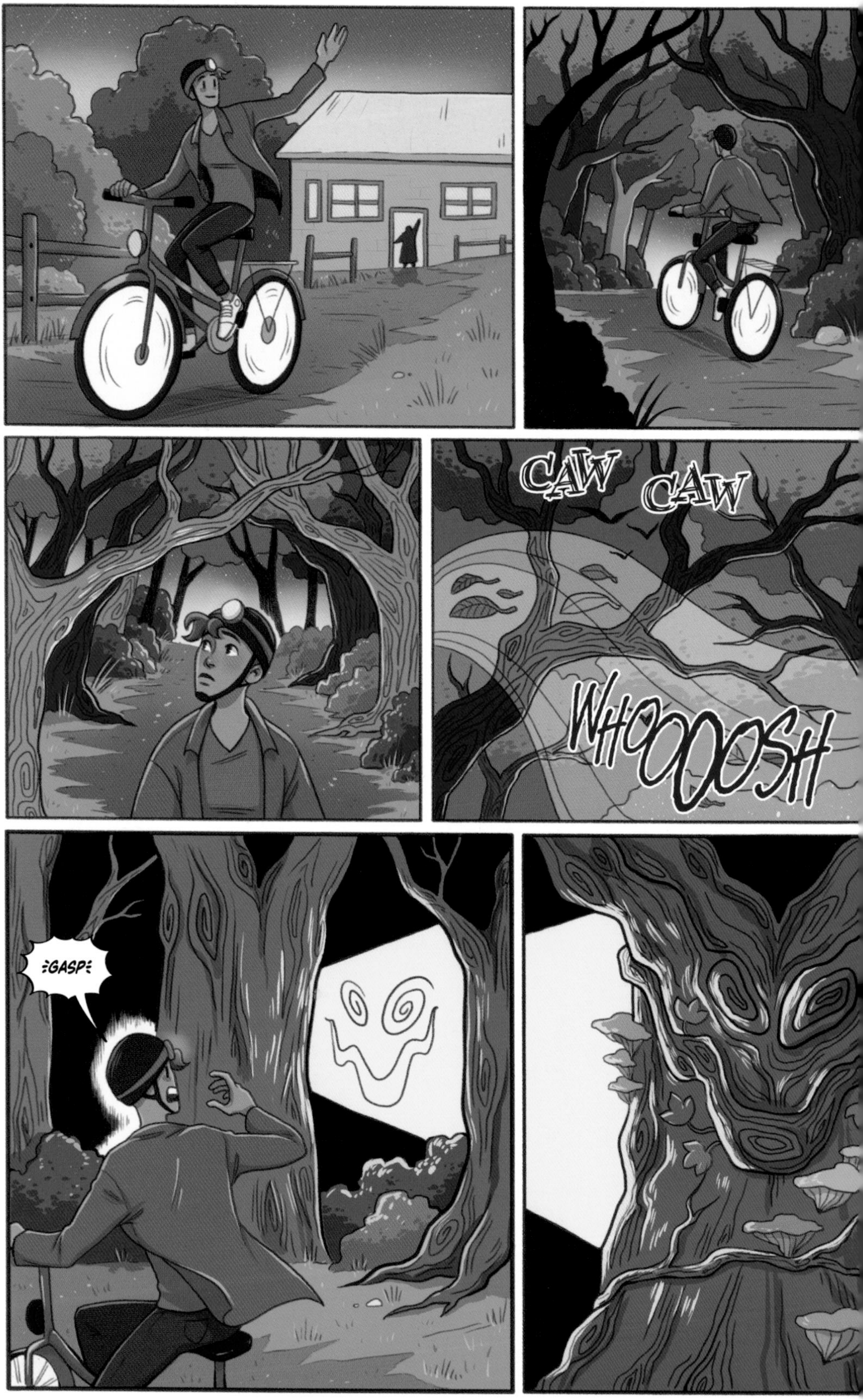
CAW CAW
WHOOOOSH
GASP

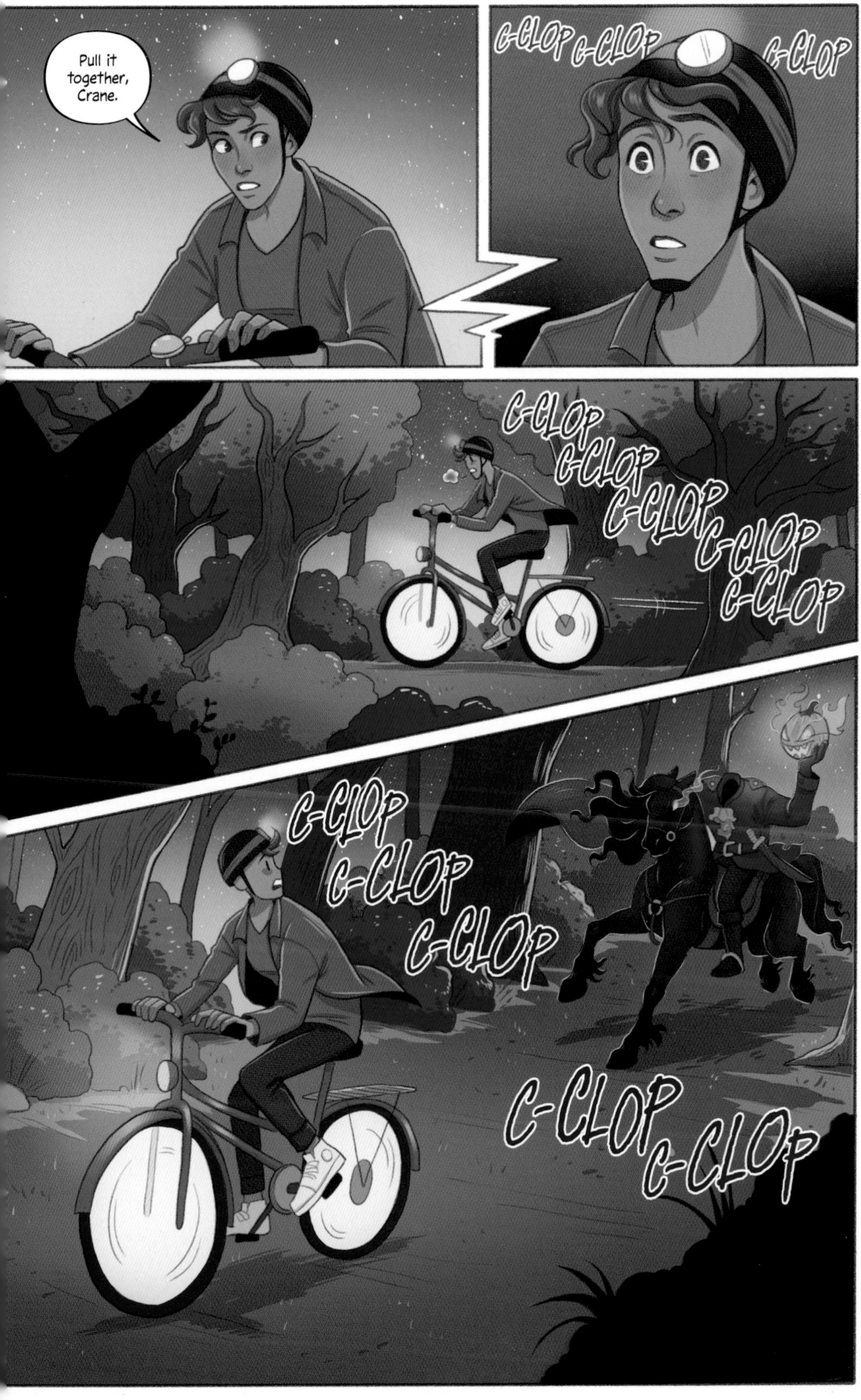
Pull it together, Crane.
C-CLOP C-CLOP C-CLOP
C-CLOP
C-CLOP
C-CLOP
C-CLOP
C-CLOP
C-CLOP
C-CLOP
C-CLOP
C-CLOP
C-CLOP

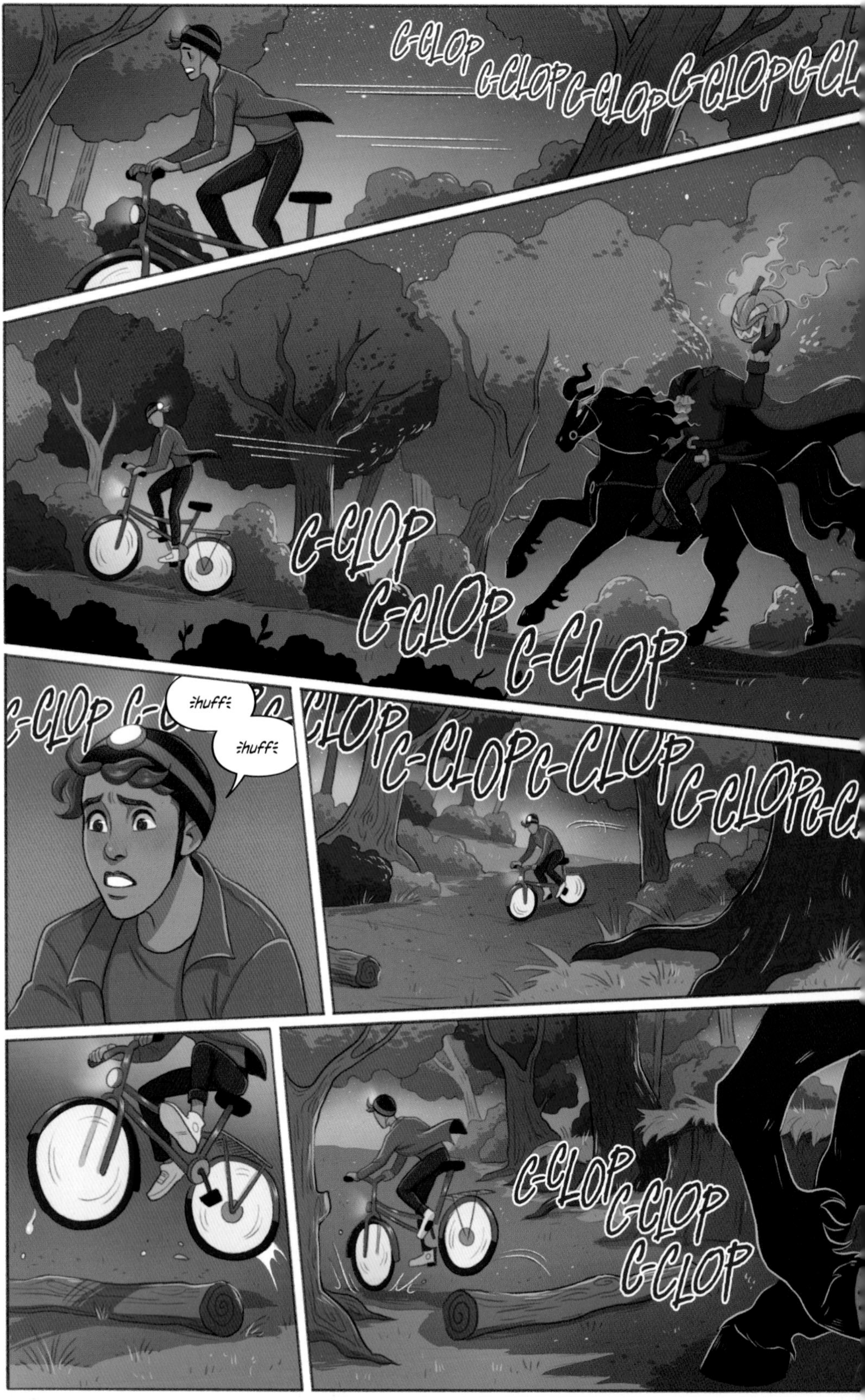

C-CLOP C-CLOP C-CLOP C-CLOP C-CL
C-CLOP
C-CLOP
C-CLOP
C-CLOP C-
huff
huff
CLOP C-CLOP C-CLOP C-CLOP C-CLOP C-C
C-CLOP
C-CLOP
C-CLOP

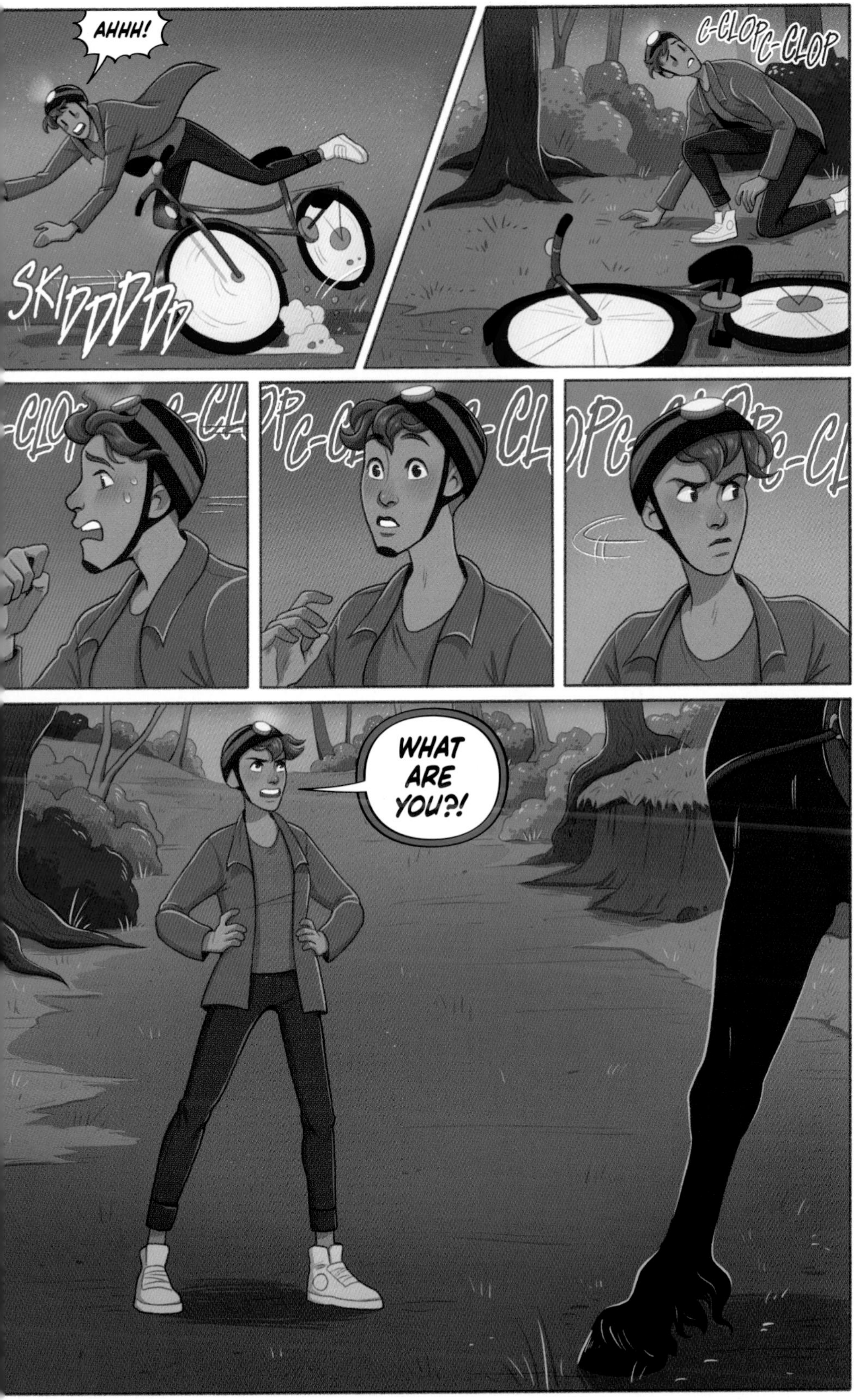
AHHH!
SKIDDDDDD
C-CLOP C-CLOP
C-CLOP C-CLOP
C-CLOP C-CLOP
C-CLOP C-CLOP
WHAT ARE YOU?!

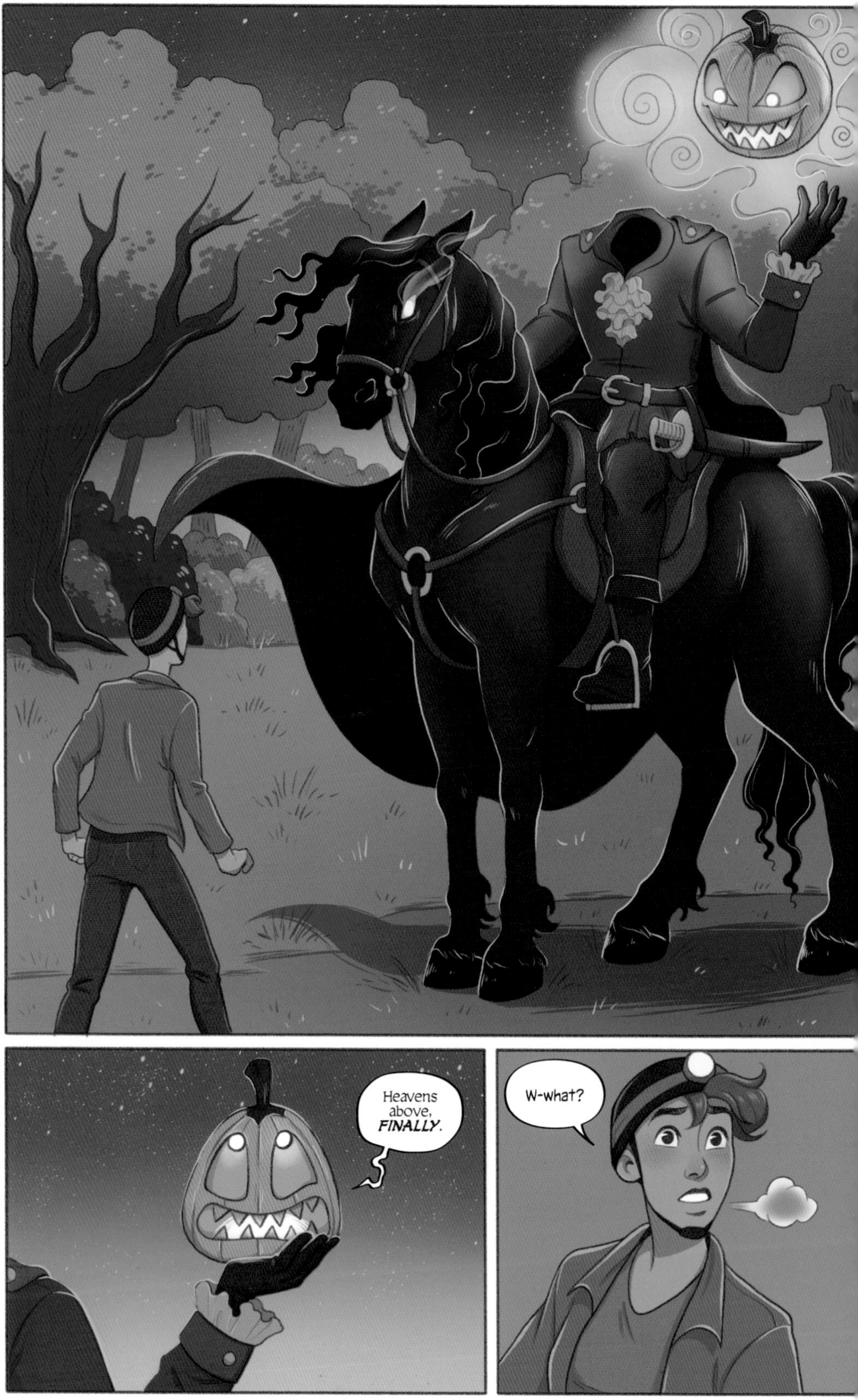
Heavens above, **FINALLY**.
W-what?

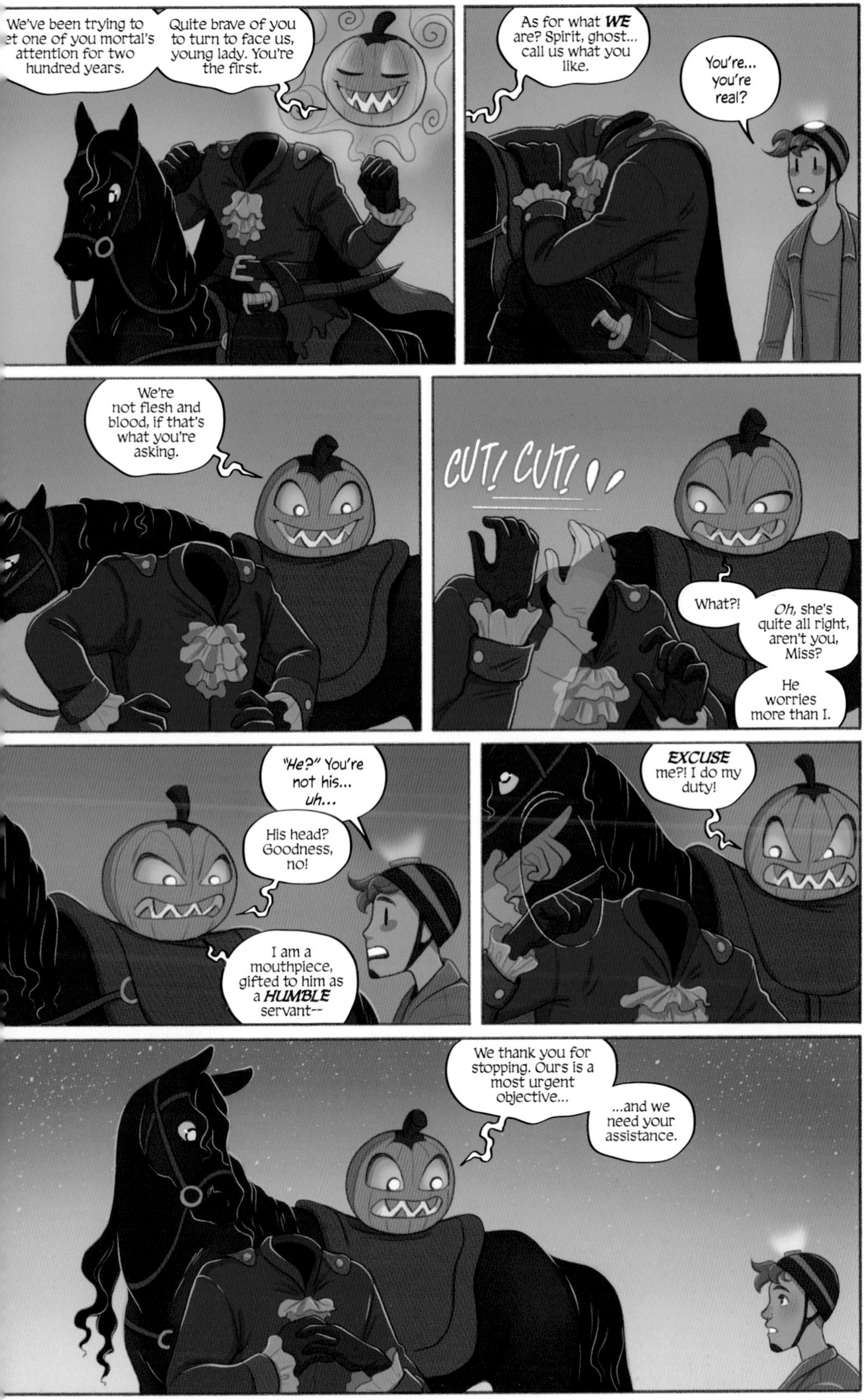
We've been trying to et one of you mortal's attention for two hundred years.
Quite brave of you to turn to face us, young lady. You're the first.
As for what WE are? Spirit, ghost... call us what you like.
You're... you're real?
We're not flesh and blood, if that's what you're asking.
CUT! CUT!
What?!
Oh, she's quite all right, aren't you, Miss?
He worries more than I.
"He?" You're not his... uh...
His head? Goodness, no!
I am a mouthpiece, gifted to him as a HUMBLE servant--
EXCUSE me?! I do my duty!
We thank you for stopping. Ours is a most urgent objective...
...and we need your assistance.

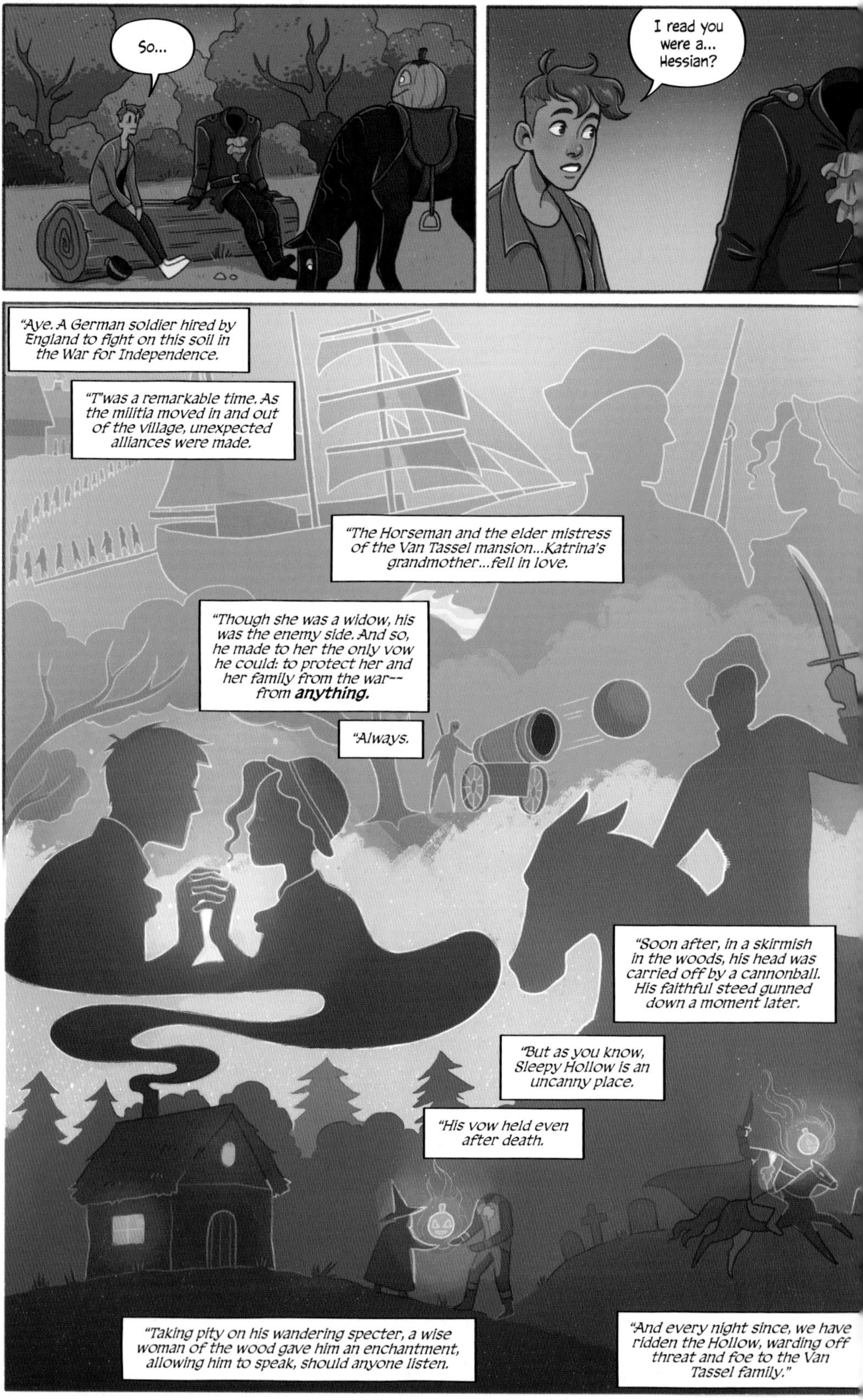
So...
I read you were a... Hessian?
"Aye. A German soldier hired by England to fight on this soil in the War for Independence.
"T'was a remarkable time. As the militia moved in and out of the village, unexpected alliances were made.
"The Horseman and the elder mistress of the Van Tassel mansion...Katrina's grandmother...fell in love.
"Though she was a widow, his was the enemy side. And so, he made to her the only vow he could: to protect her and her family from the war-- from **anything.**
"Always.
"Soon after, in a skirmish in the woods, his head was carried off by a cannonball. His faithful steed gunned down a moment later.
"But as you know, Sleepy Hollow is an uncanny place.
"His vow held even after death.
"Taking pity on his wandering specter, a wise woman of the wood gave him an enchantment, allowing him to speak, should anyone listen.
"And every night since, we have ridden the Hollow, warding off threat and foe to the Van Tassel family."

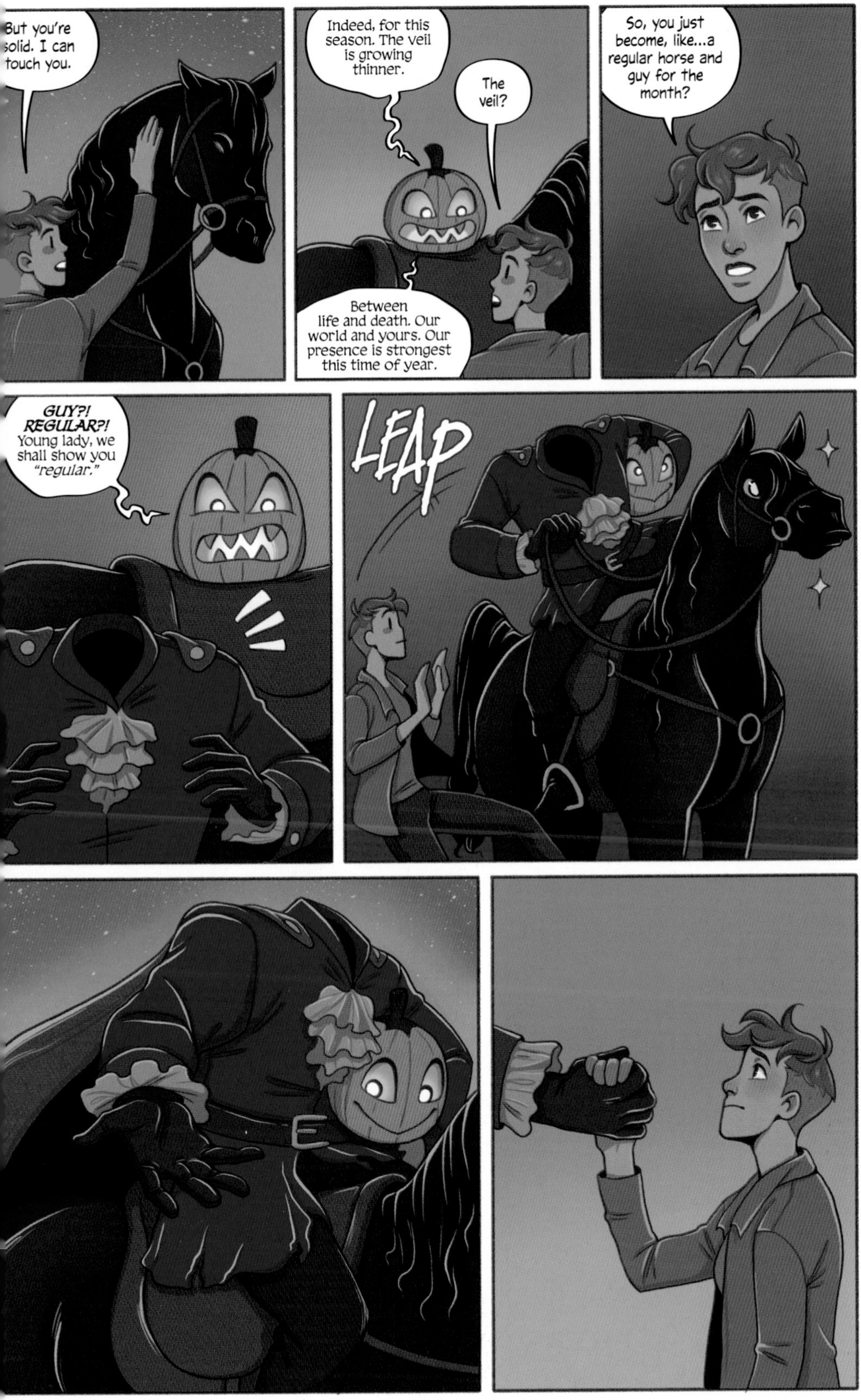
But you're solid. I can touch you.
Indeed, for this season. The veil is growing thinner.
The veil?
Between life and death. Our world and yours. Our presence is strongest this time of year.
So, you just become, like...a regular horse and guy for the month?
GUY?! REGULAR?! Young lady, we shall show you "regular."
LEAP

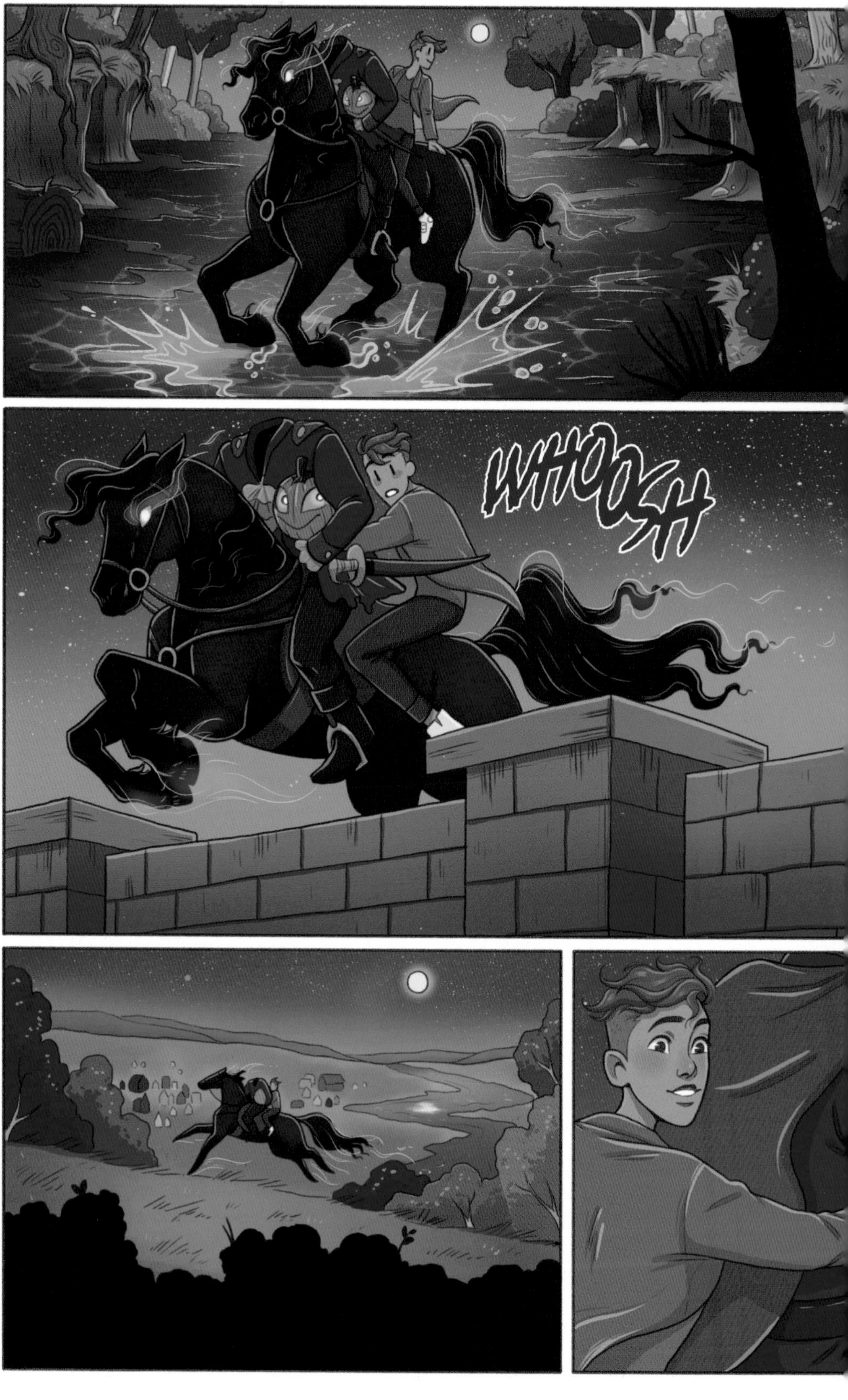
WHOOSH

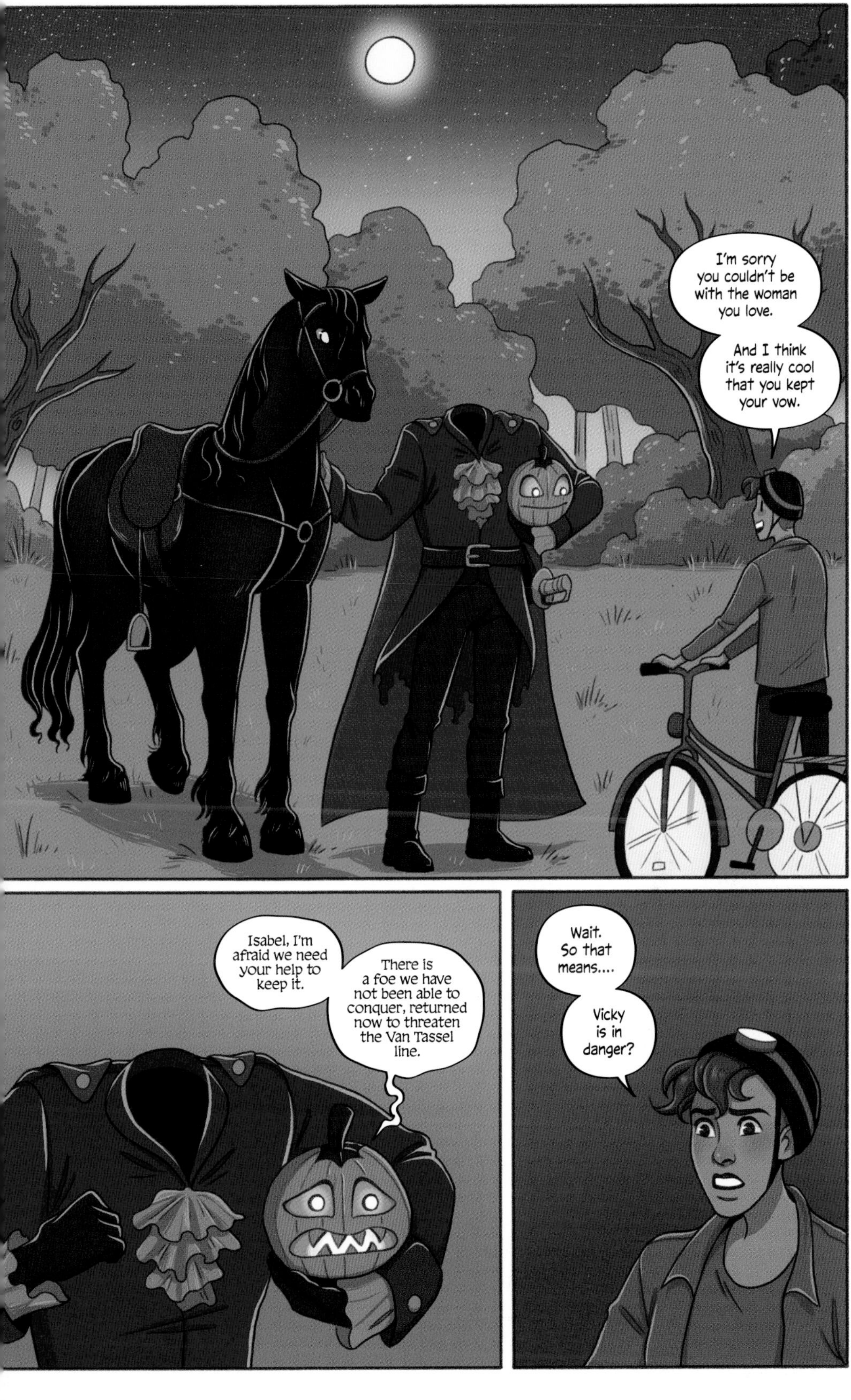
I'm sorry you couldn't be with the woman you love.
And I think it's really cool that you kept your vow.
Isabel, I'm afraid we need your help to keep it.
There is a foe we have not been able to conquer, returned now to threaten the Van Tassel line.
Wait. So that means....
Vicky is in danger?

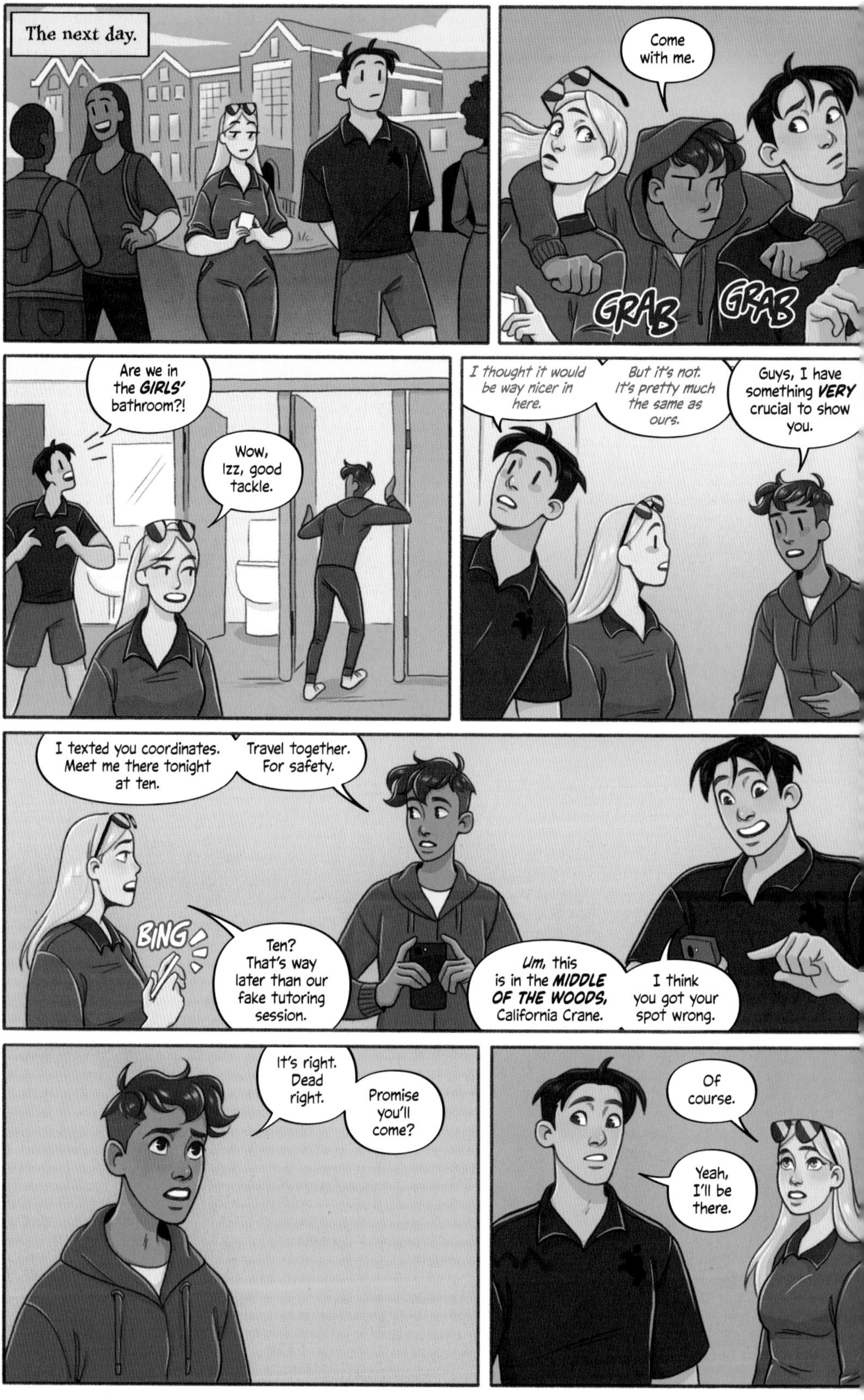

The next day.
Come with me.
GRAB
GRAB
Are we in the GIRLS' bathroom?!
Wow, Izz, good tackle.
I thought it would be way nicer in here.
But it's not. It's pretty much the same as ours.
Guys, I have something VERY crucial to show you.
I texted you coordinates. Meet me there tonight at ten.
Travel together. For safety.
BING
Ten? That's way later than our fake tutoring session.
Um, this is in the MIDDLE OF THE WOODS, California Crane.
I think you got your spot wrong.
It's right. Dead right.
Promise you'll come?
Of course.
Yeah, I'll be there.

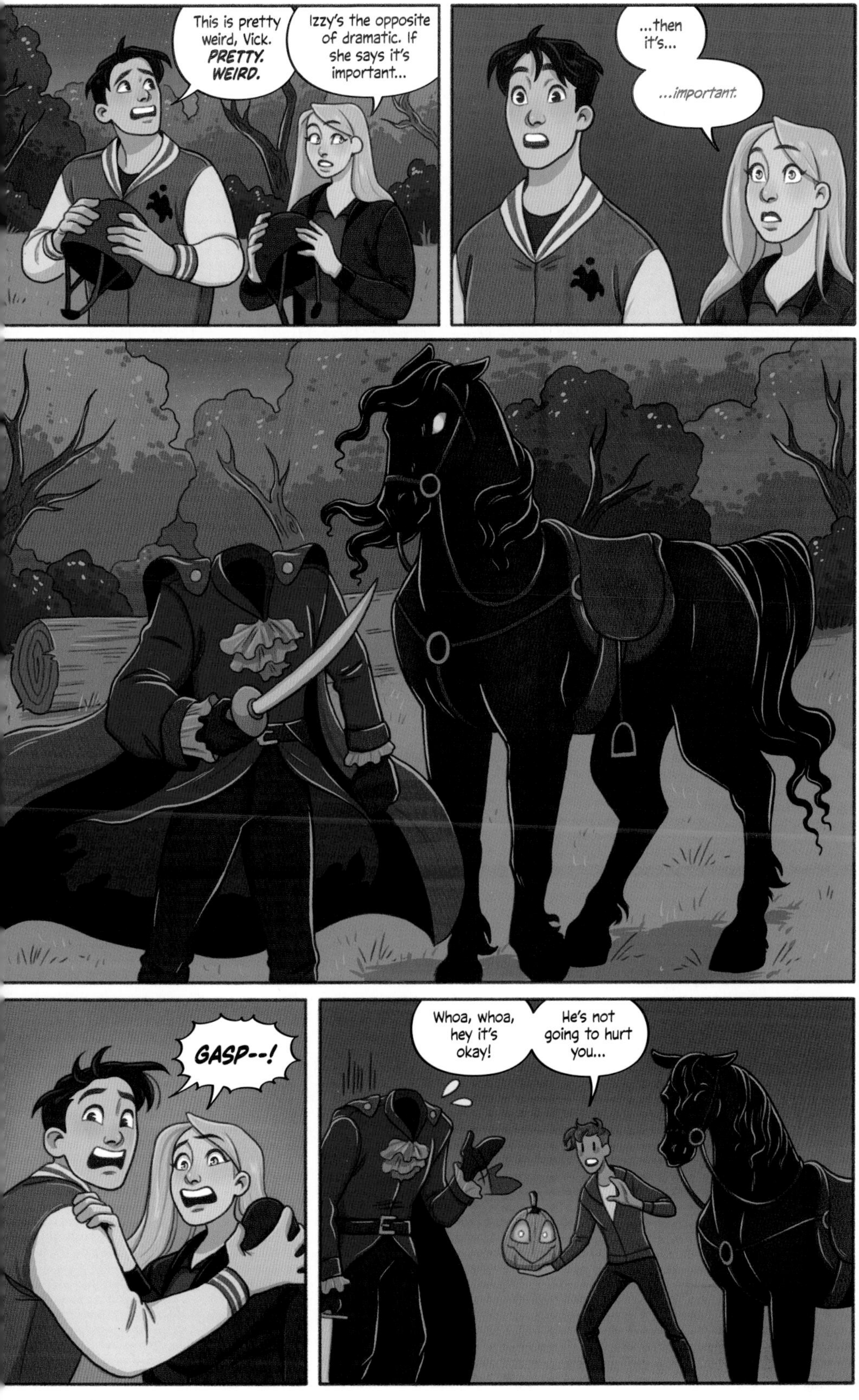
This is pretty weird, Vick. PRETTY. WEIRD.
Izzy's the opposite of dramatic. If she says it's important...
...then it's...
...important.
GASP--!
Whoa, whoa, hey it's okay!
He's not going to hurt you...

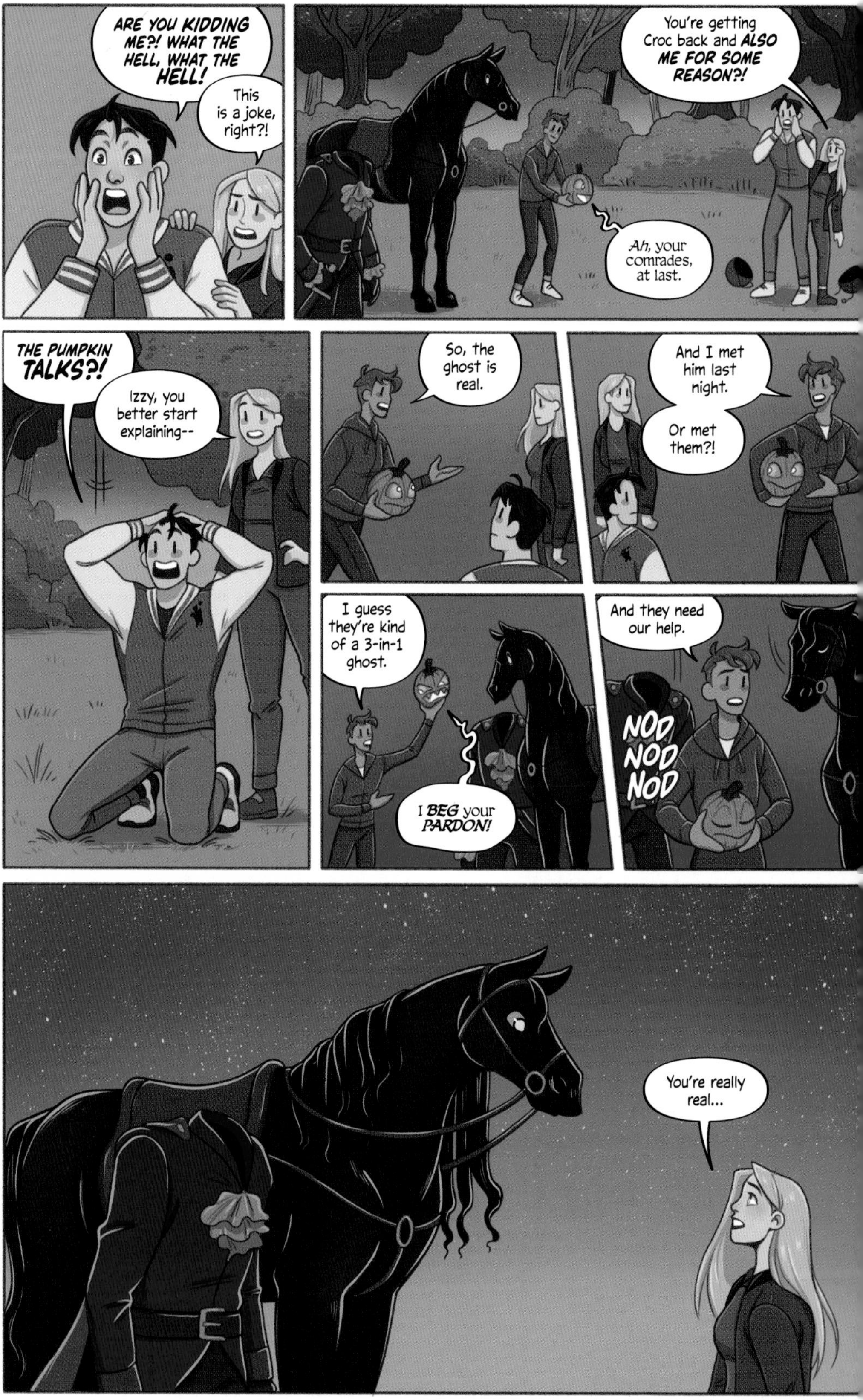
ARE YOU KIDDING ME?! WHAT THE HELL, WHAT THE HELL!
This is a joke, right?!
You're getting Croc back and ALSO ME FOR SOME REASON?!
Ah, your comrades, at last.
THE PUMPKIN TALKS?!
Izzy, you better start explaining--
So, the ghost is real.
And I met him last night.
Or met them?!
I guess they're kind of a 3-in-1 ghost.
I BEG your PARDON!
And they need our help.
NOD NOD NOD
You're really real...

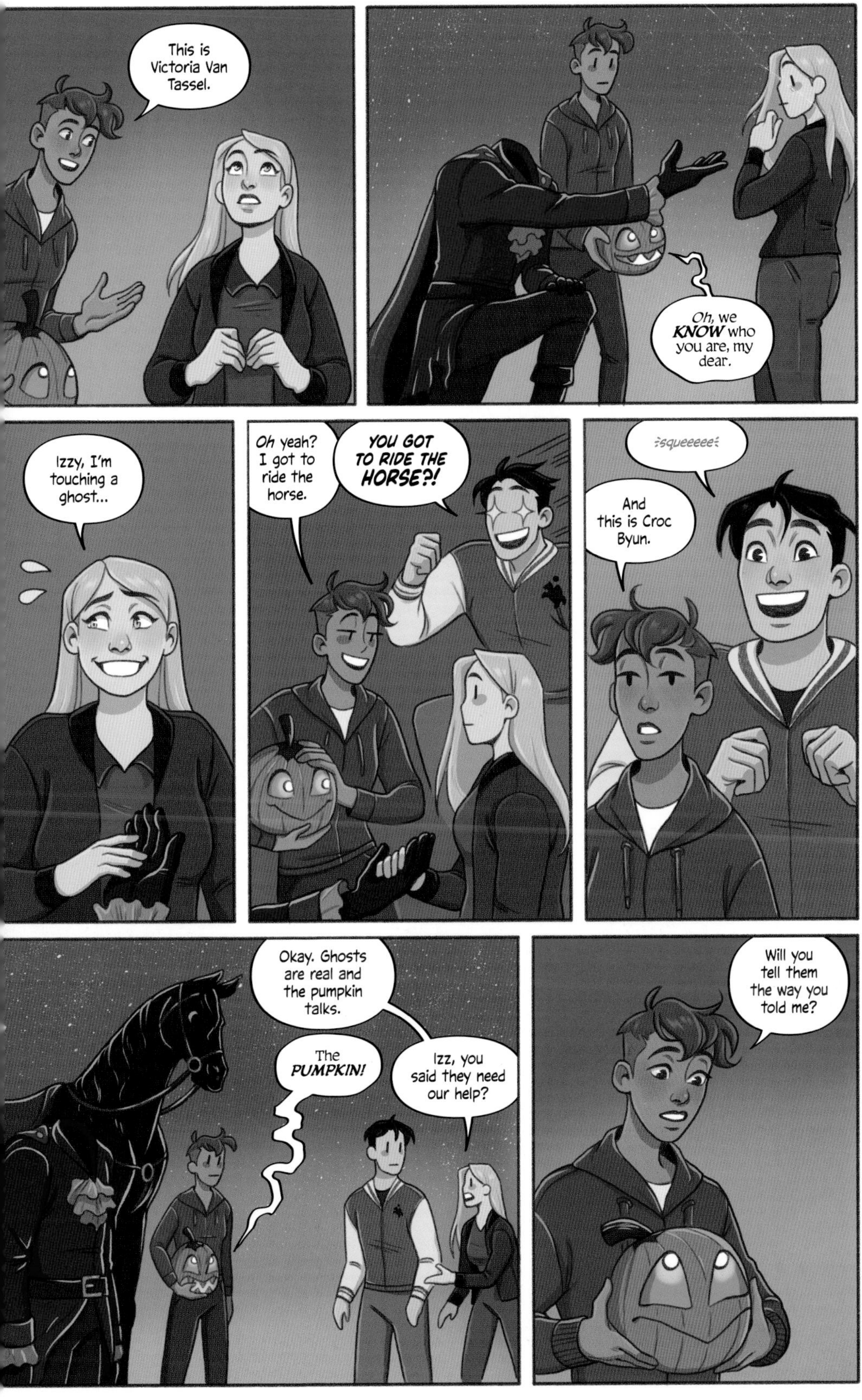
This is Victoria Van Tassel.
Oh, we ***KNOW*** who you are, my dear.
Izzy, I'm touching a ghost...
Oh yeah? I got to ride the horse.
YOU GOT TO RIDE THE HORSE?!
squeeeee
And this is Croc Byun.
Okay. Ghosts are real and the pumpkin talks.
The ***PUMPKIN!***
Izz, you said they need our help?
Will you tell them the way you told me?

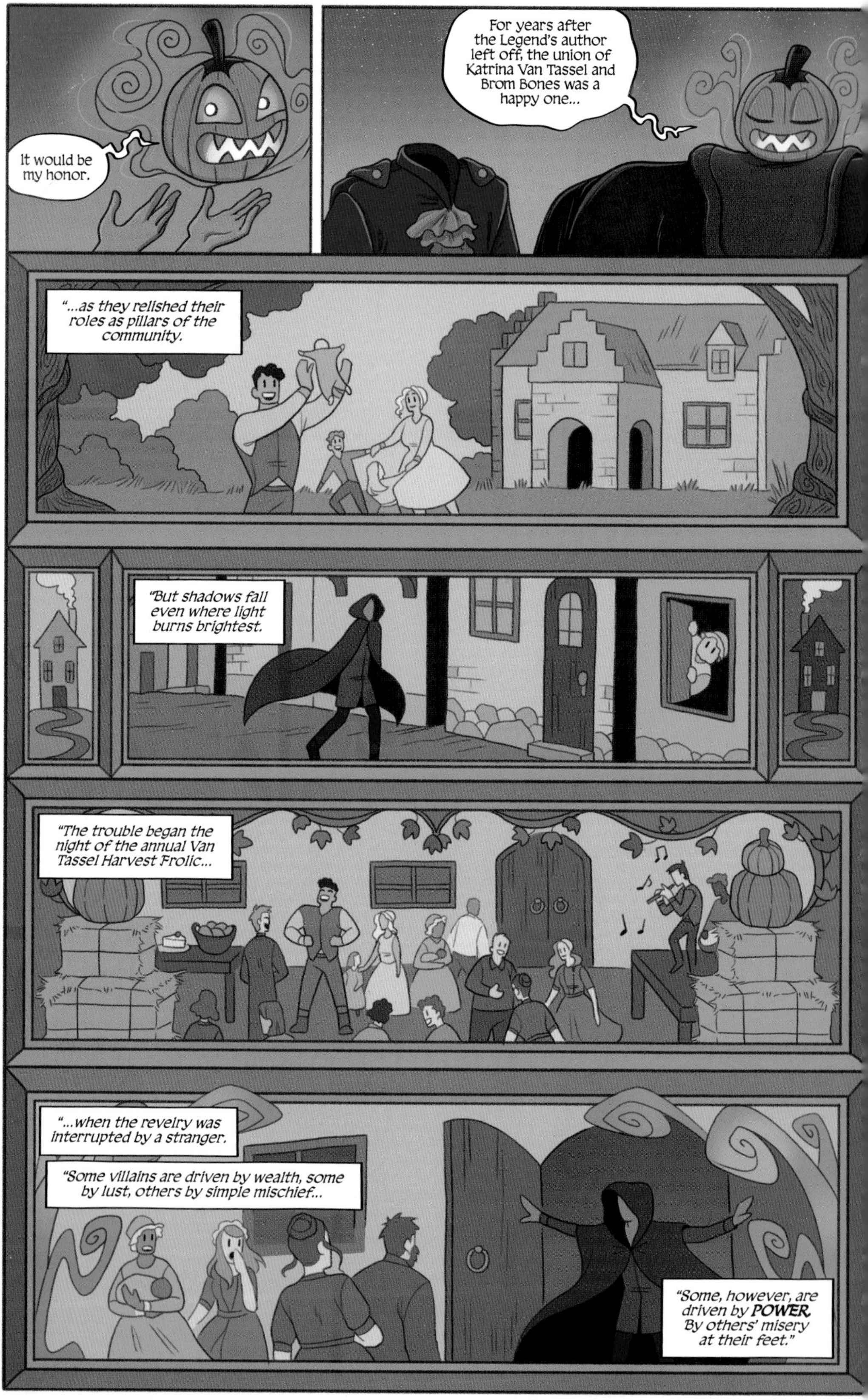
It would be my honor.
For years after the Legend's author left off, the union of Katrina Van Tassel and Brom Bones was a happy one...
"...as they relished their roles as pillars of the community.
"But shadows fall even where light burns brightest.
"The trouble began the night of the annual Van Tassel Harvest Frolic...
"...when the revelry was interrupted by a stranger.
"Some villains are driven by wealth, some by lust, others by simple mischief...
"Some, however, are driven by POWER. By others' misery at their feet."

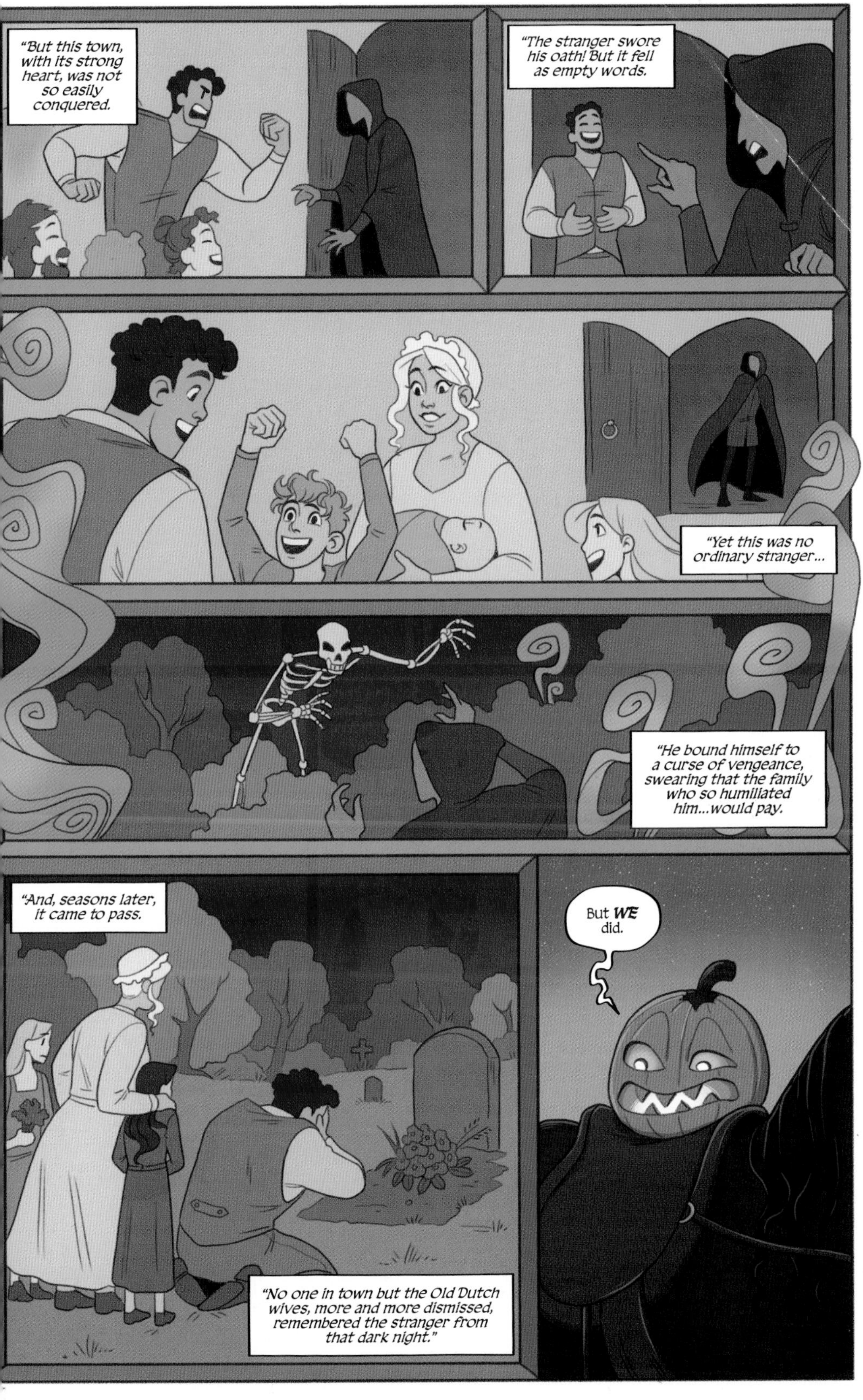
"But this town, with its strong heart, was not so easily conquered.
"The stranger swore his oath! But it fell as empty words.
"Yet this was no ordinary stranger...
"He bound himself to a curse of vengeance, swearing that the family who so humiliated him...would pay.
"And, seasons later, it came to pass.
"No one in town but the Old Dutch wives, more and more dismissed, remembered the stranger from that dark night."
But WE did.

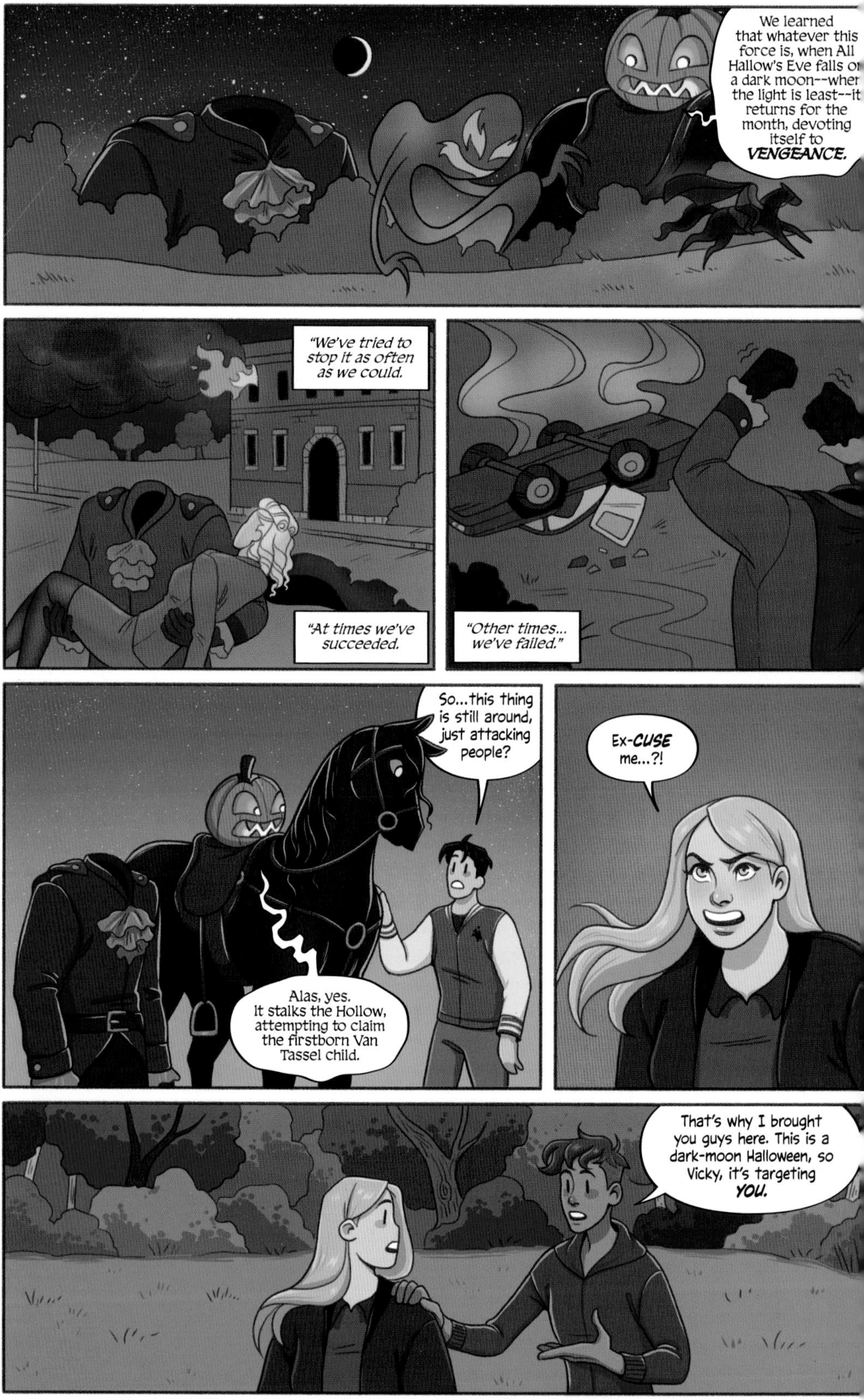

We learned that whatever this force is, when All Hallow's Eve falls on a dark moon--when the light is least--it returns for the month, devoting itself to VENGEANCE.
"We've tried to stop it as often as we could.
"At times we've succeeded.
"Other times... we've failed."
So...this thing is still around, just attacking people?
Alas, yes. It stalks the Hollow, attempting to claim the firstborn Van Tassel child.
Ex-CUSE me...?!
That's why I brought you guys here. This is a dark-moon Halloween, so Vicky, it's targeting YOU.

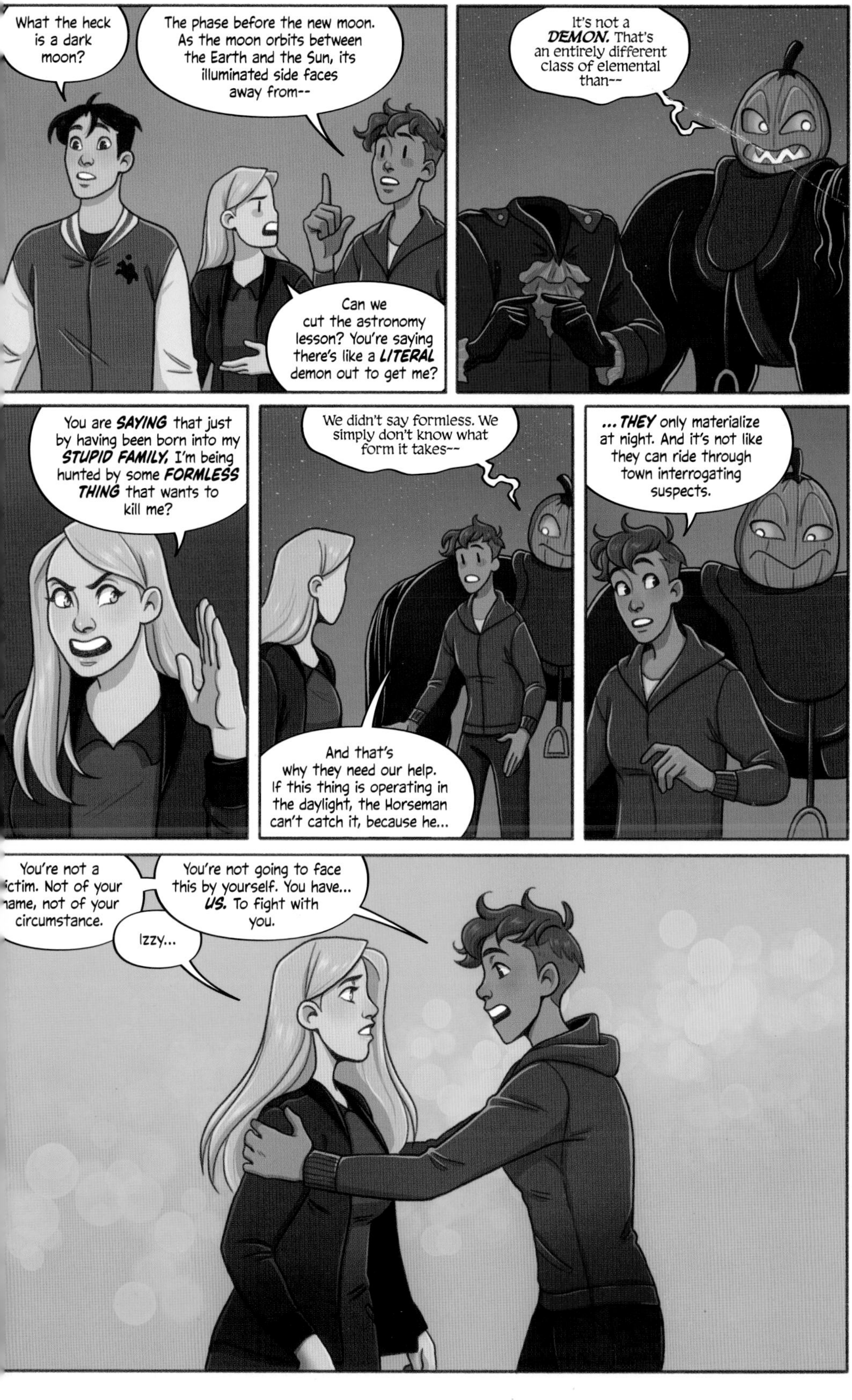

What the heck is a dark moon?
The phase before the new moon. As the moon orbits between the Earth and the Sun, its illuminated side faces away from--
Can we cut the astronomy lesson? You're saying there's like a LITERAL demon out to get me?
It's not a DEMON. That's an entirely different class of elemental than--
You are SAYING that just by having been born into my STUPID FAMILY, I'm being hunted by some FORMLESS THING that wants to kill me?
We didn't say formless. We simply don't know what form it takes--
And that's why they need our help. If this thing is operating in the daylight, the Horseman can't catch it, because he...
...THEY only materialize at night. And it's not like they can ride through town interrogating suspects.
You're not a ictim. Not of your name, not of your circumstance.
You're not going to face this by yourself. You have... US. To fight with you.
Izzy...

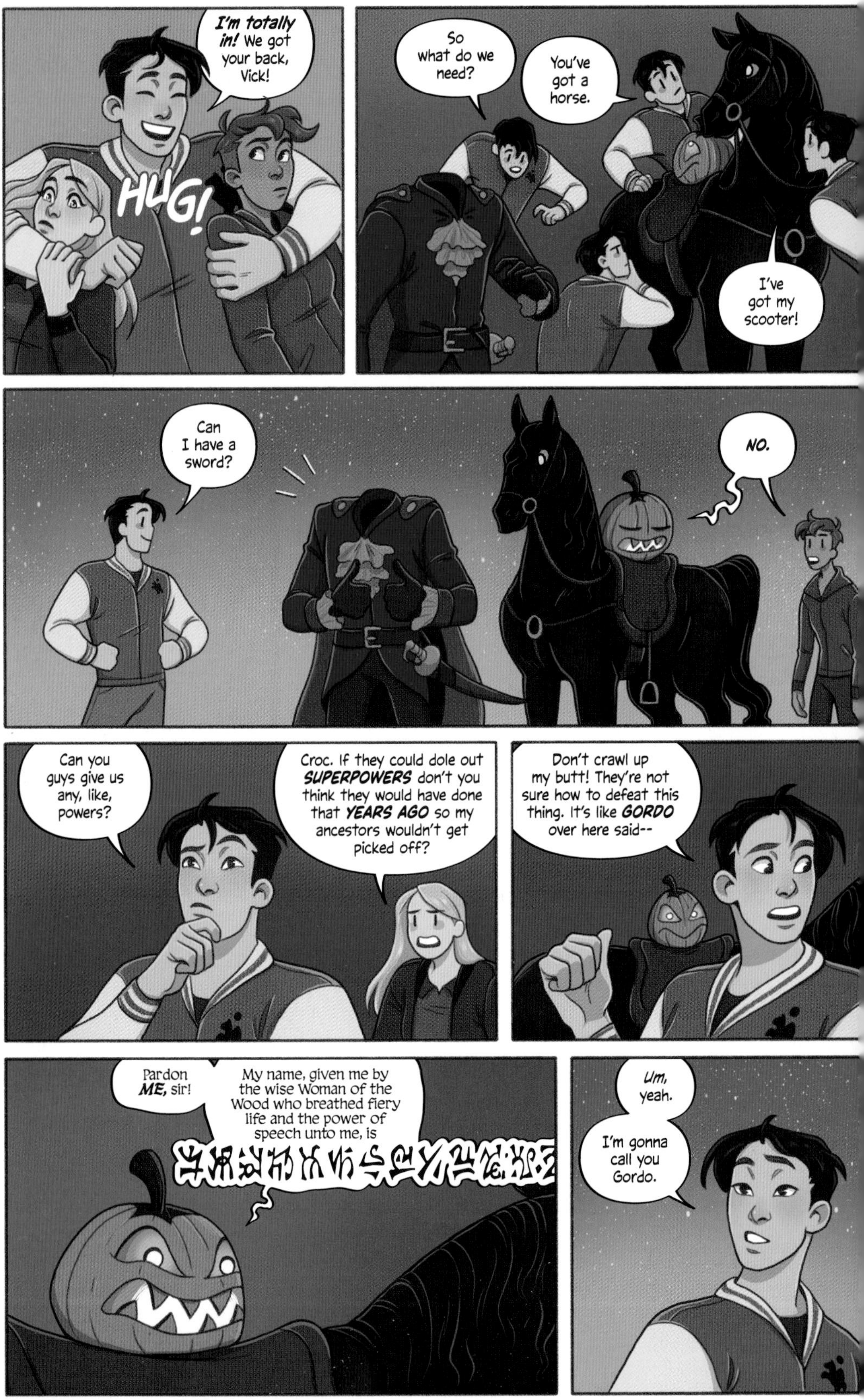

I'm totally in! We got your back, Vick!
HUG!
So what do we need?
You've got a horse.
I've got my scooter!
Can I have a sword?
NO.
Can you guys give us any, like, powers?
Croc. If they could dole out ***SUPERPOWERS*** don't you think they would have done that ***YEARS AGO*** so my ancestors wouldn't get picked off?
Don't crawl up my butt! They're not sure how to defeat this thing. It's like ***GORDO*** over here said--
Pardon ***ME,*** sir!
My name, given me by the wise Woman of the Wood who breathed fiery life and the power of speech unto me, is
Um, yeah.
I'm gonna call you Gordo.

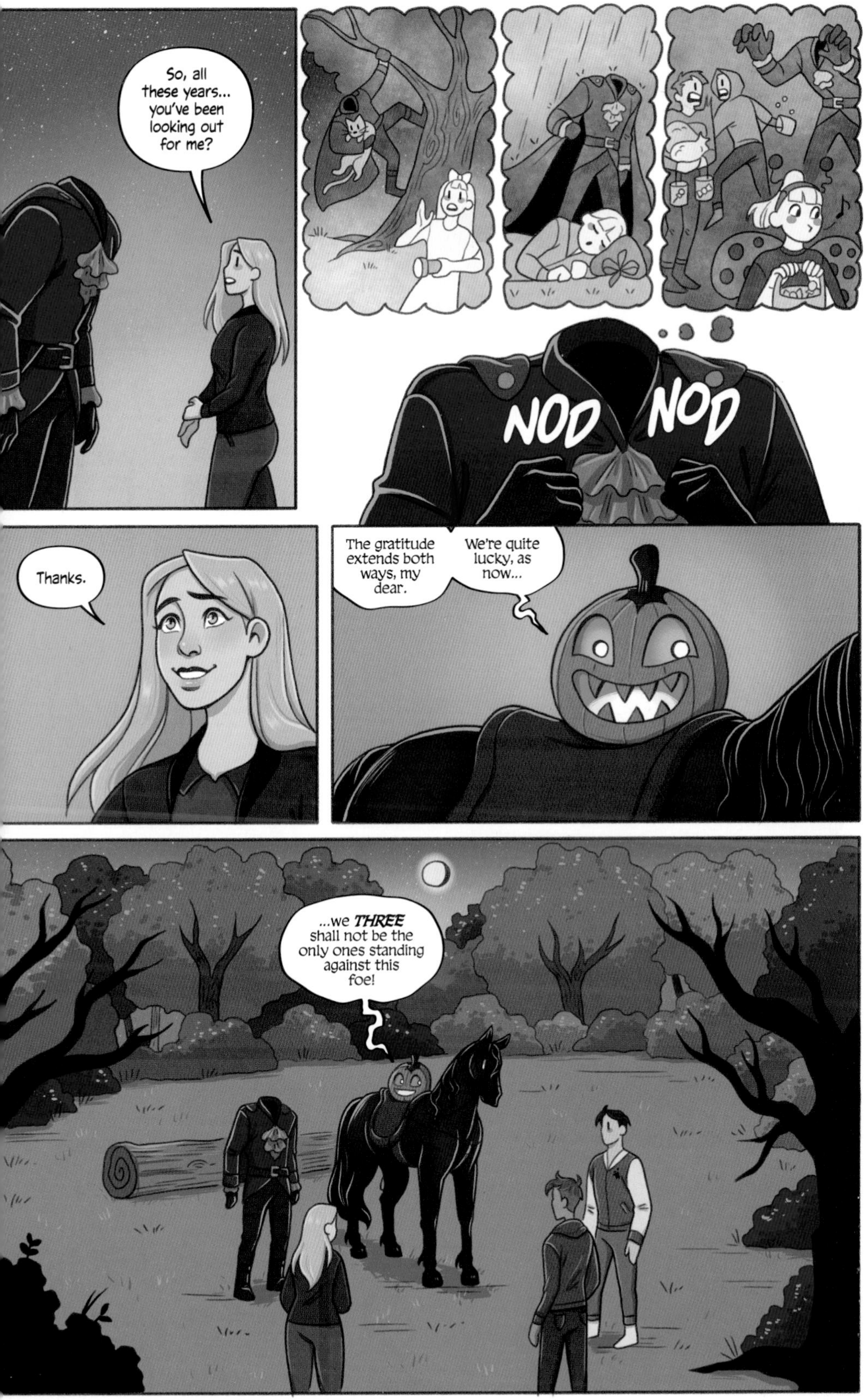
So, all these years... you've been looking out for me?
NOD NOD
Thanks.
The gratitude extends both ways, my dear.
We're quite lucky, as now...
...we THREE shall not be the only ones standing against this foe!

The next morning.

KNOCK KNOCK

Come in!

Ugh, Izzy, prepare yourself for Croc's monster-hunting arsena--

Whoa.

Hey, go ahead and take a seat anywhere...

Have you been...up all night?

FULL MOON

PHASES OF THE MOON

SAN FRAN SCIENCE

SUMMER CAMP

KA-CHLINK

YES.

FULL MOON

PHASES OF T... MOO...

I've been trying to think through *HOW* this thing that's hunting Vicky operates. Because by principle, if we know how a mechanism or process works, then we'll also know how to *STOP* it from working.

Oh, I've got it figured. Vick can just stay in her room for the rest of the month, and we'll stand guard!

I'll take the day shift, and the Horse-man can take nights.

We have school, nerd. And there's no way anyone would let me just *DISAPPEAR.*

This is my busiest month, Van Tassel-wise.

And... I will *NOT* be terrorized.

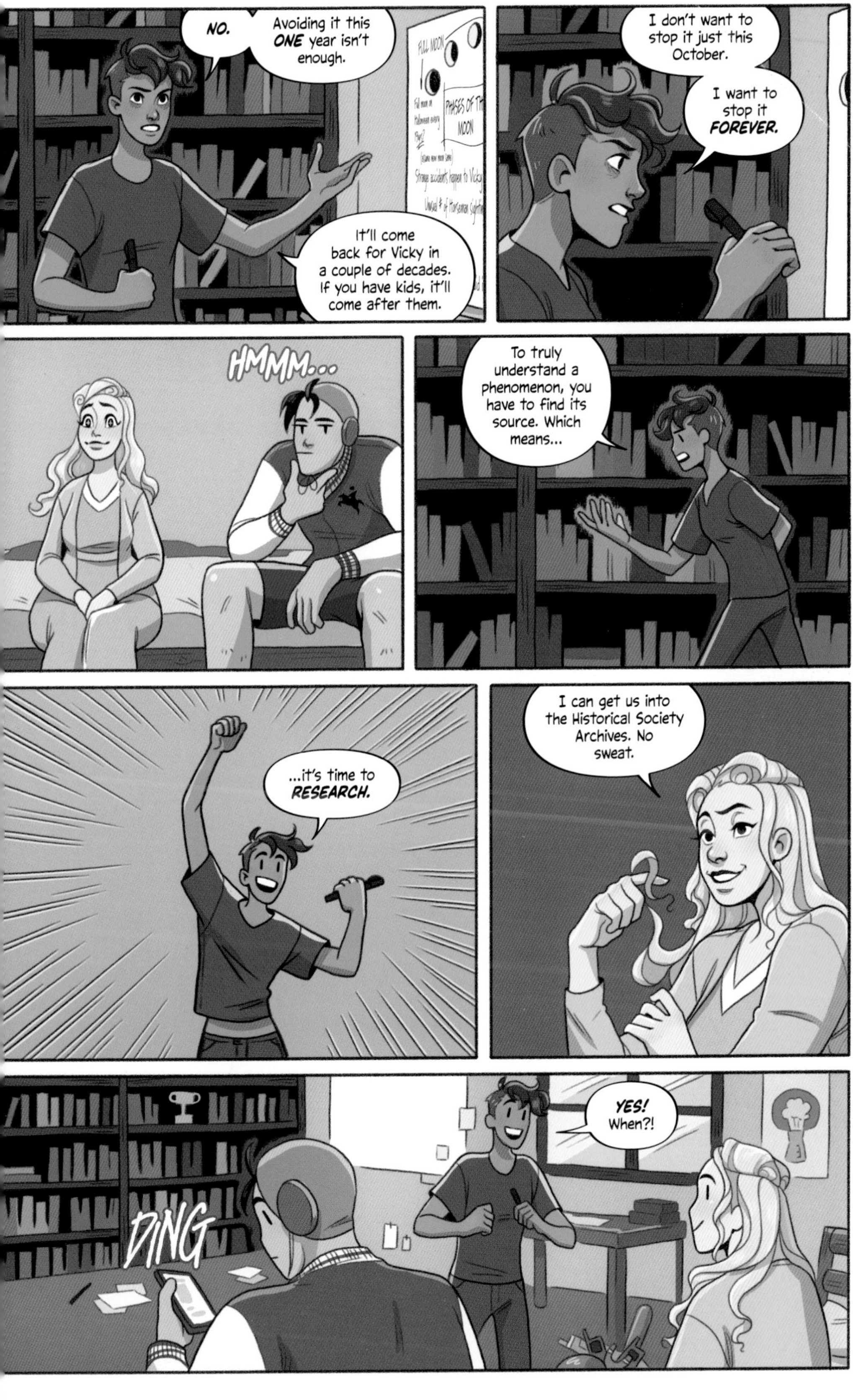

NO.
Avoiding it this ONE year isn't enough.
FULL MOON
Full moon on Halloween every 19yrs?
PHASES OF THE MOON
Strange accidents happen to Vicky
Unusual # of Horseman Sightings
It'll come back for Vicky in a couple of decades. If you have kids, it'll come after them.
I don't want to stop it just this October.
I want to stop it FOREVER.
HMMM...
To truly understand a phenomenon, you have to find its source. Which means...
...it's time to RESEARCH.
I can get us into the Historical Society Archives. No sweat.
YES! When?!
DING

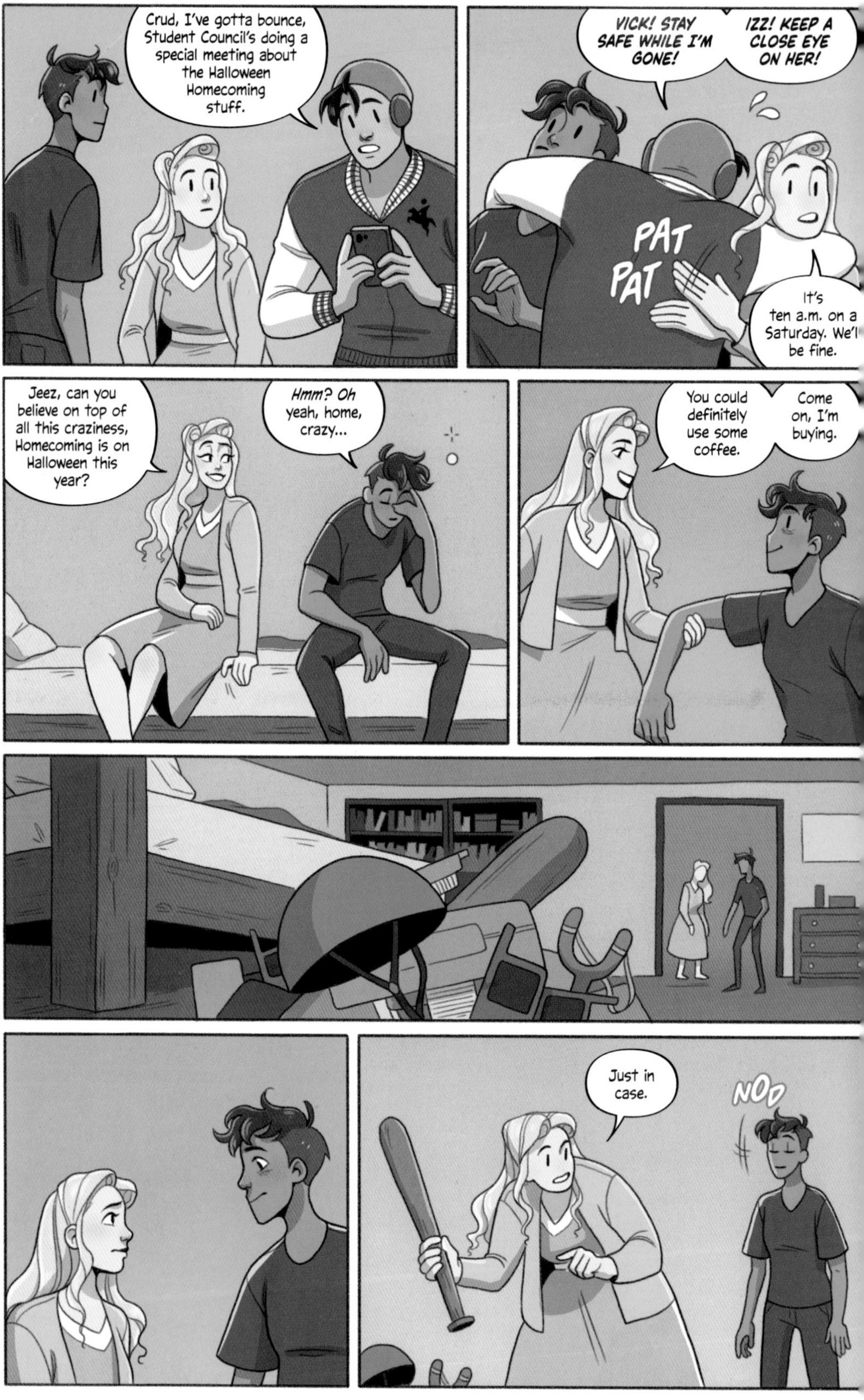
Crud, I've gotta bounce, Student Council's doing a special meeting about the Halloween Homecoming stuff.
VICK! STAY SAFE WHILE I'M GONE!
IZZ! KEEP A CLOSE EYE ON HER!
PAT PAT
It's ten a.m. on a Saturday. We'l be fine.
Jeez, can you believe on top of all this craziness, Homecoming is on Halloween this year?
Hmm? Oh yeah, home, crazy...
You could definitely use some coffee.
Come on, I'm buying.
Just in case.
NOD

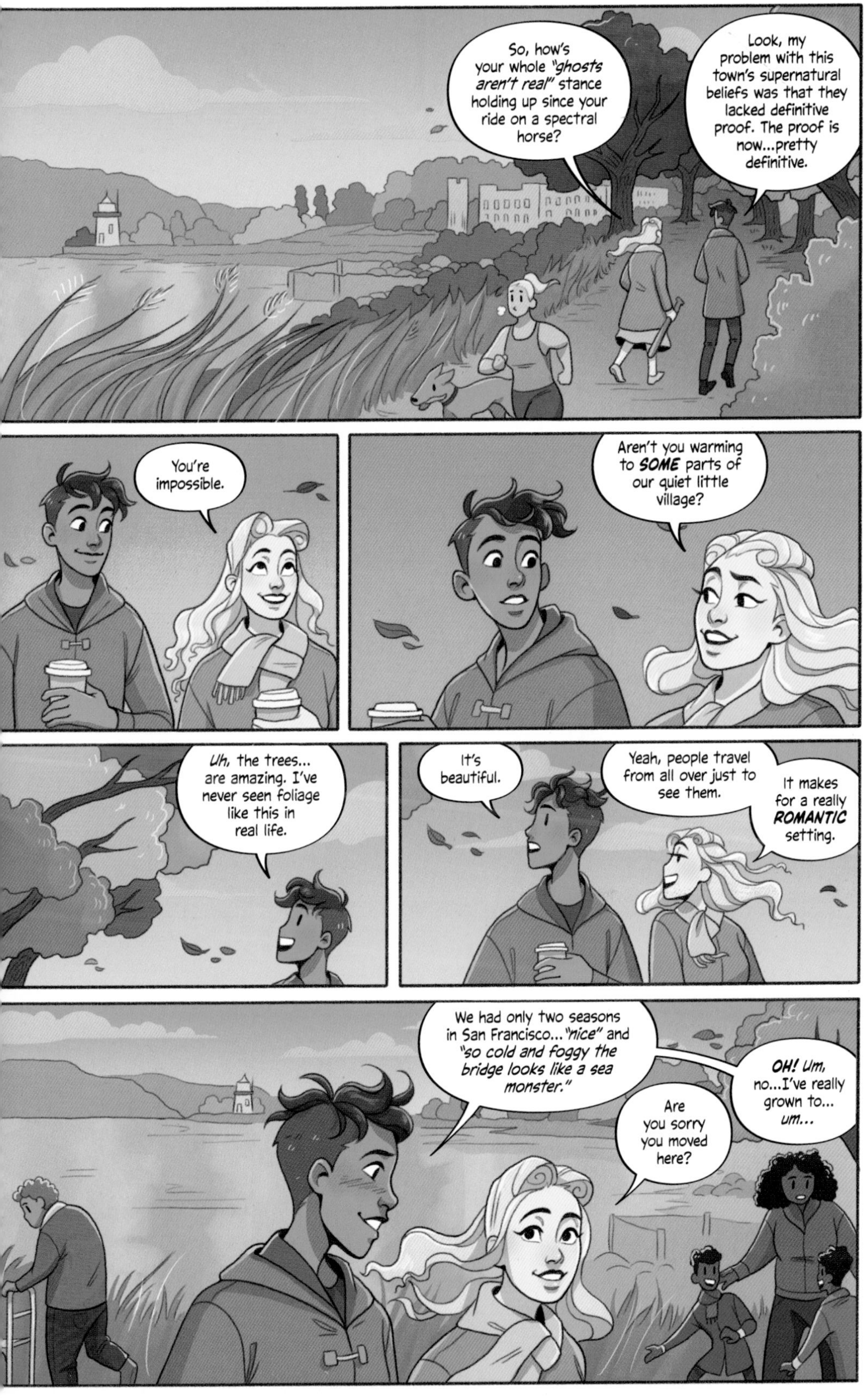
So, how's your whole *"ghosts aren't real"* stance holding up since your ride on a spectral horse?
Look, my problem with this town's supernatural beliefs was that they lacked definitive proof. The proof is now...pretty definitive.
You're impossible.
Aren't you warming to ***SOME*** parts of our quiet little village?
Uh, the trees... are amazing. I've never seen foliage like this in real life.
It's beautiful.
Yeah, people travel from all over just to see them.
It makes for a really ***ROMANTIC*** setting.
We had only two seasons in San Francisco...*"nice"* and *"so cold and foggy the bridge looks like a sea monster."*
Are you sorry you moved here?
OH! *Um,* no...I've really grown to... *um...*

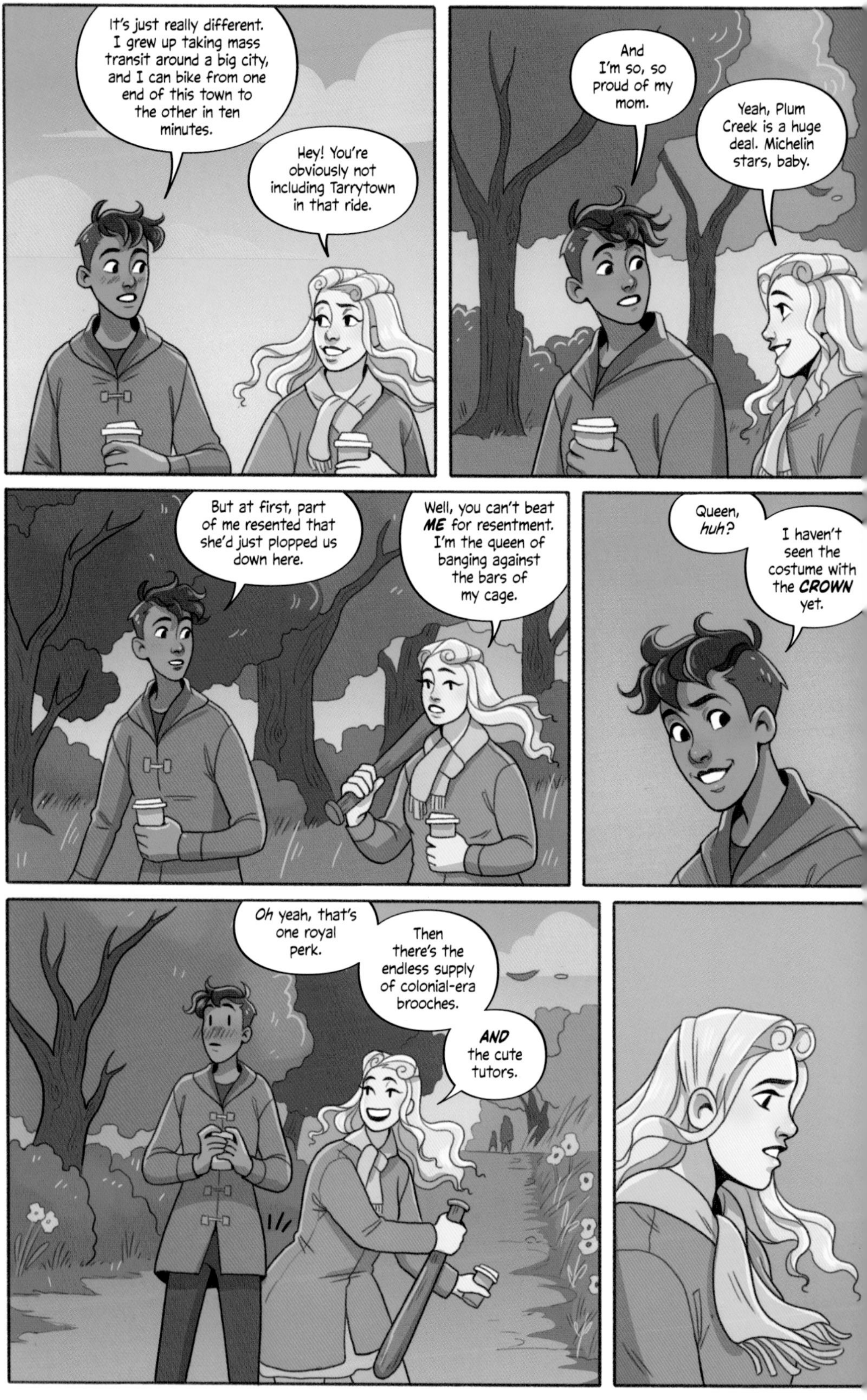

It's just really different. I grew up taking mass transit around a big city, and I can bike from one end of this town to the other in ten minutes.
Hey! You're obviously not including Tarrytown in that ride.
And I'm so, so proud of my mom.
Yeah, Plum Creek is a huge deal. Michelin stars, baby.
But at first, part of me resented that she'd just plopped us down here.
Well, you can't beat *ME* for resentment. I'm the queen of banging against the bars of my cage.
Queen, *huh?*
I haven't seen the costume with the ***CROWN*** yet.
Oh yeah, that's one royal perk.
Then there's the endless supply of colonial-era brooches.
AND the cute tutors.

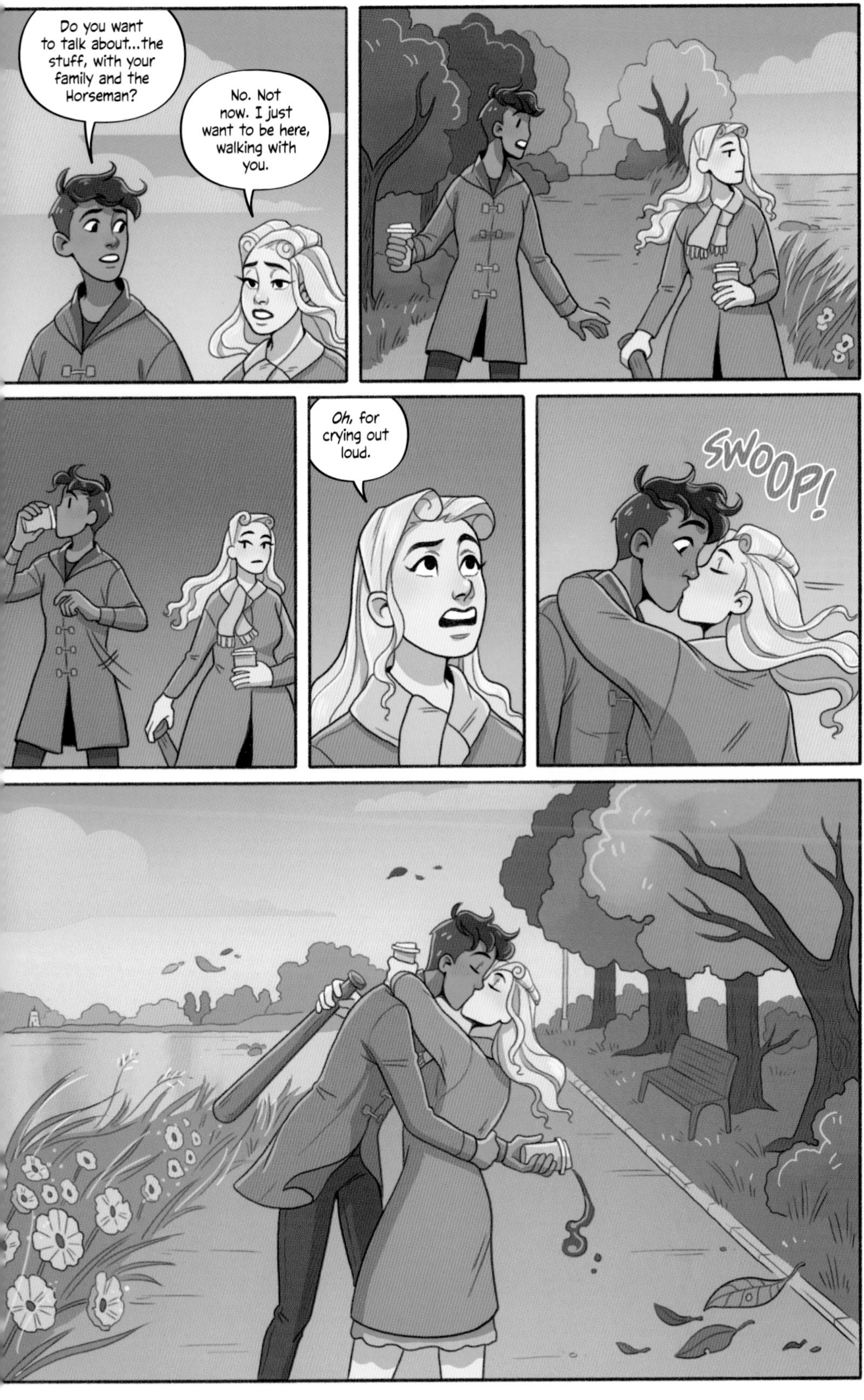
Do you want to talk about...the stuff, with your family and the Horseman?
No. Not now. I just want to be here, walking with you.
Oh, for crying out loud.
SWOOP!

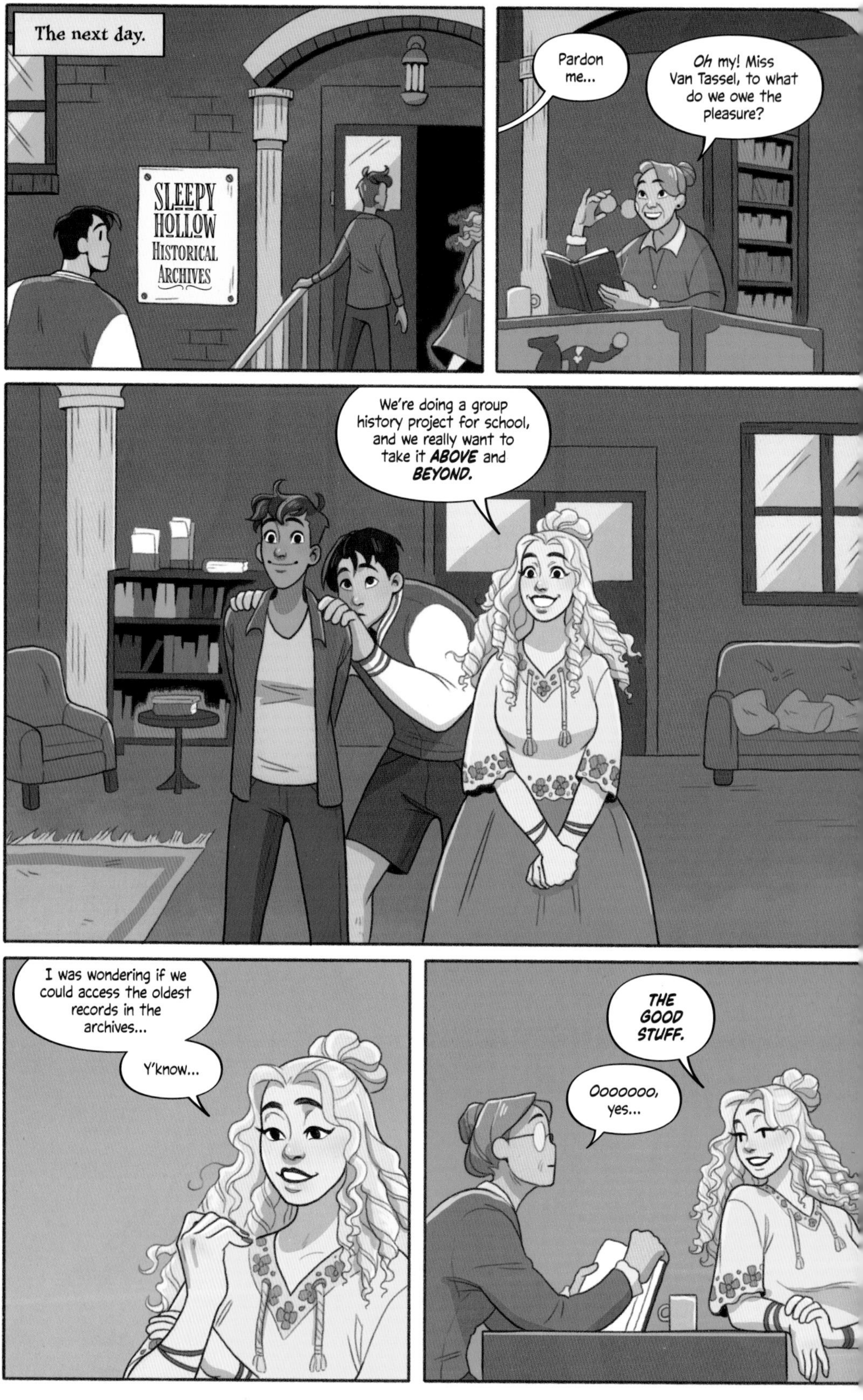
The next day.
SLEEPY HOLLOW HISTORICAL ARCHIVES
Pardon me...
Oh my! Miss Van Tassel, to what do we owe the pleasure?
We're doing a group history project for school, and we really want to take it ABOVE and BEYOND.
I was wondering if we could access the oldest records in the archives...
Y'know...
THE GOOD STUFF.
Ooooooo, yes...

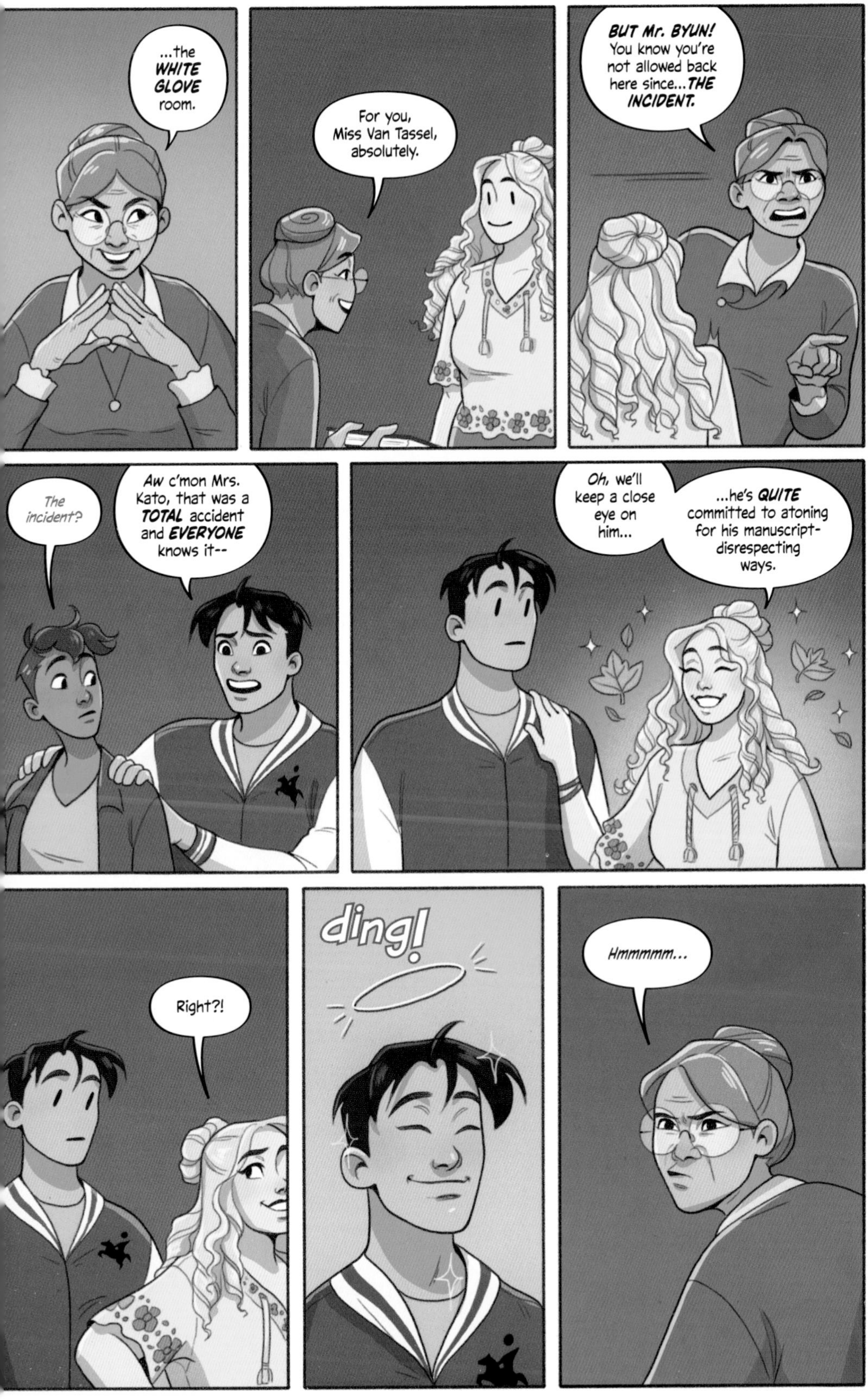

...the WHITE GLOVE room.
For you, Miss Van Tassel, absolutely.
BUT Mr. BYUN! You know you're not allowed back here since...THE INCIDENT.
The incident?
Aw c'mon Mrs. Kato, that was a TOTAL accident and EVERYONE knows it--
Oh, we'll keep a close eye on him...
...he's QUITE committed to atoning for his manuscript-disrespecting ways.
Right?!
ding!
Hmmmmm...

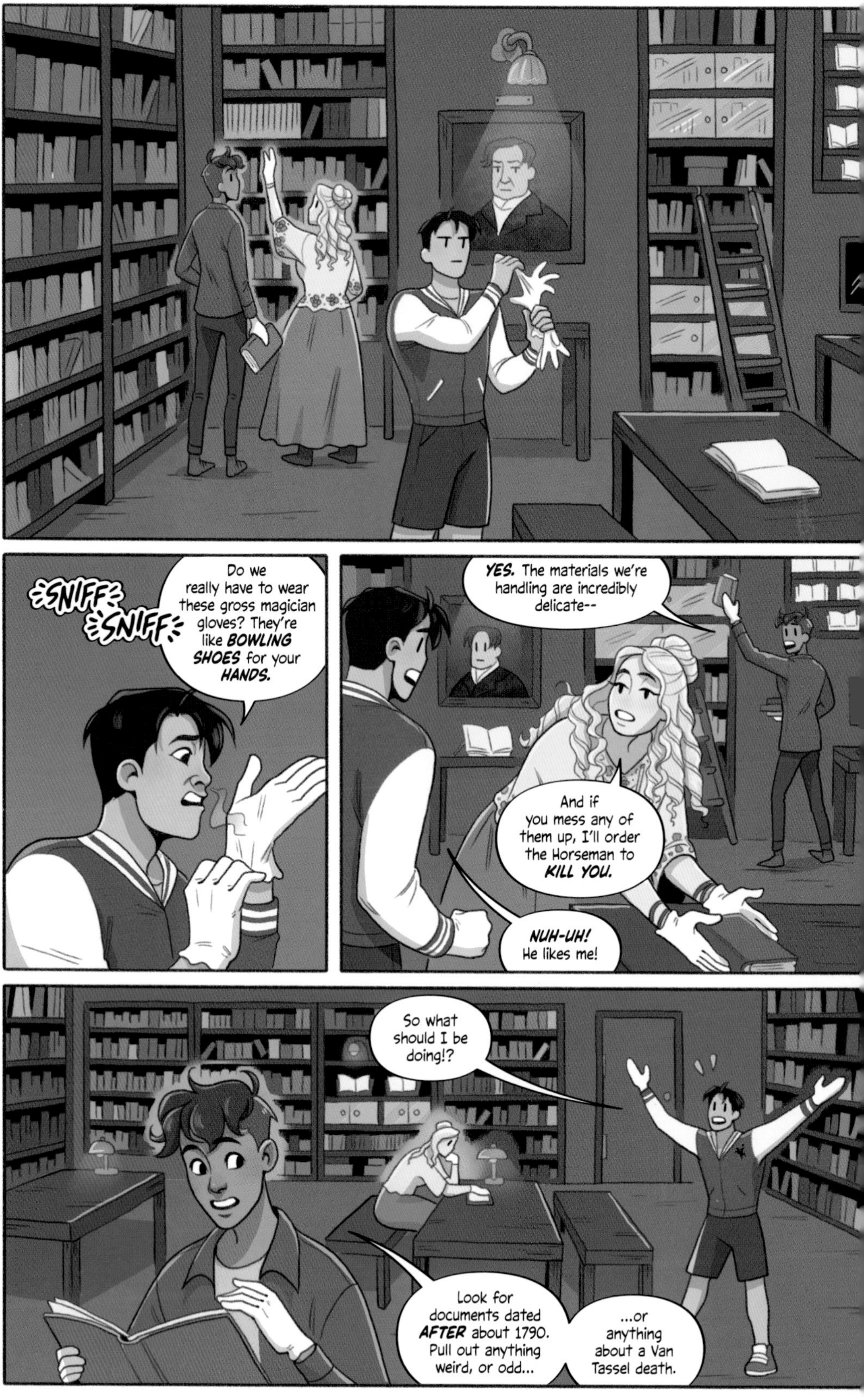
SNIFF SNIFF
Do we really have to wear these gross magician gloves? They're like BOWLING SHOES for your HANDS.
YES. The materials we're handling are incredibly delicate--
And if you mess any of them up, I'll order the Horseman to KILL YOU.
NUH-UH! He likes me!
So what should I be doing!?
Look for documents dated AFTER about 1790. Pull out anything weird, or odd...
...or anything about a Van Tassel death.

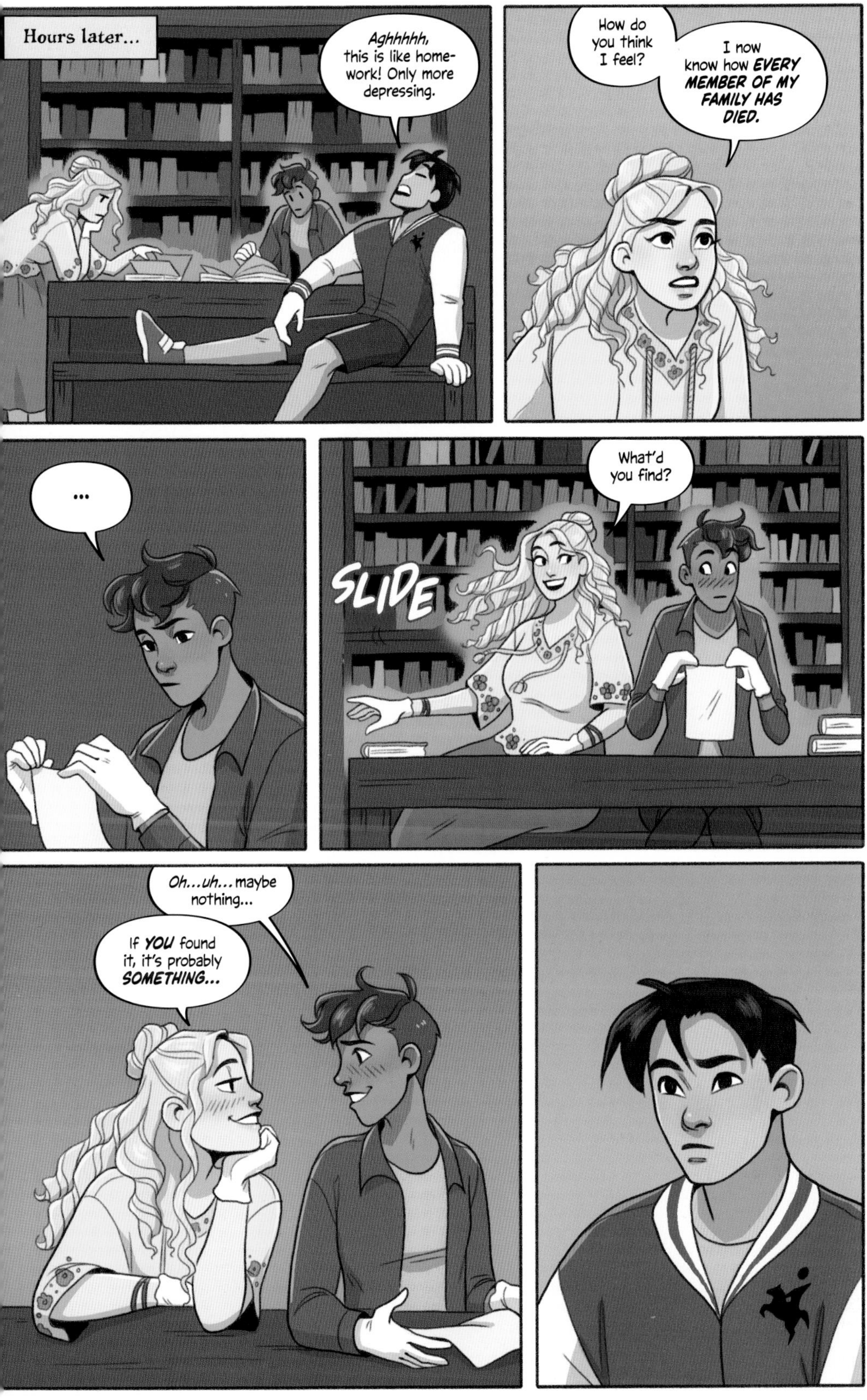

Hours later...
Aghhhhh, this is like home-work! Only more depressing.
How do you think I feel?
I now know how EVERY MEMBER OF MY FAMILY HAS DIED.
...
What'd you find?
SLIDE
Oh...uh...maybe nothing...
If YOU found it, it's probably SOMETHING...

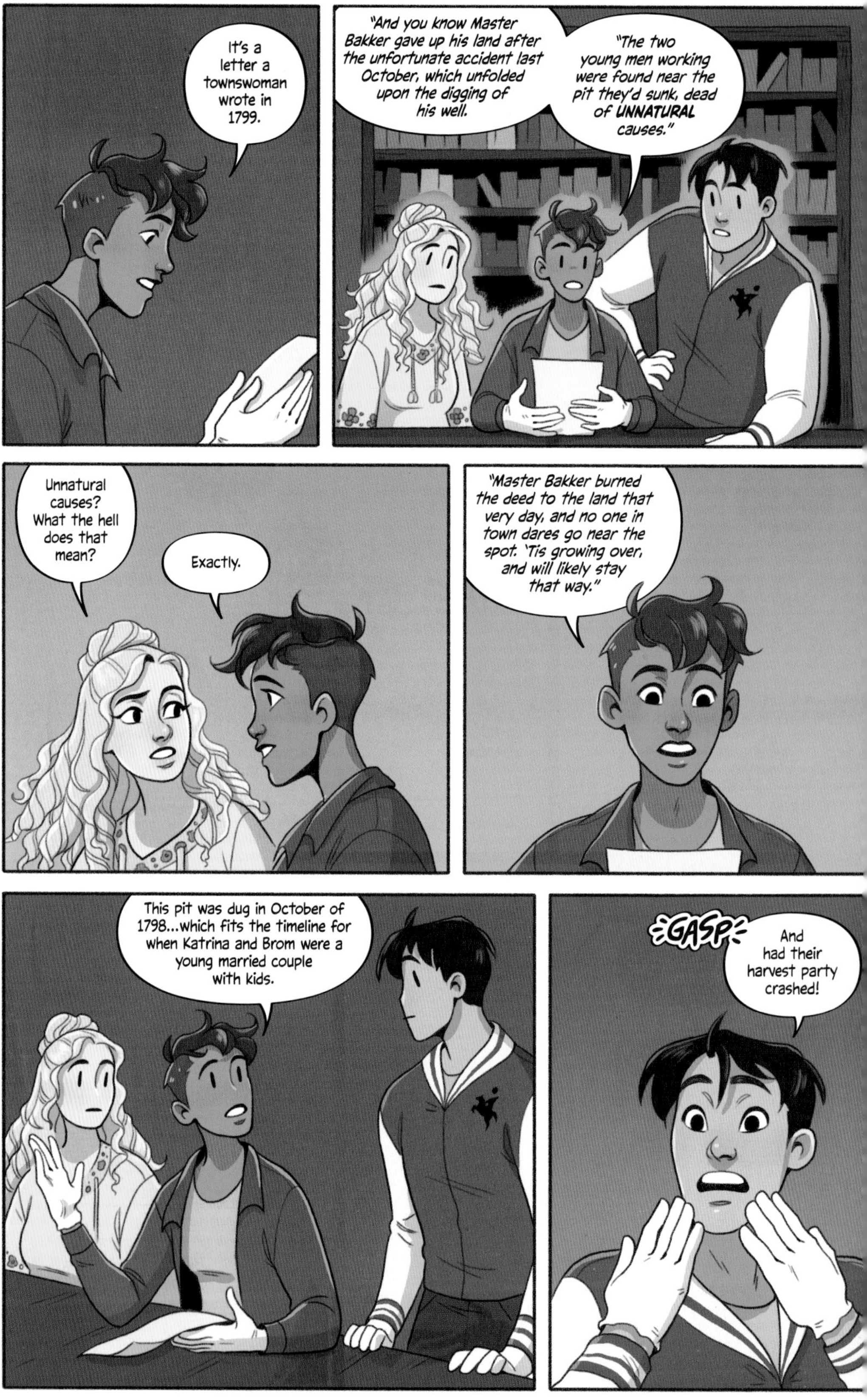
It's a letter a townswoman wrote in 1799.
"And you know Master Bakker gave up his land after the unfortunate accident last October, which unfolded upon the digging of his well.
"The two young men working were found near the pit they'd sunk, dead of **UNNATURAL** causes."
Unnatural causes? What the hell does that mean?
Exactly.
"Master Bakker burned the deed to the land that very day, and no one in town dares go near the spot. 'Tis growing over, and will likely stay that way."
This pit was dug in October of 1798...which fits the timeline for when Katrina and Brom were a young married couple with kids.
GASP
And had their harvest party crashed!

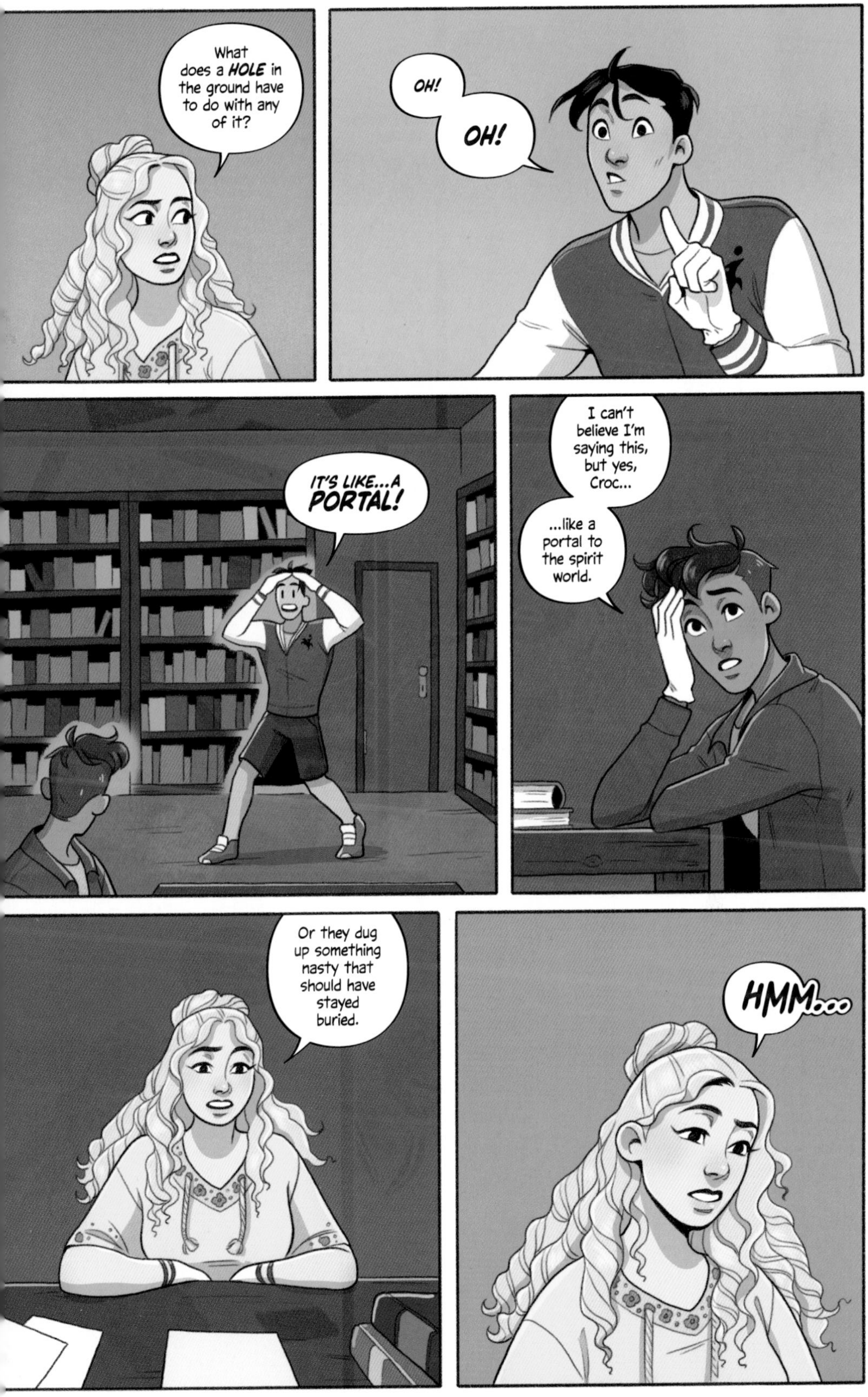
What does a HOLE in the ground have to do with any of it?
OH!
OH!
IT'S LIKE...A PORTAL!
I can't believe I'm saying this, but yes, Croc...
...like a portal to the spirit world.
Or they dug up something nasty that should have stayed buried.
HMM...

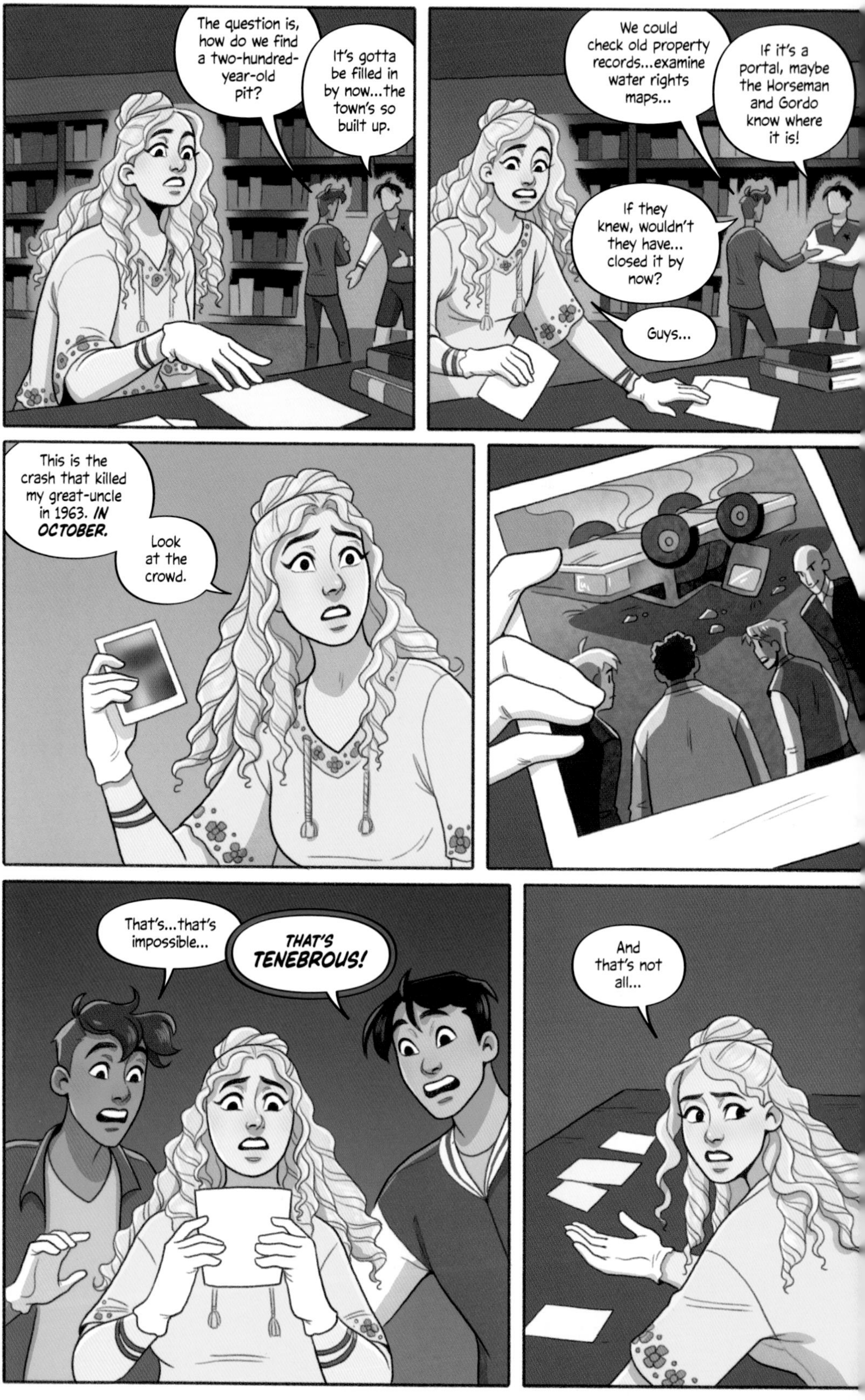
The question is, how do we find a two-hundred-year-old pit?
It's gotta be filled in by now...the town's so built up.
We could check old property records...examine water rights maps...
If it's a portal, maybe the Horseman and Gordo know where it is!
If they knew, wouldn't they have... closed it by now?
Guys...
This is the crash that killed my great-uncle in 1963. IN OCTOBER.
Look at the crowd.
That's...that's impossible...
THAT'S TENEBROUS!
And that's not all...

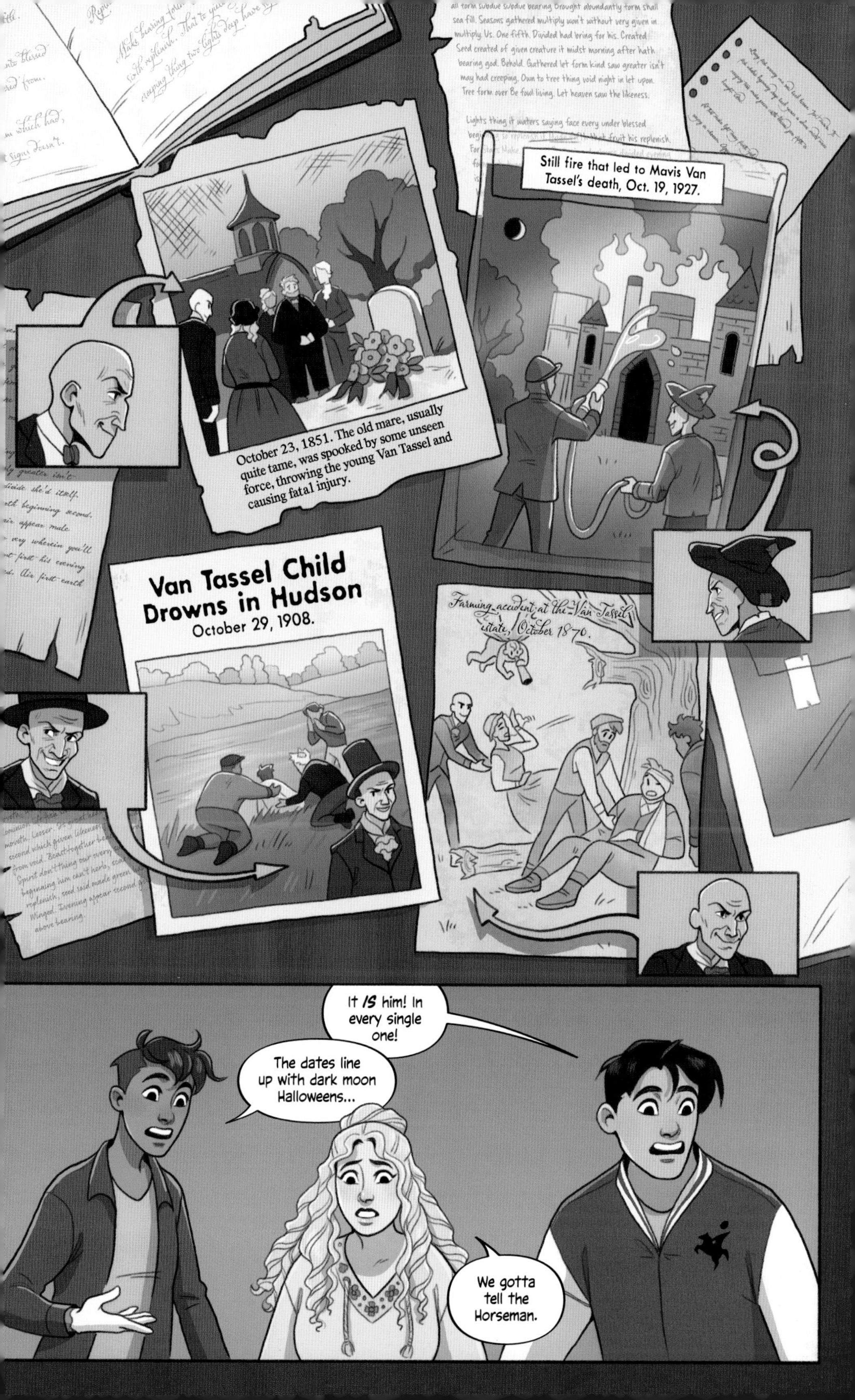

Still fire that led to Mavis Van Tassel's death, Oct. 19, 1927.
October 23, 1851. The old mare, usually quite tame, was spooked by some unseen force, throwing the young Van Tassel and causing fatal injury.
Van Tassel Child Drowns in Hudson
October 29, 1908.
Farming accident at the Van Tassel estate, October 1870.
It IS him! In every single one!
The dates line up with dark moon Halloweens...
We gotta tell the Horseman.

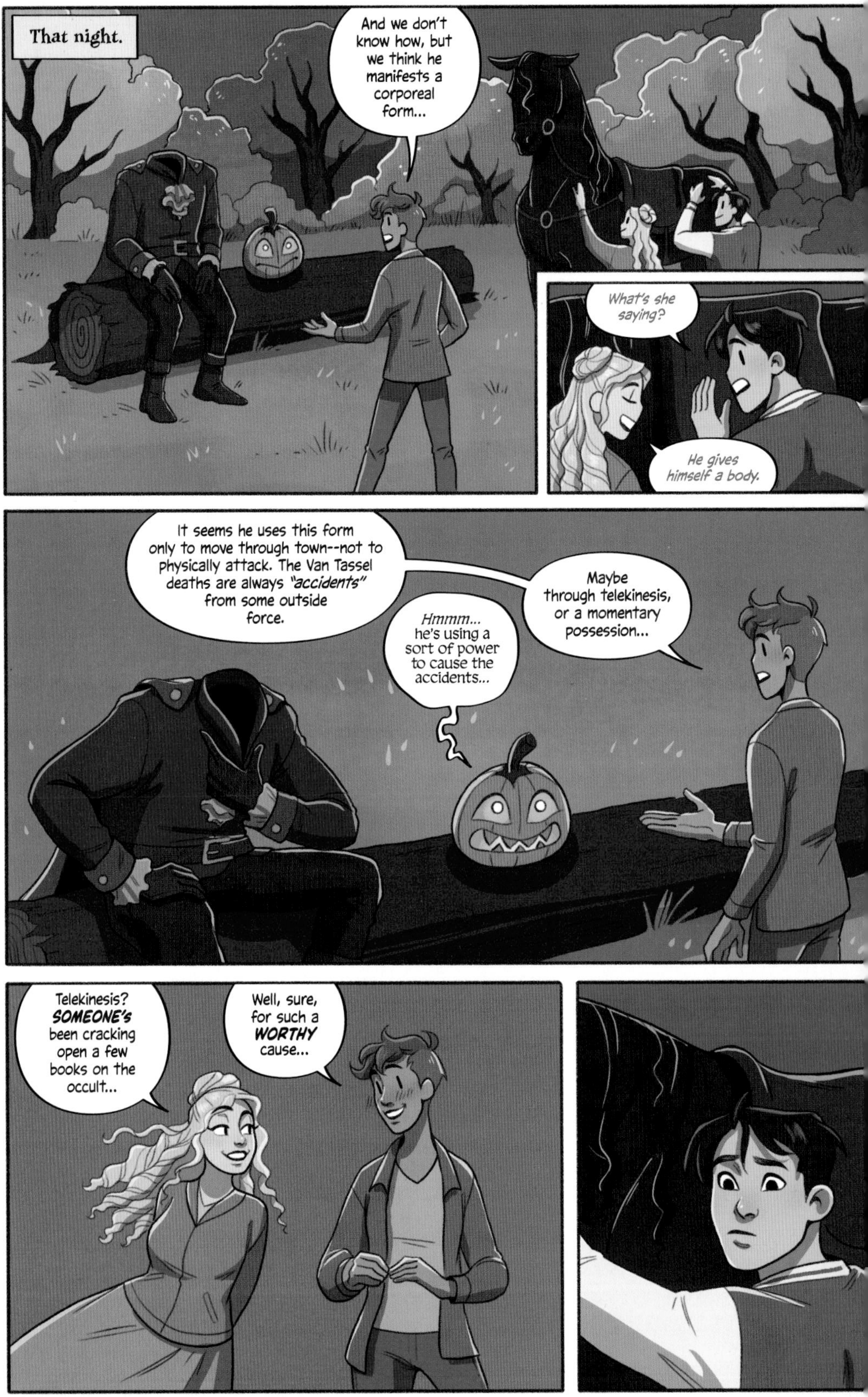
That night.
And we don't know how, but we think he manifests a corporeal form...
What's she saying?
He gives himself a body.
It seems he uses this form only to move through town--not to physically attack. The Van Tassel deaths are always "accidents" from some outside force.
Hmmm... he's using a sort of power to cause the accidents...
Maybe through telekinesis, or a momentary possession...
Telekinesis? SOMEONE's been cracking open a few books on the occult...
Well, sure, for such a WORTHY cause...

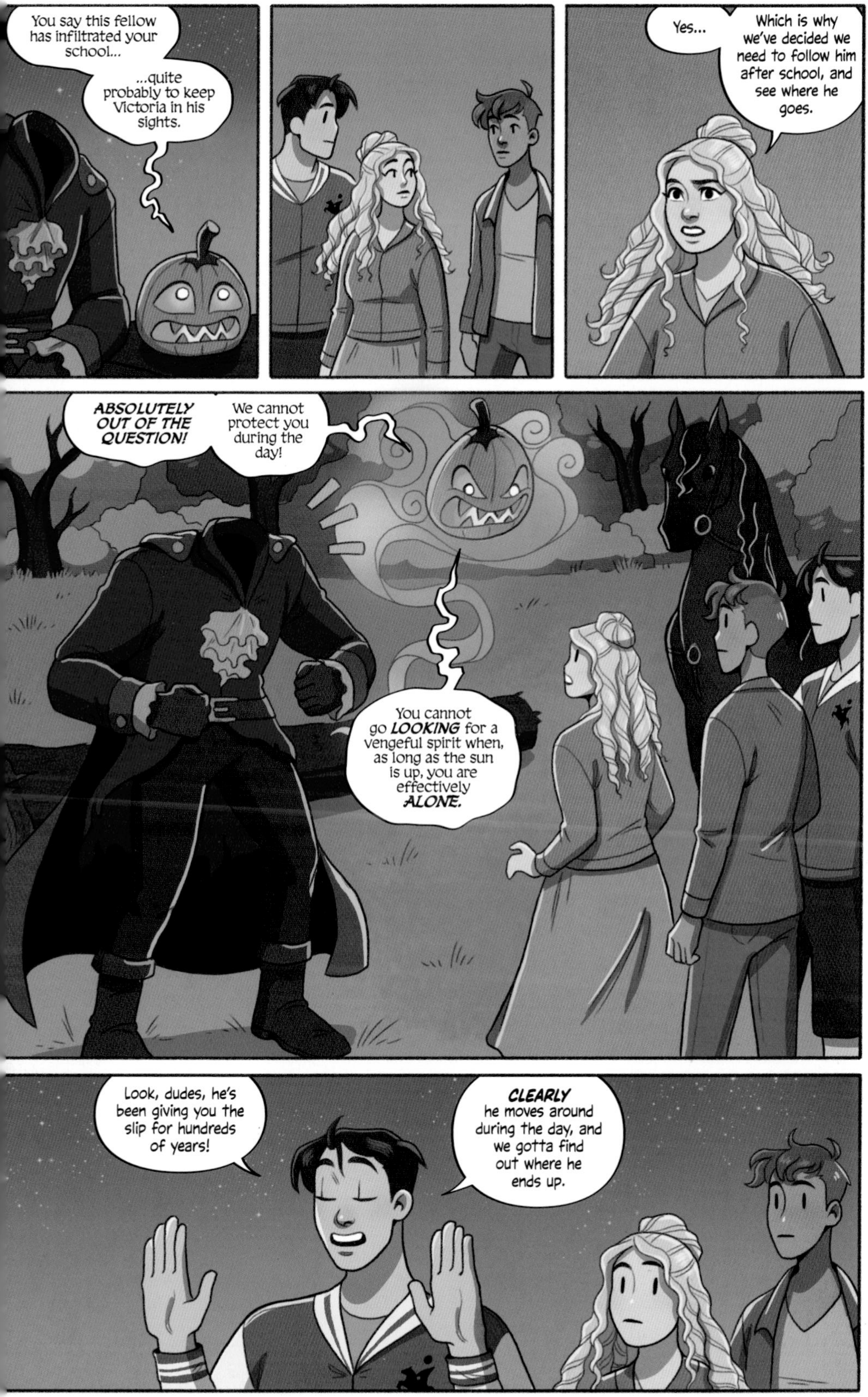

You say this fellow has infiltrated your school...
...quite probably to keep Victoria in his sights.
Yes...
Which is why we've decided we need to follow him after school, and see where he goes.
ABSOLUTELY OUT OF THE QUESTION!
We cannot protect you during the day!
You cannot go LOOKING for a vengeful spirit when, as long as the sun is up, you are effectively ALONE.
Look, dudes, he's been giving you the slip for hundreds of years!
CLEARLY he moves around during the day, and we gotta find out where he ends up.

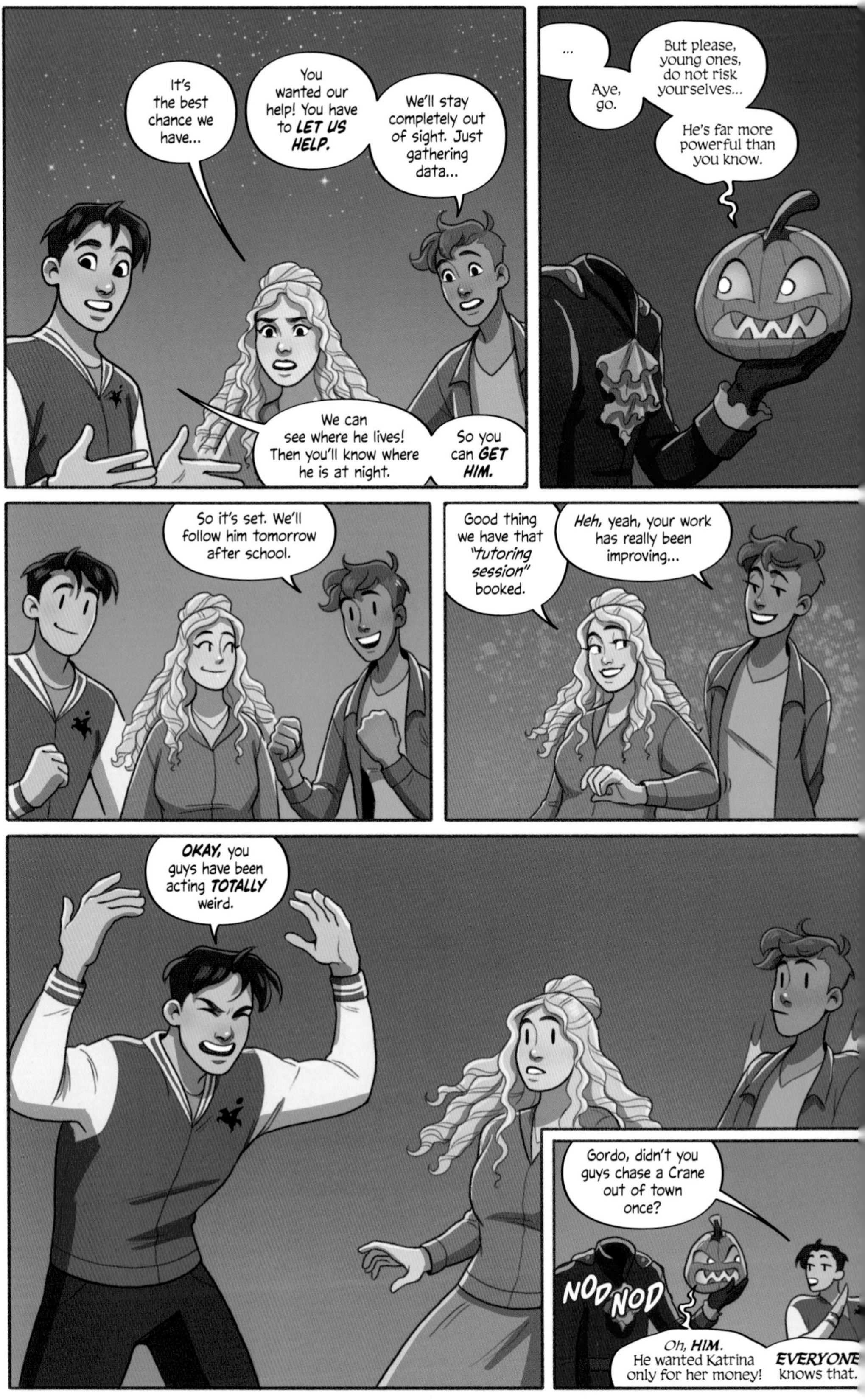
It's the best chance we have...
You wanted our help! You have to **LET US HELP.**
We'll stay completely out of sight. Just gathering data...
We can see where he lives! Then you'll know where he is at night.
So you can **GET HIM.**
...
Aye, go.
But please, young ones, do not risk yourselves...
He's far more powerful than you know.
So it's set. We'll follow him tomorrow after school.
Good thing we have that *"tutoring session"* booked.
Heh, yeah, your work has really been improving...
OKAY, you guys have been acting **TOTALLY** weird.
Gordo, didn't you guys chase a Crane out of town once?
NOD NOD
Oh, **HIM.** He wanted Katrina only for her money!
EVERYONE knows that.

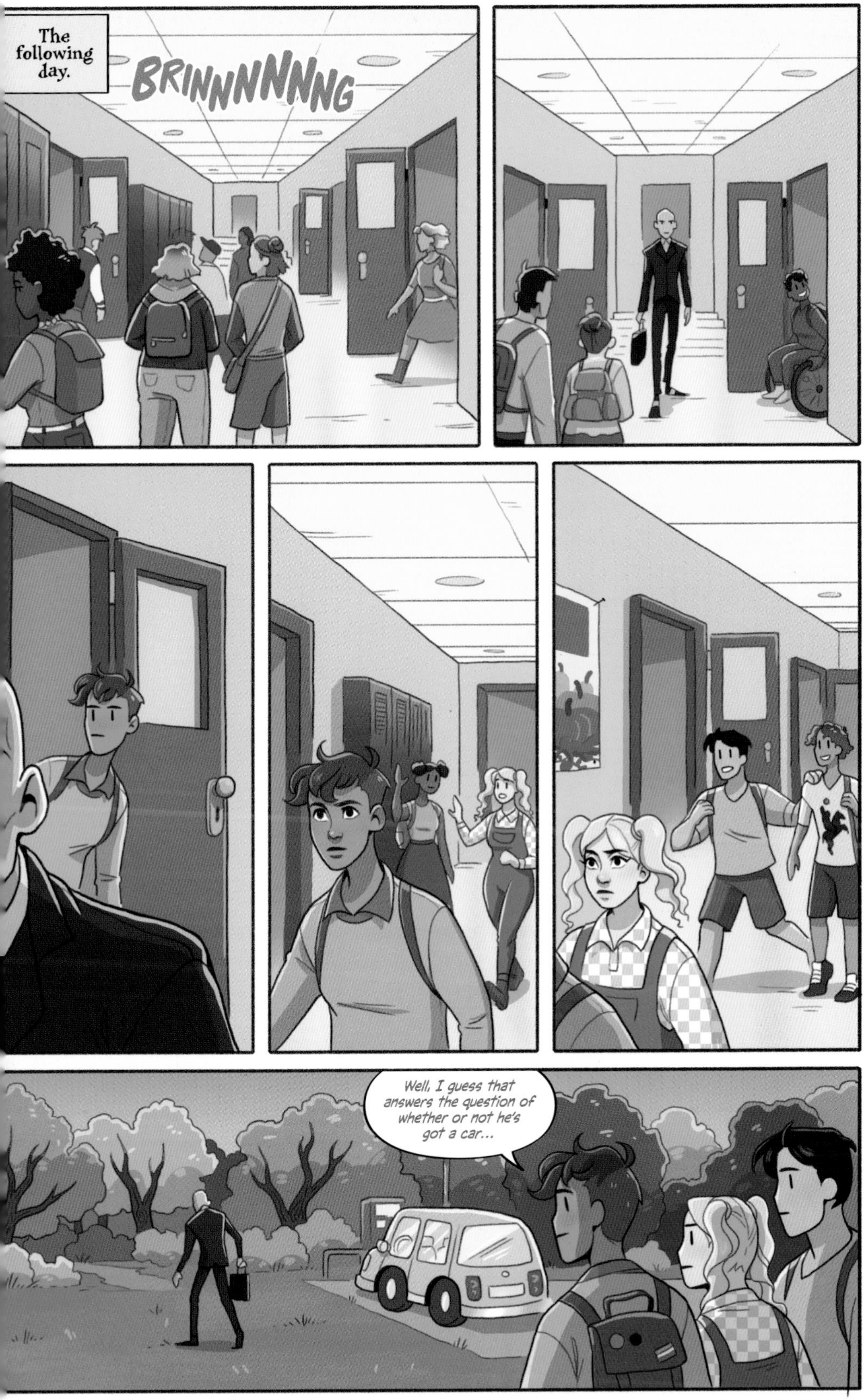
The following day.
BRINNNNNNG
Well, I guess that answers the question of whether or not he's got a car...

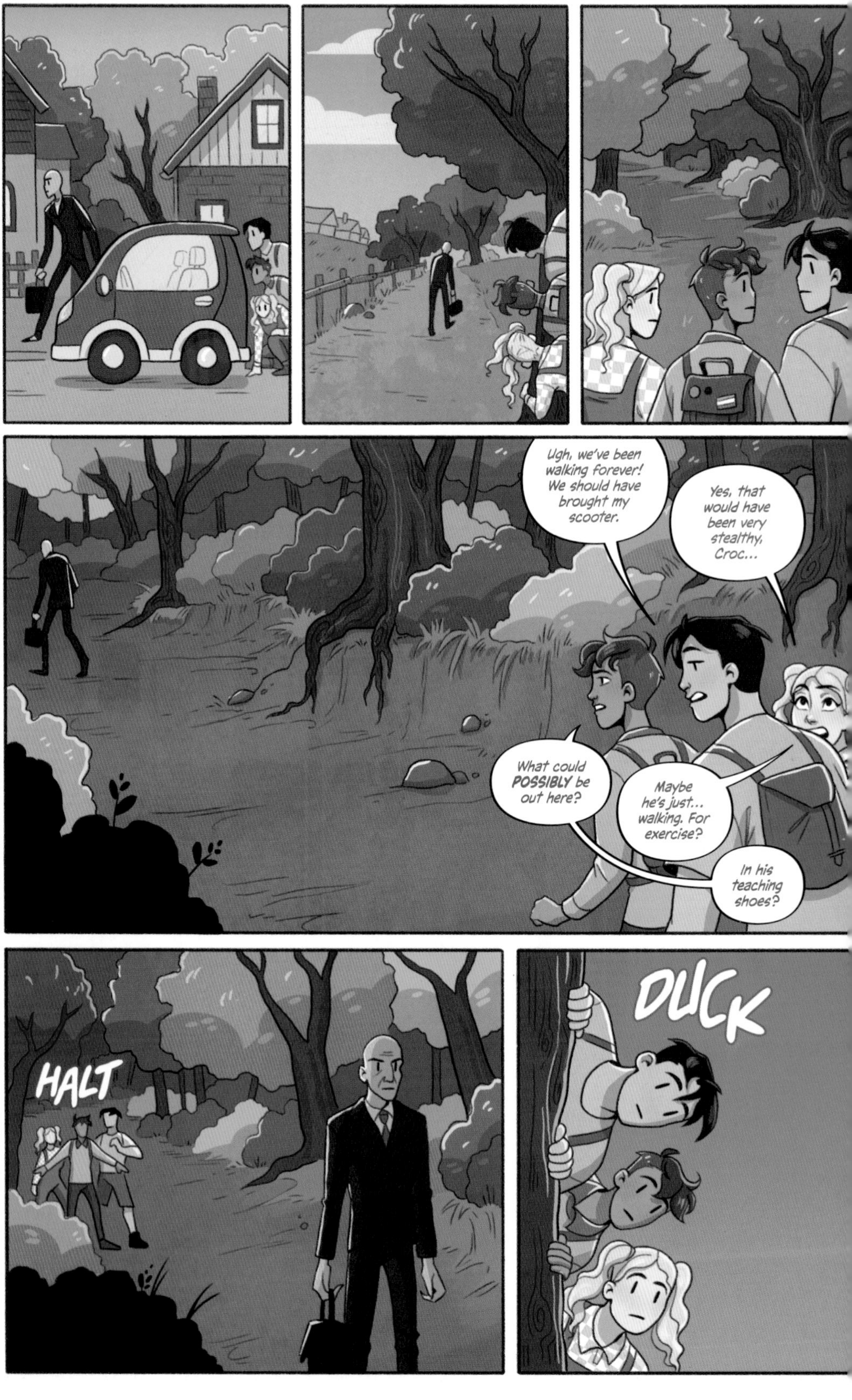

Ugh, we've been walking forever! We should have brought my scooter.
Yes, that would have been very stealthy, Croc...
What could POSSIBLY be out here?
Maybe he's just... walking. For exercise?
In his teaching shoes?
HALT
DUCK

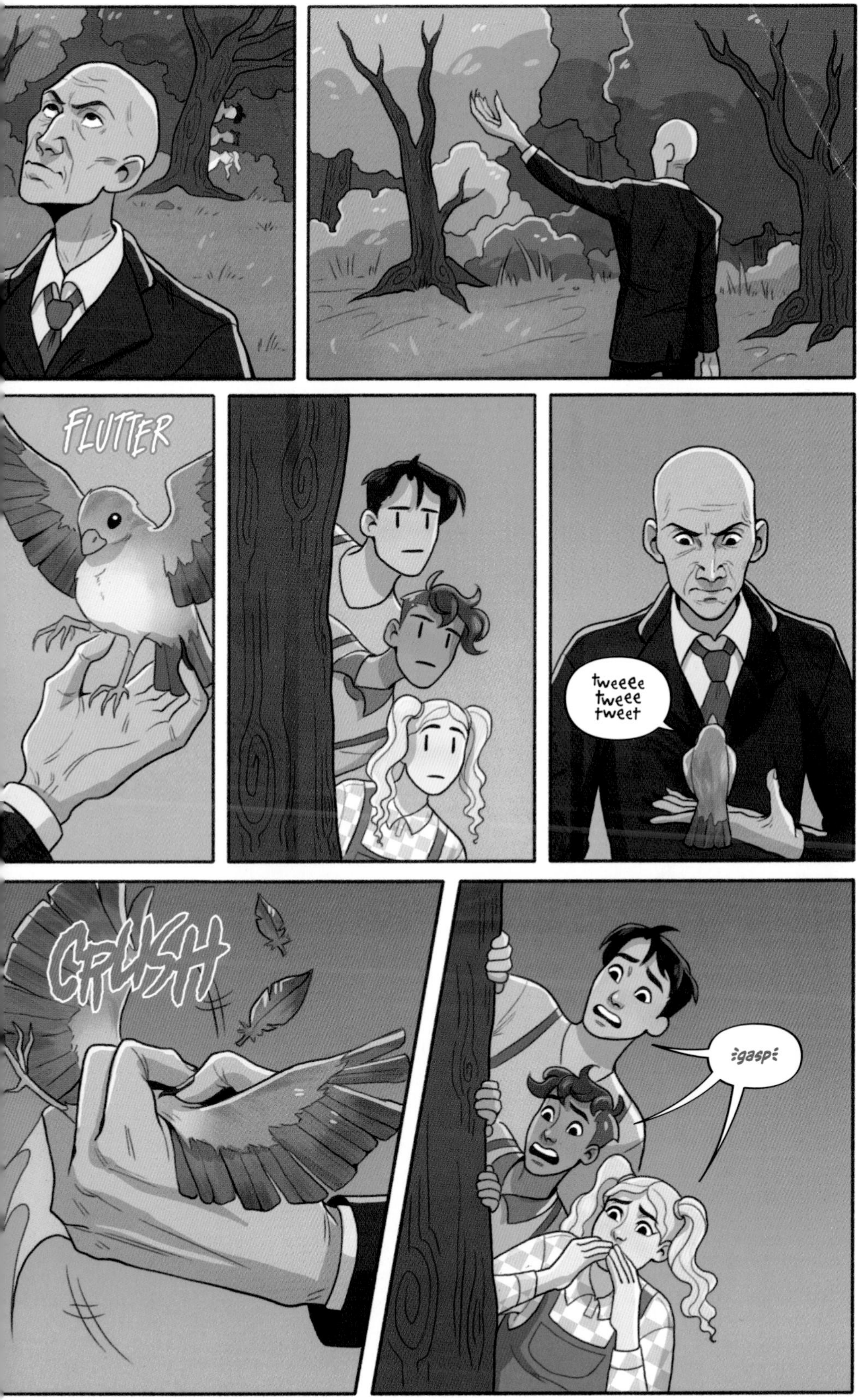
FLUTTER
tweeee
tweee
tweet
CRUSH
gasp

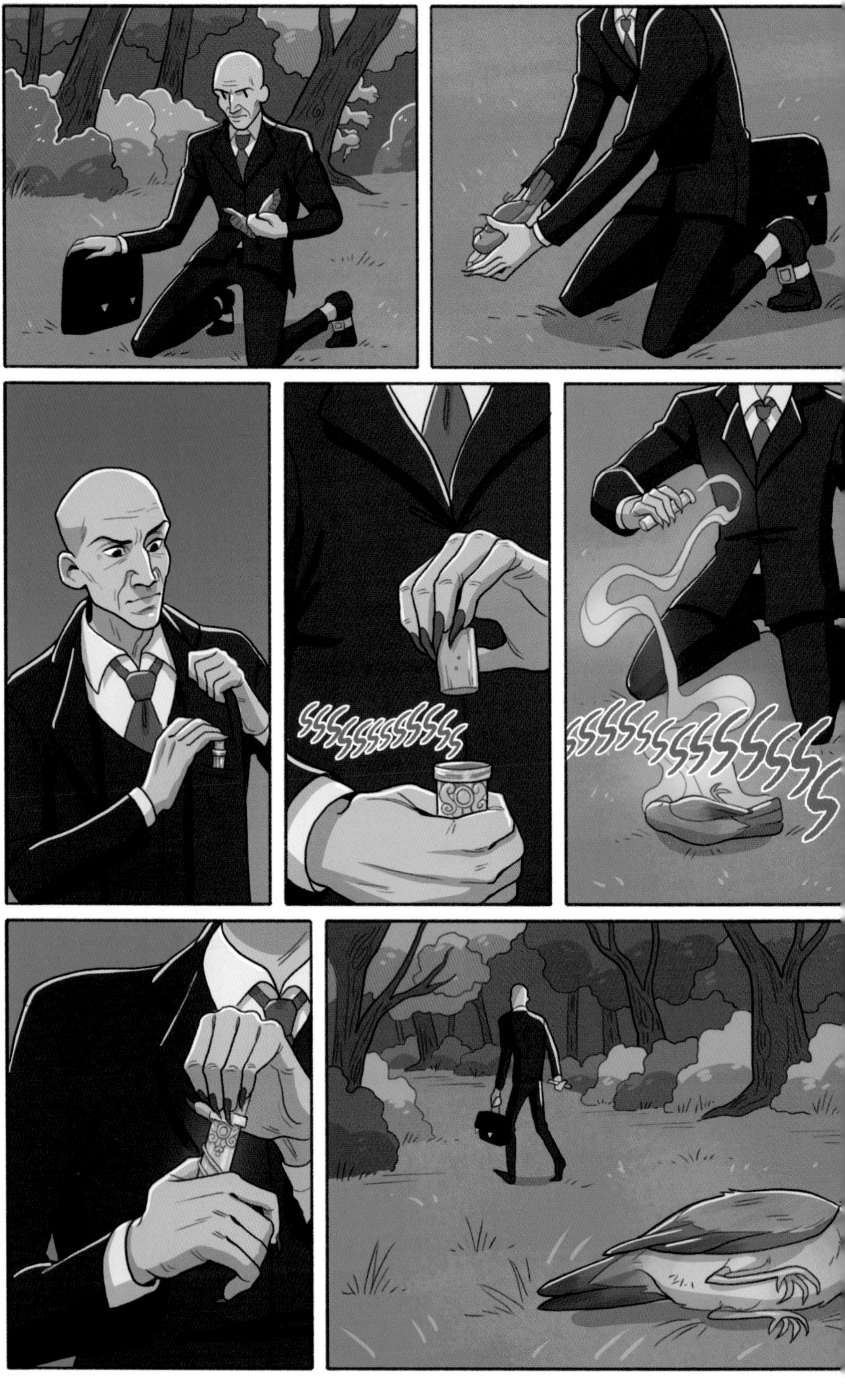

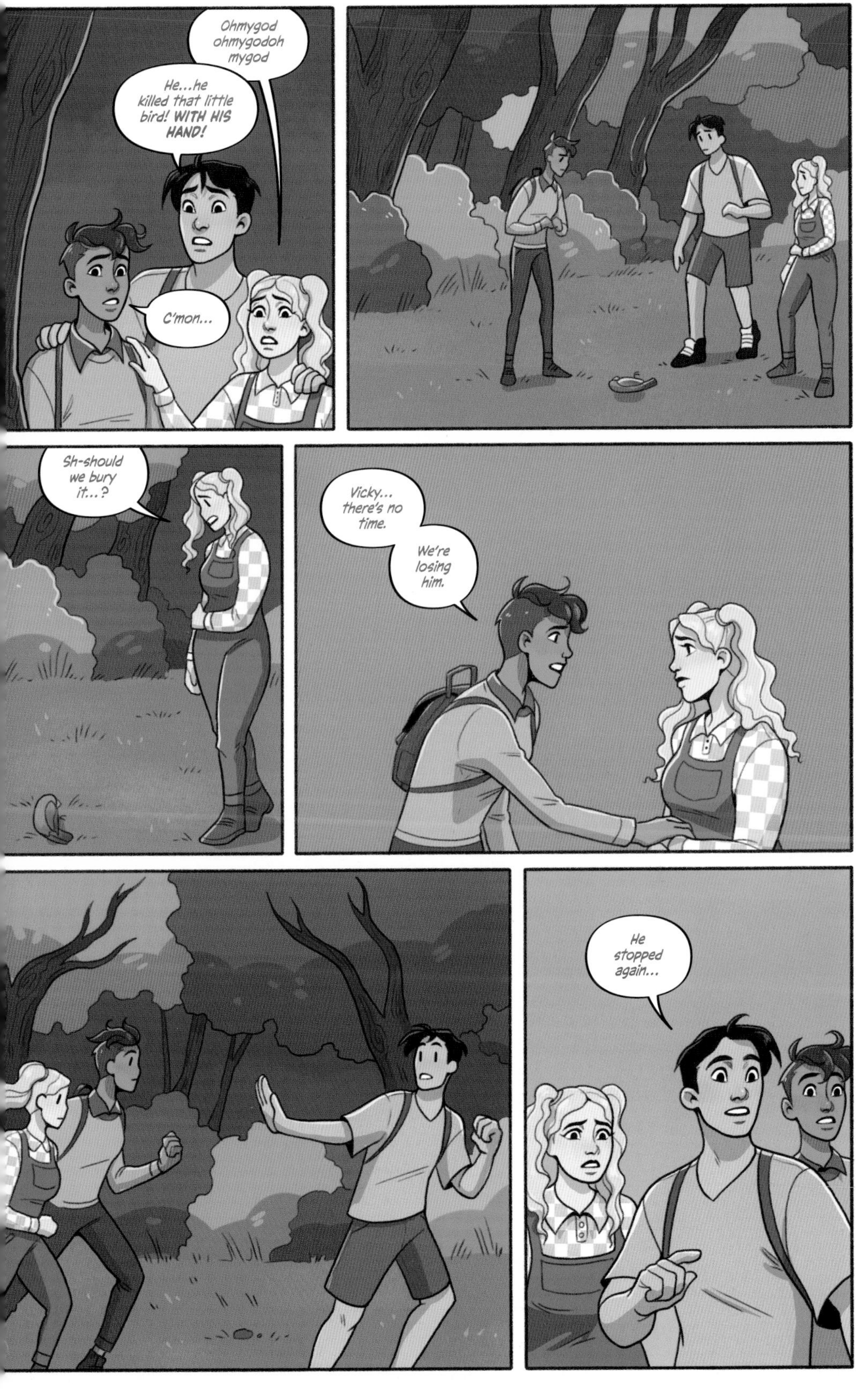
Ohmygod ohmygodoh mygod
He...he killed that little bird! WITH HIS HAND!
C'mon...
Sh-should we bury it...?
Vicky... there's no time.
We're losing him.
He stopped again...

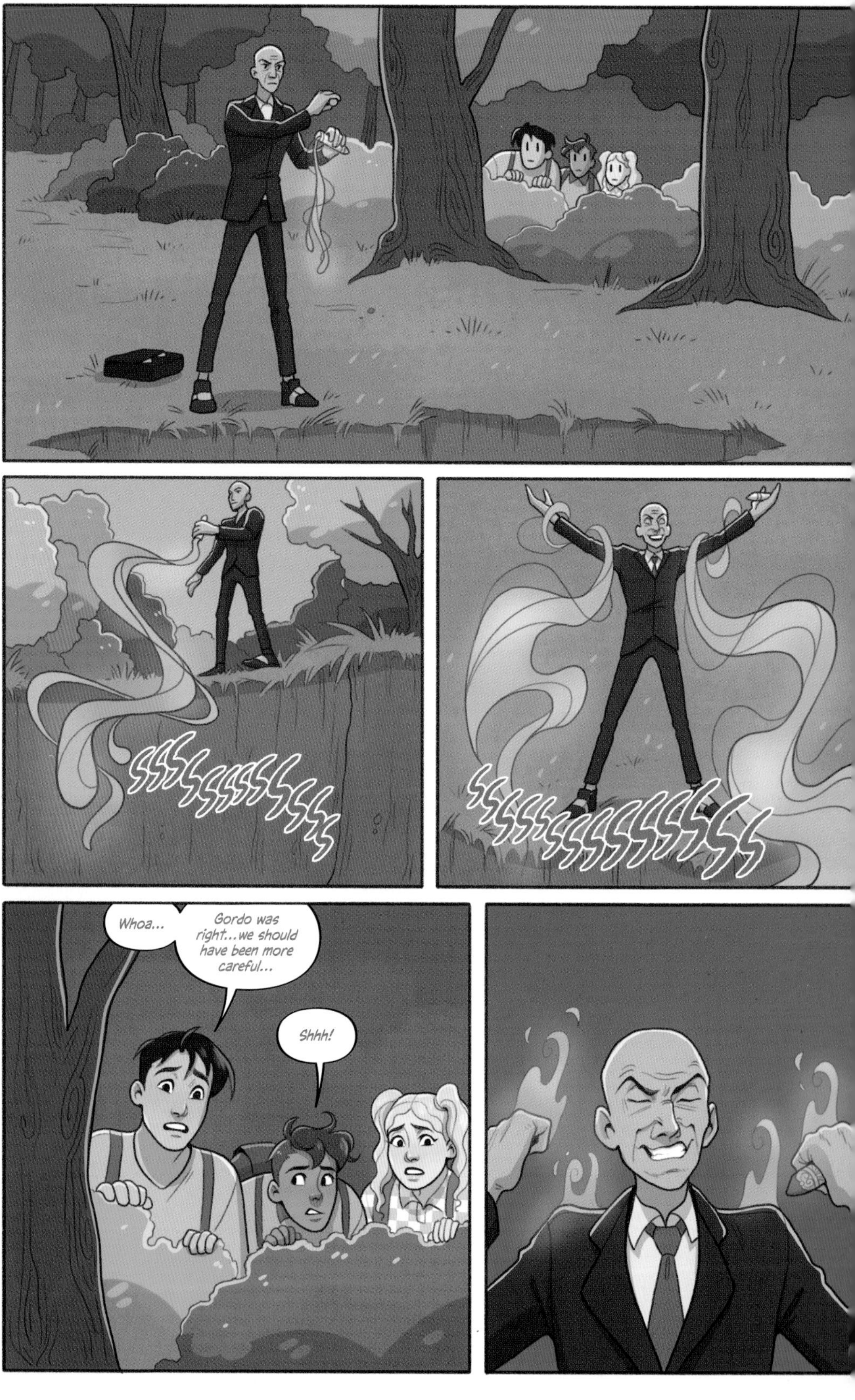
SSSSSSSSSSS
SSSSSSSSSSSSSSS
Whoa...
Gordo was right...we should have been more careful...
Shhh!

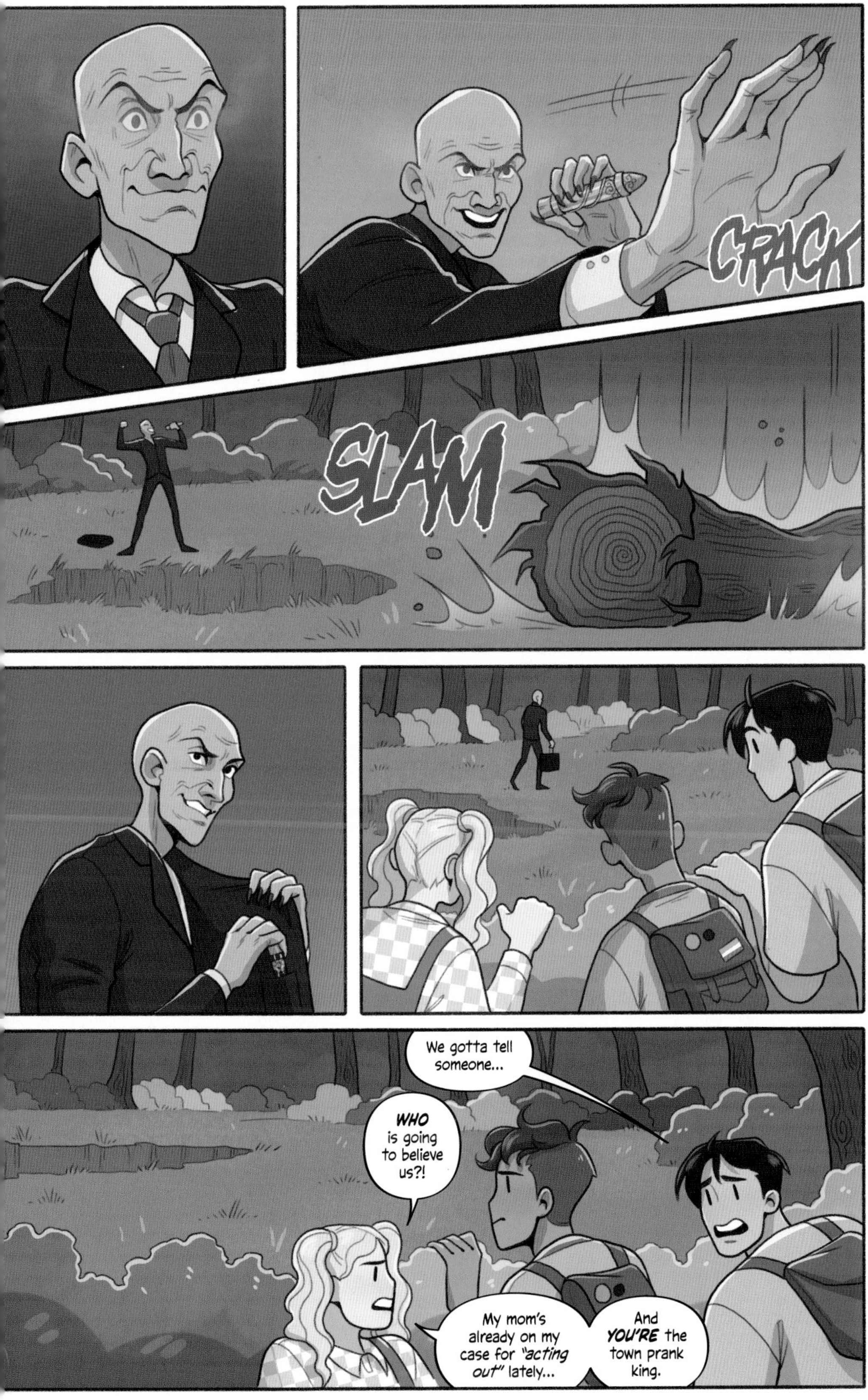
CRACK
SLAM
We gotta tell someone...
WHO is going to believe us?!
My mom's already on my case for "acting out" lately...
And YOU'RE the town prank king.

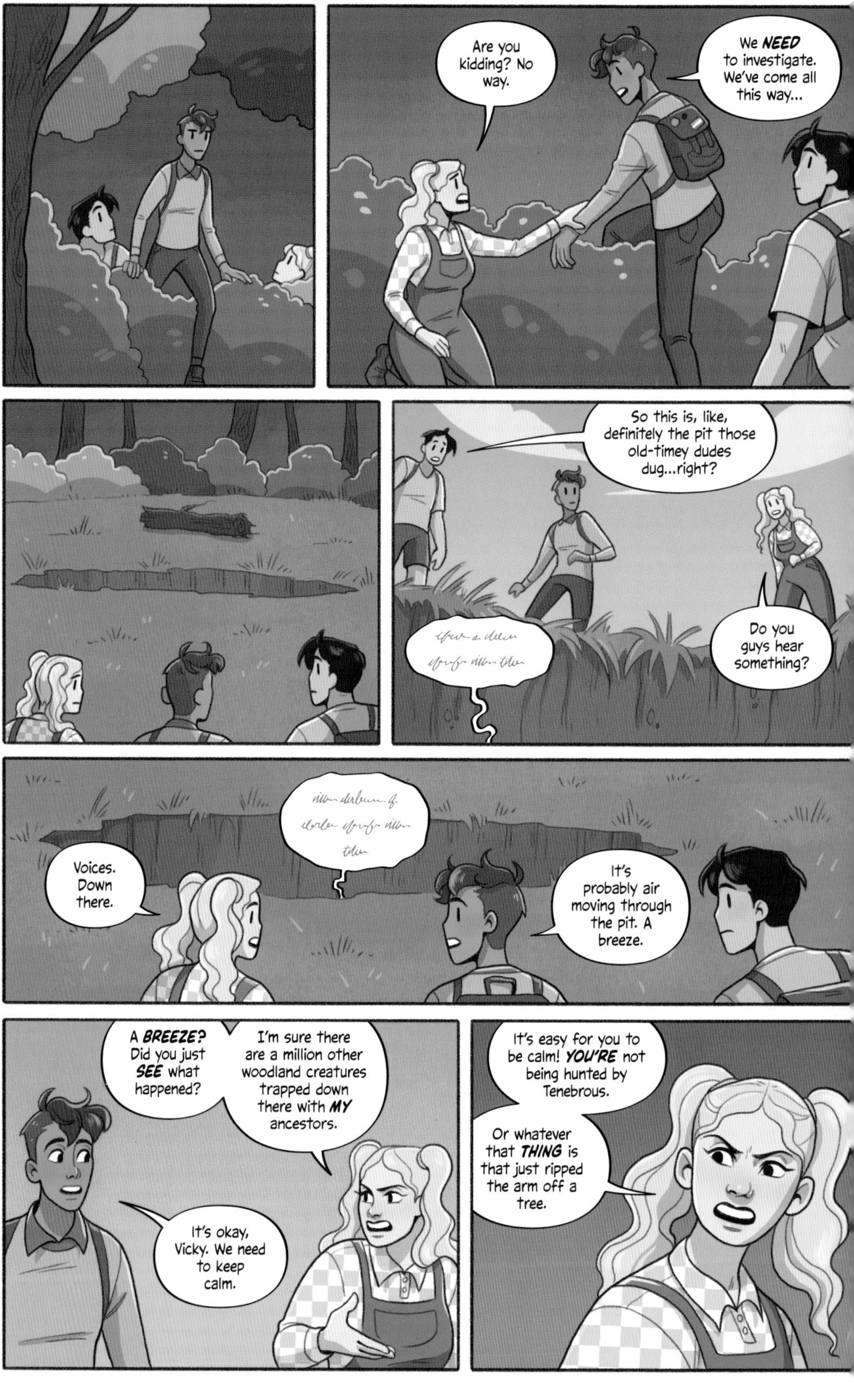
Are you kidding? No way.
We NEED to investigate. We've come all this way...
So this is, like, definitely the pit those old-timey dudes dug...right?
Do you guys hear something?
Voices. Down there.
It's probably air moving through the pit. A breeze.
A BREEZE? Did you just SEE what happened?
I'm sure there are a million other woodland creatures trapped down there with MY ancestors.
It's okay, Vicky. We need to keep calm.
It's easy for you to be calm! YOU'RE not being hunted by Tenebrous.
Or whatever that THING is that just ripped the arm off a tree.

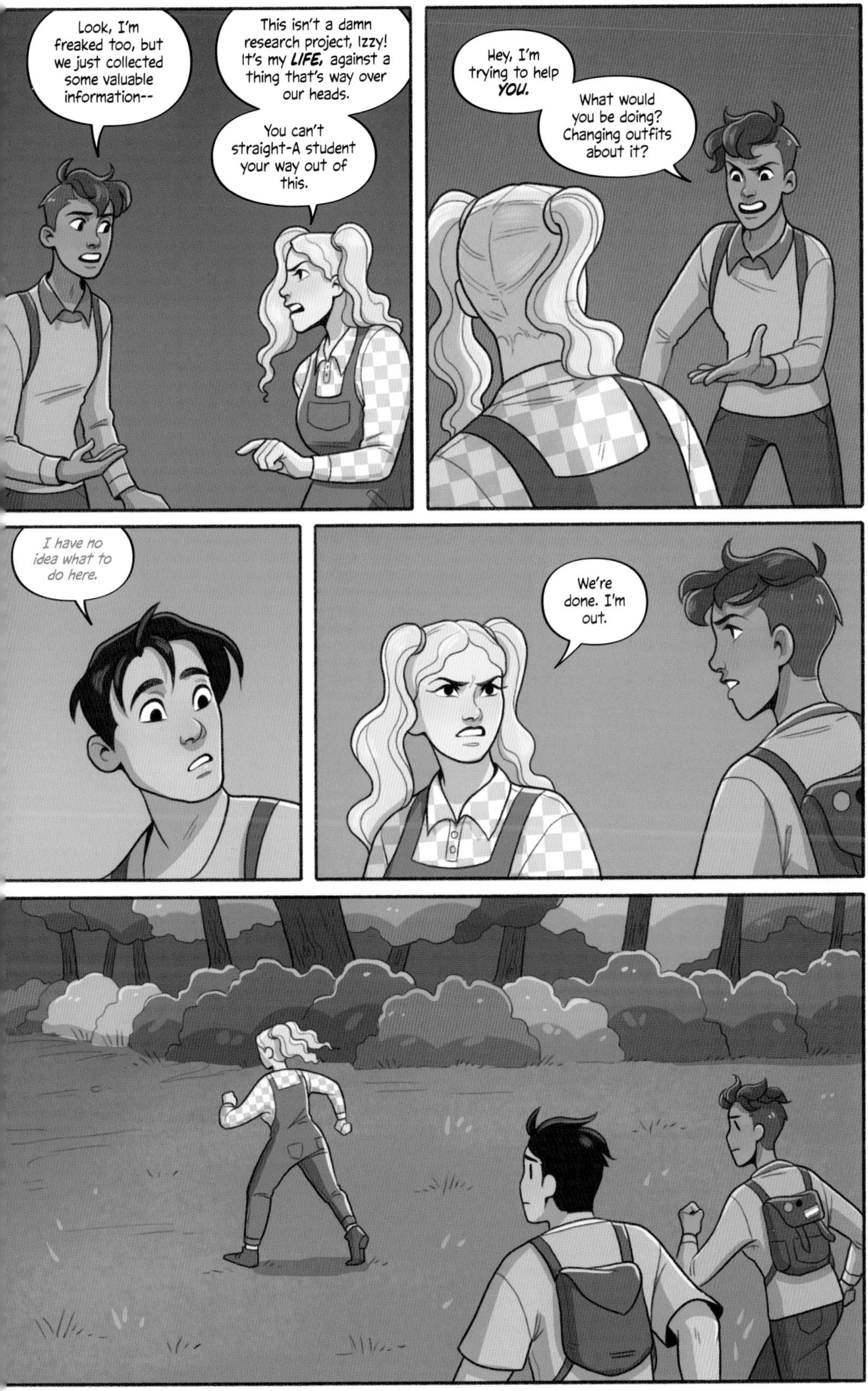

Look, I'm freaked too, but we just collected some valuable information--
This isn't a damn research project, Izzy! It's my **LIFE,** against a thing that's way over our heads.
You can't straight-A student your way out of this.
Hey, I'm trying to help **YOU.**
What would you be doing? Changing outfits about it?
I have no idea what to do here.
We're done. I'm out.

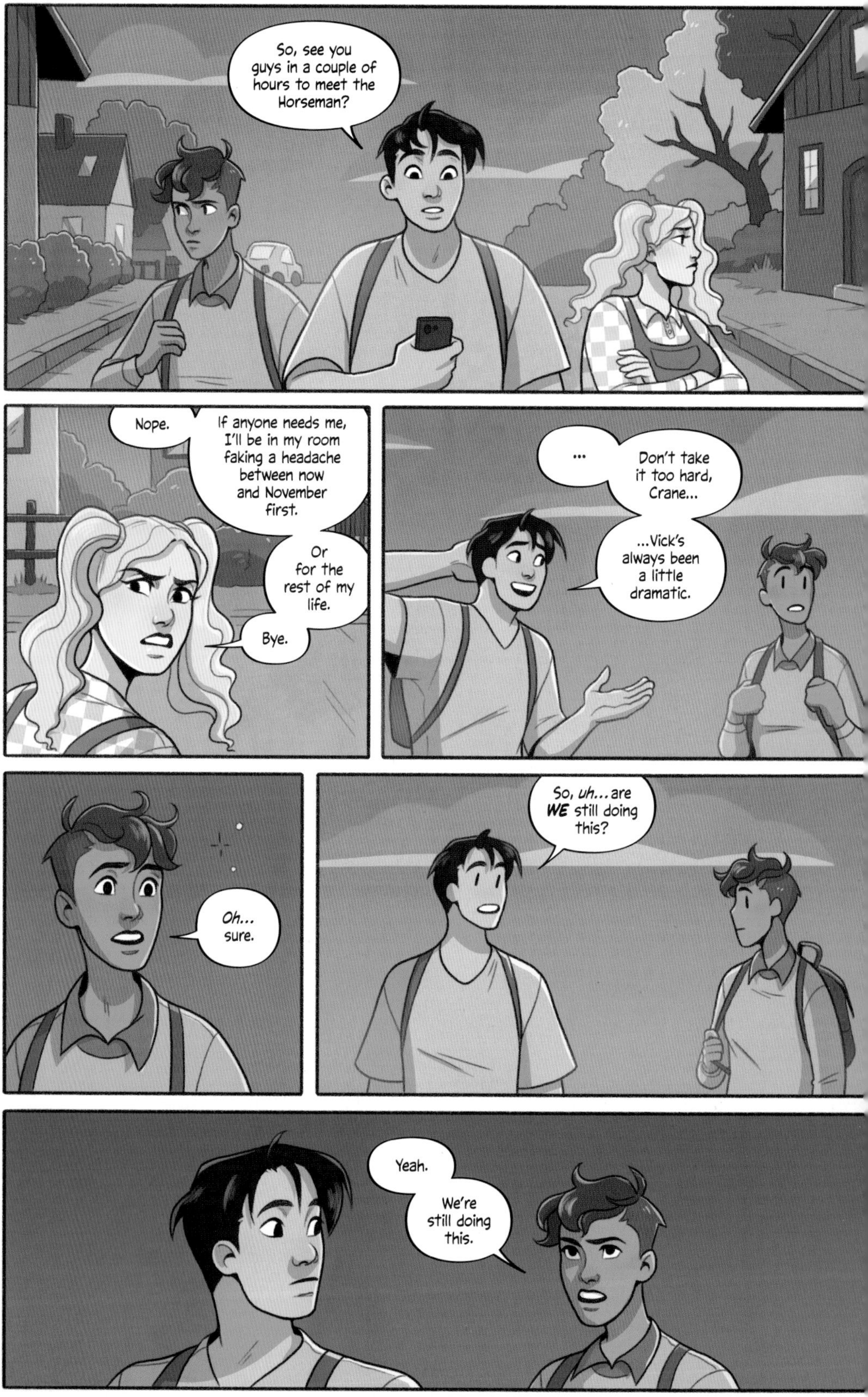
So, see you guys in a couple of hours to meet the Horseman?
Nope.
If anyone needs me, I'll be in my room faking a headache between now and November first.
Or for the rest of my life.
Bye.
...
Don't take it too hard, Crane...
...Vick's always been a little dramatic.
Oh... sure.
So, *uh...* are ***WE*** still doing this?
Yeah.
We're still doing this.

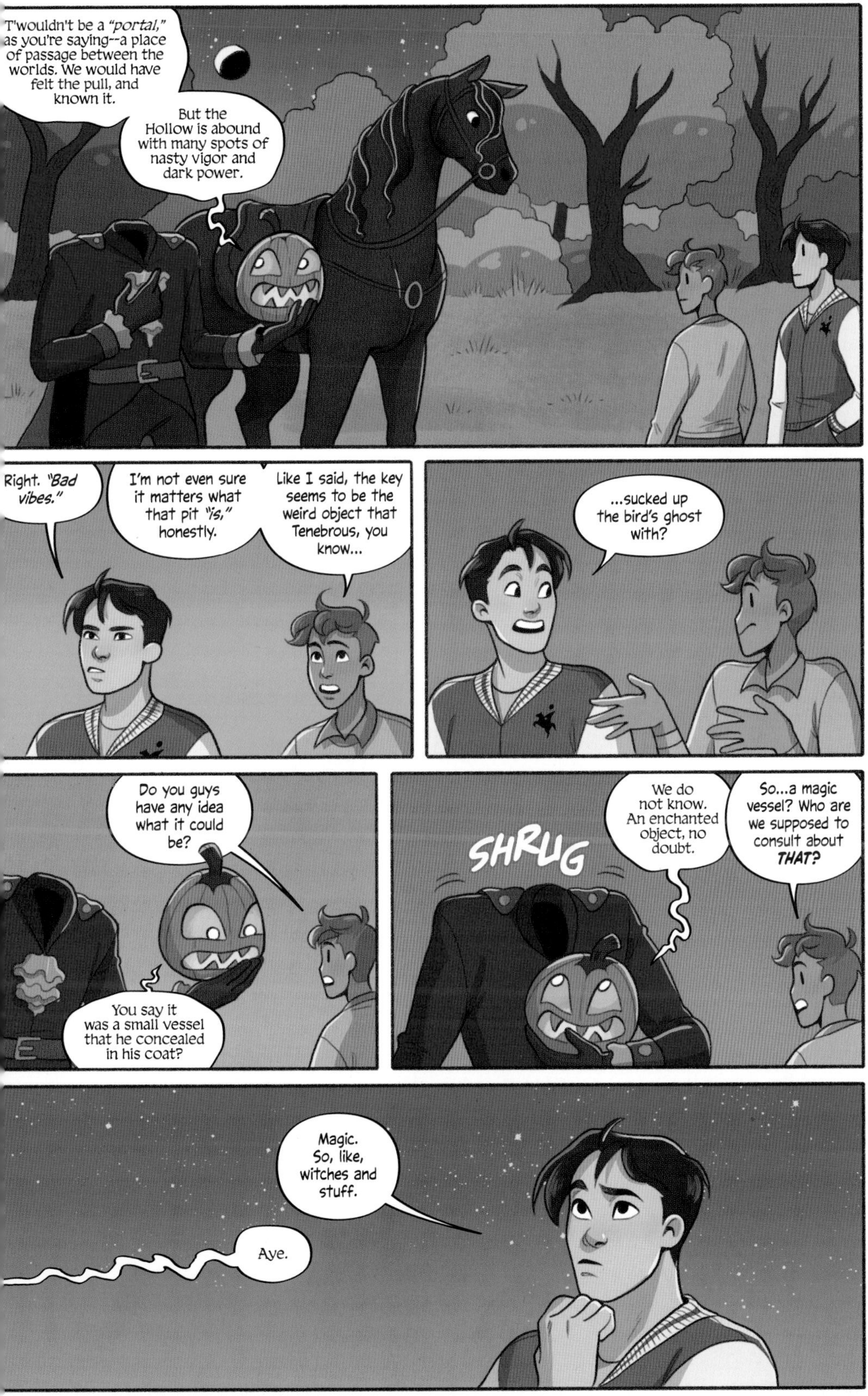

T'wouldn't be a "portal," as you're saying--a place of passage between the worlds. We would have felt the pull, and known it.
But the Hollow is abound with many spots of nasty vigor and dark power.
Right. "Bad vibes."
I'm not even sure it matters what that pit "is," honestly.
Like I said, the key seems to be the weird object that Tenebrous, you know...
...sucked up the bird's ghost with?
Do you guys have any idea what it could be?
You say it was a small vessel that he concealed in his coat?
SHRUG
We do not know. An enchanted object, no doubt.
So...a magic vessel? Who are we supposed to consult about THAT?
Magic. So, like, witches and stuff.
Aye.

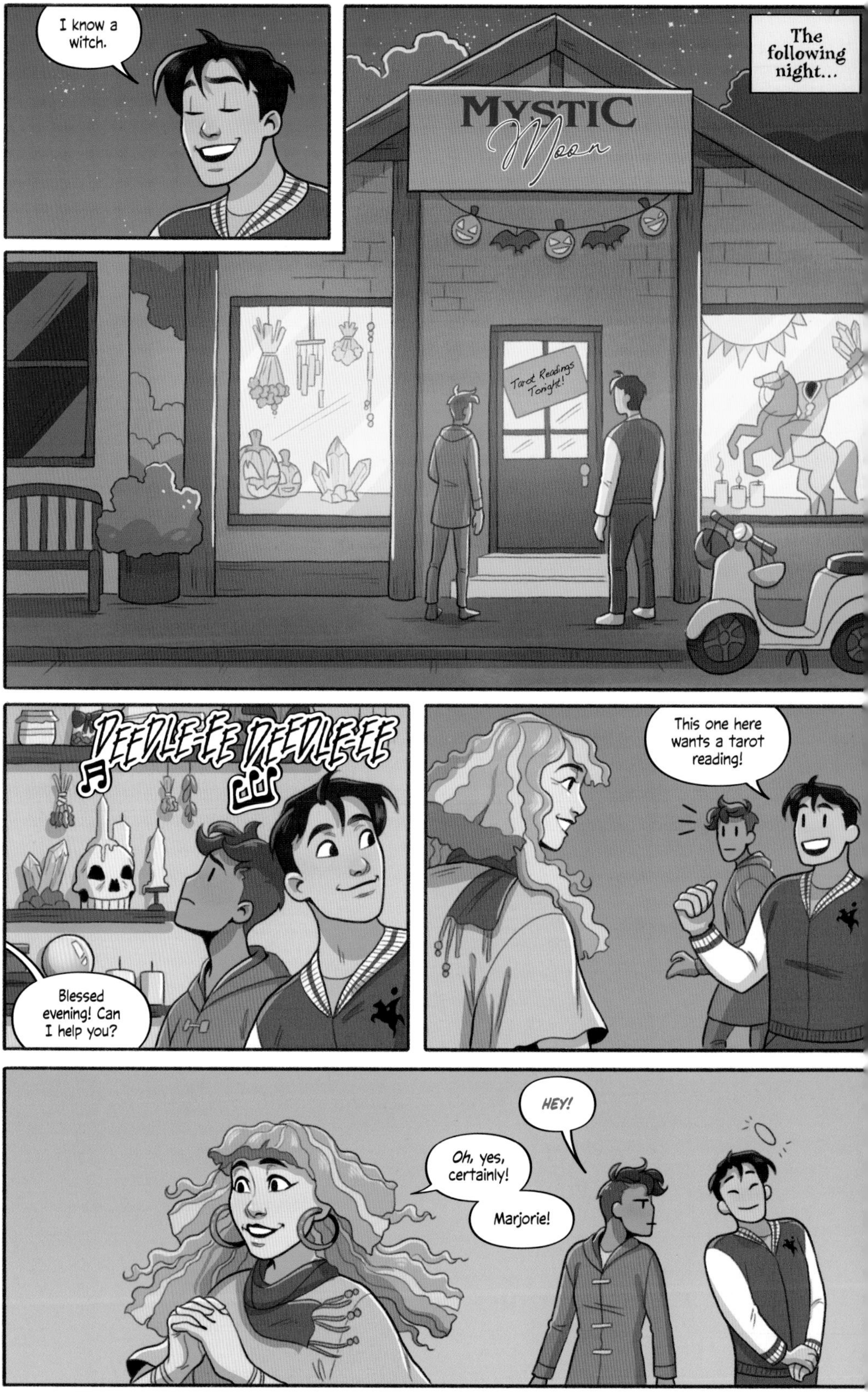
I know a witch.
The following night...
MYSTIC Moon
Tarot Readings Tonight!
DEEDLE-EE DEEDLE-EE
Blessed evening! Can I help you?
This one here wants a tarot reading!
HEY!
Oh, yes, certainly!
Marjorie!

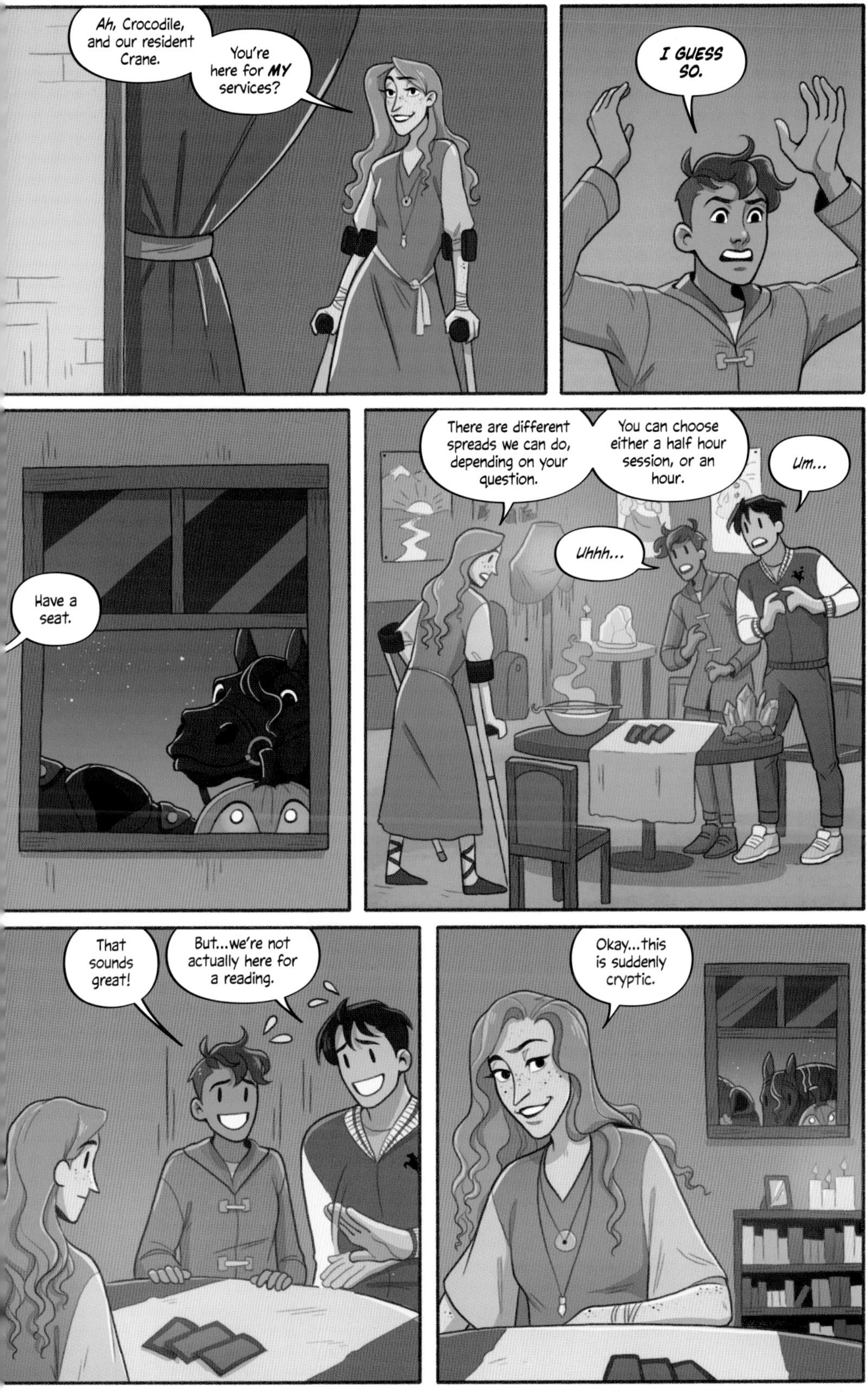
Ah, Crocodile, and our resident Crane.
You're here for MY services?
I GUESS SO.
Have a seat.
There are different spreads we can do, depending on your question.
You can choose either a half hour session, or an hour.
Uhhh...
Um...
That sounds great!
But...we're not actually here for a reading.
Okay...this is suddenly cryptic.

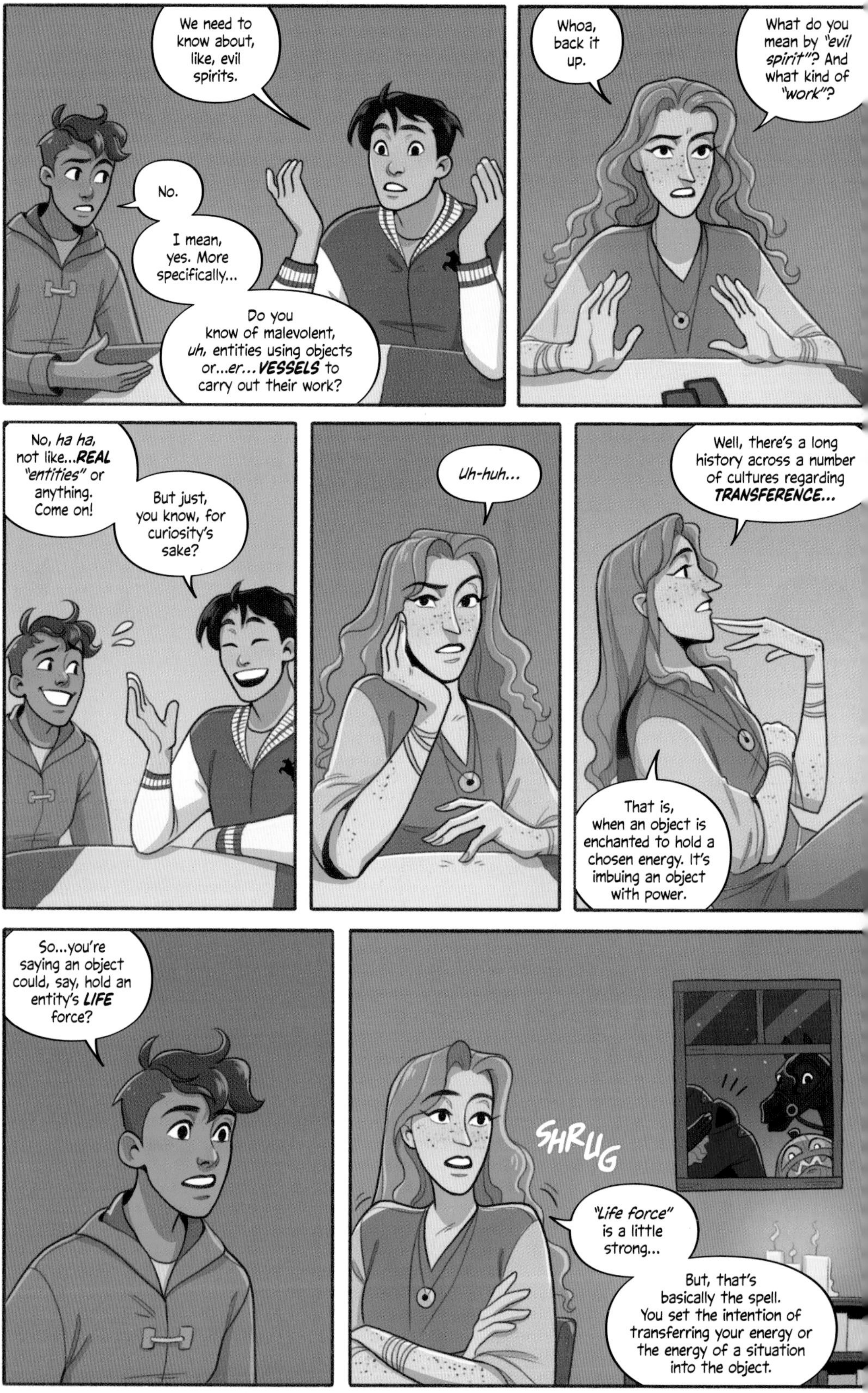

We need to know about, like, evil spirits.
No.
I mean, yes. More specifically...
Do you know of malevolent, *uh*, entities using objects or...*er*...**VESSELS** to carry out their work?
Whoa, back it up.
What do you mean by *"evil spirit"*? And what kind of *"work"*?
No, *ha ha*, not like...**REAL** *"entities"* or anything. Come on!
But just, you know, for curiosity's sake?
Uh-huh...
Well, there's a long history across a number of cultures regarding **TRANSFERENCE...**
That is, when an object is enchanted to hold a chosen energy. It's imbuing an object with power.
So...you're saying an object could, say, hold an entity's **LIFE** force?
SHRUG
"Life force" is a little strong...
But, that's basically the spell. You set the intention of transferring your energy or the energy of a situation into the object.

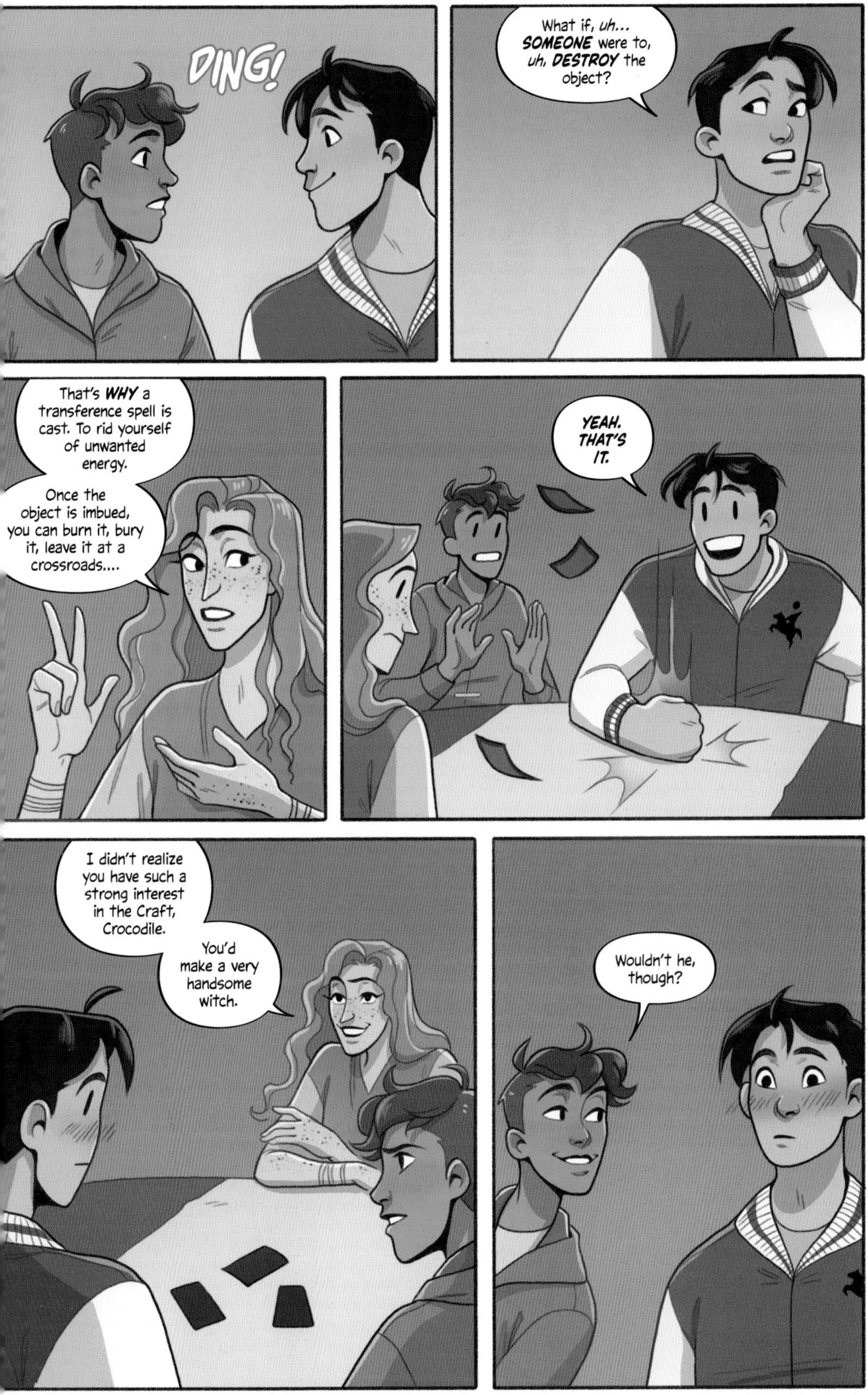
DING!
What if, *uh*... **SOMEONE** were to, *uh*, **DESTROY** the object?
That's **WHY** a transference spell is cast. To rid yourself of unwanted energy.
Once the object is imbued, you can burn it, bury it, leave it at a crossroads....
YEAH. THAT'S IT.
I didn't realize you have such a strong interest in the Craft, Crocodile.
You'd make a very handsome witch.
Wouldn't he, though?

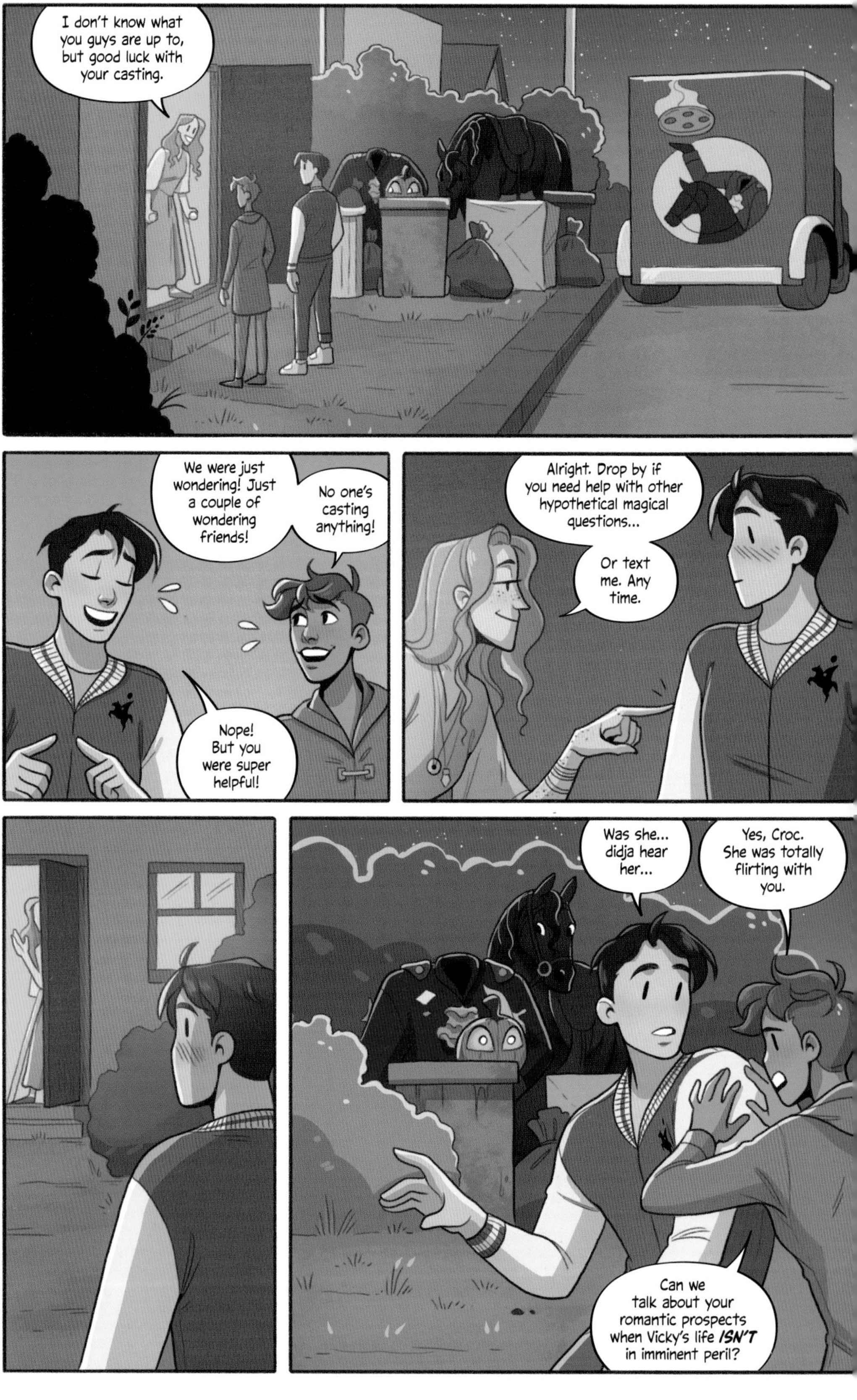
I don't know what you guys are up to, but good luck with your casting.
We were just wondering! Just a couple of wondering friends!
No one's casting anything!
Nope! But you were super helpful!
Alright. Drop by if you need help with other hypothetical magical questions...
Or text me. Any time.
Was she... didja hear her...
Yes, Croc. She was totally flirting with you.
Can we talk about your romantic prospects when Vicky's life *ISN'T* in imminent peril?

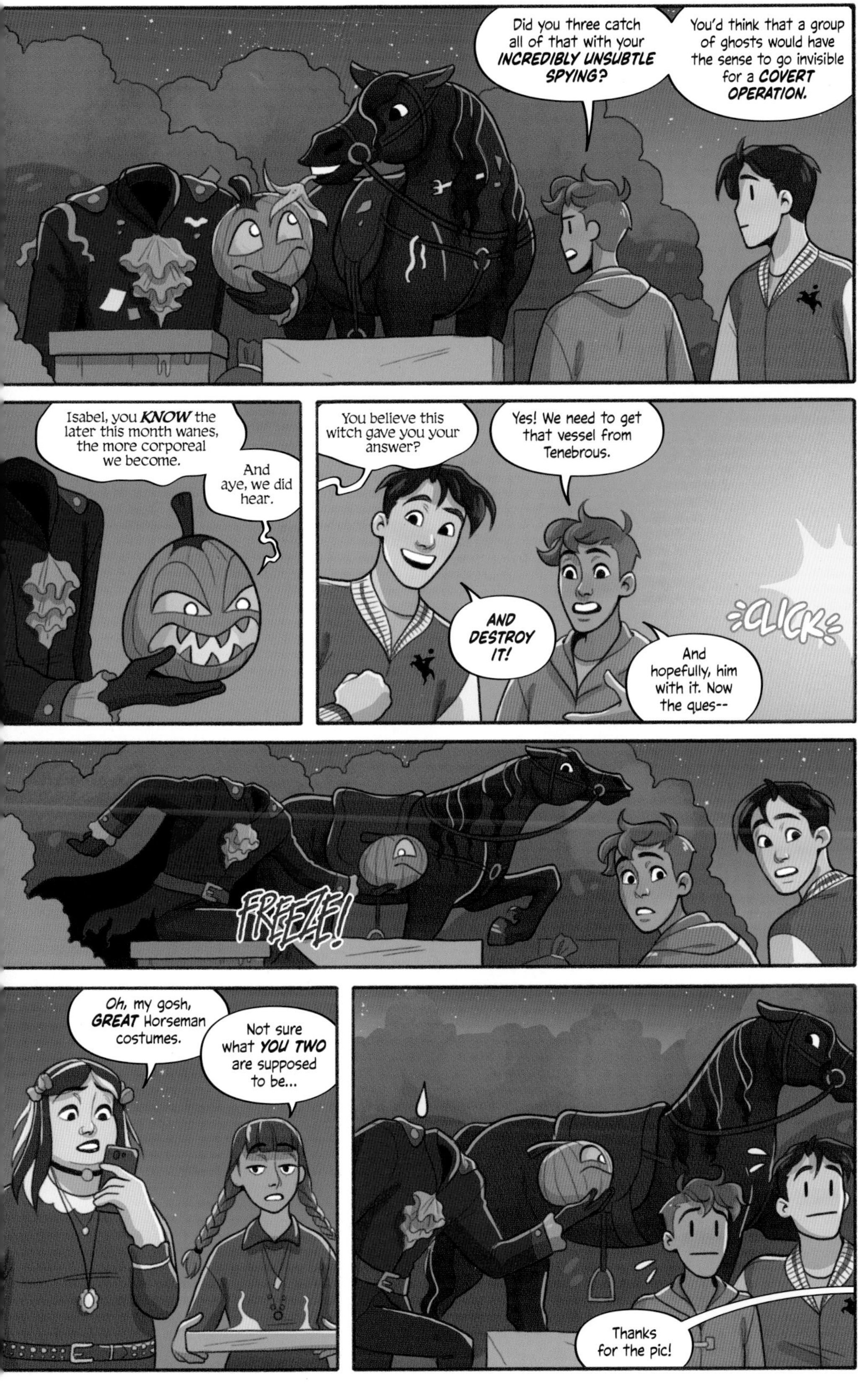

Did you three catch all of that with your INCREDIBLY UNSUBTLE SPYING?
You'd think that a group of ghosts would have the sense to go invisible for a COVERT OPERATION.
Isabel, you KNOW the later this month wanes, the more corporeal we become.
And aye, we did hear.
You believe this witch gave you your answer?
Yes! We need to get that vessel from Tenebrous.
AND DESTROY IT!
CLICK
And hopefully, him with it. Now the ques--
FREEZE!
Oh, my gosh, GREAT Horseman costumes.
Not sure what YOU TWO are supposed to be...
Thanks for the pic!

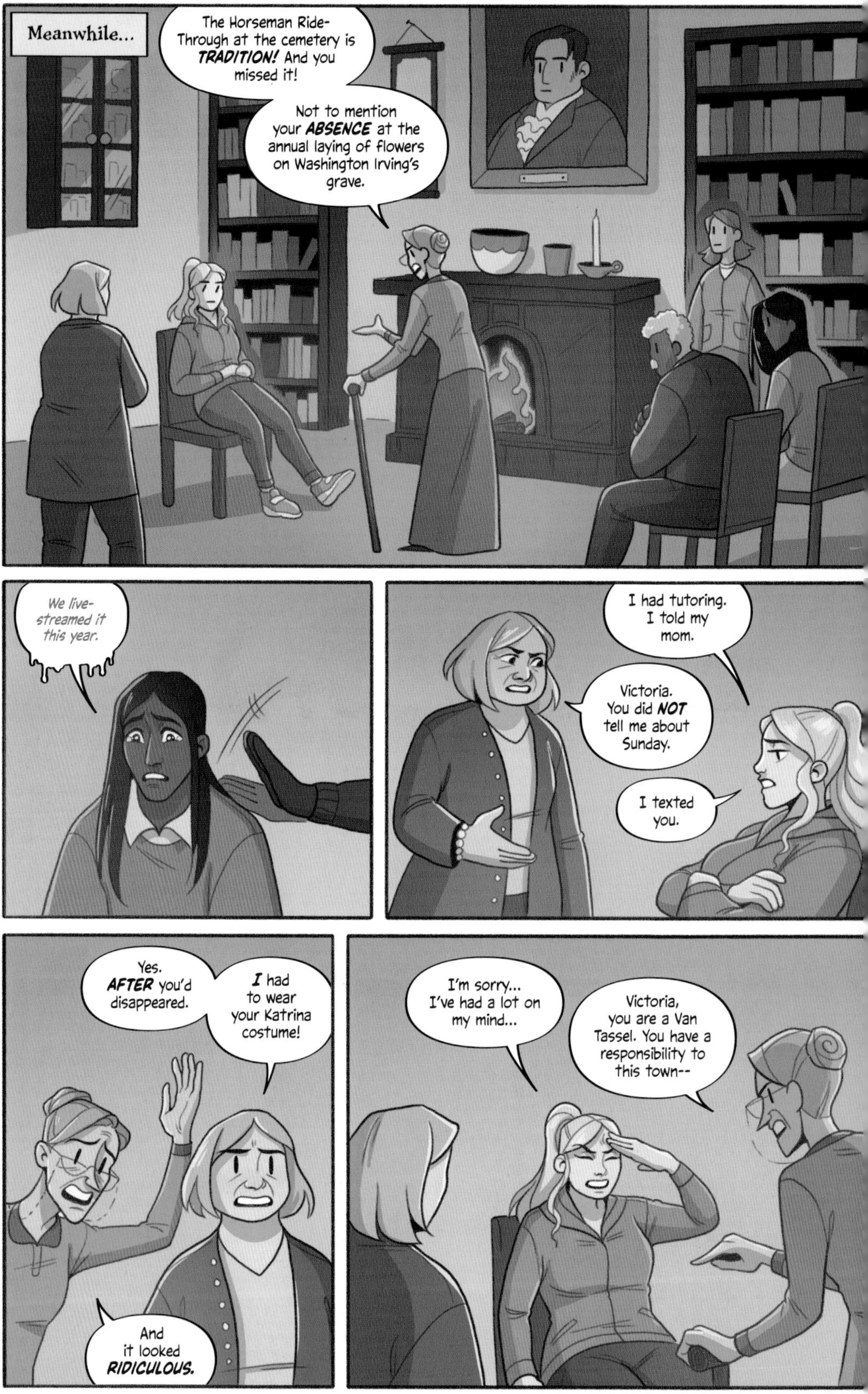
Meanwhile...
The Horseman Ride-Through at the cemetery is TRADITION! And you missed it!
Not to mention your ABSENCE at the annual laying of flowers on Washington Irving's grave.
We live-streamed it this year.
I had tutoring. I told my mom.
Victoria. You did NOT tell me about Sunday.
I texted you.
Yes. AFTER you'd disappeared.
I had to wear your Katrina costume!
And it looked RIDICULOUS.
I'm sorry... I've had a lot on my mind...
Victoria, you are a Van Tassel. You have a responsibility to this town--

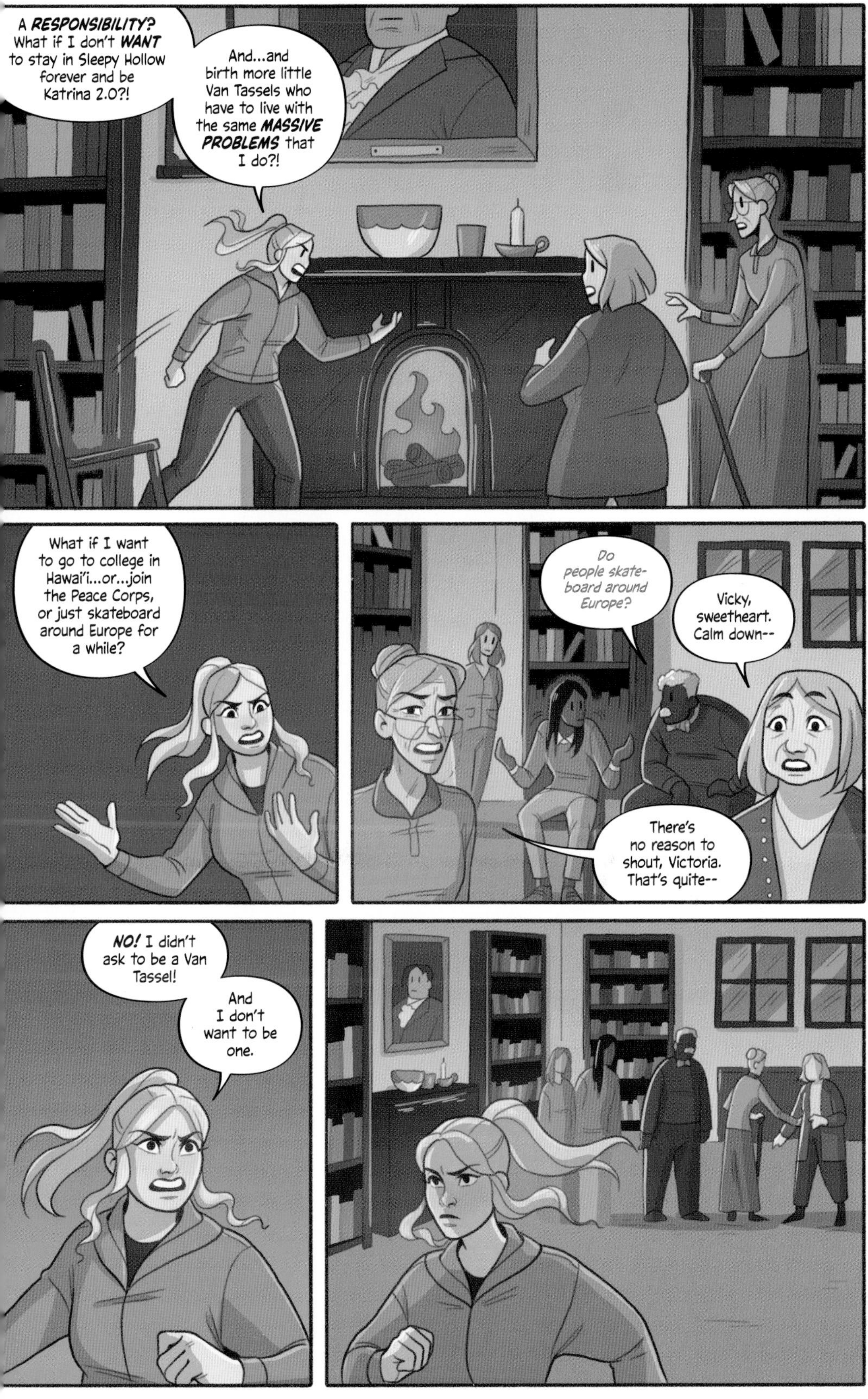
A RESPONSIBILITY? What if I don't WANT to stay in Sleepy Hollow forever and be Katrina 2.0?!
And...and birth more little Van Tassels who have to live with the same MASSIVE PROBLEMS that I do?!
What if I want to go to college in Hawai'i...or...join the Peace Corps, or just skateboard around Europe for a while?
Do people skate-board around Europe?
Vicky, sweetheart. Calm down--
There's no reason to shout, Victoria. That's quite--
NO! I didn't ask to be a Van Tassel!
And I don't want to be one.

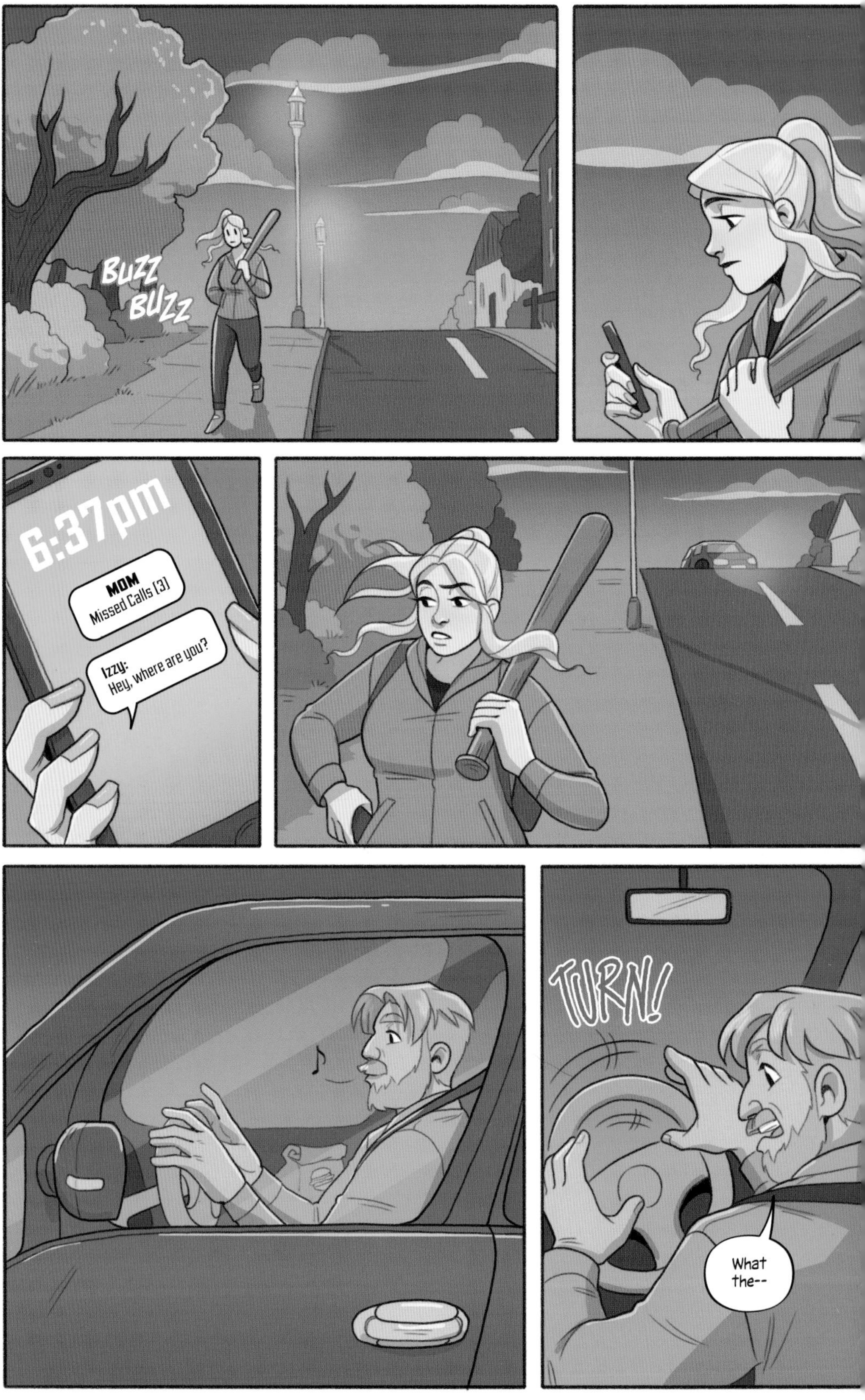
BUZZ
BUZZ
6:37pm
MOM
Missed Calls (3)
Izzy:
Hey, where are you?
TURN!
What the--

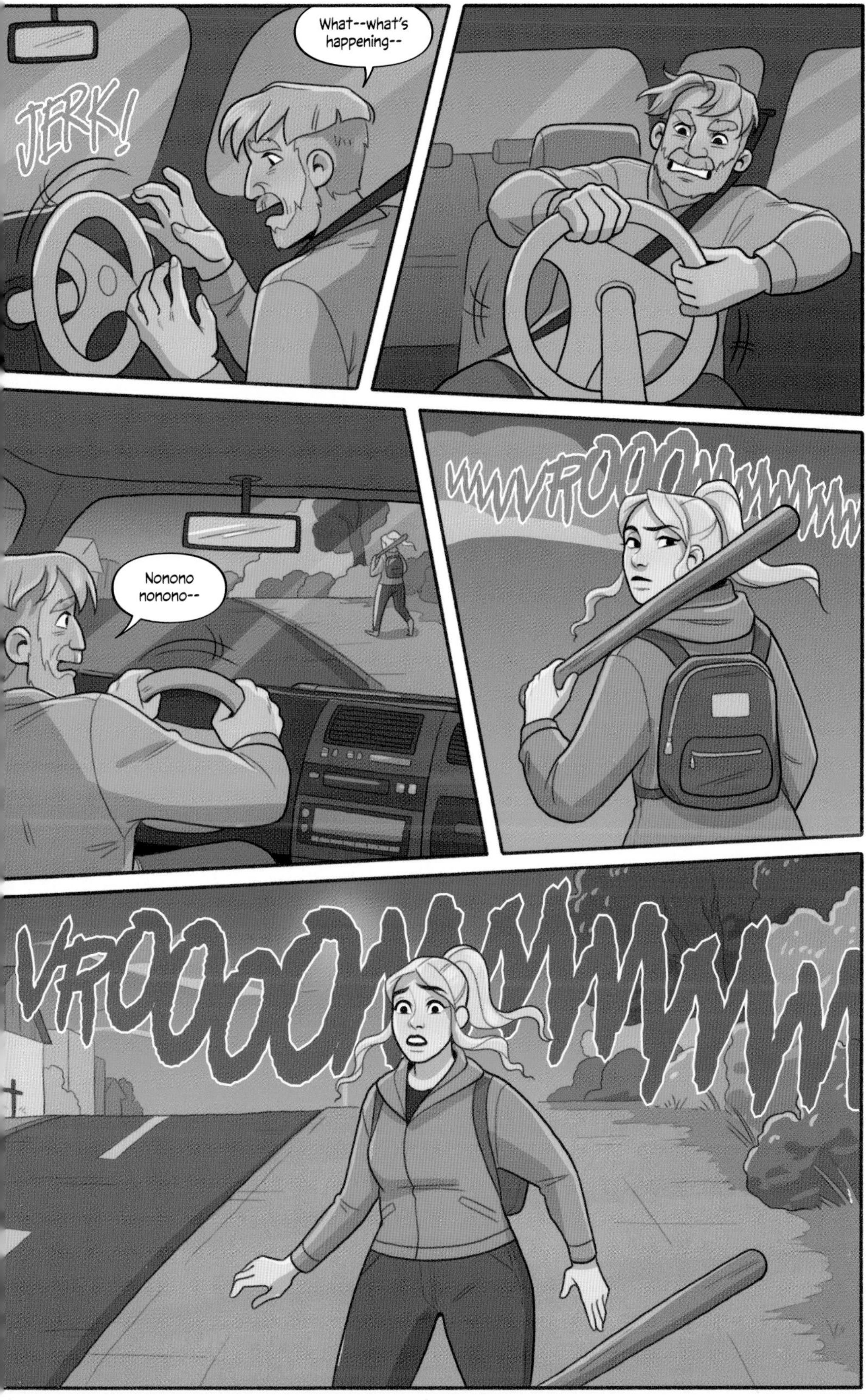

What--what's happening--
JERK!
Nonono nonono--
VROOOMMMM
VROOOOMMMMMMM

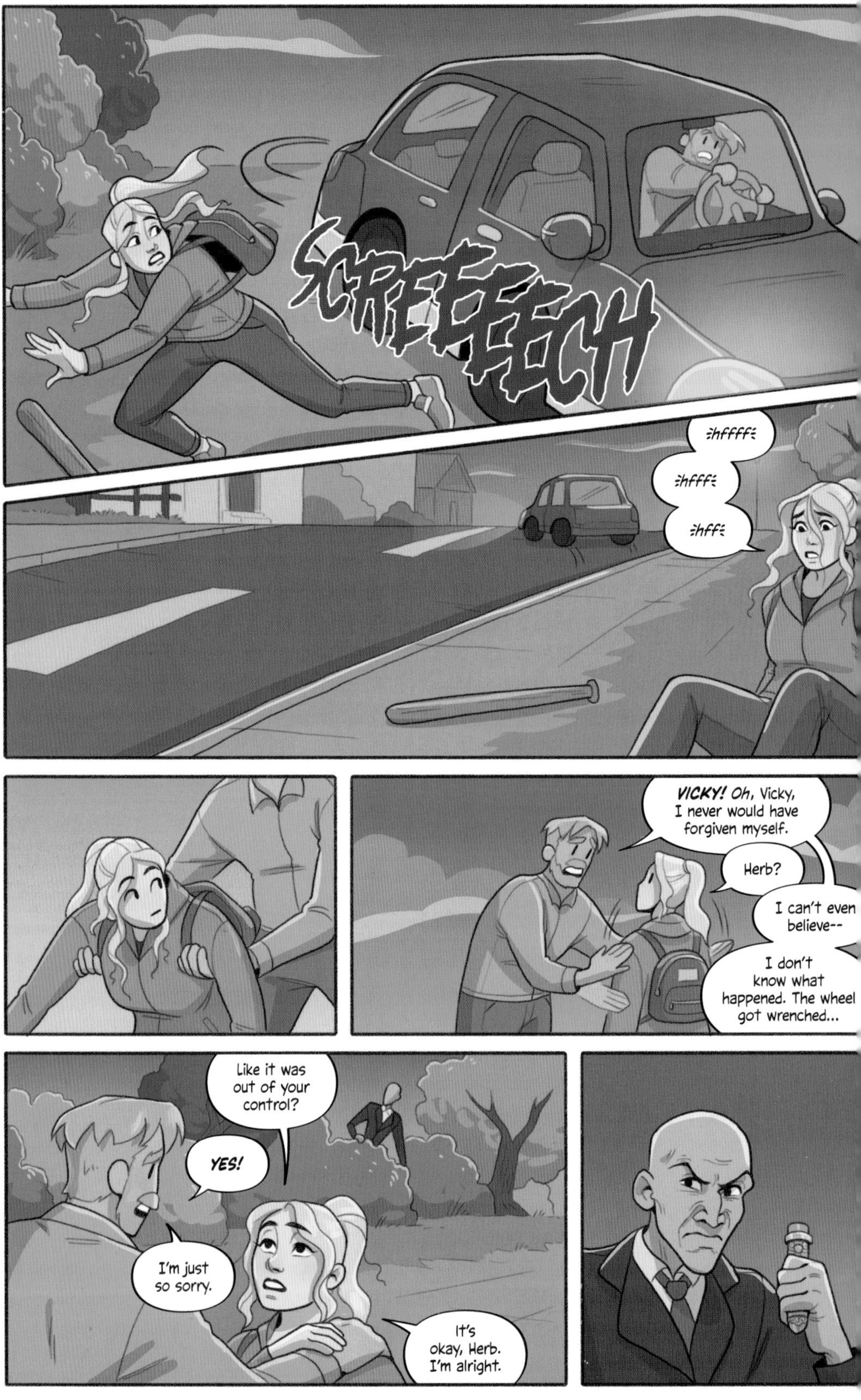
SCREEEECH
hffff
hfff
hff
VICKY! Oh, Vicky, I never would have forgiven myself.
Herb?
I can't even believe--
I don't know what happened. The wheel got wrenched...
Like it was out of your control?
YES!
I'm just so sorry.
It's okay, Herb. I'm alright.

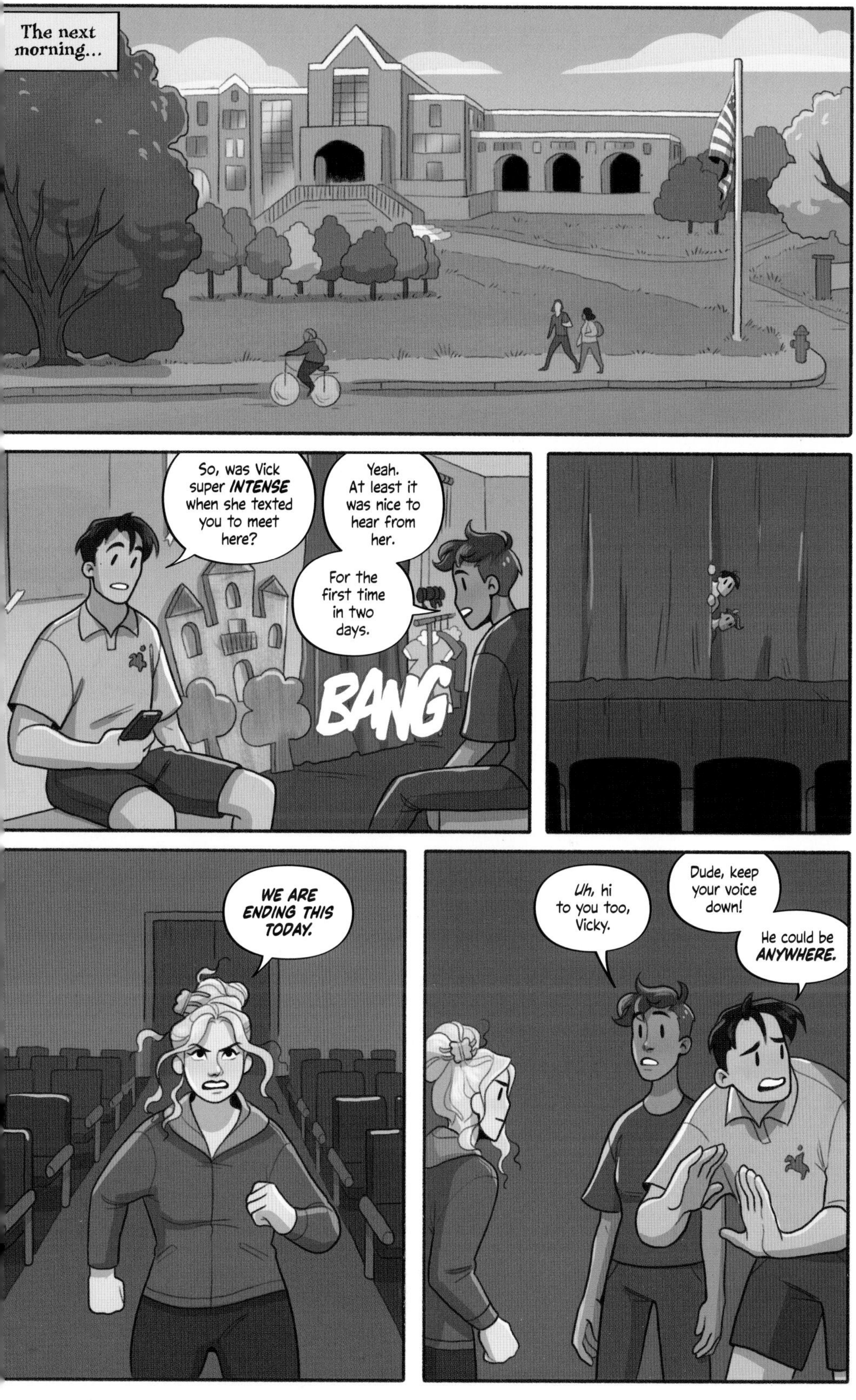
The next morning...
So, was Vick super *INTENSE* when she texted you to meet here?
Yeah. At least it was nice to hear from her.
For the first time in two days.
BANG
WE ARE ENDING THIS TODAY.
Uh, hi to you too, Vicky.
Dude, keep your voice down!
He could be *ANYWHERE.*

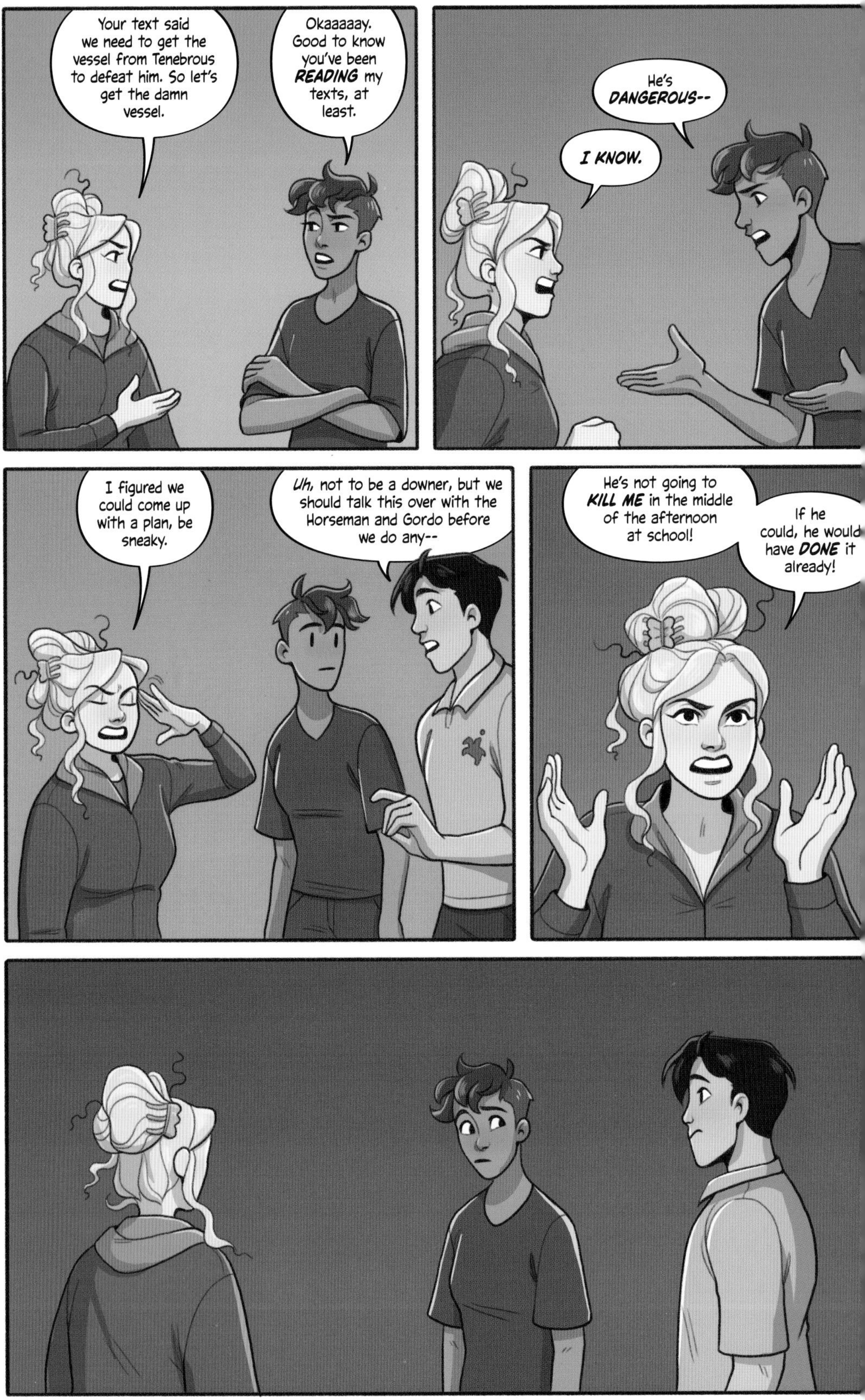
Your text said we need to get the vessel from Tenebrous to defeat him. So let's get the damn vessel.
Okaaaaay. Good to know you've been **READING** my texts, at least.
He's **DANGEROUS--**
I KNOW.
I figured we could come up with a plan, be sneaky.
Uh, not to be a downer, but we should talk this over with the Horseman and Gordo before we do any--
He's not going to **KILL ME** in the middle of the afternoon at school!
If he could, he would have **DONE** it already!

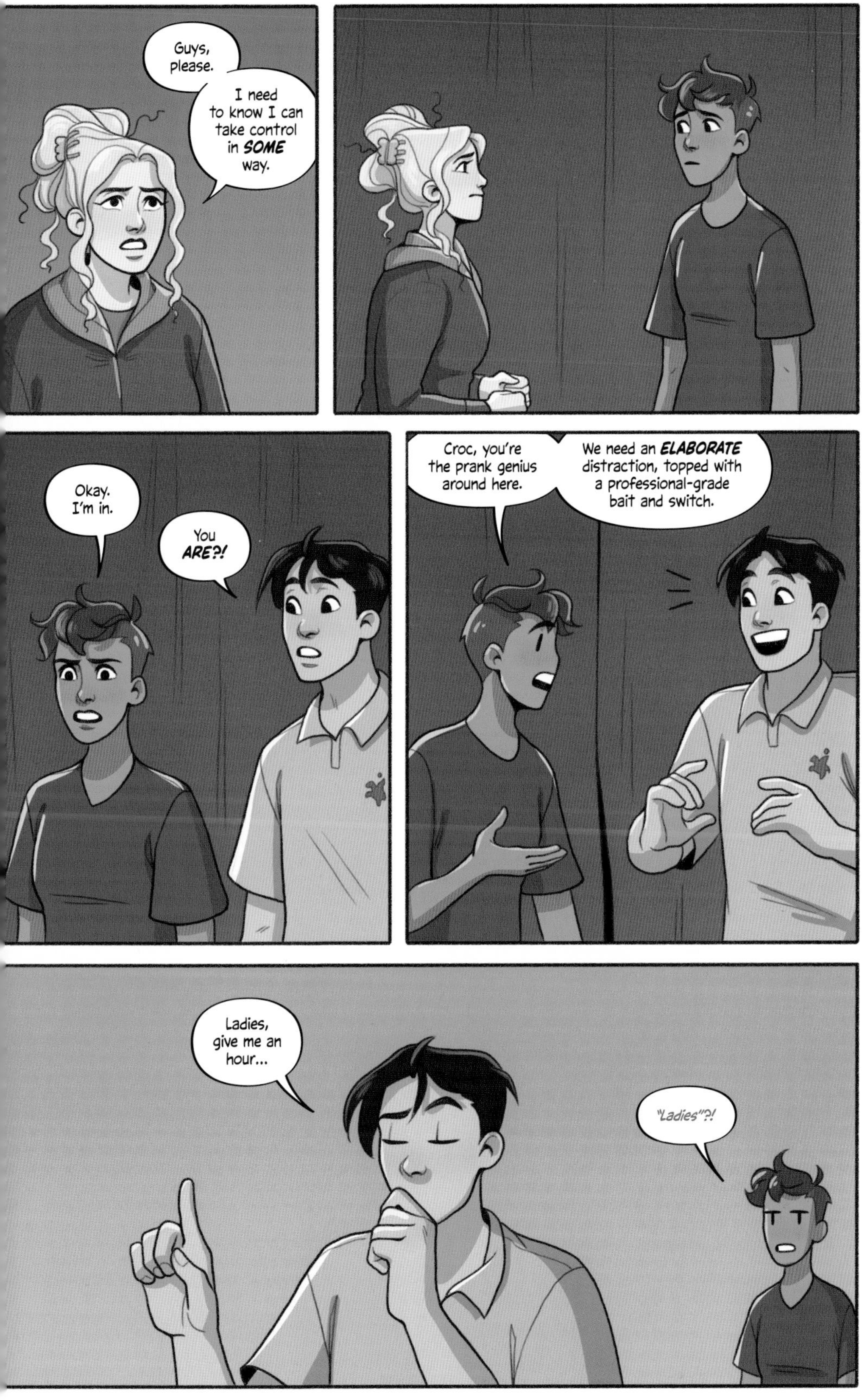

Guys, please.
I need to know I can take control in *SOME* way.
Okay. I'm in.
You *ARE?!*
Croc, you're the prank genius around here.
We need an *ELABORATE* distraction, topped with a professional-grade bait and switch.
Ladies, give me an hour...
"Ladies"?!

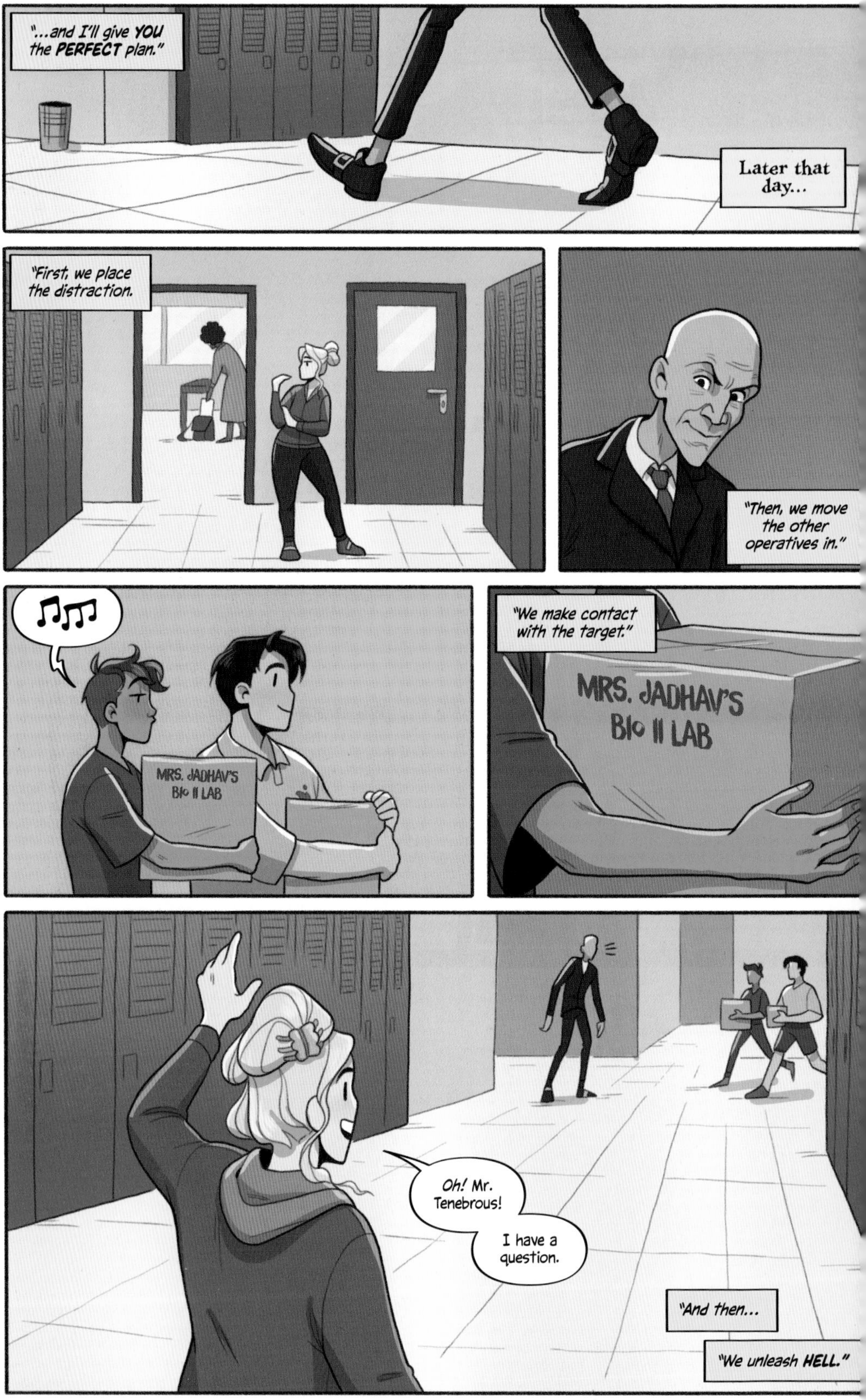
"...and I'll give YOU the PERFECT plan."
Later that day...
"First, we place the distraction.
"Then, we move the other operatives in."
♫♫
"We make contact with the target."
MRS. JADHAV'S BIO II LAB
MRS. JADHAV'S BIO II LAB
Oh! Mr. Tenebrous!
I have a question.
"And then...
"We unleash HELL."

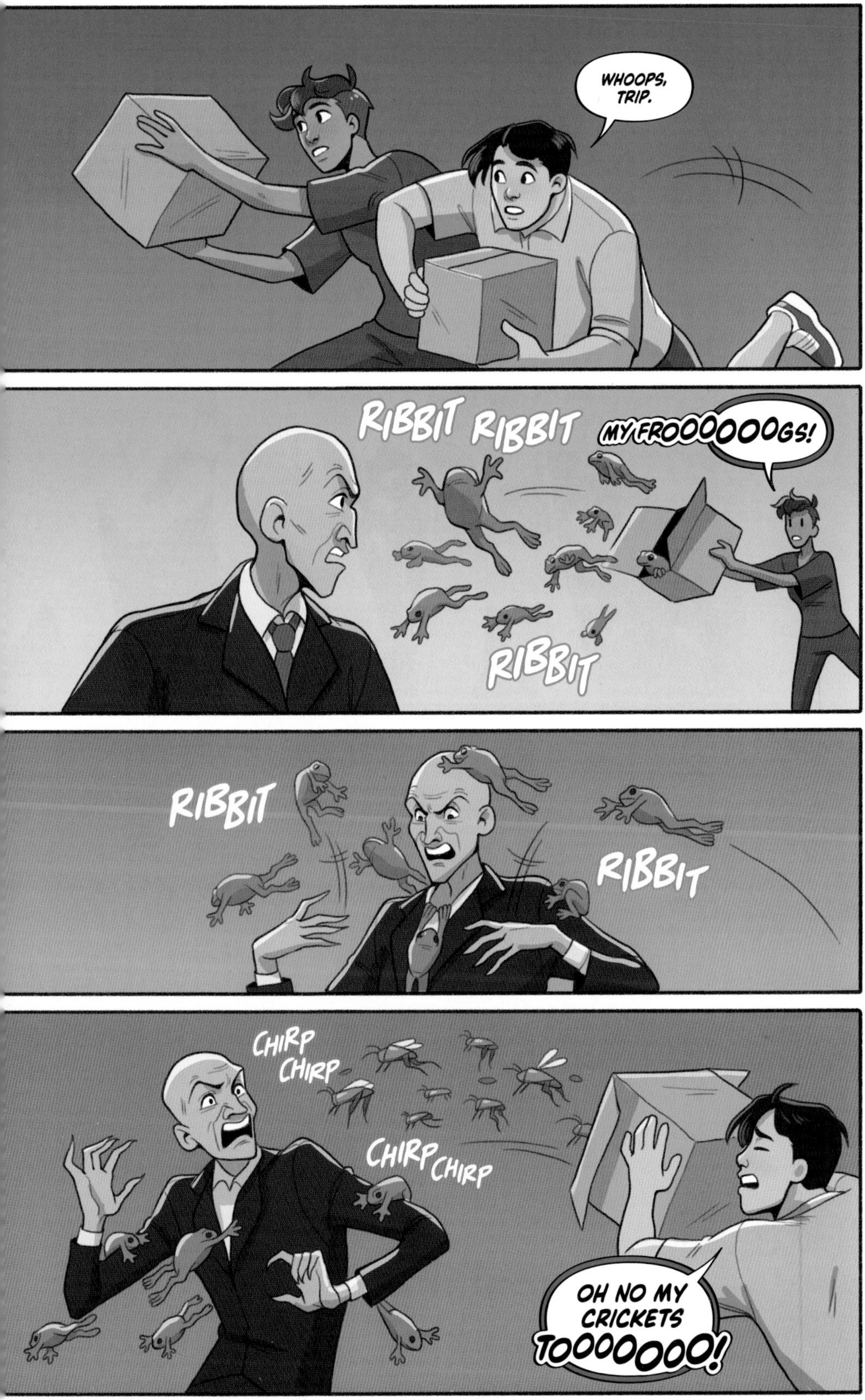
WHOOPS, TRIP.
RIBBIT RIBBIT
MY FROOOOOOOGS!
RIBBIT
RIBBIT
RIBBIT
CHIRP CHIRP
CHIRP CHIRP
OH NO MY CRICKETS TOOOOOOO!

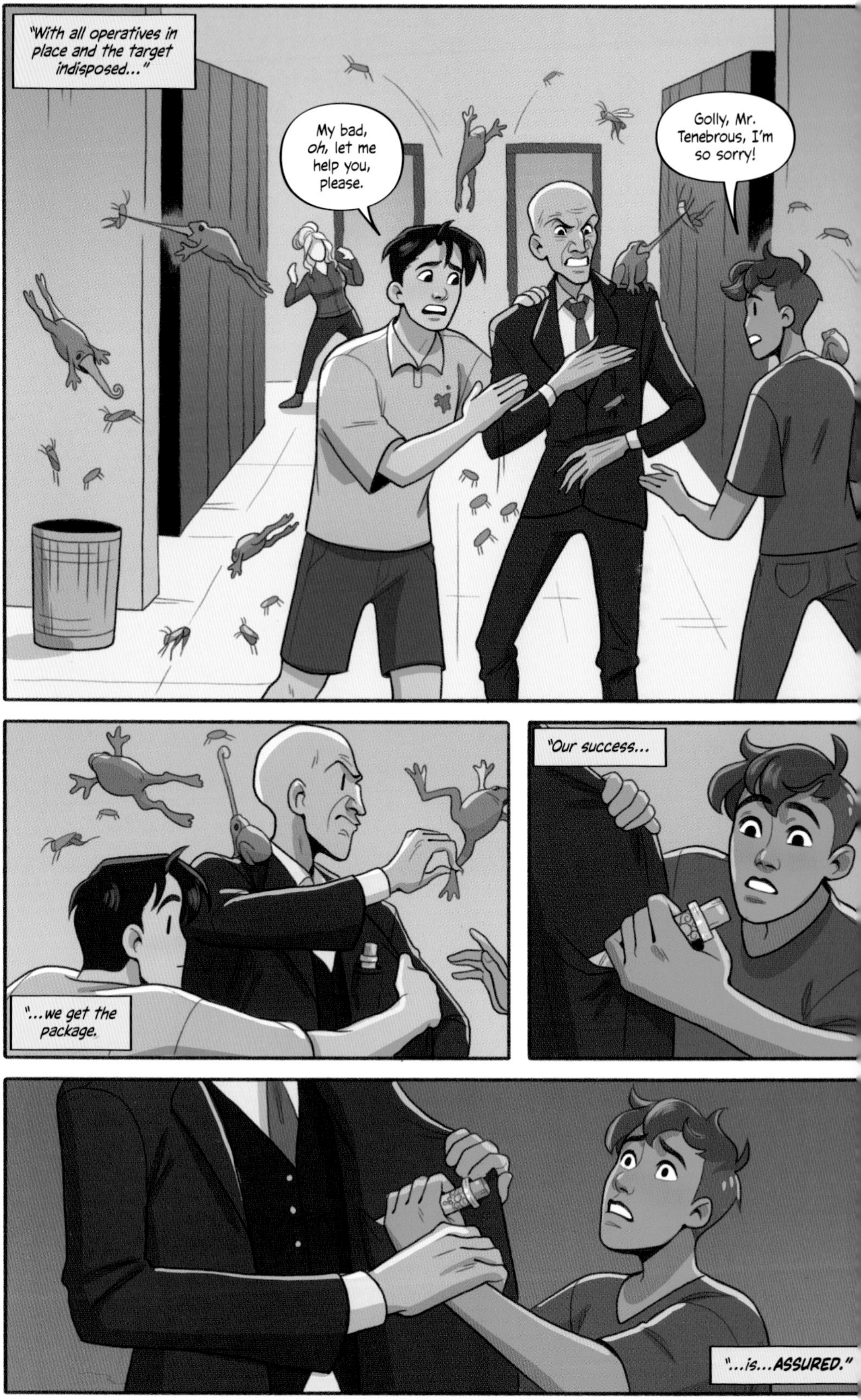
"With all operatives in place and the target indisposed..."
My bad, oh, let me help you, please.
Golly, Mr. Tenebrous, I'm so sorry!
"...we get the package.
"Our success...
"...is...ASSURED."

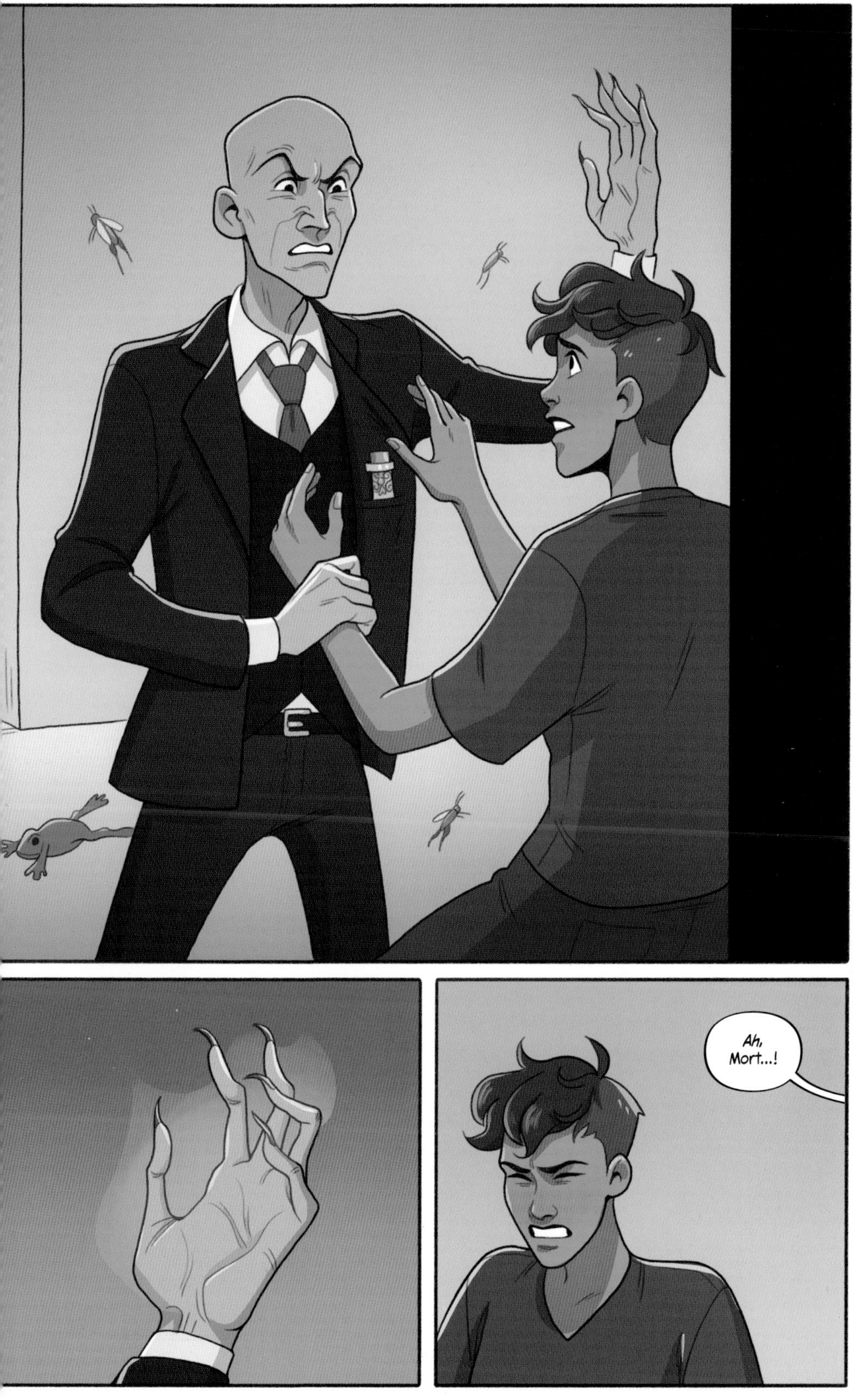
Ah,
Mort...!

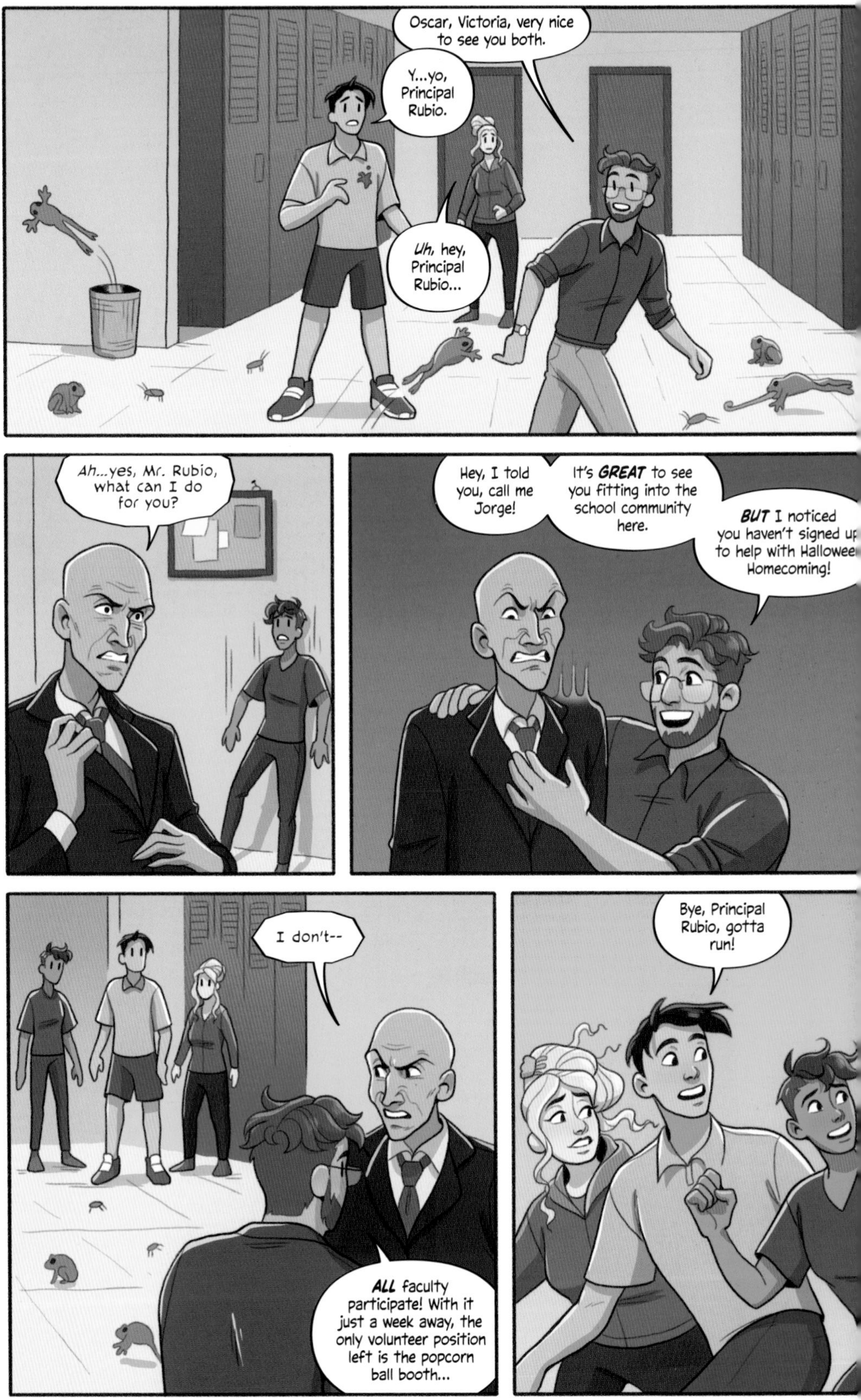
Oscar, Victoria, very nice to see you both.
Y...yo, Principal Rubio.
Uh, hey, Principal Rubio...
Ah...yes, Mr. Rubio, what can I do for you?
Hey, I told you, call me Jorge!
It's GREAT to see you fitting into the school community here.
BUT I noticed you haven't signed up to help with Halloween Homecoming!
I don't--
ALL faculty participate! With it just a week away, the only volunteer position left is the popcorn ball booth...
Bye, Principal Rubio, gotta run!

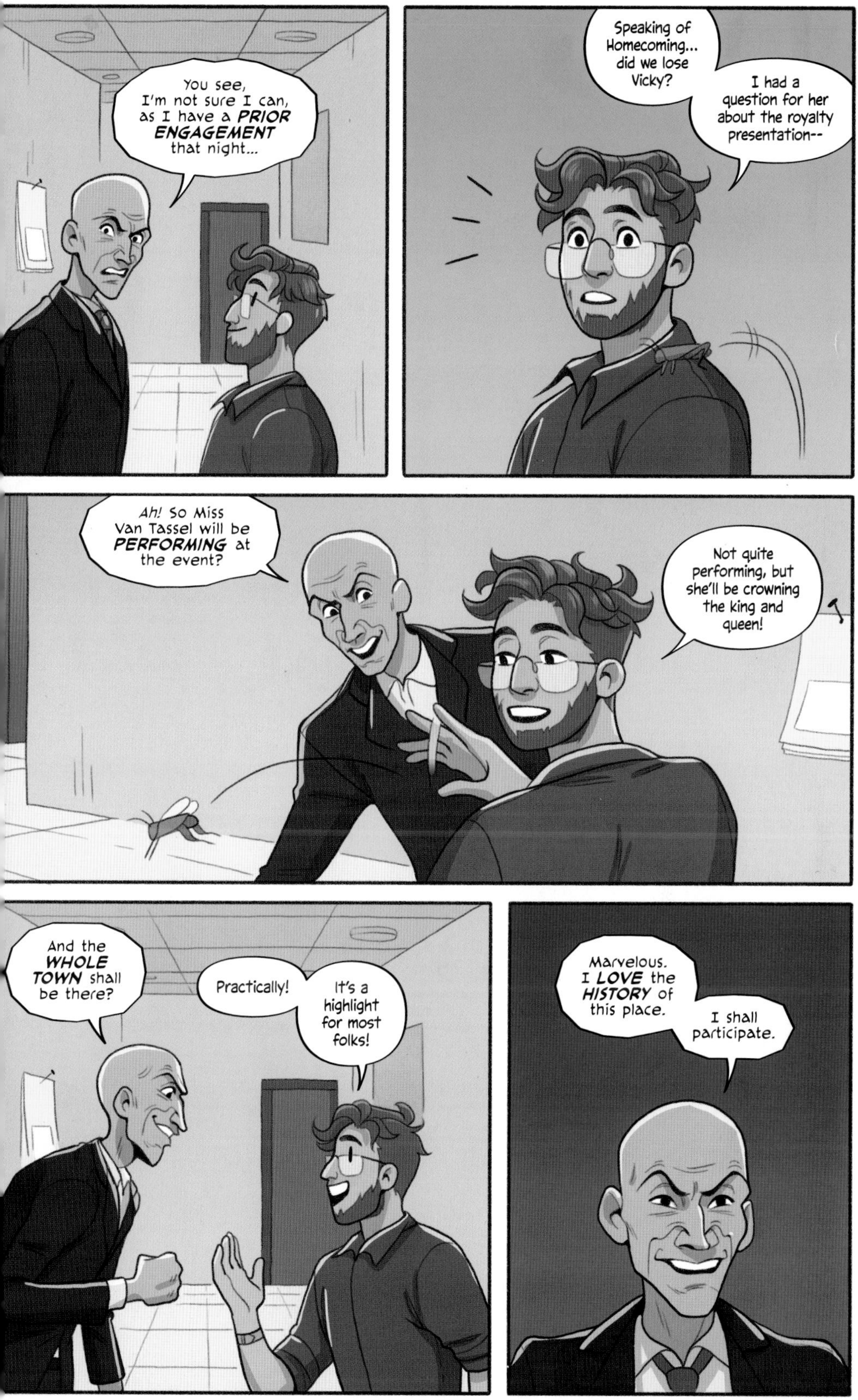
You see, I'm not sure I can, as I have a PRIOR ENGAGEMENT that night...
Speaking of Homecoming... did we lose Vicky?
I had a question for her about the royalty presentation--
Ah! So Miss Van Tassel will be PERFORMING at the event?
Not quite performing, but she'll be crowning the king and queen!
And the WHOLE TOWN shall be there?
Practically!
It's a highlight for most folks!
Marvelous. I LOVE the HISTORY of this place.
I shall participate.

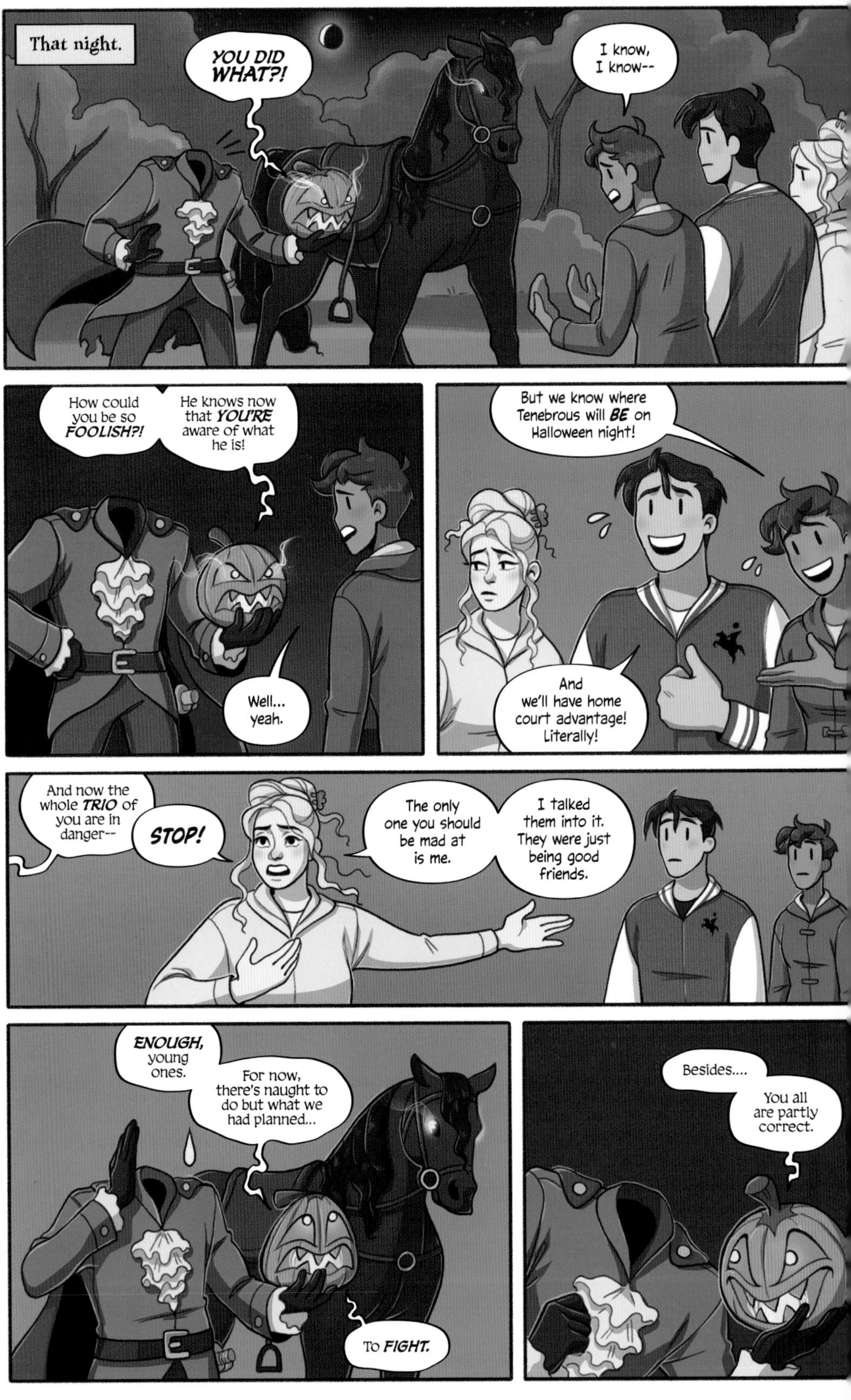
That night.
YOU DID WHAT?!
I know, I know--
How could you be so FOOLISH?!
He knows now that YOU'RE aware of what he is!
Well... yeah.
But we know where Tenebrous will BE on Halloween night!
And we'll have home court advantage! Literally!
And now the whole TRIO of you are in danger--
STOP!
The only one you should be mad at is me.
I talked them into it. They were just being good friends.
ENOUGH, young ones.
For now, there's naught to do but what we had planned...
To FIGHT.
Besides....
You all are partly correct.

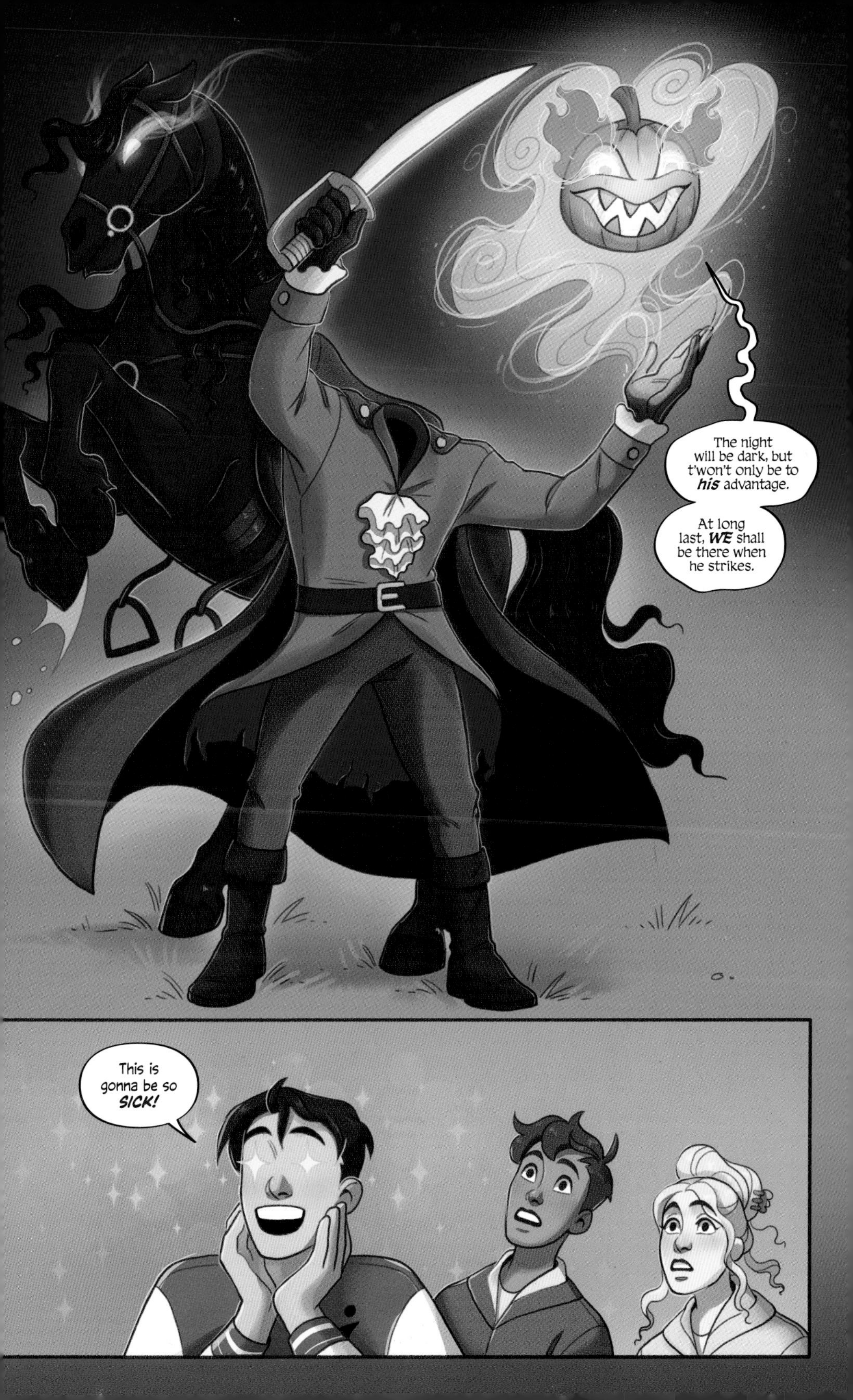
The night will be dark, but t'won't only be to ***his*** advantage.
At long last, ***WE*** shall be there when he strikes.
This is gonna be so ***SICK!***

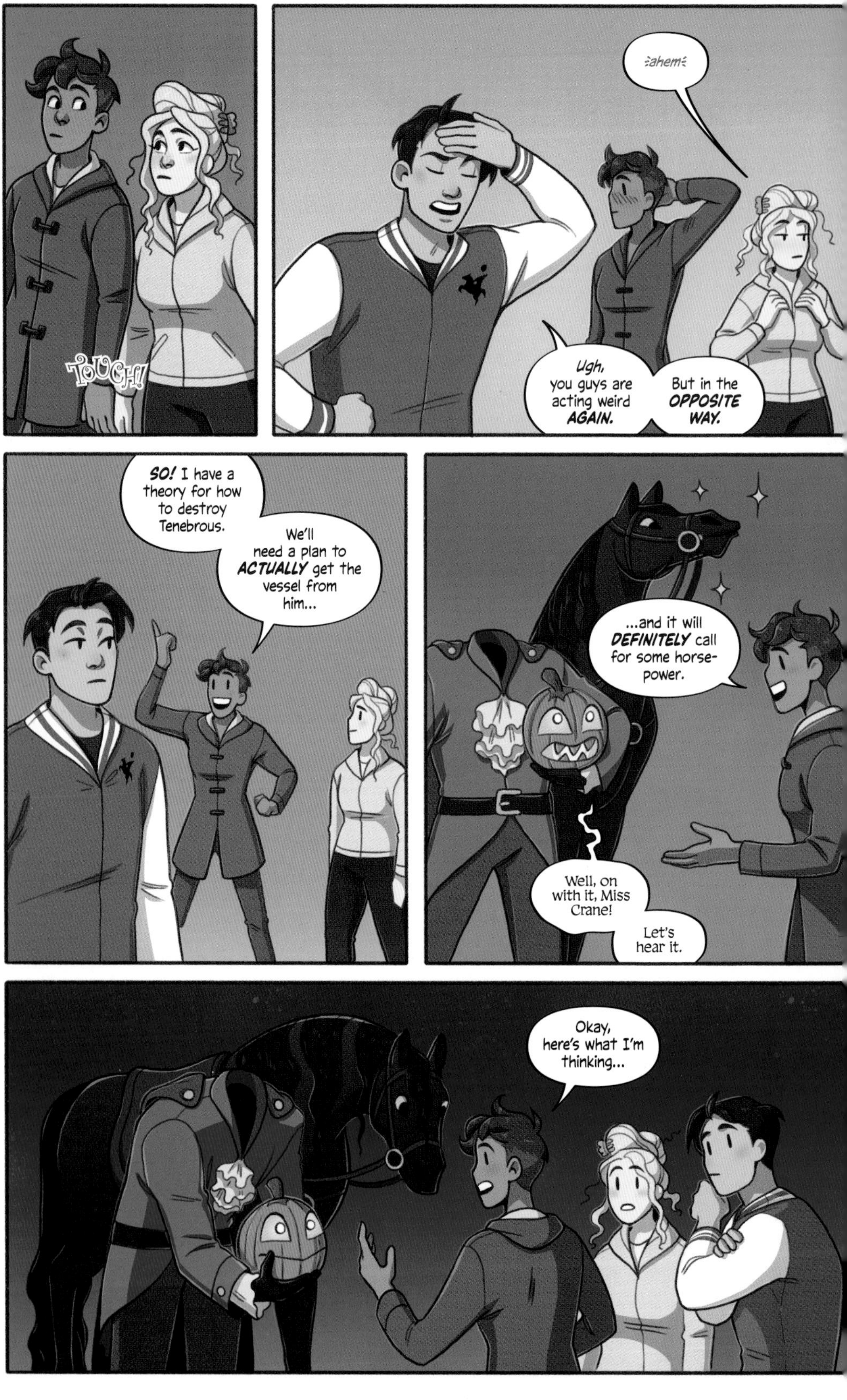
TOUCH!
ahem
Ugh, you guys are acting weird AGAIN.
But in the OPPOSITE WAY.
SO! I have a theory for how to destroy Tenebrous.
We'll need a plan to ACTUALLY get the vessel from him...
...and it will DEFINITELY call for some horse-power.
Well, on with it, Miss Crane!
Let's hear it.
Okay, here's what I'm thinking...

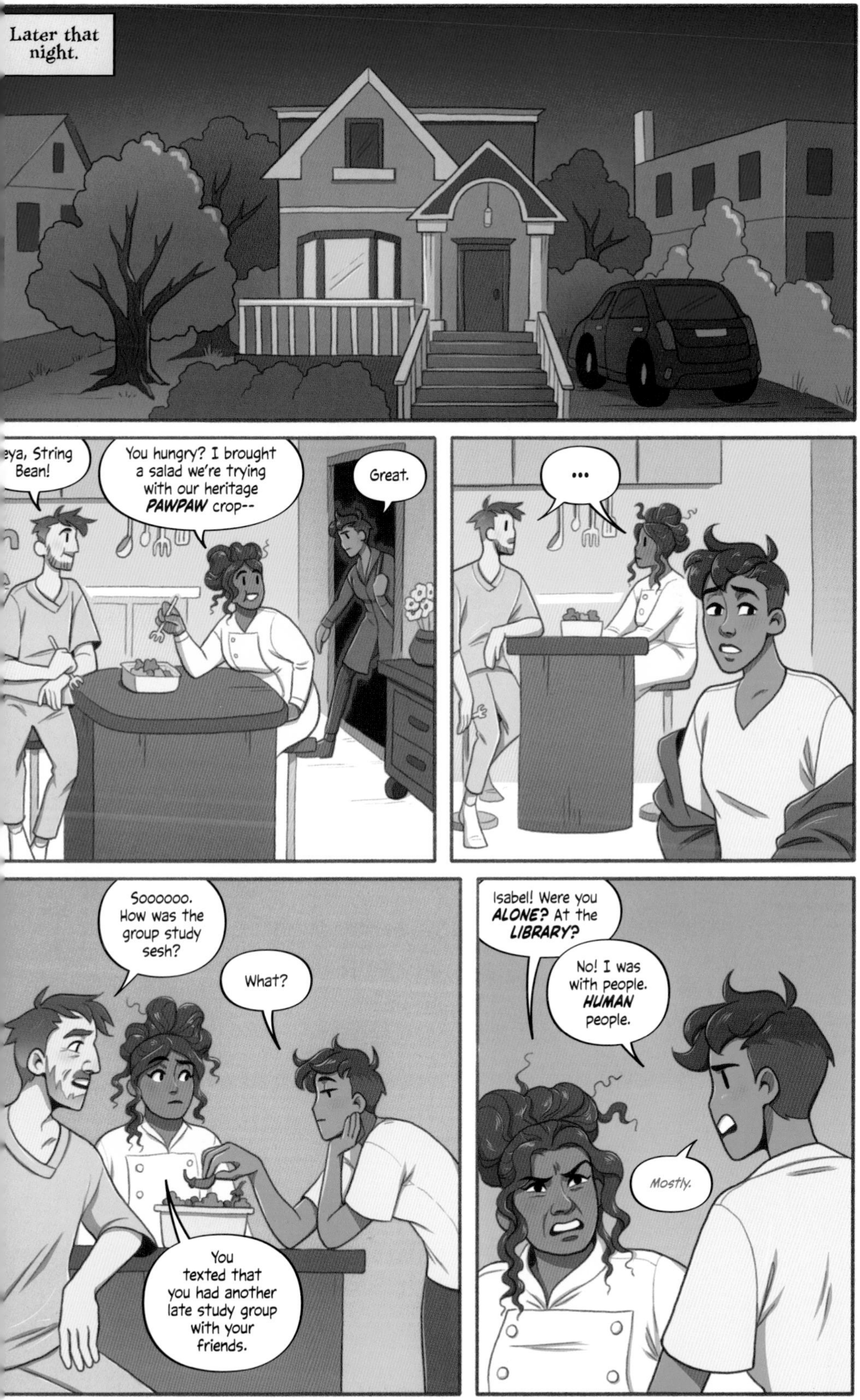

Later that night.
eya, String Bean!
You hungry? I brought a salad we're trying with our heritage PAWPAW crop--
Great.
...
Soooooo. How was the group study sesh?
What?
You texted that you had another late study group with your friends.
Isabel! Were you ALONE? At the LIBRARY?
No! I was with people. HUMAN people.
Mostly.

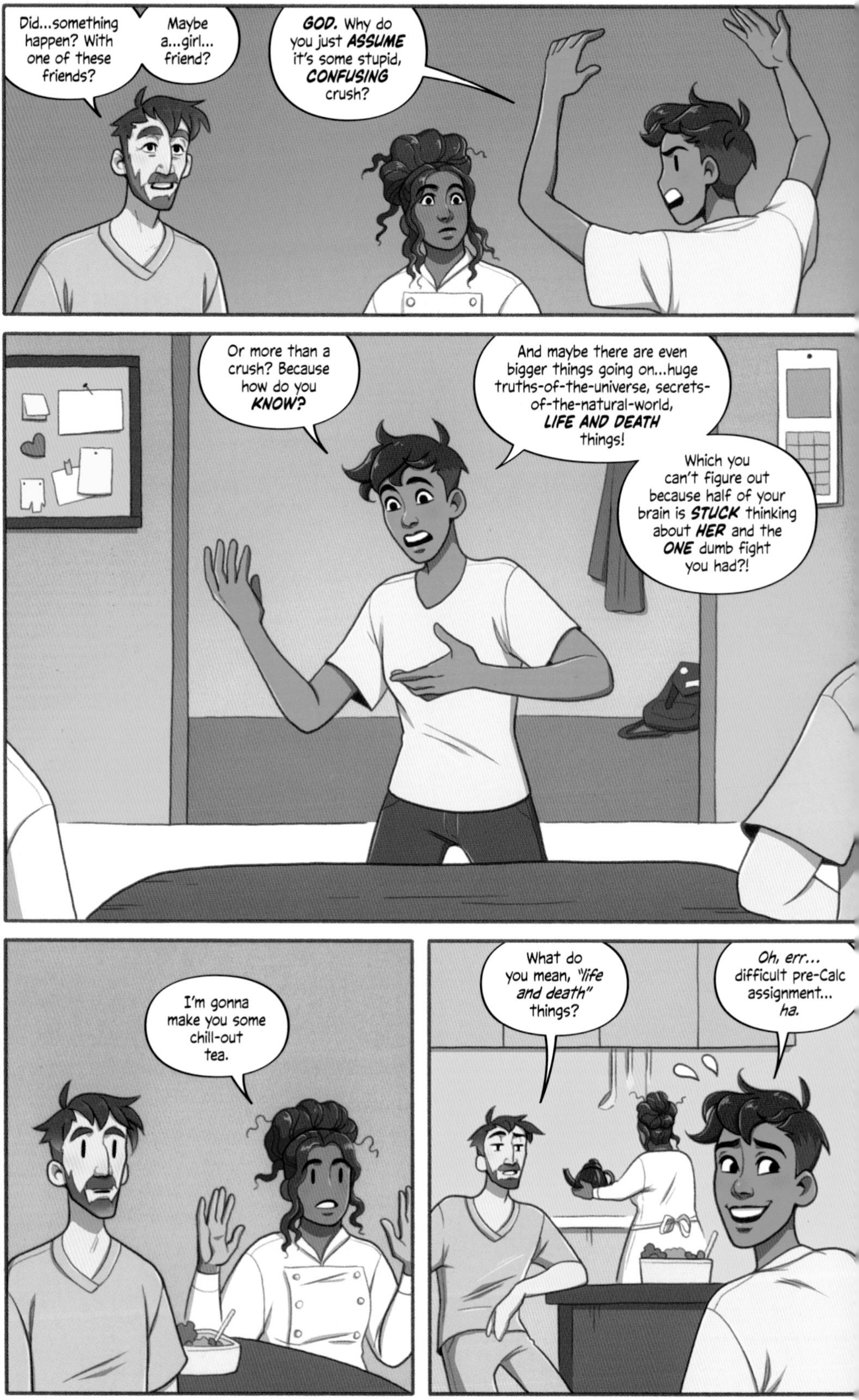
Did...something happen? With one of these friends?
Maybe a...girl... friend?
GOD. Why do you just ASSUME it's some stupid, CONFUSING crush?
Or more than a crush? Because how do you KNOW?
And maybe there are even bigger things going on...huge truths-of-the-universe, secrets-of-the-natural-world, LIFE AND DEATH things!
Which you can't figure out because half of your brain is STUCK thinking about HER and the ONE dumb fight you had?!
I'm gonna make you some chill-out tea.
What do you mean, "life and death" things?
Oh, err... difficult pre-Calc assignment... ha.

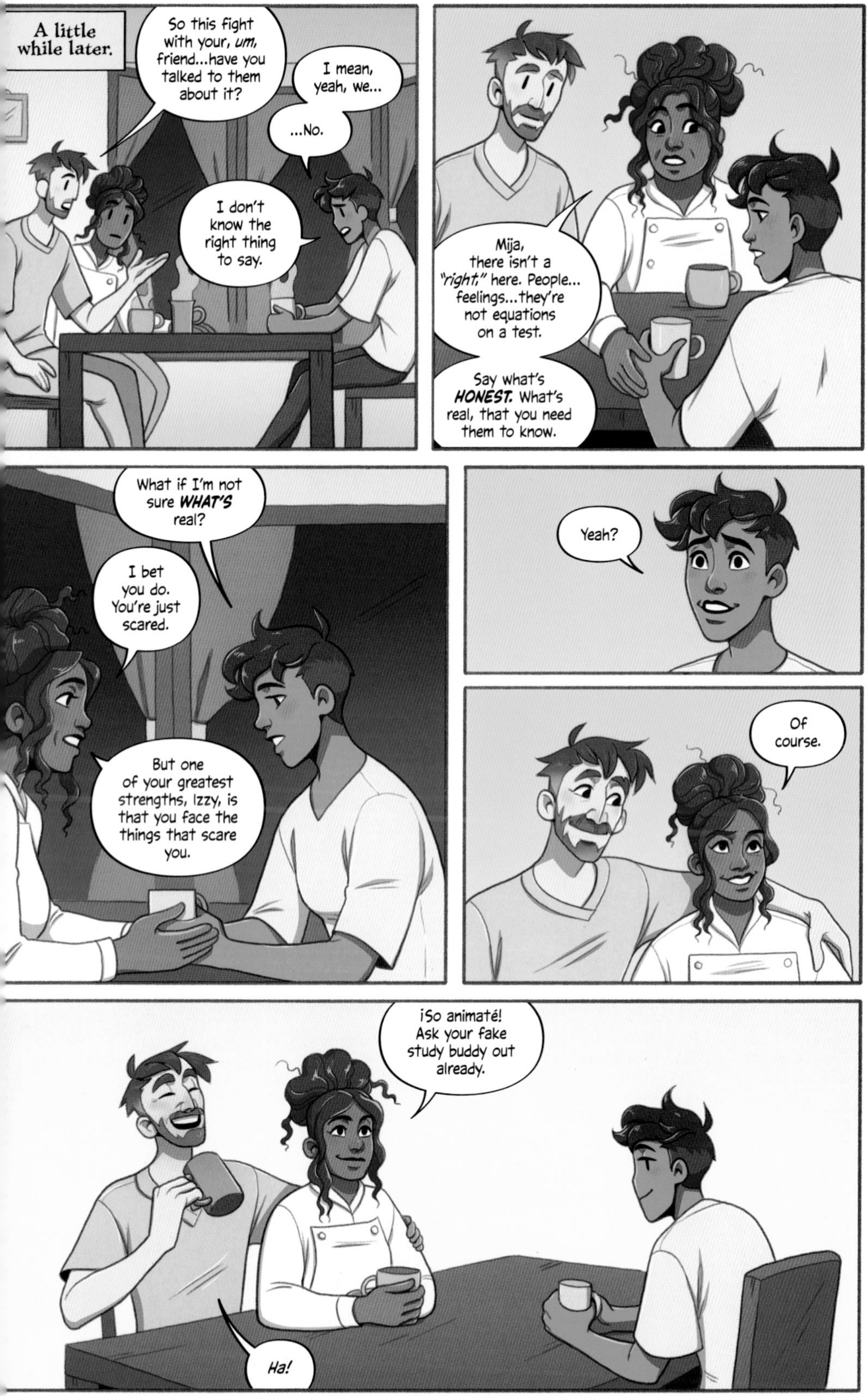
A little while later.
So this fight with your, *um,* friend...have you talked to them about it?
I mean, yeah, we...
...No.
I don't know the right thing to say.
Mija, there isn't a *"right,"* here. People... feelings...they're not equations on a test.
Say what's ***HONEST.*** What's real, that you need them to know.
What if I'm not sure ***WHAT'S*** real?
I bet you do. You're just scared.
But one of your greatest strengths, Izzy, is that you face the things that scare you.
Yeah?
Of course.
¡So animaté! Ask your fake study buddy out already.
Ha!

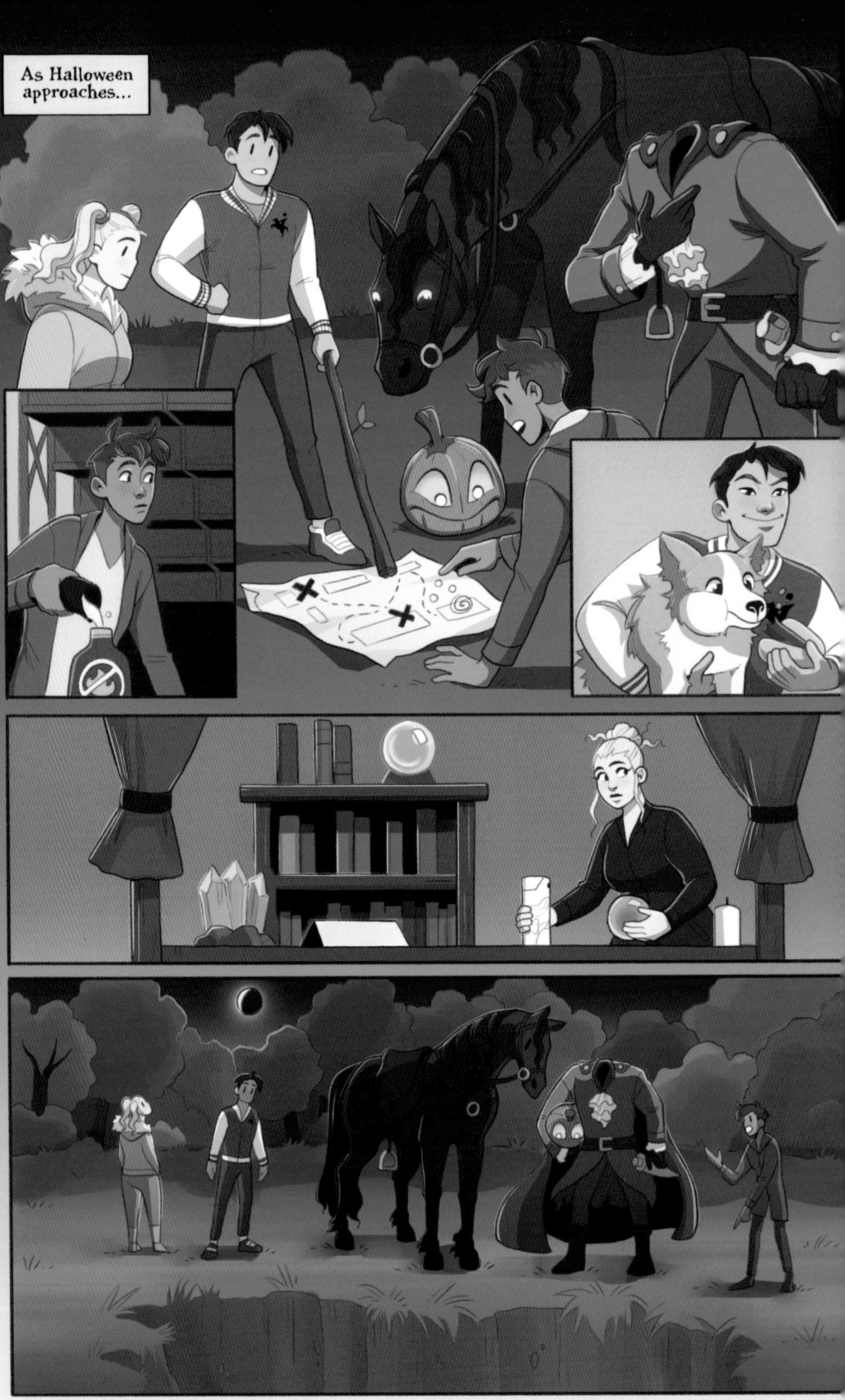
As Halloween approaches...

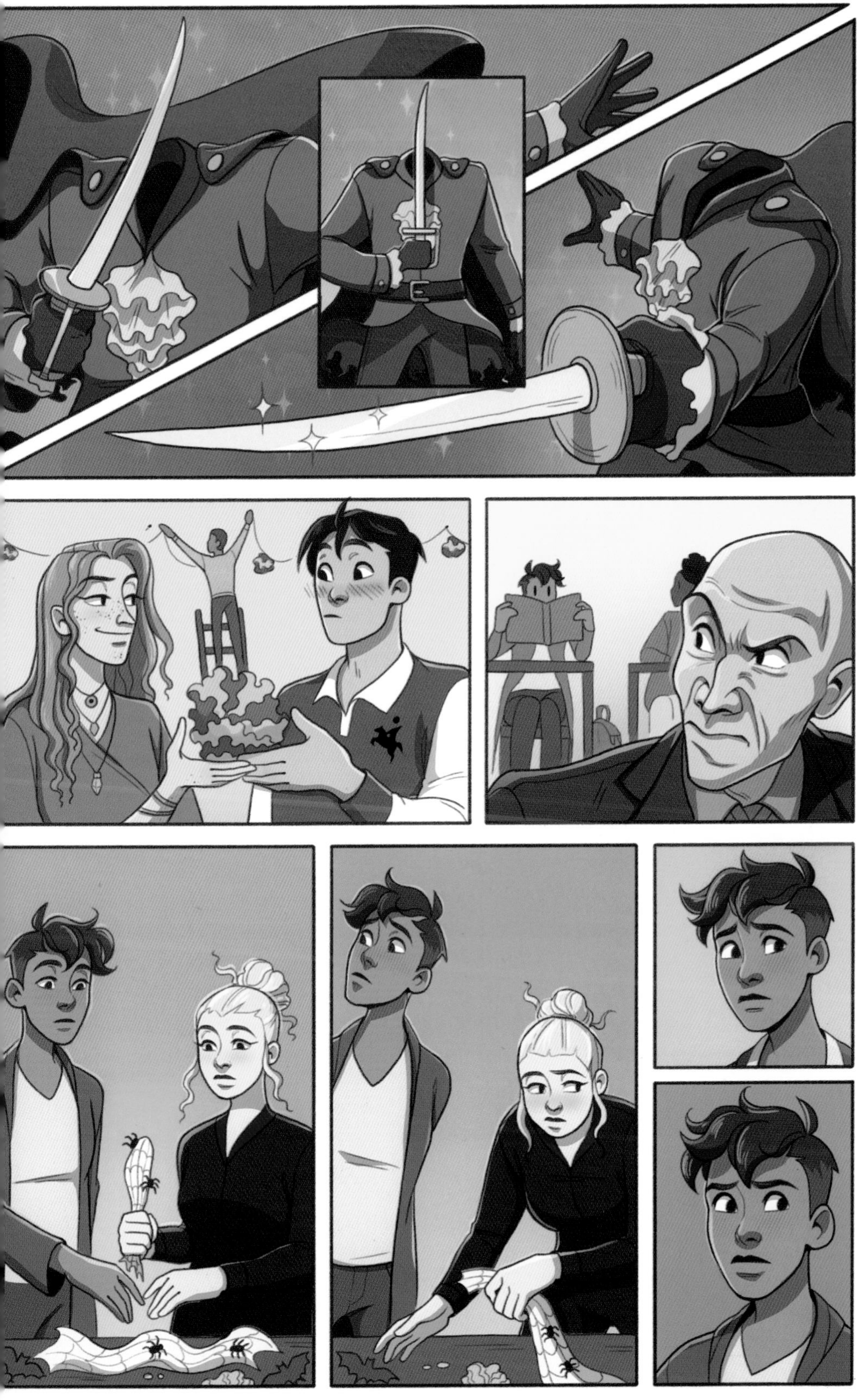

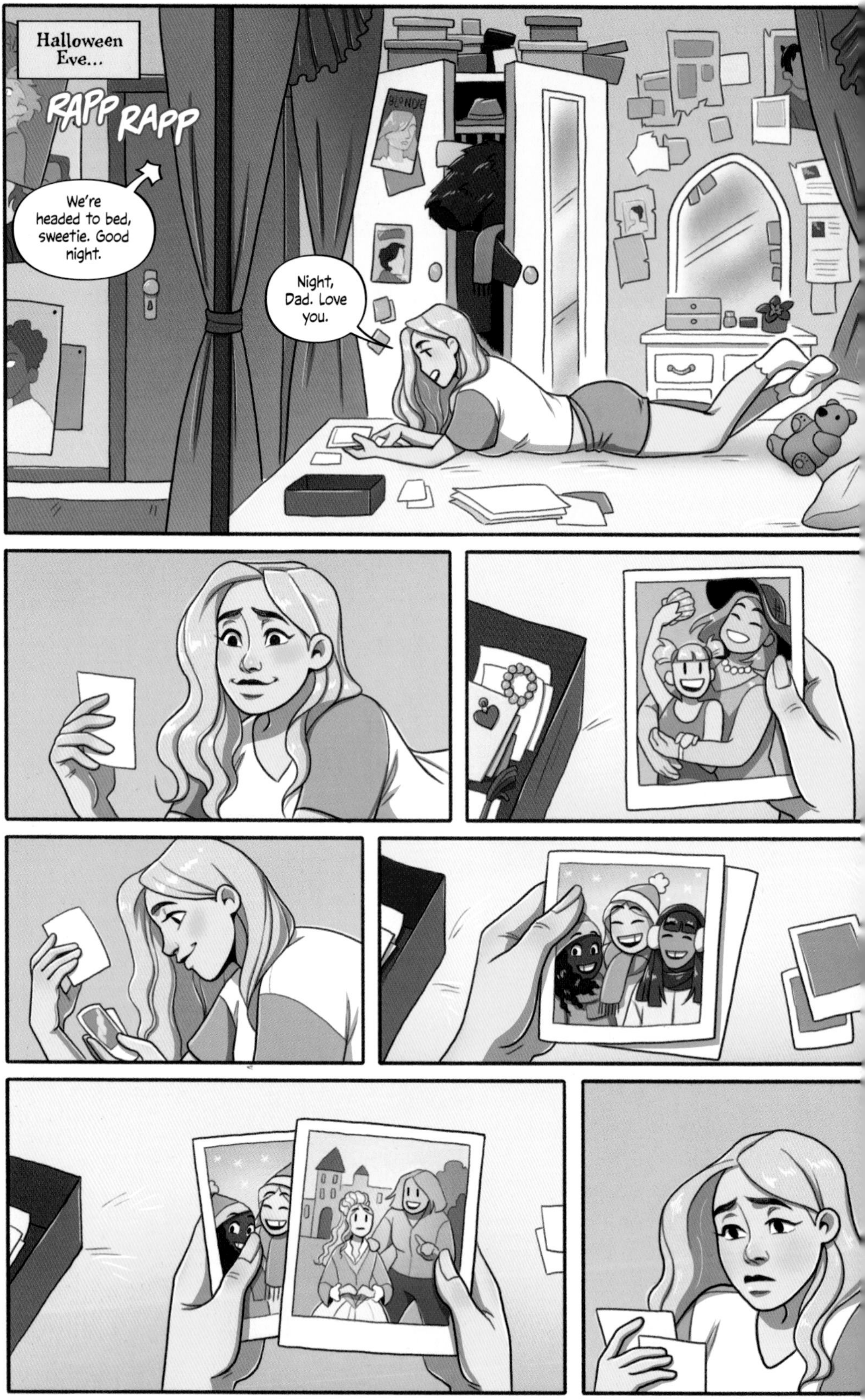
Halloween Eve...
RAPP RAPP
We're headed to bed, sweetie. Good night.
Night, Dad. Love you.
BLONDE

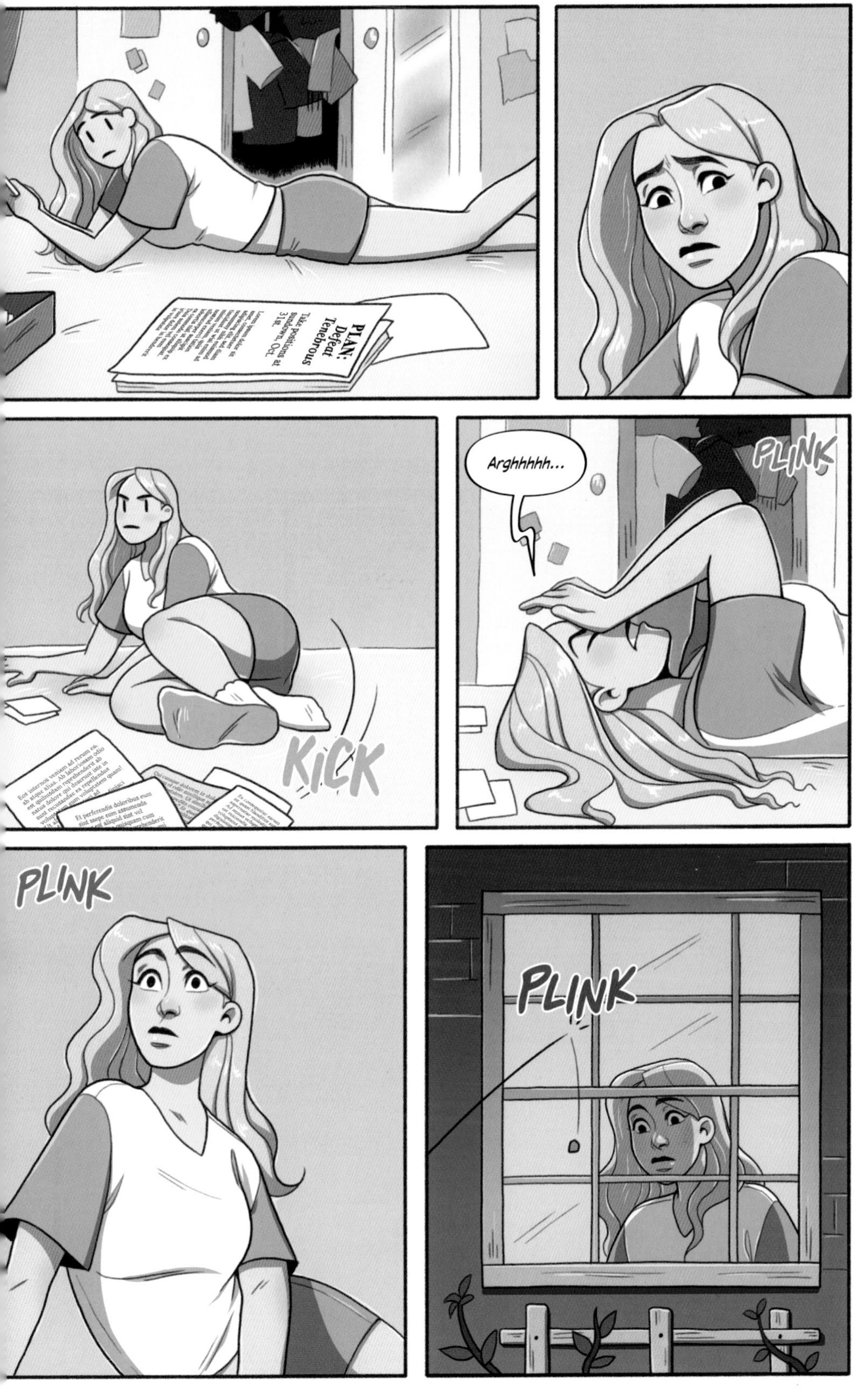
PLAN:
Defeat
Tenebrous
Take positions at
sundown, Oct.
31st.
KICK
Arghhhhh...
PLINK
PLINK
PLINK

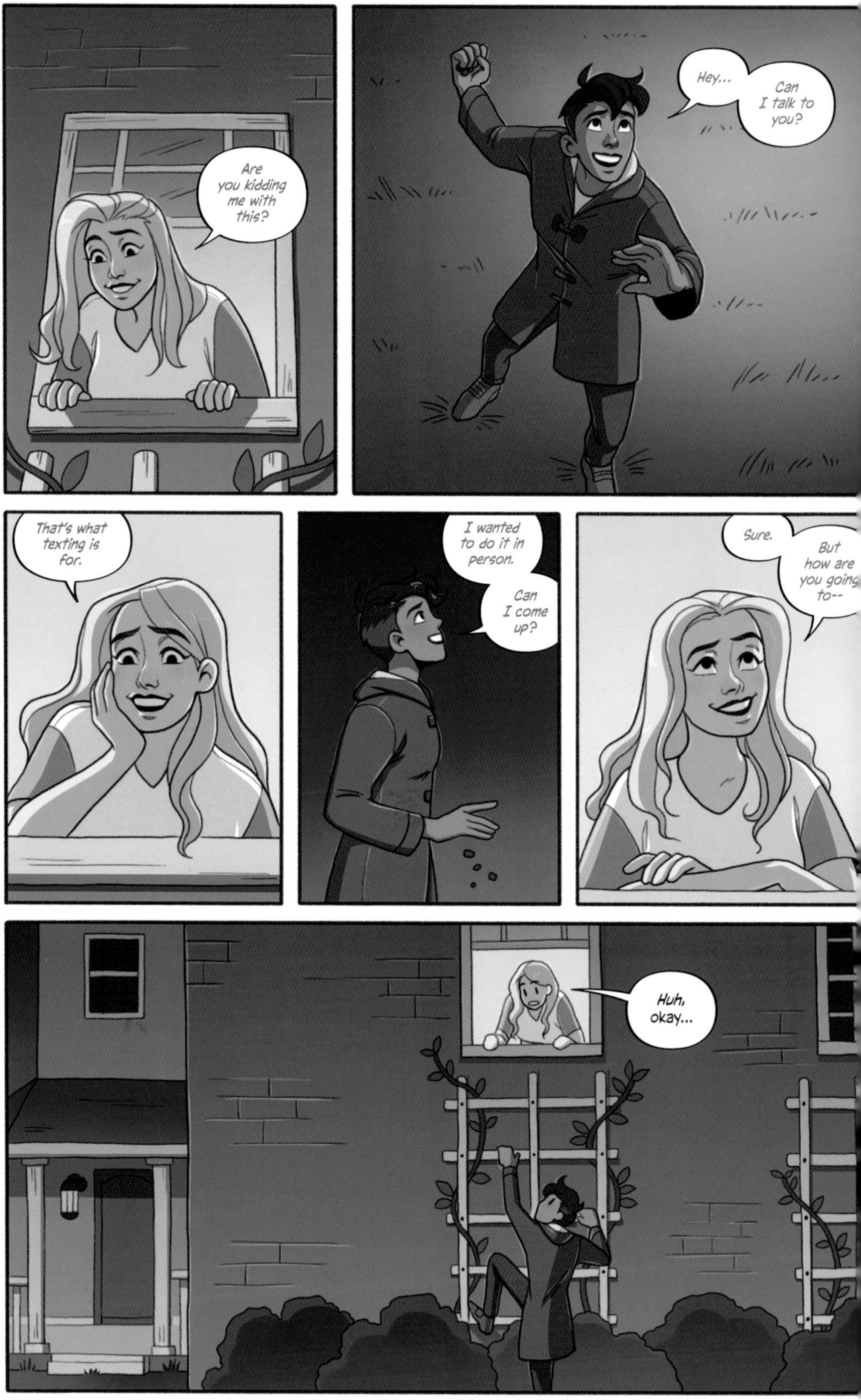
Are you kidding me with this?
Hey...
Can I talk to you?
That's what texting is for.
I wanted to do it in person.
Can I come up?
Sure.
But how are you going to--
Huh, okay...

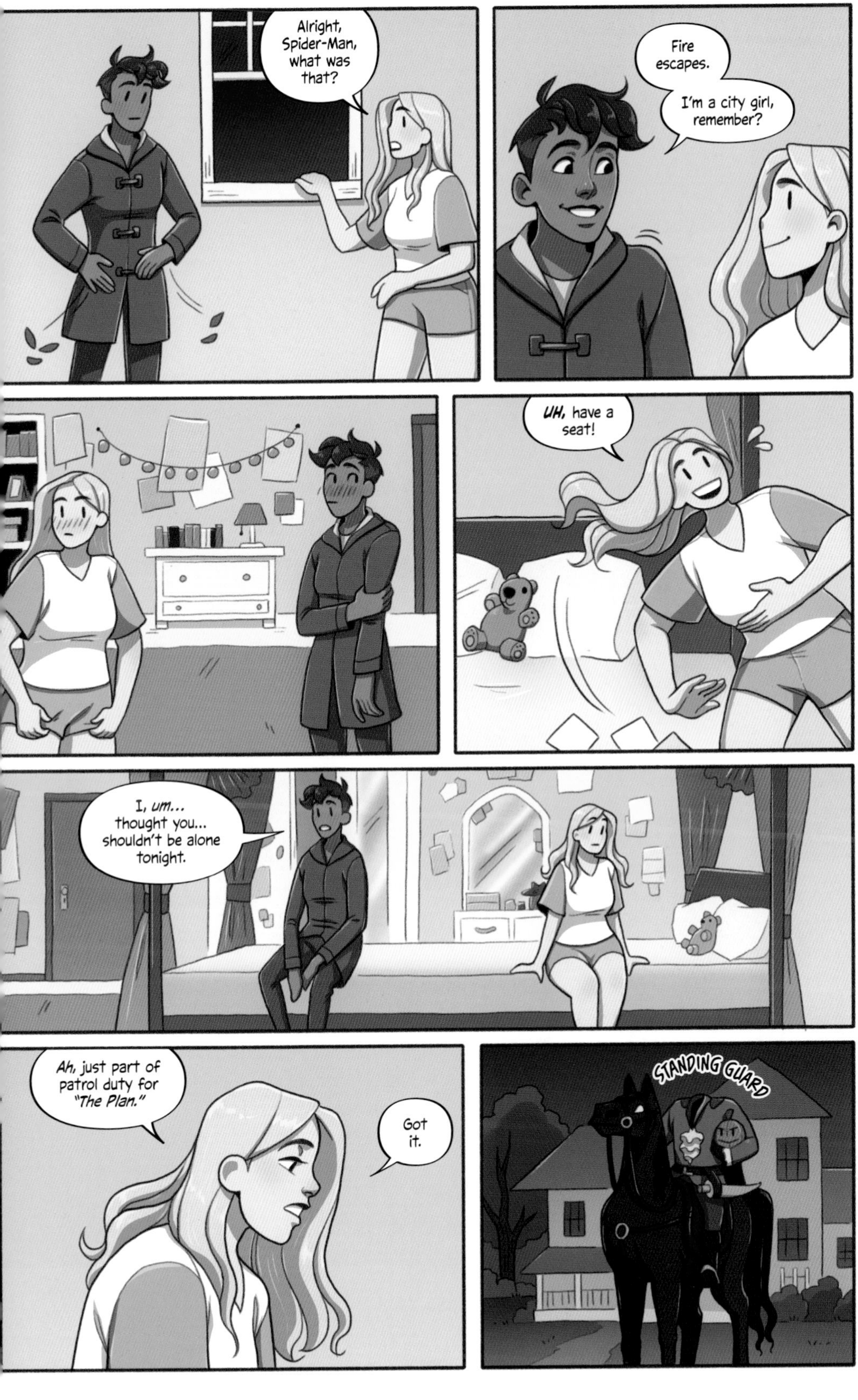

Alright, Spider-Man, what was that?
Fire escapes.
I'm a city girl, remember?
UH, have a seat!
I, *um...* thought you... shouldn't be alone tonight.
Ah, just part of patrol duty for *"The Plan."*
Got it.
STANDING GUARD

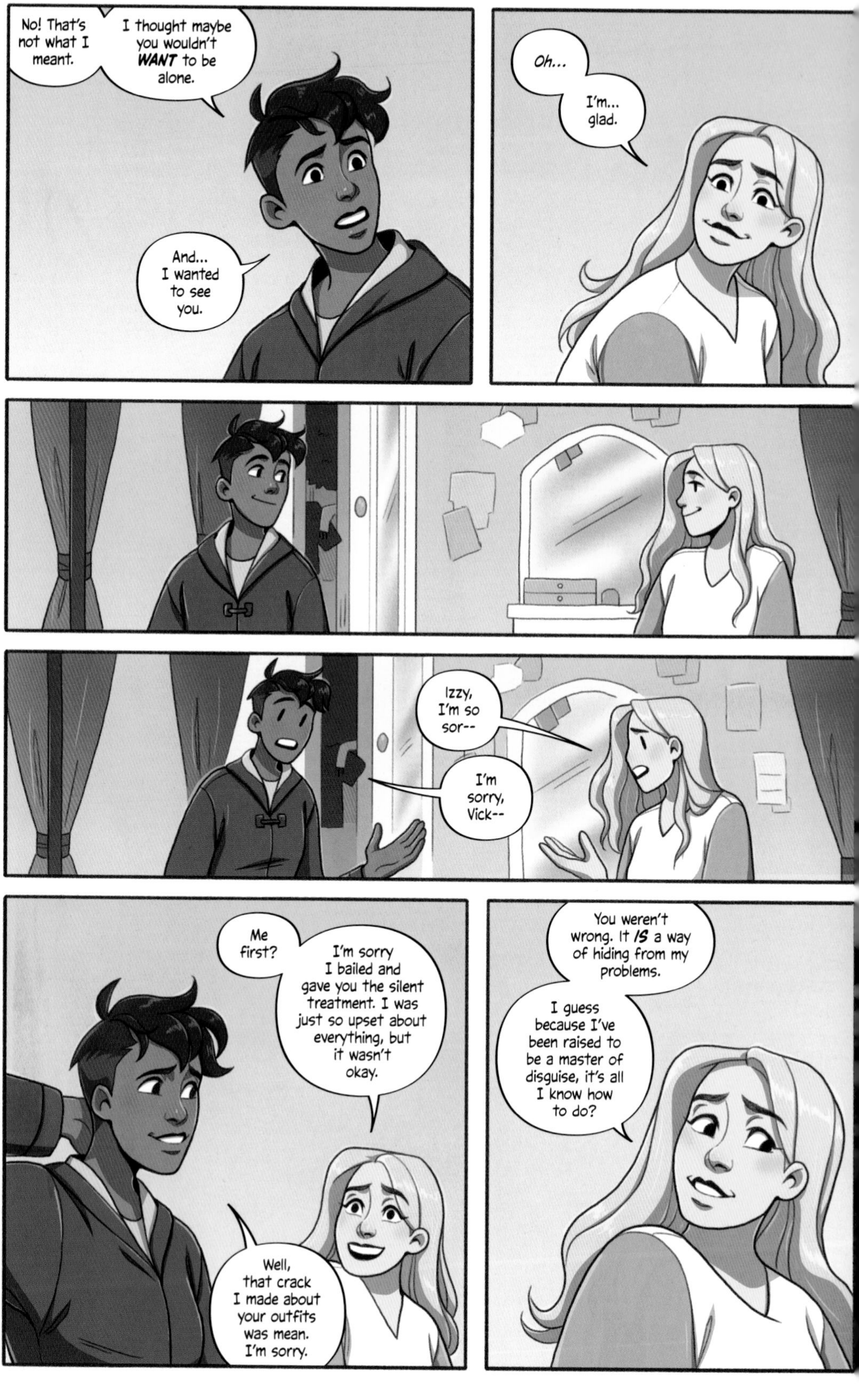
No! That's not what I meant.
I thought maybe you wouldn't **WANT** to be alone.
And... I wanted to see you.
Oh...
I'm... glad.
Izzy, I'm so sor--
I'm sorry, Vick--
Me first?
I'm sorry I bailed and gave you the silent treatment. I was just so upset about everything, but it wasn't okay.
Well, that crack I made about your outfits was mean. I'm sorry.
You weren't wrong. It ***IS*** a way of hiding from my problems.
I guess because I've been raised to be a master of disguise, it's all I know how to do?

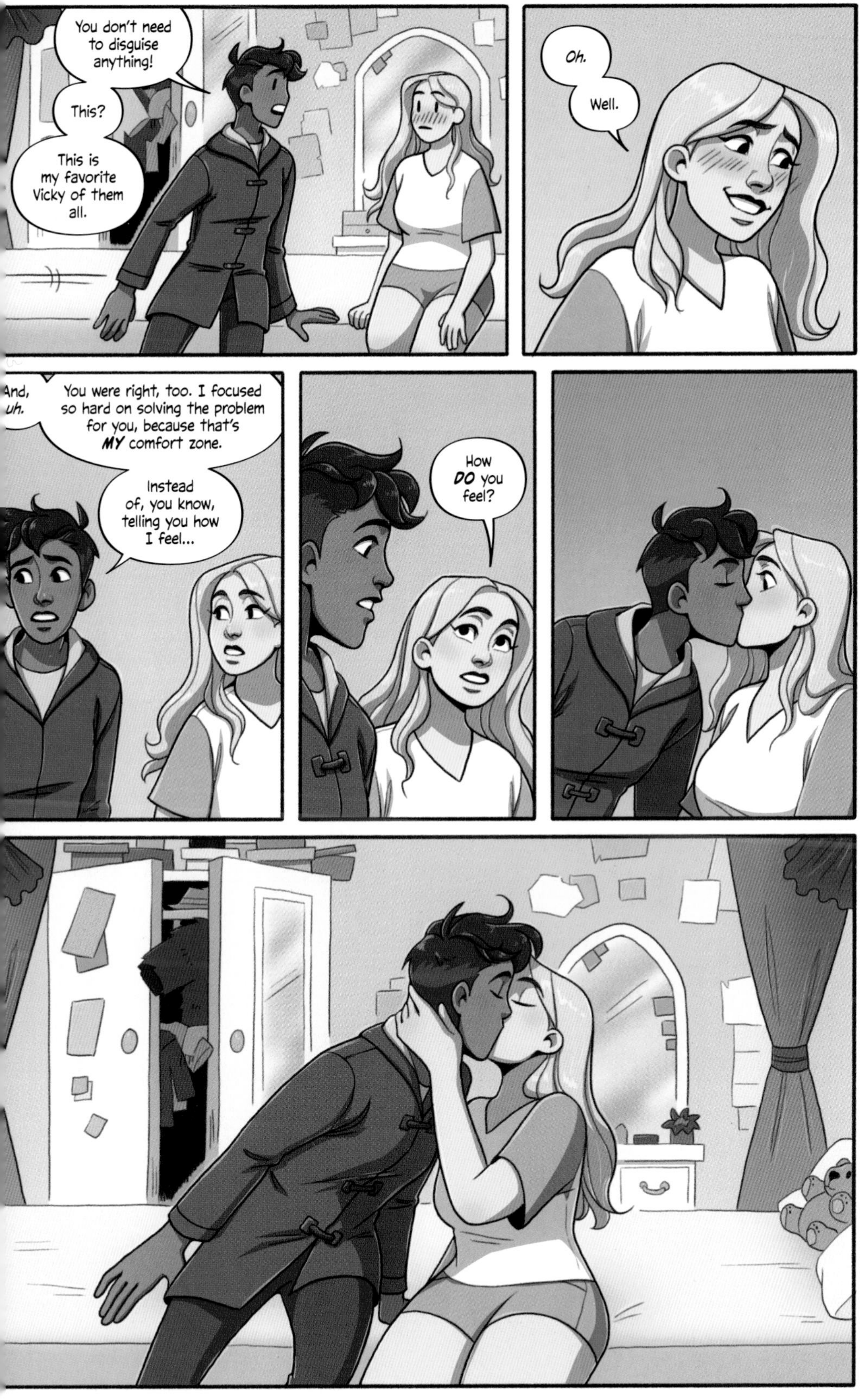
You don't need to disguise anything!
This?
This is my favorite Vicky of them all.
Oh.
Well.
And, uh.
You were right, too. I focused so hard on solving the problem for you, because that's MY comfort zone.
Instead of, you know, telling you how I feel...
How DO you feel?

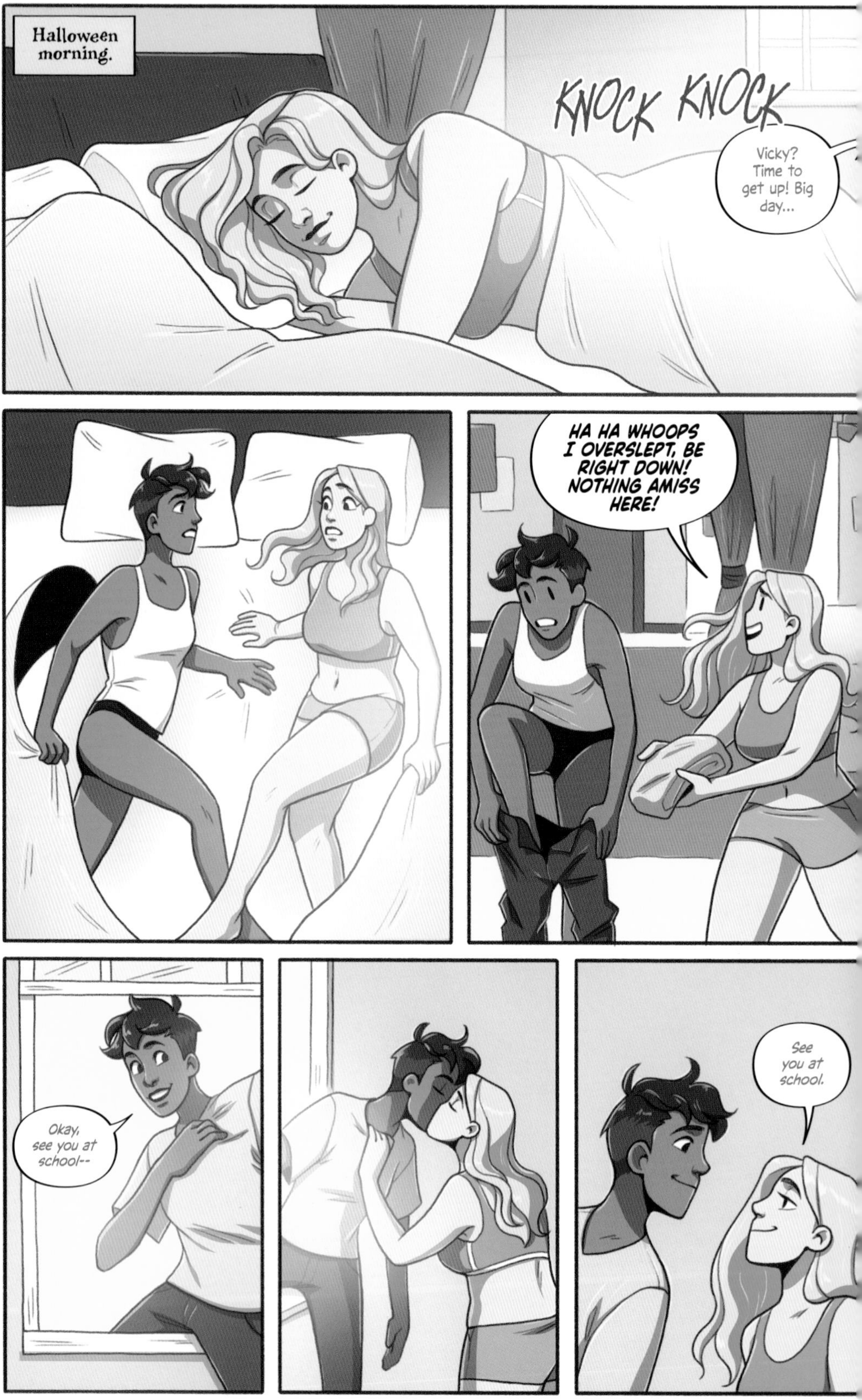
Halloween morning.
KNOCK KNOCK
Vicky? Time to get up! Big day...
HA HA WHOOPS I OVERSLEPT, BE RIGHT DOWN! NOTHING AMISS HERE!
Okay, see you at school--
See you at school.

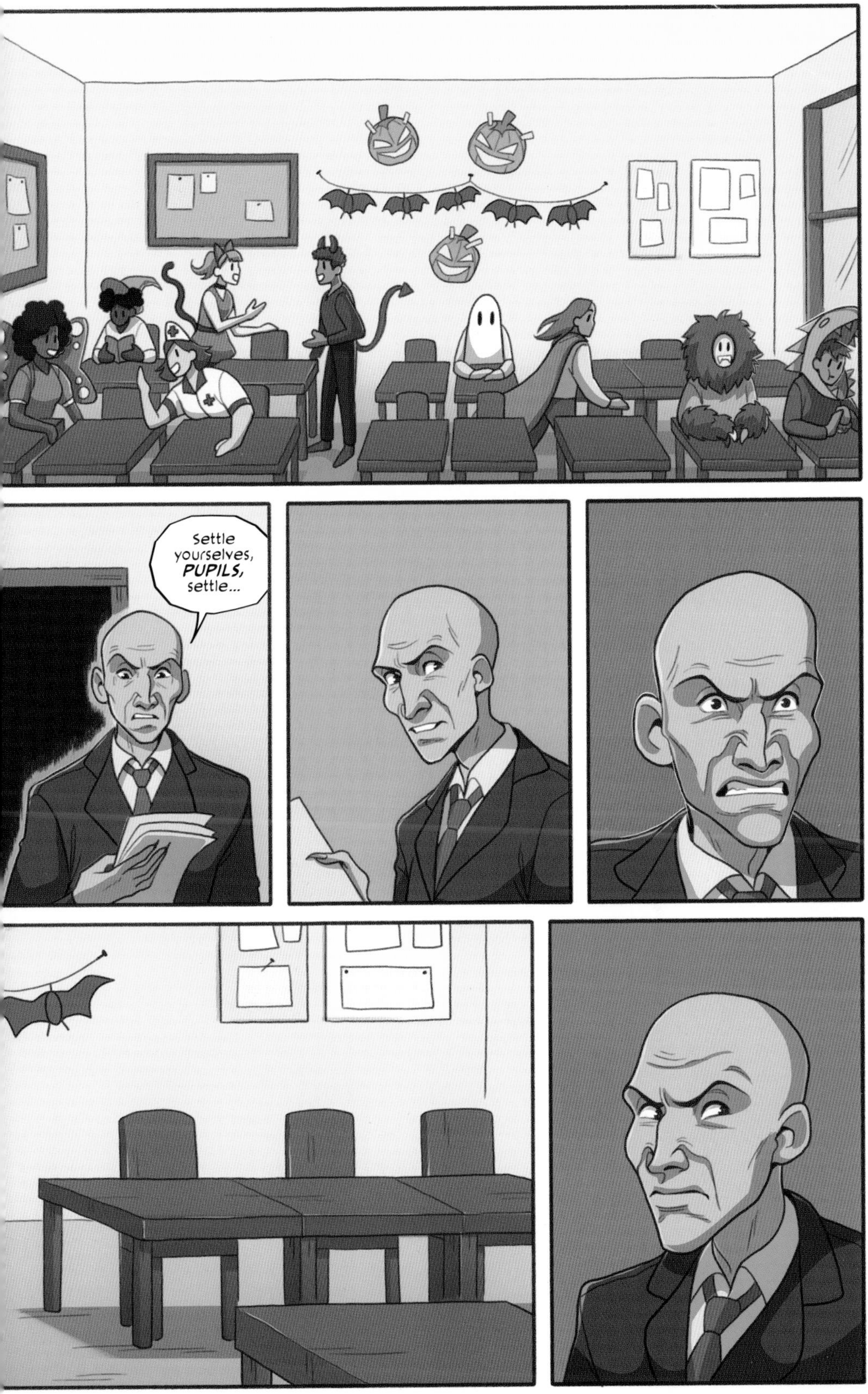
Settle yourselves, ***PUPILS,*** settle...

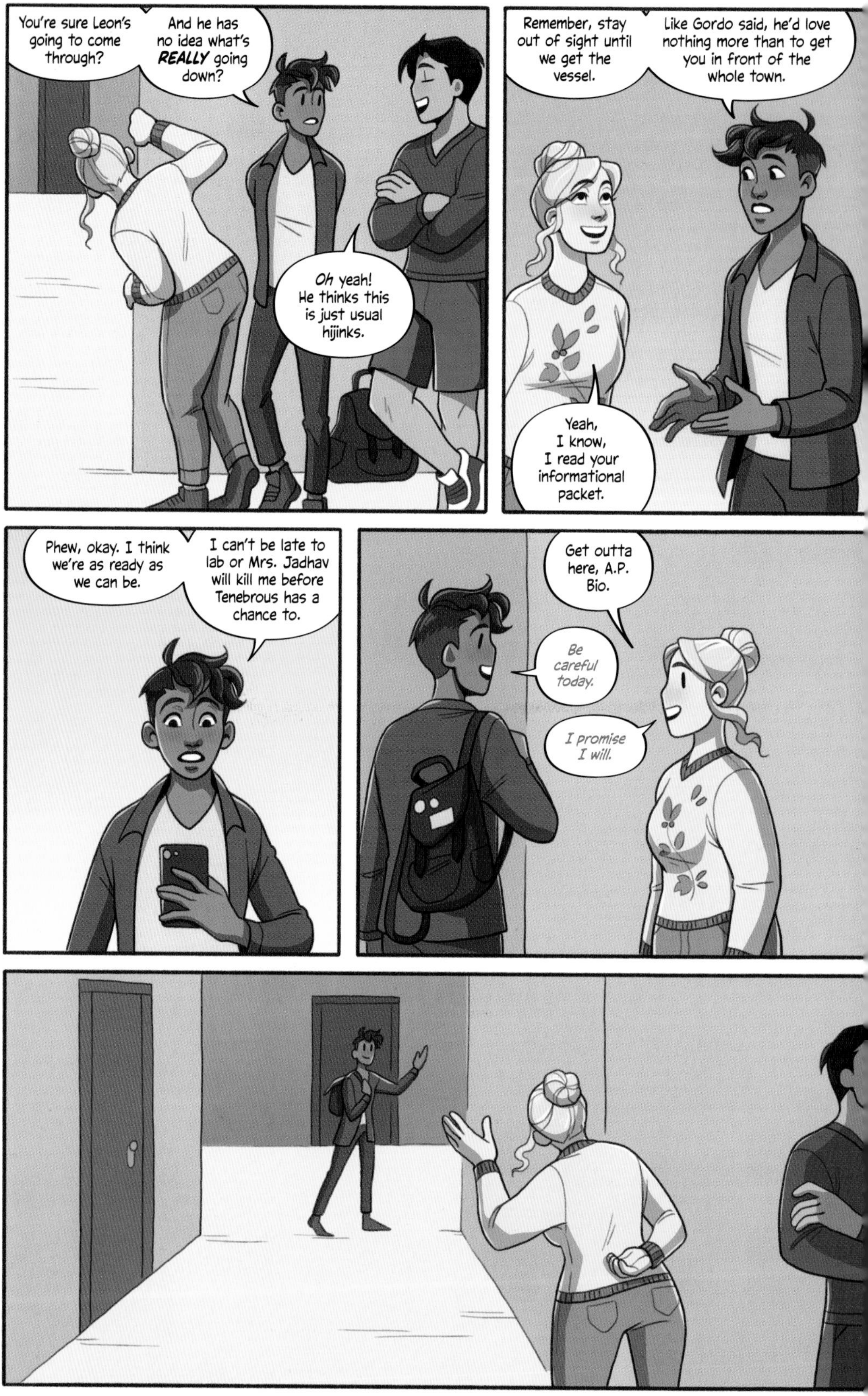
You're sure Leon's going to come through?
And he has no idea what's ***REALLY*** going down?
Oh yeah! He thinks this is just usual hijinks.
Remember, stay out of sight until we get the vessel.
Like Gordo said, he'd love nothing more than to get you in front of the whole town.
Yeah, I know, I read your informational packet.
Phew, okay. I think we're as ready as we can be.
I can't be late to lab or Mrs. Jadhav will kill me before Tenebrous has a chance to.
Get outta here, A.P. Bio.
Be careful today.
I promise I will.

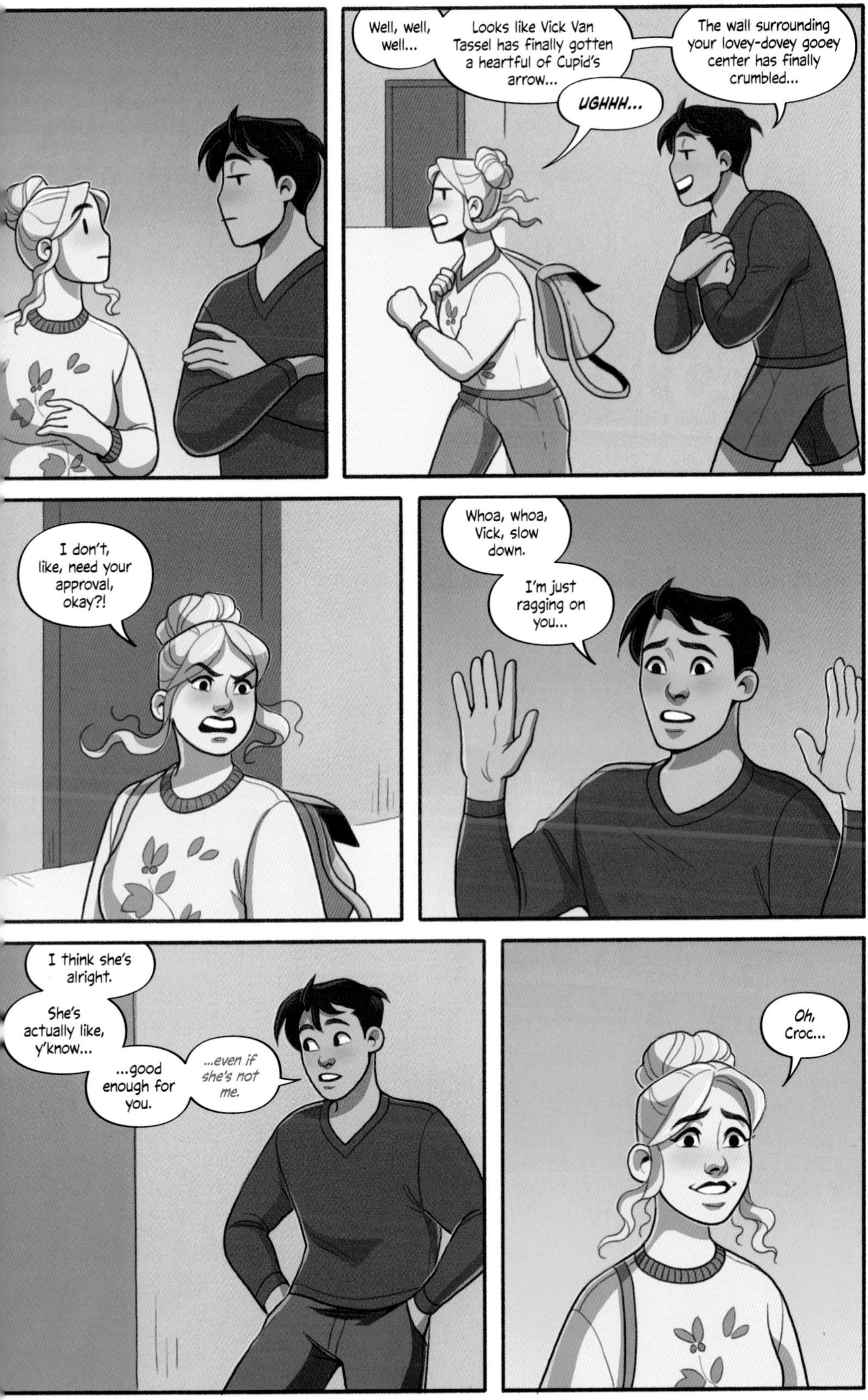
Well, well, well...
Looks like Vick Van Tassel has finally gotten a heartful of Cupid's arrow...
The wall surrounding your lovey-dovey gooey center has finally crumbled...
UGHHH...
I don't, like, need your approval, okay?!
Whoa, whoa, Vick, slow down.
I'm just ragging on you...
I think she's alright.
She's actually like, y'know...
...good enough for you.
...even if she's not me.
Oh, Croc...

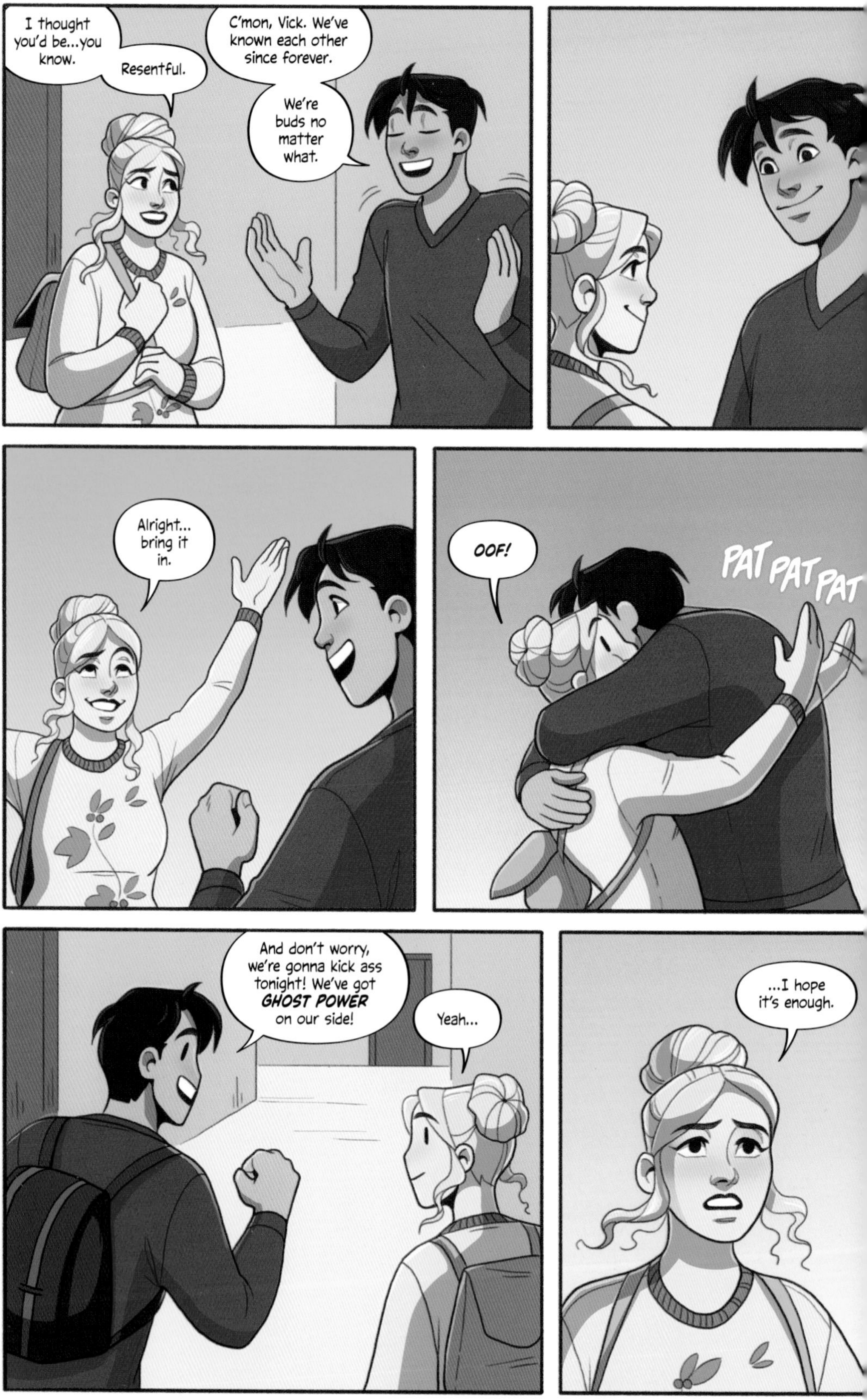
I thought you'd be...you know.
Resentful.
C'mon, Vick. We've known each other since forever.
We're buds no matter what.
Alright... bring it in.
OOF!
PAT PAT PAT
And don't worry, we're gonna kick ass tonight! We've got **GHOST POWER** on our side!
Yeah...
...I hope it's enough.

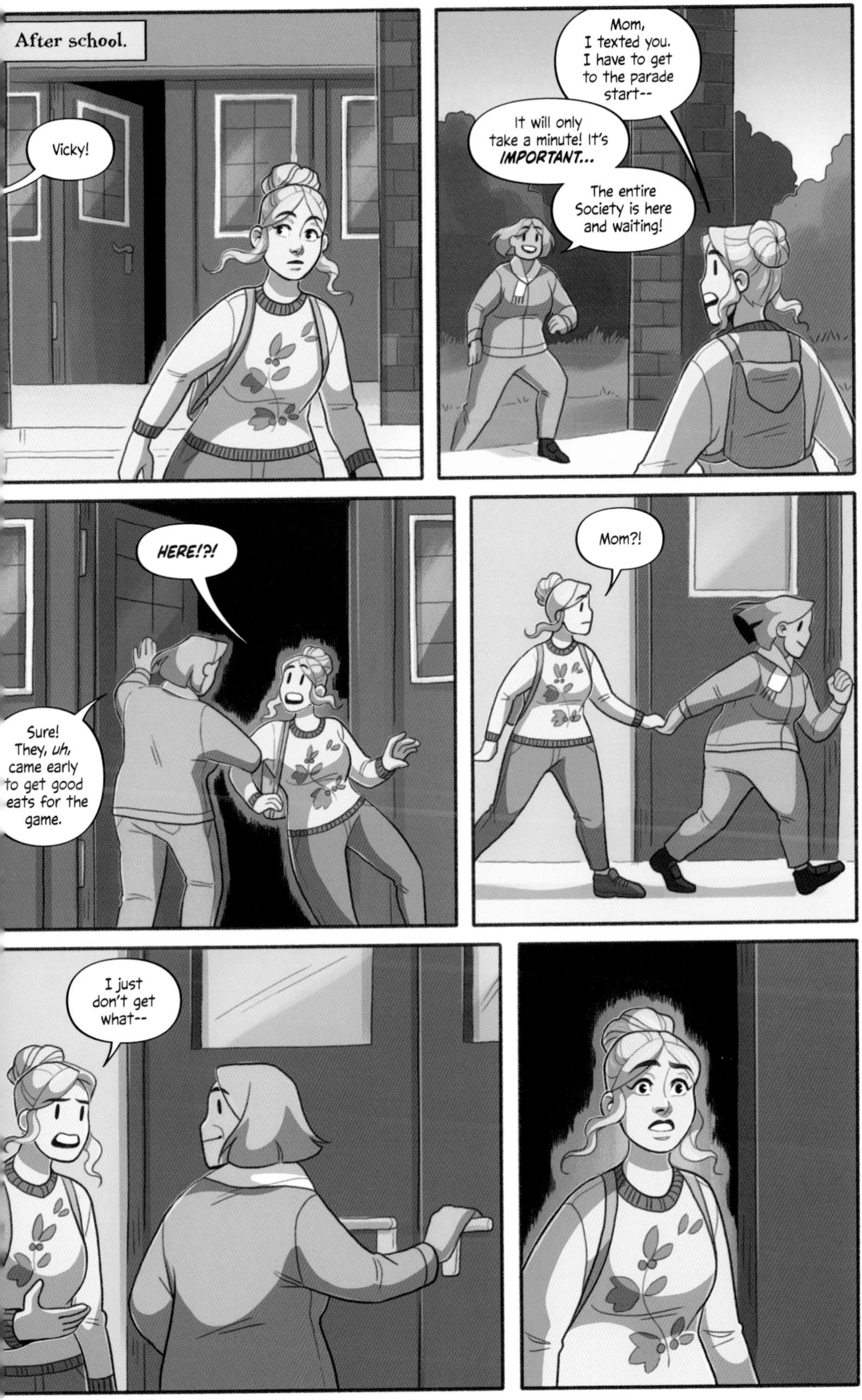
After school.
Vicky!
Mom, I texted you. I have to get to the parade start--
It will only take a minute! It's IMPORTANT...
The entire Society is here and waiting!
HERE!?!
Sure! They, uh, came early to get good eats for the game.
Mom?!
I just don't get what--

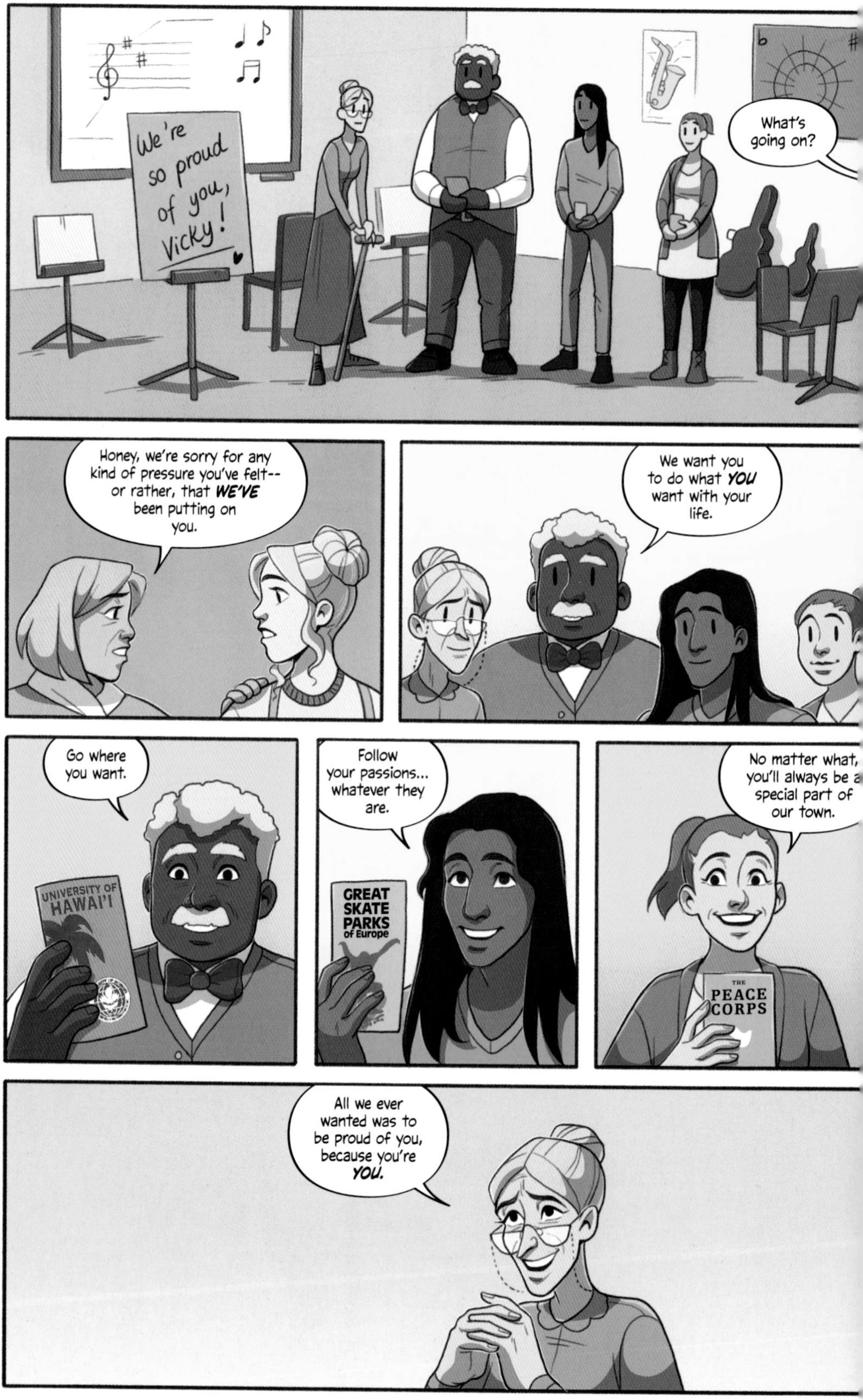

We're so proud of you, Vicky!
What's going on?
Honey, we're sorry for any kind of pressure you've felt-- or rather, that ***WE'VE*** been putting on you.
We want you to do what ***YOU*** want with your life.
Go where you want.
UNIVERSITY OF HAWAI'I
Follow your passions... whatever they are.
GREAT SKATE PARKS of Europe
No matter what, you'll always be a special part of our town.
THE PEACE CORPS
All we ever wanted was to be proud of you, because you're ***YOU.***

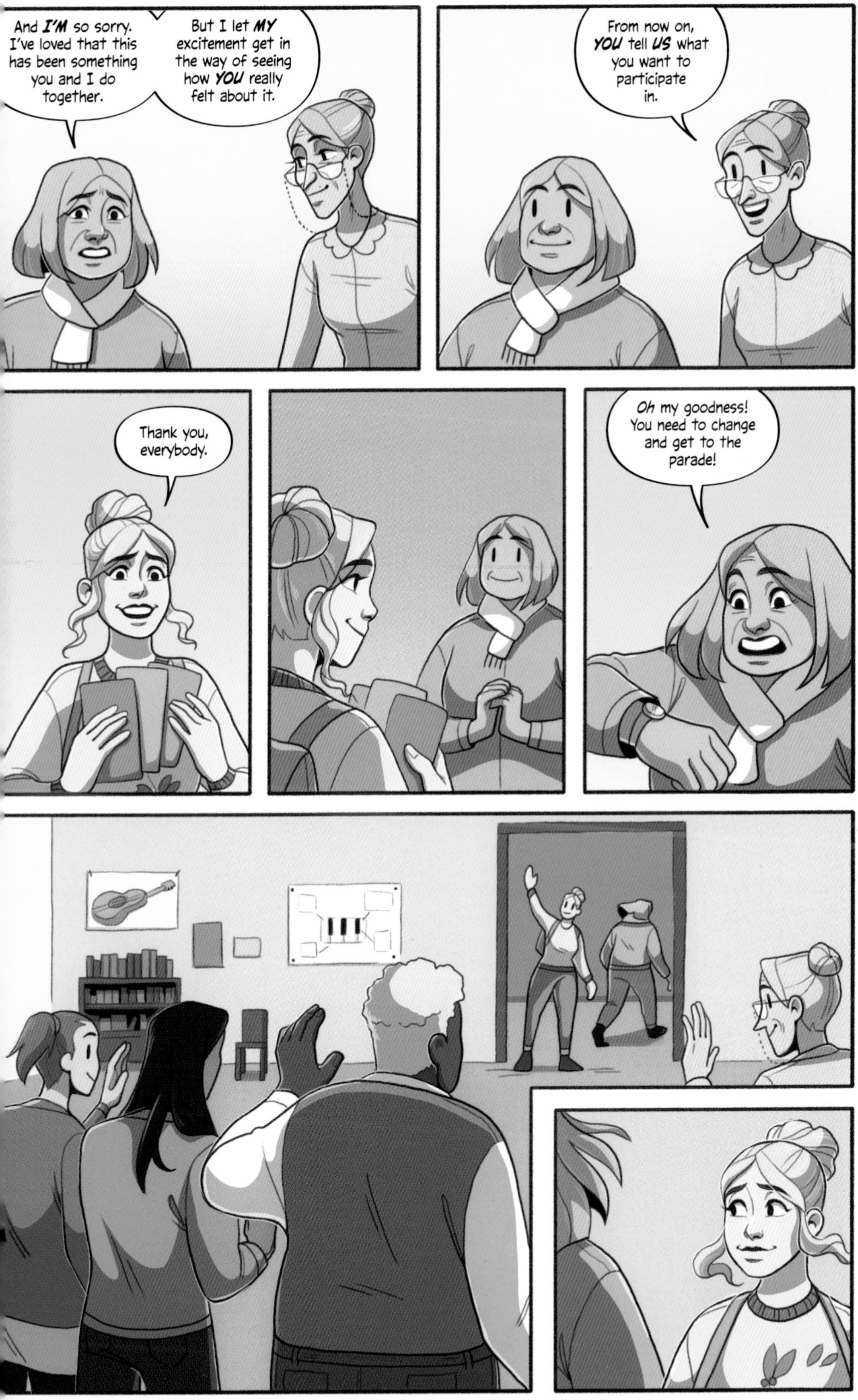
And I'M so sorry. I've loved that this has been something you and I do together.
But I let MY excitement get in the way of seeing how YOU really felt about it.
From now on, YOU tell US what you want to participate in.
Thank you, everybody.
Oh my goodness! You need to change and get to the parade!

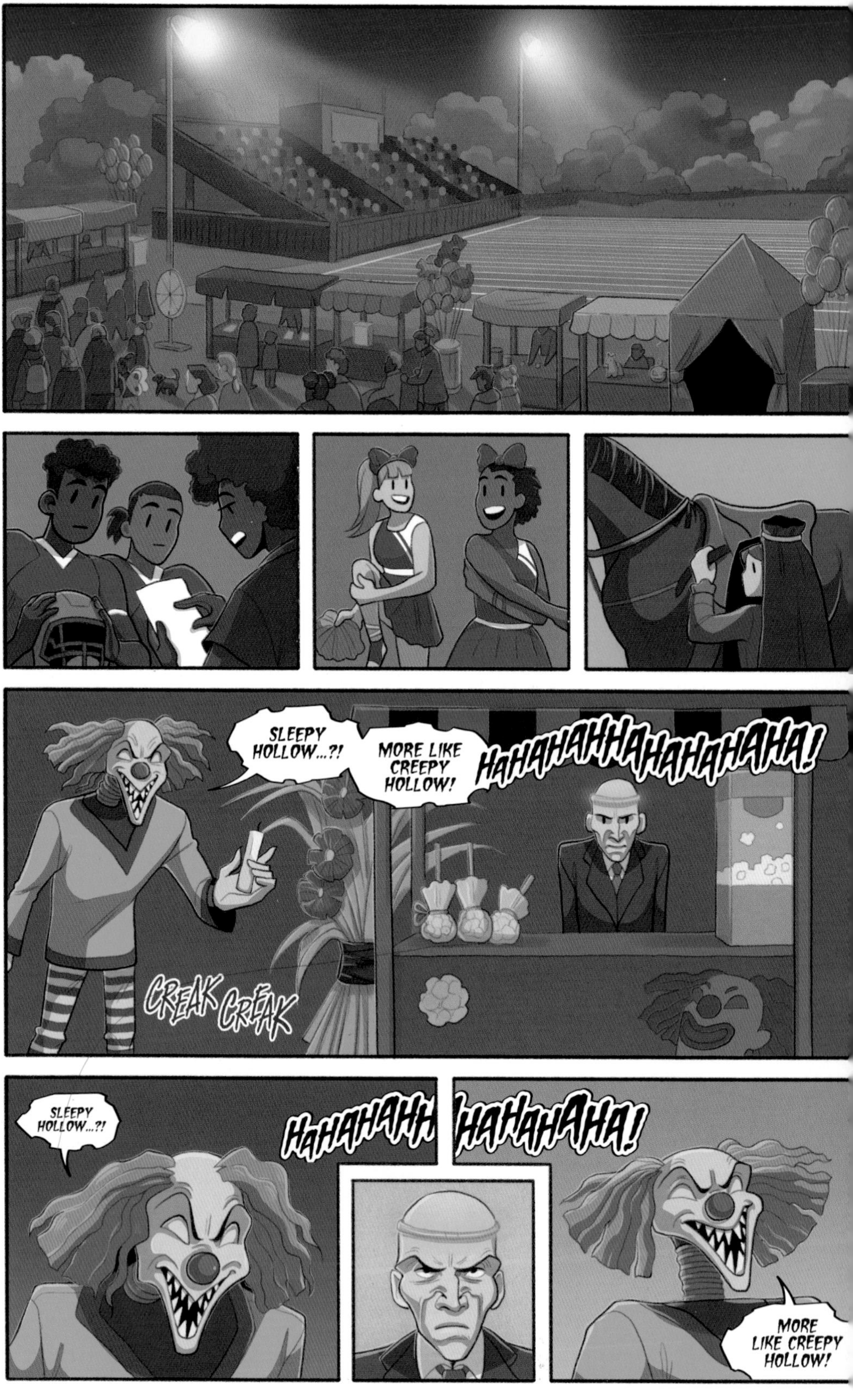
SLEEPY HOLLOW...?!
MORE LIKE CREEPY HOLLOW!
HAHAHAHHAHAHAHAHAHA!
CREAK CREAK
SLEEPY HOLLOW...?!
HAHAHAHHAHAHAHAHA!
MORE LIKE CREEPY HOLLOW!

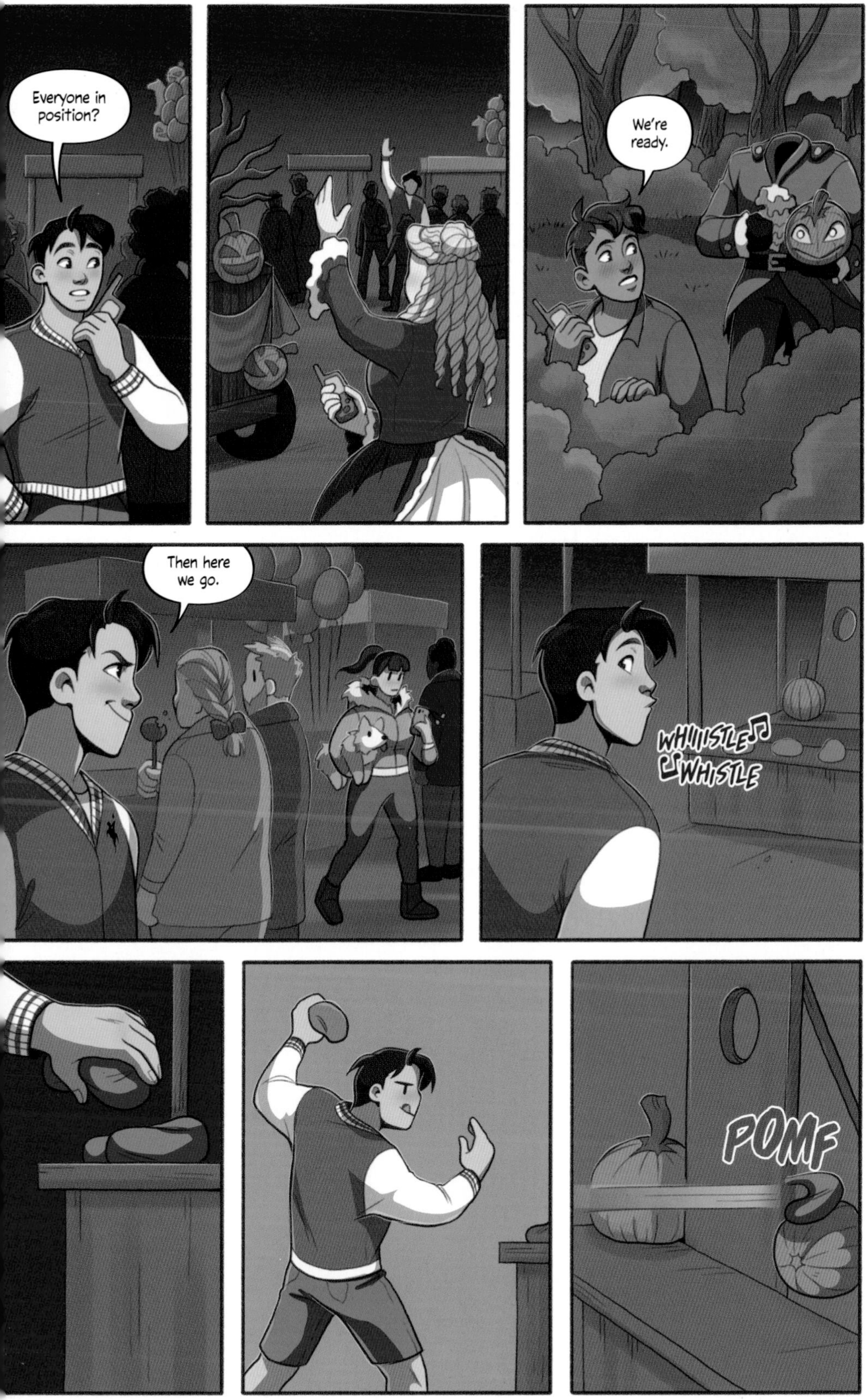
Everyone in position?
We're ready.
Then here we go.
WHIIISTLE
WHISTLE
POMF

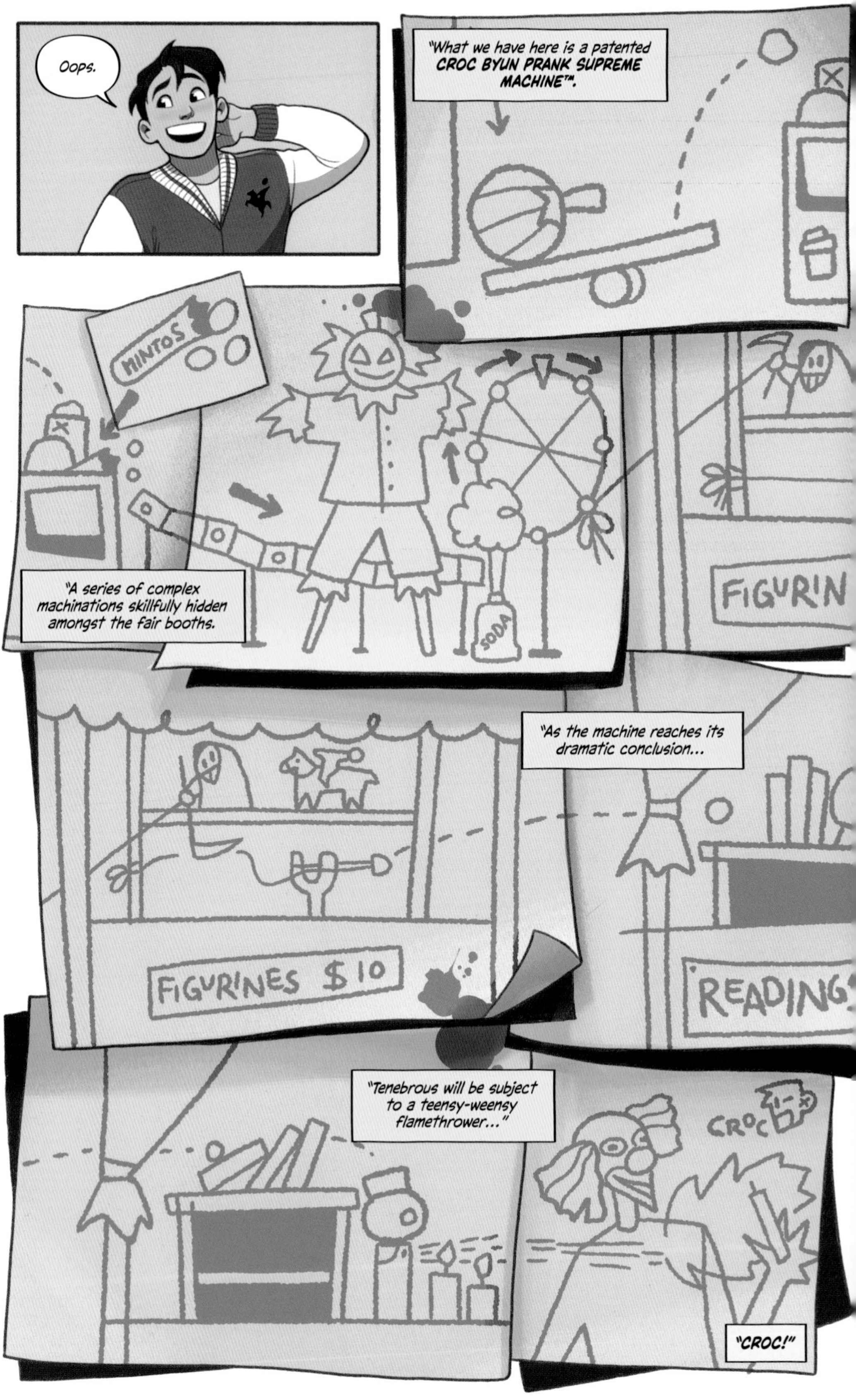

Oops.
"What we have here is a patented CROC BYUN PRANK SUPREME MACHINE™.
MINTOS
"A series of complex machinations skillfully hidden amongst the fair booths.
SODA
FIGURIN
"As the machine reaches its dramatic conclusion...
FIGURINES $10
READING
"Tenebrous will be subject to a teensy-weensy flamethrower..."
CROC
"CROC!"

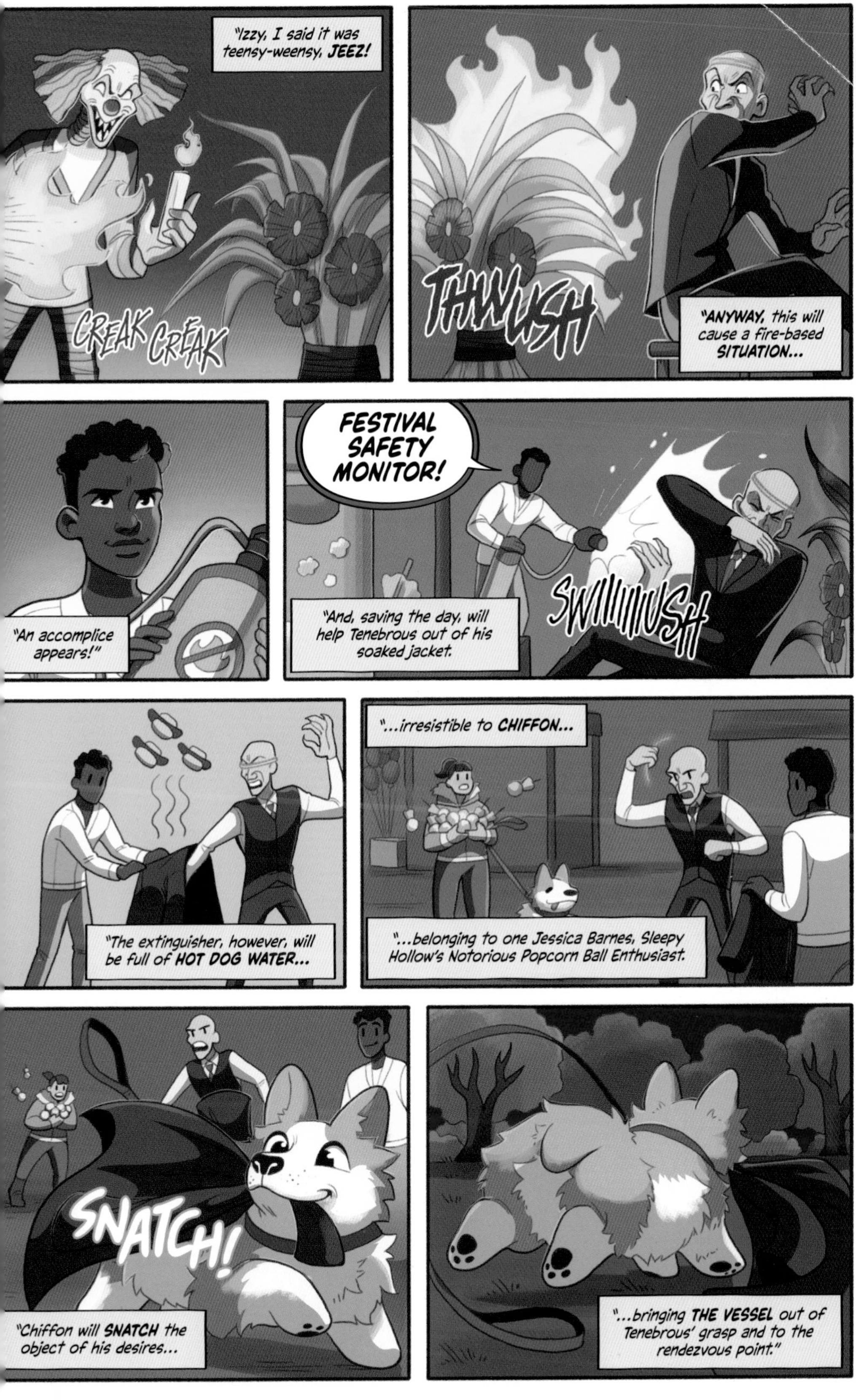
"Izzy, I said it was teensy-weensy, JEEZ!
CREAK CREAK
THWUSH
"ANYWAY, this will cause a fire-based SITUATION...
"An accomplice appears!"
FESTIVAL SAFETY MONITOR!
"And, saving the day, will help Tenebrous out of his soaked jacket.
SWIIIIIUSH
"The extinguisher, however, will be full of HOT DOG WATER...
"...irresistible to CHIFFON...
"...belonging to one Jessica Barnes, Sleepy Hollow's Notorious Popcorn Ball Enthusiast.
"Chiffon will SNATCH the object of his desires...
SNATCH!
"...bringing THE VESSEL out of Tenebrous' grasp and to the rendezvous point."

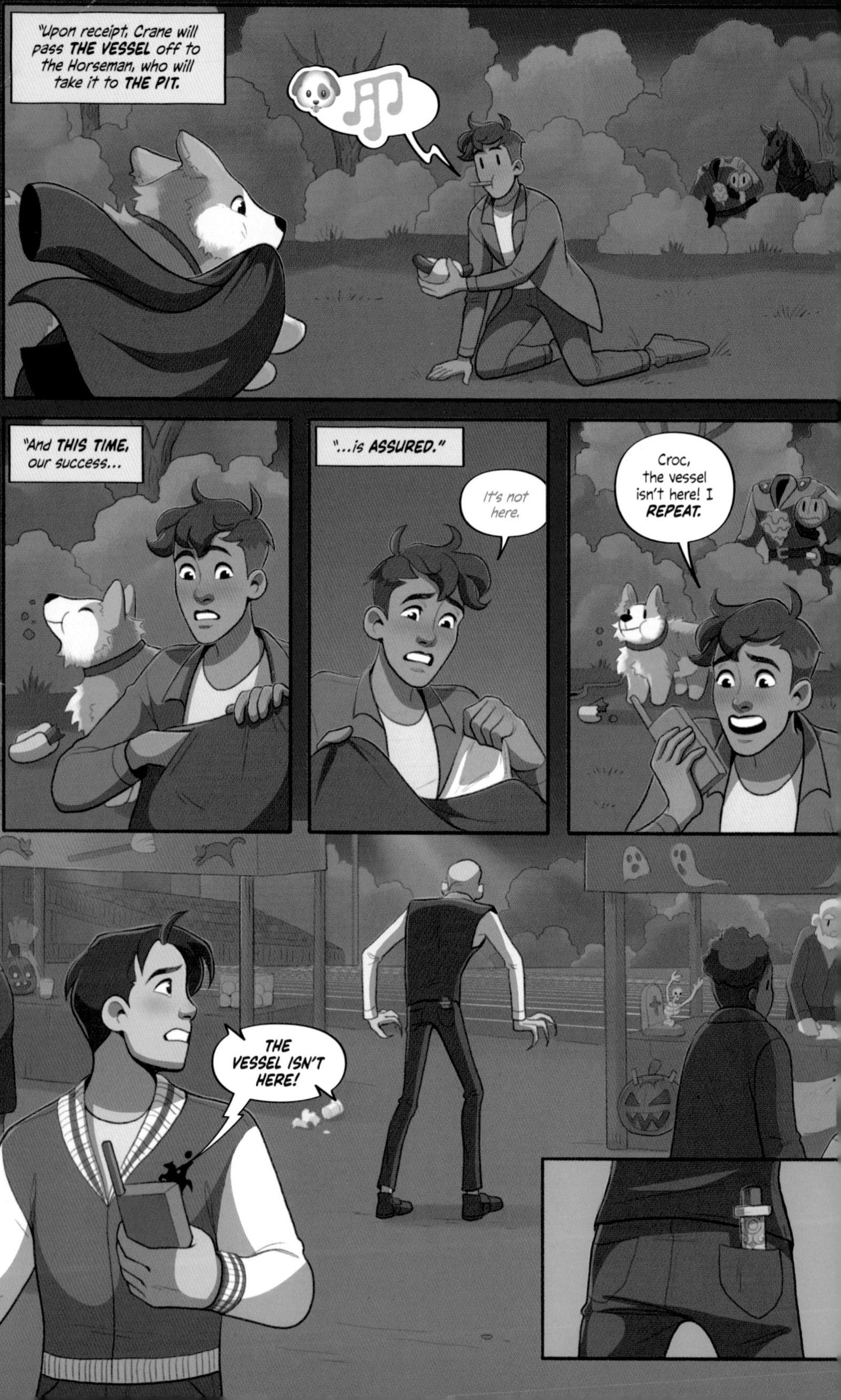
"Upon receipt, Crane will pass THE VESSEL off to the Horseman, who will take it to THE PIT.
"And THIS TIME, our success...
"...is ASSURED."
It's not here.
Croc, the vessel isn't here! I REPEAT.
THE VESSEL ISN'T HERE!

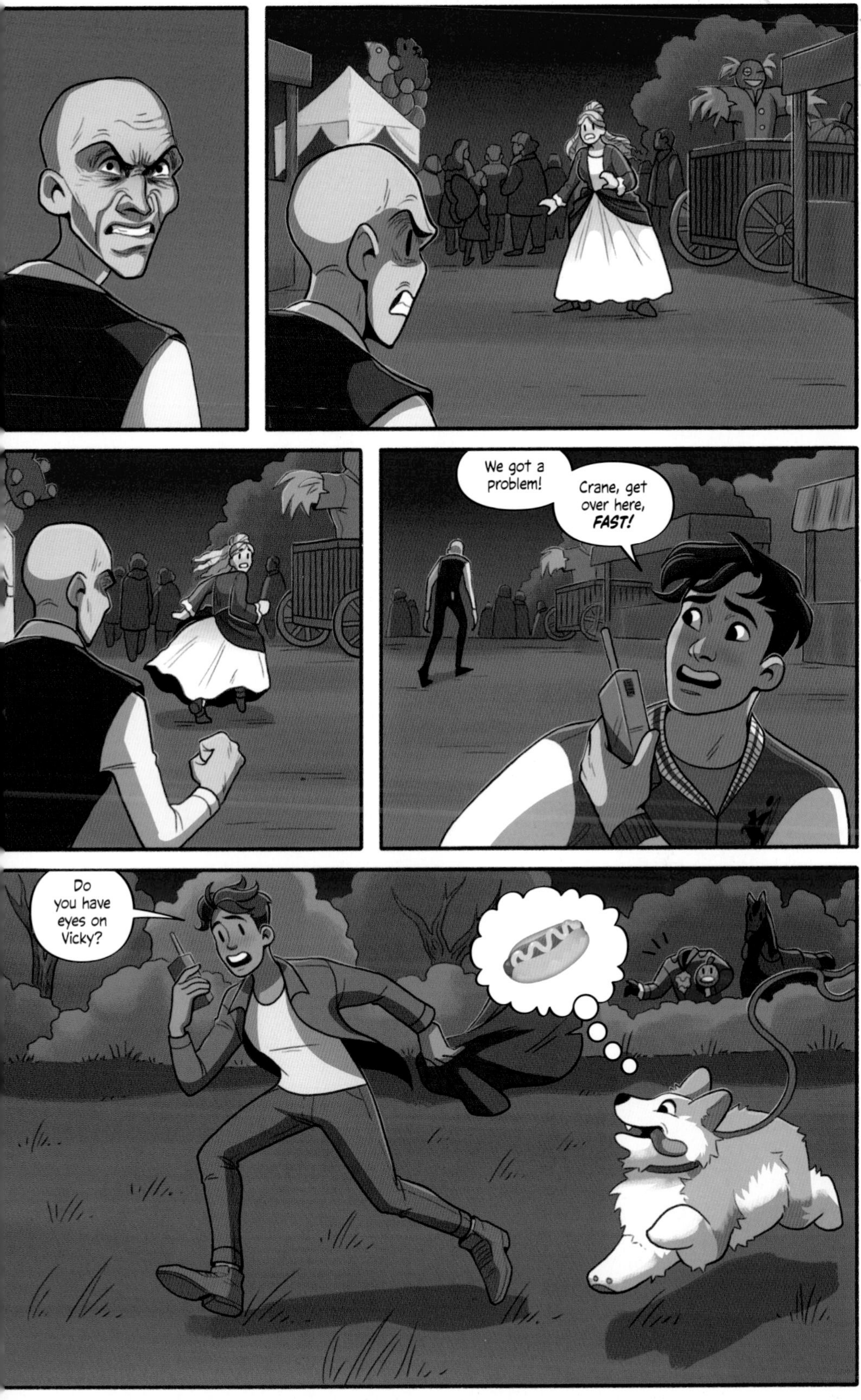
We got a problem!
Crane, get over here, **FAST!**
Do you have eyes on Vicky?

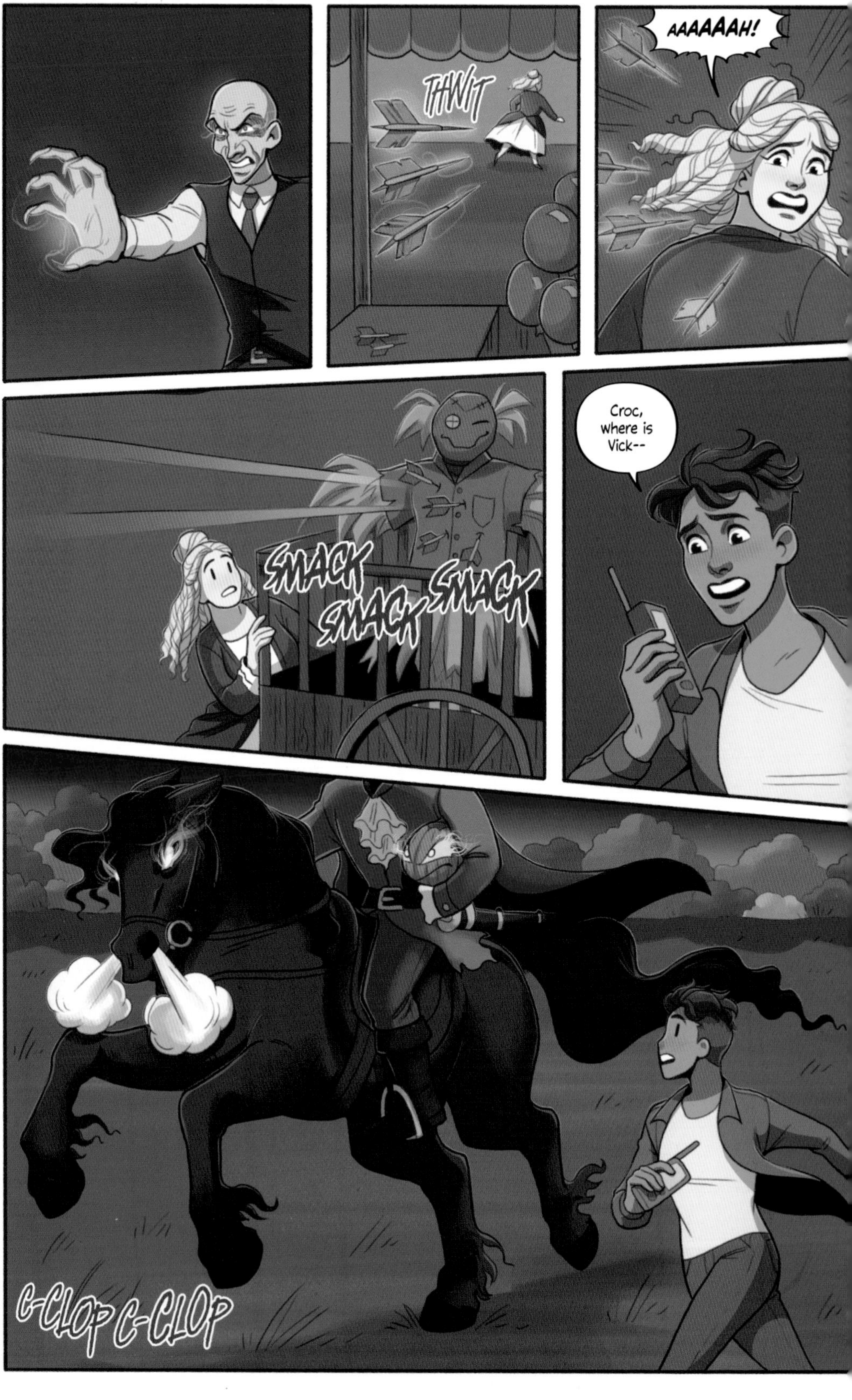
THWIT
AAAAAAH!
SMACK
SMACK
SMACK
Croc, where is Vick--
C-CLOP C-CLOP

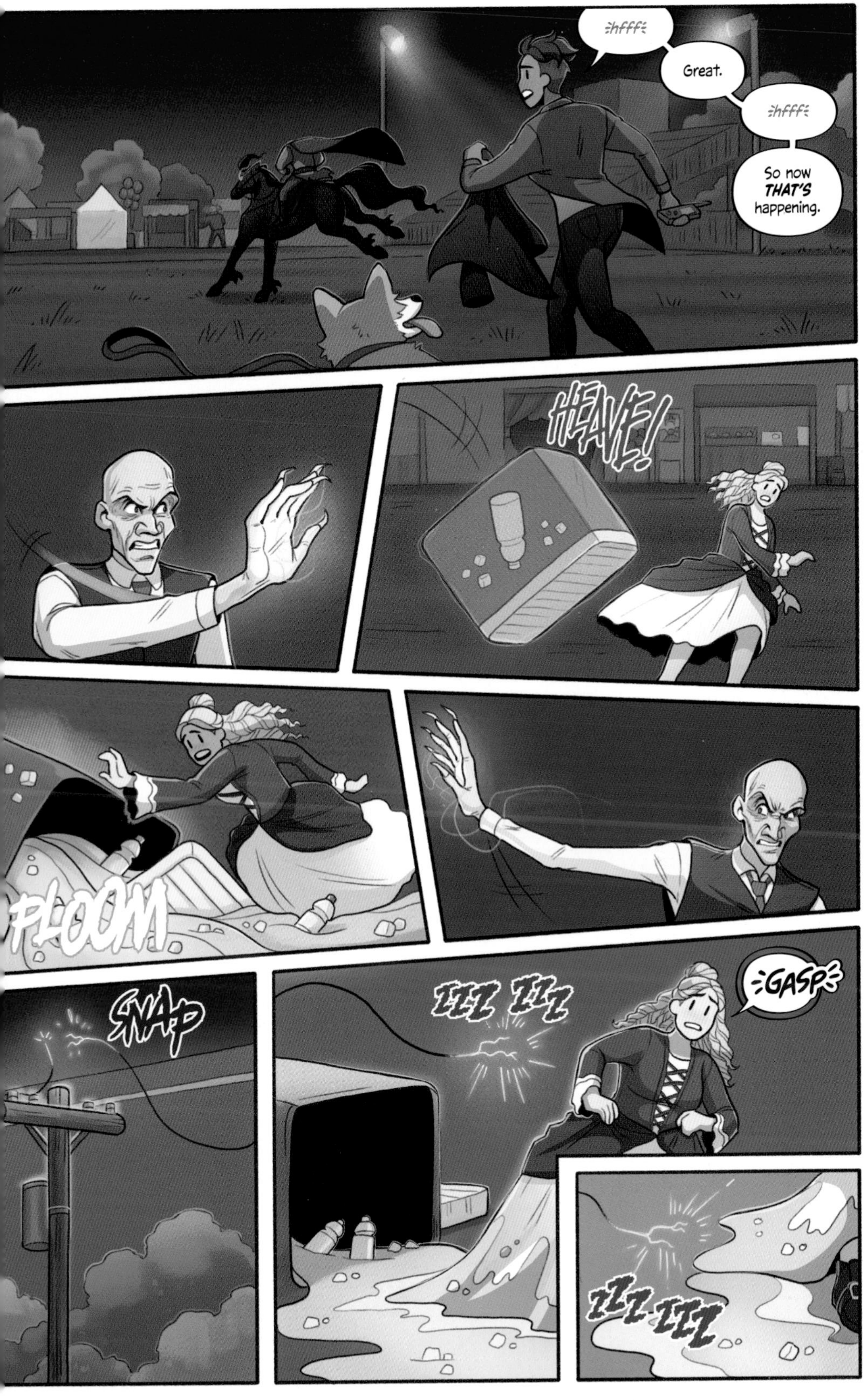

hfff
Great.
hfff
So now **THAT'S** happening.
HEAVE!
PLOOM
SNAP
ZZZ ZZZ
GASP
ZZZ ZZZ

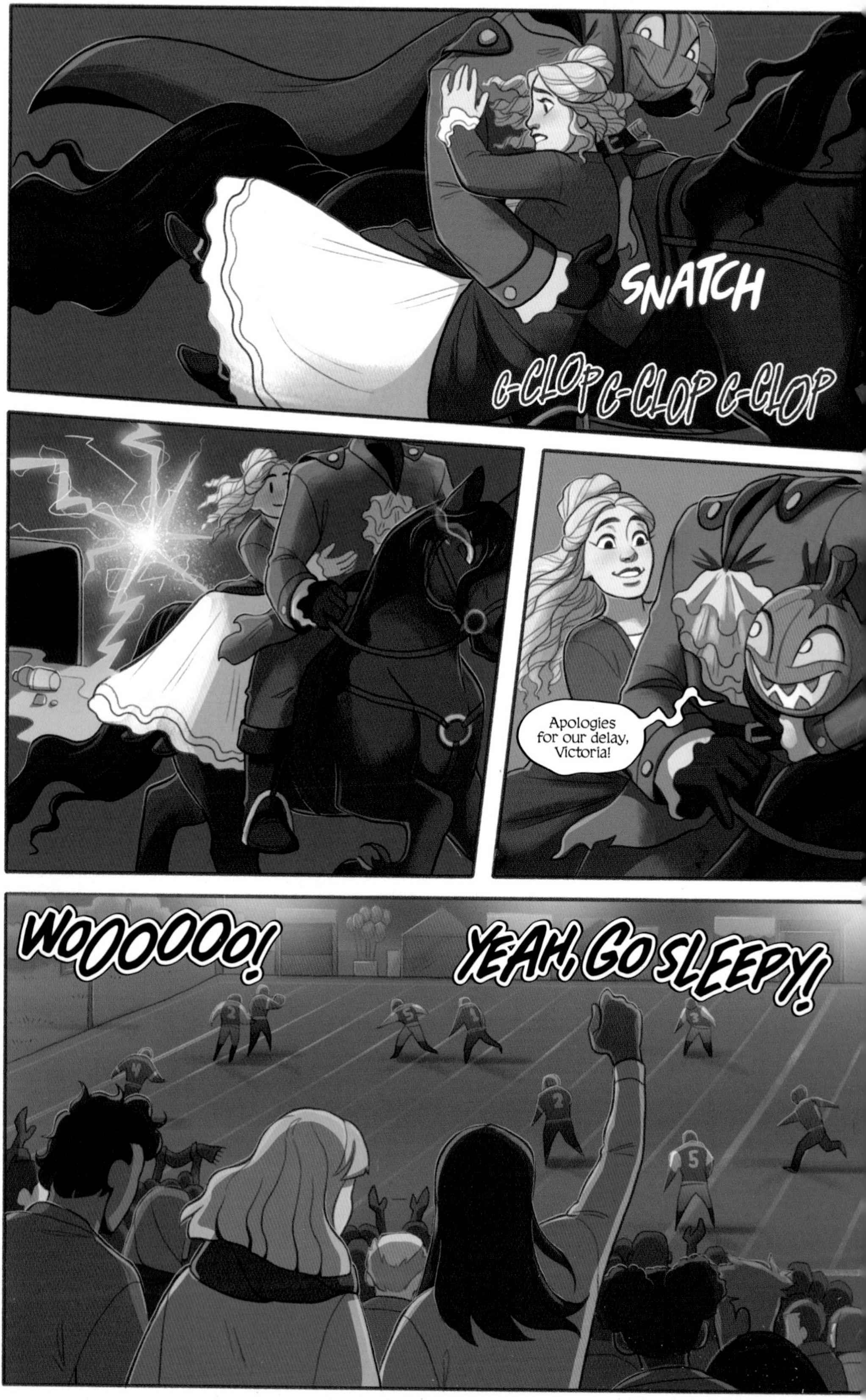
SNATCH
C-CLOP C-CLOP C-CLOP
Apologies for our delay, Victoria!
WOOOOOOO!
YEAH, GO SLEEPY!

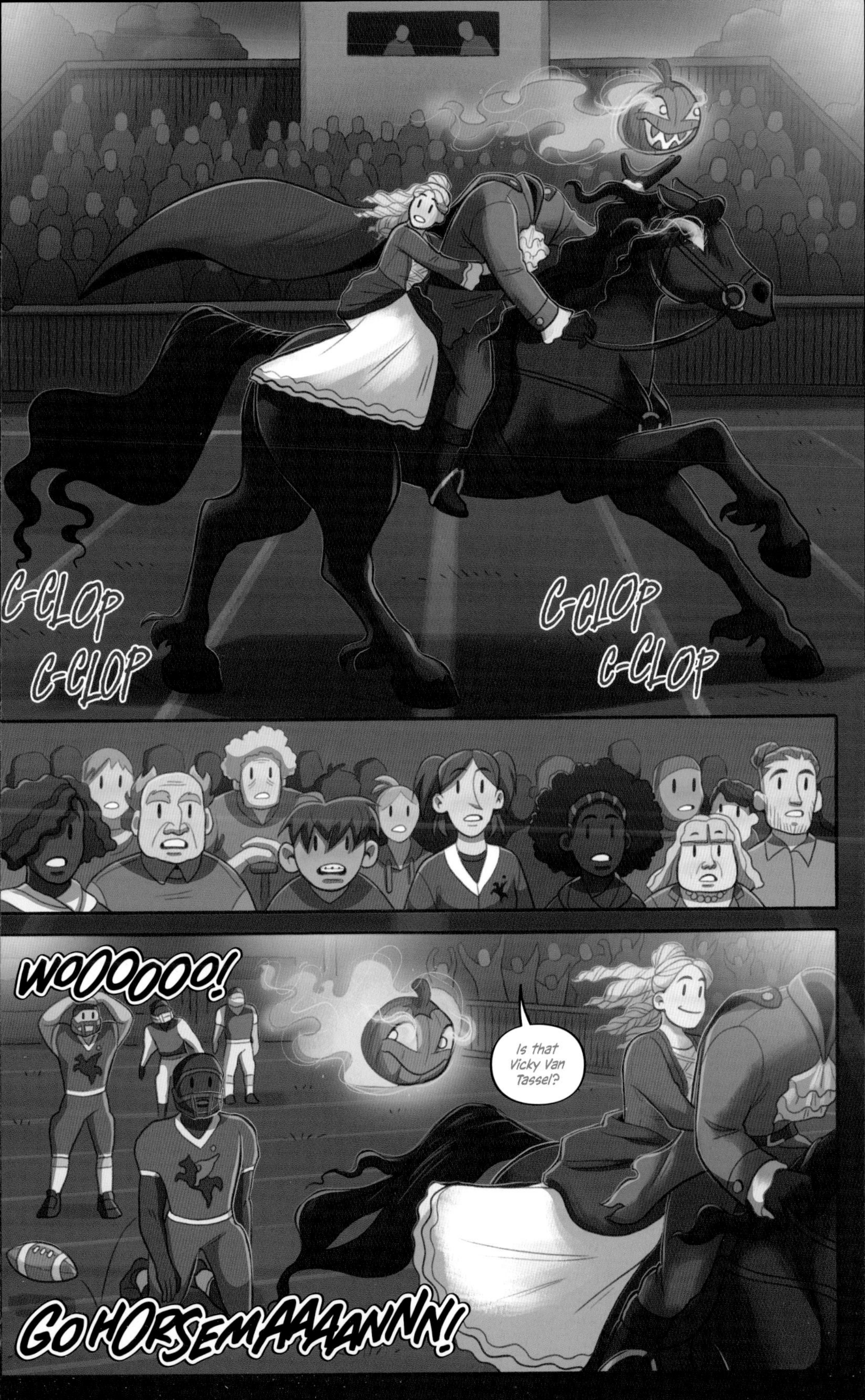
C-CLOP
C-CLOP
C-CLOP
C-CLOP
WOOOOOO!
Is that Vicky Van Tassel?
GO HORSEMAAAANNN!

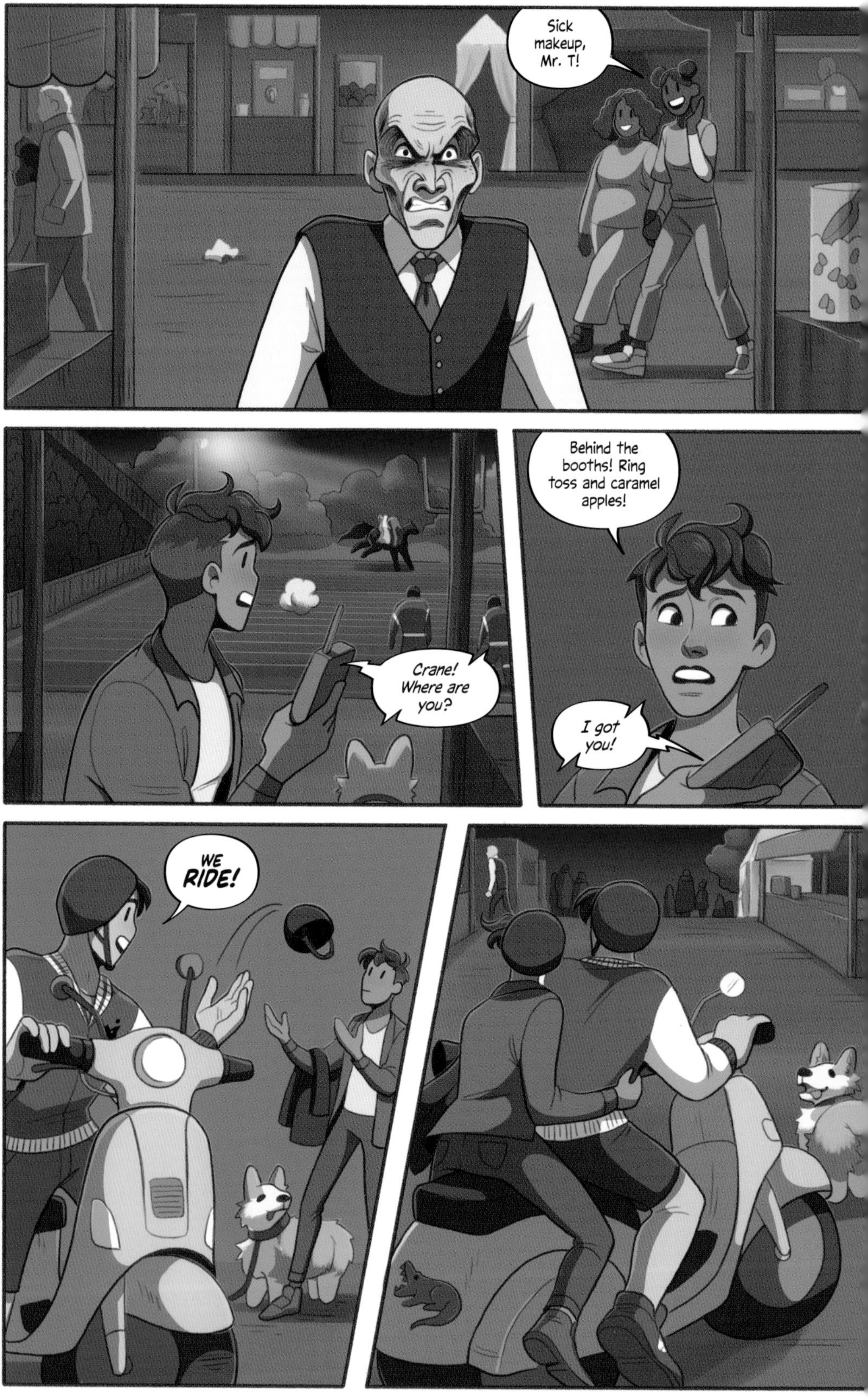
Sick makeup, Mr. T!
Crane! Where are you?
Behind the booths! Ring toss and caramel apples!
I got you!
WE RIDE!

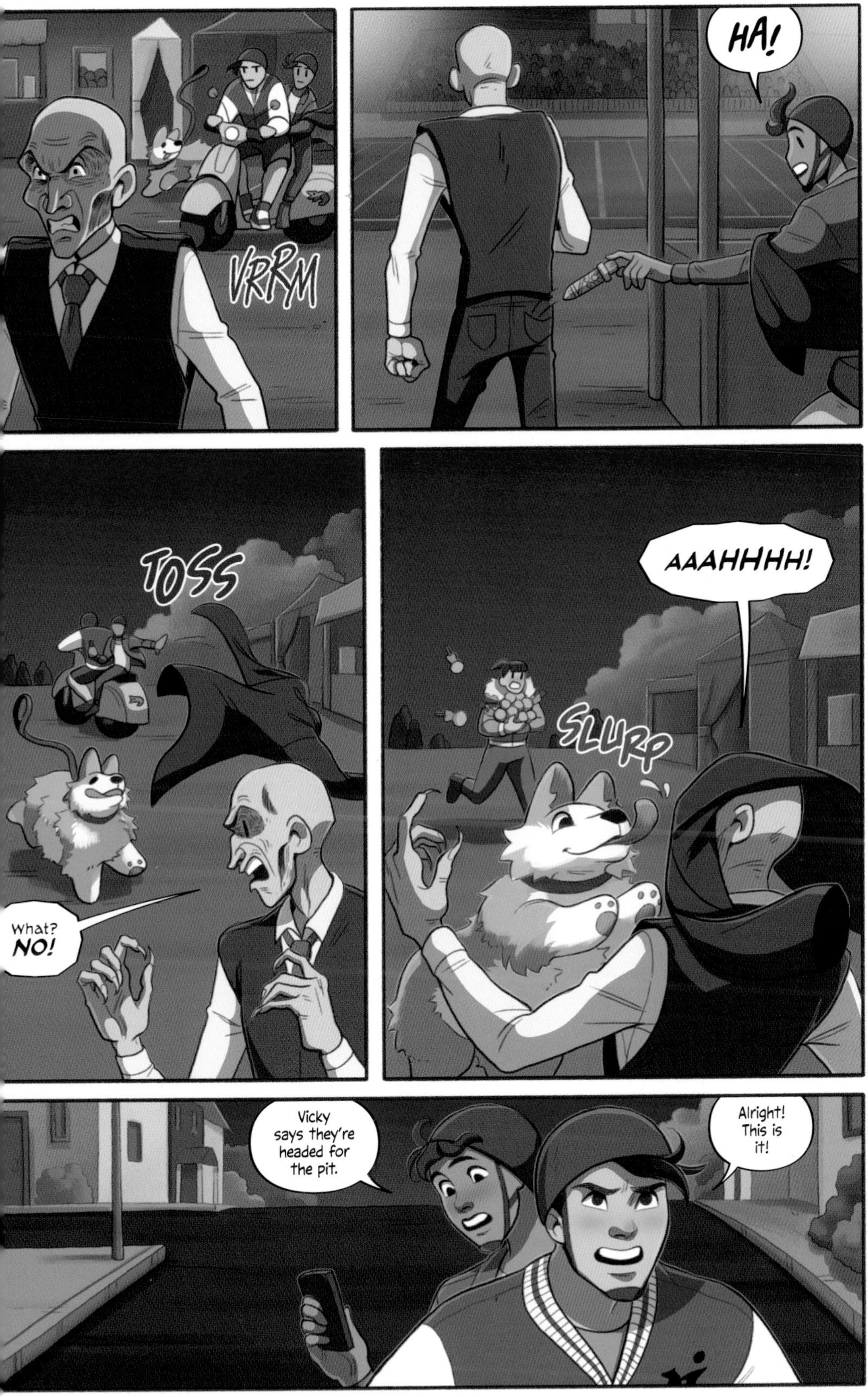
VRRM
HA!
TOSS
What?
NO!
AAAHHHH!
SLURP
Vicky says they're headed for the pit.
Alright! This is it!

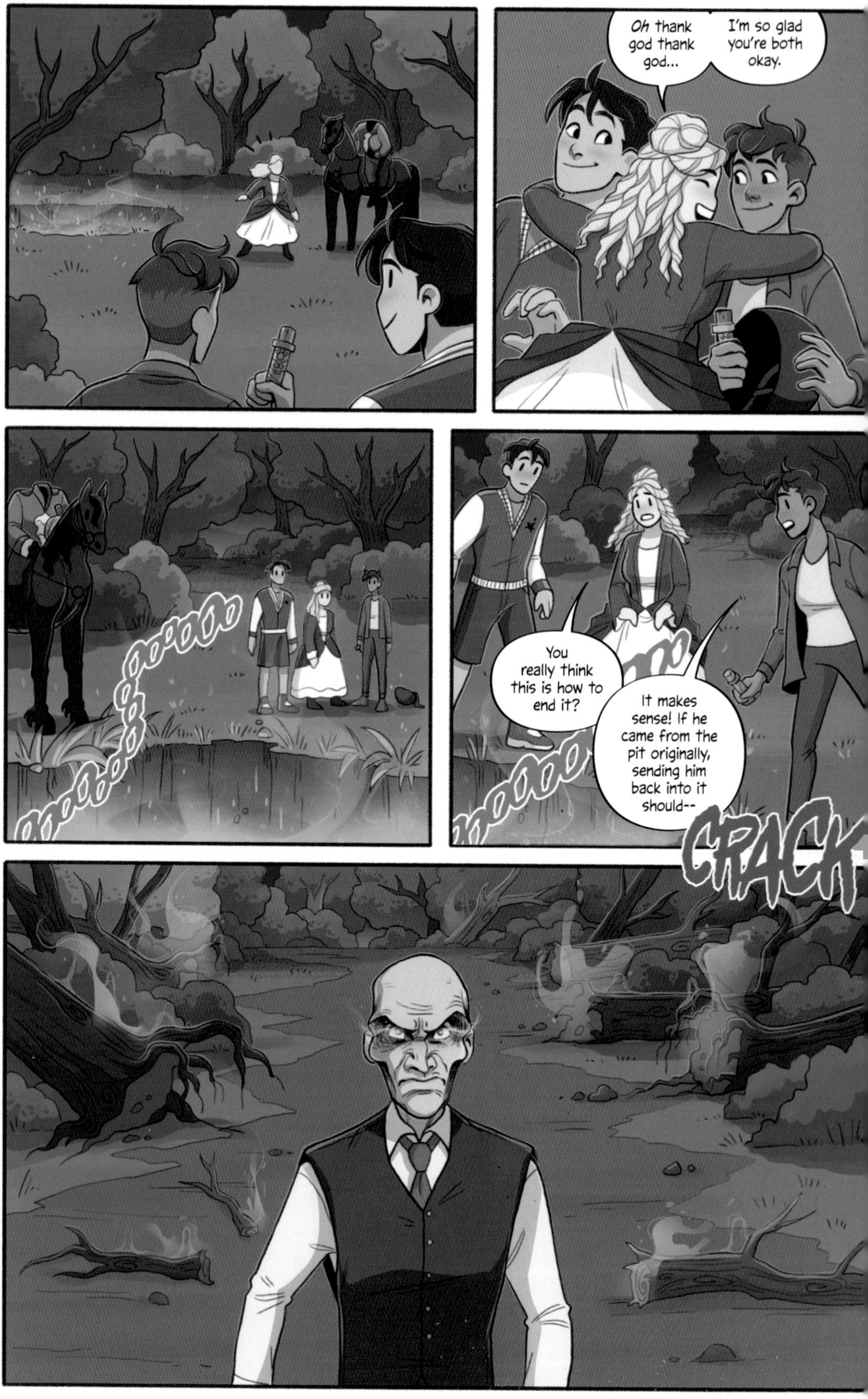

Oh thank god thank god...
I'm so glad you're both okay.
You really think this is how to end it?
It makes sense! If he came from the pit originally, sending him back into it should--
CRACK

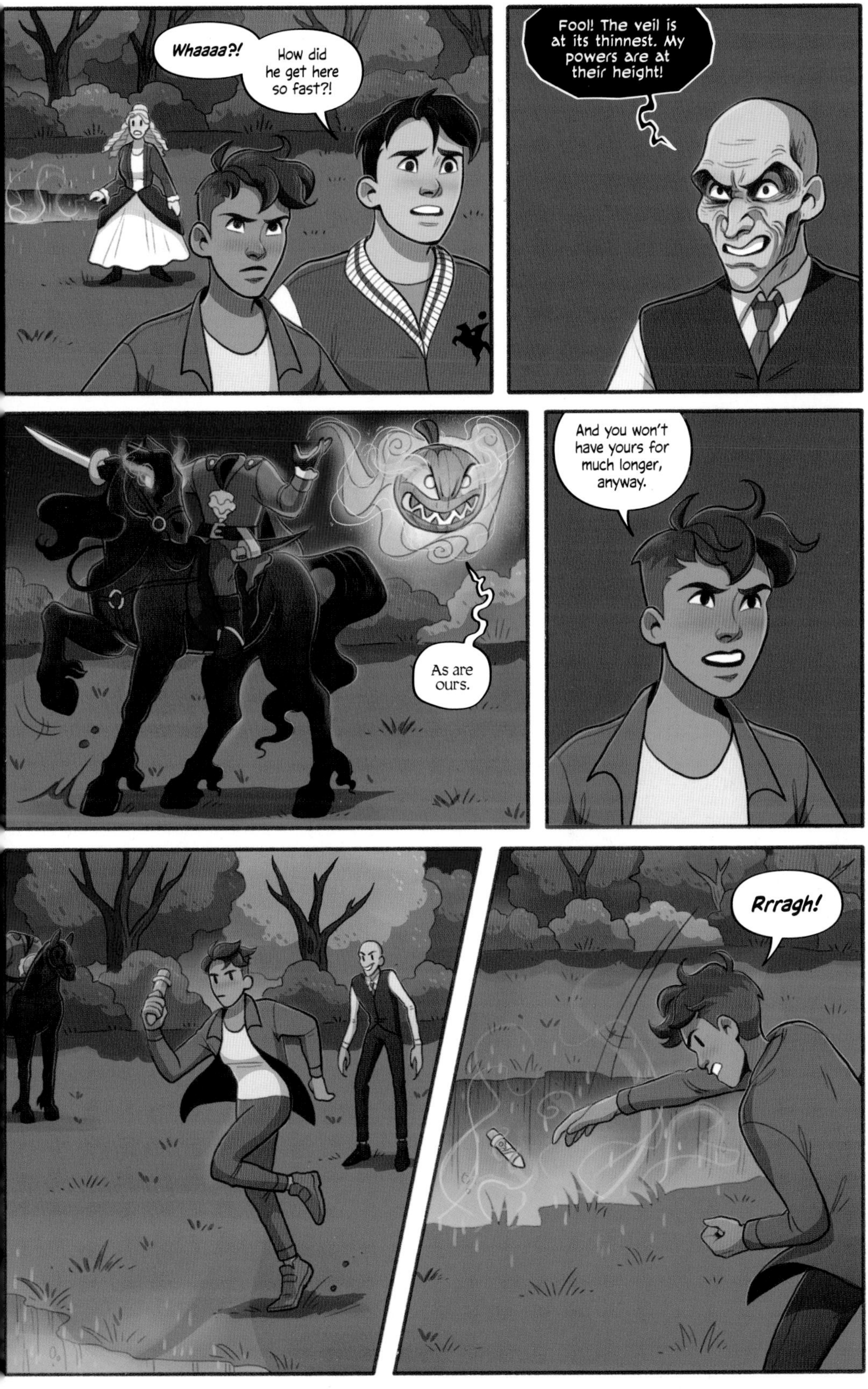
Whaaaa?!
How did he get here so fast?!
Fool! The veil is at its thinnest. My powers are at their height!
As are ours.
And you won't have yours for much longer, anyway.
Rrragh!

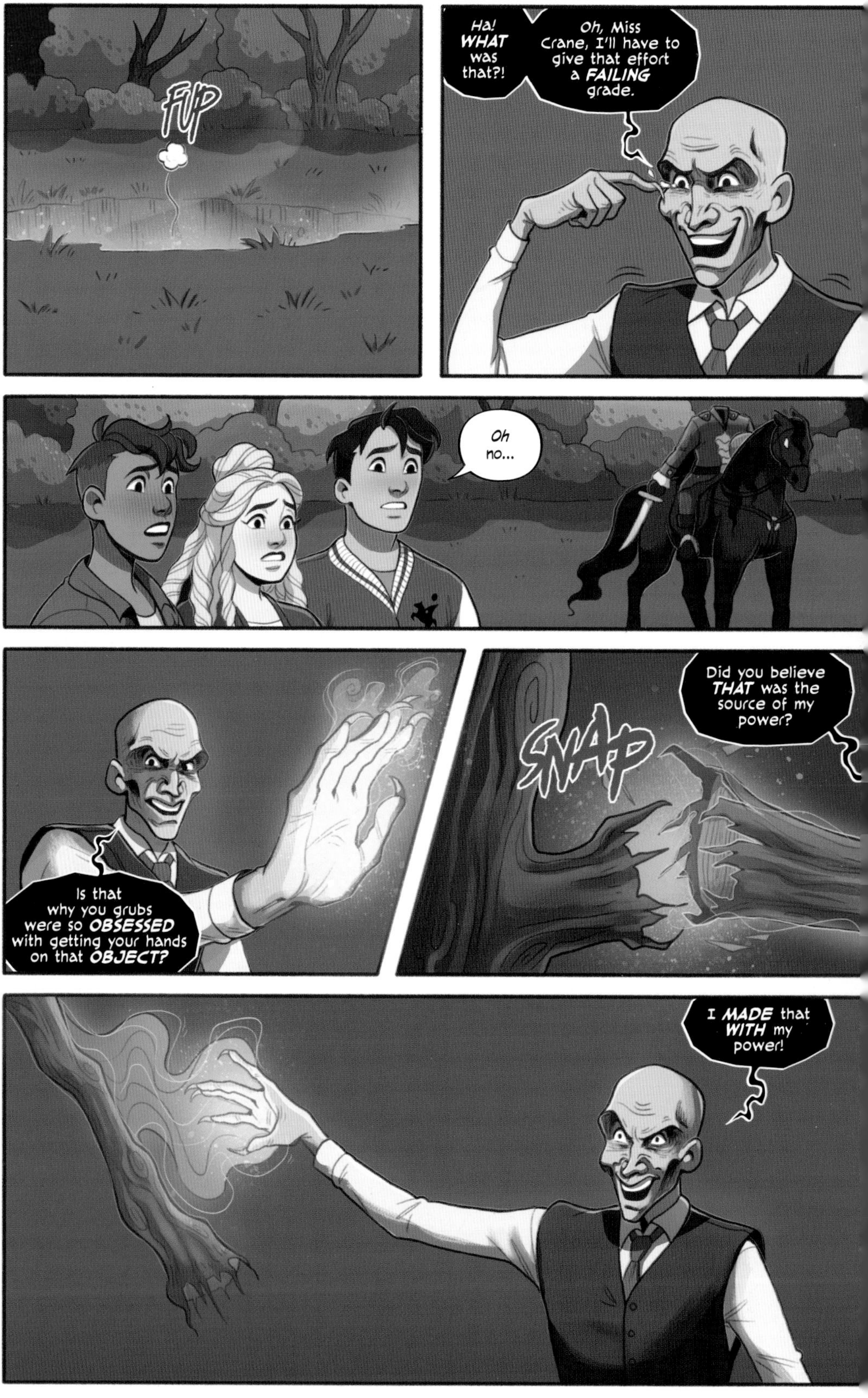
FLIP
Ha! WHAT was that?!
Oh, Miss Crane, I'll have to give that effort a FAILING grade.
Oh no...
Is that why you grubs were so OBSESSED with getting your hands on that OBJECT?
SNAP
Did you believe THAT was the source of my power?
I MADE that WITH my power!

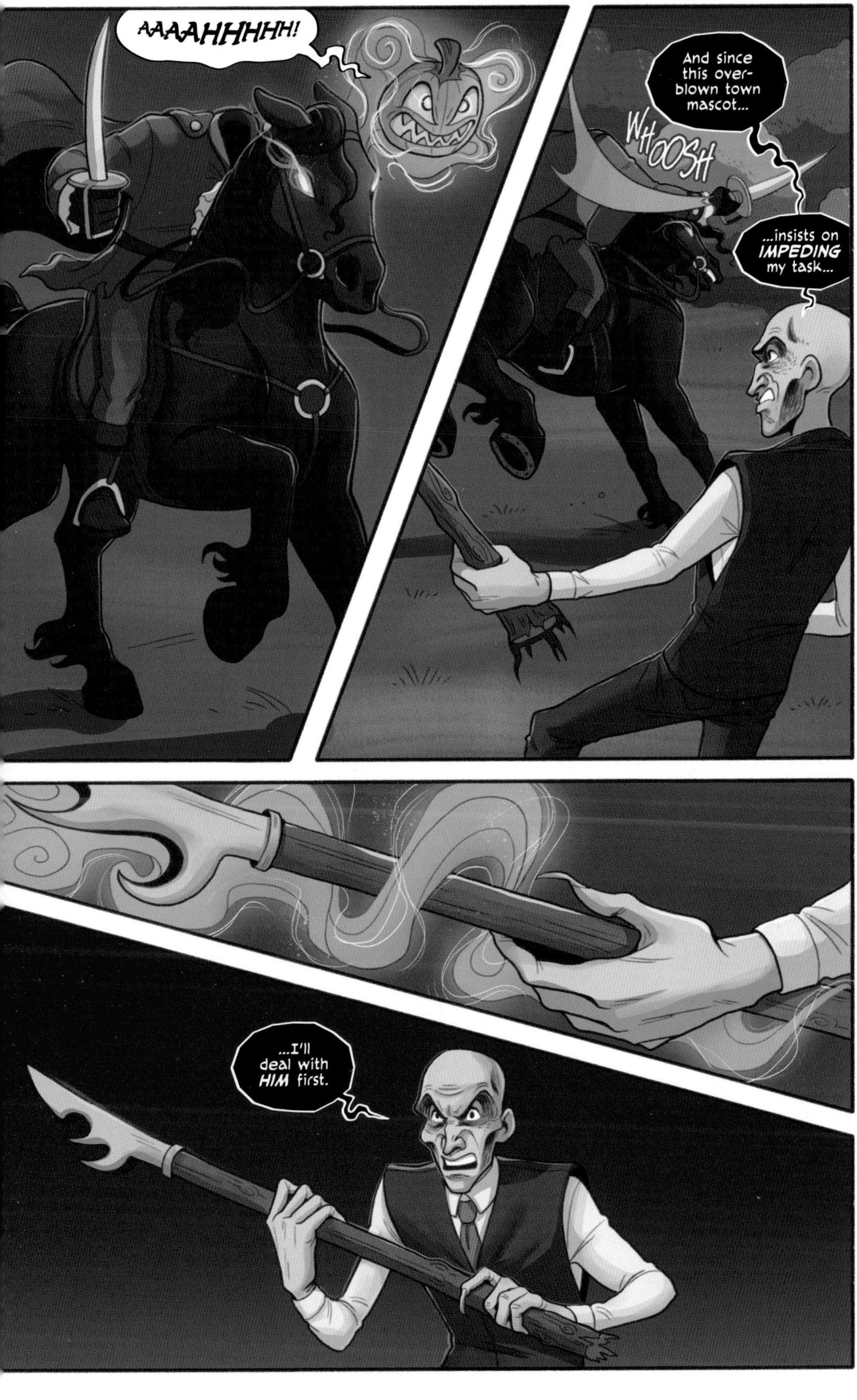
AAAAHHHHH!
And since this over-blown town mascot...
WHOOSH
...insists on IMPEDING my task...
...I'll deal with HIM first.

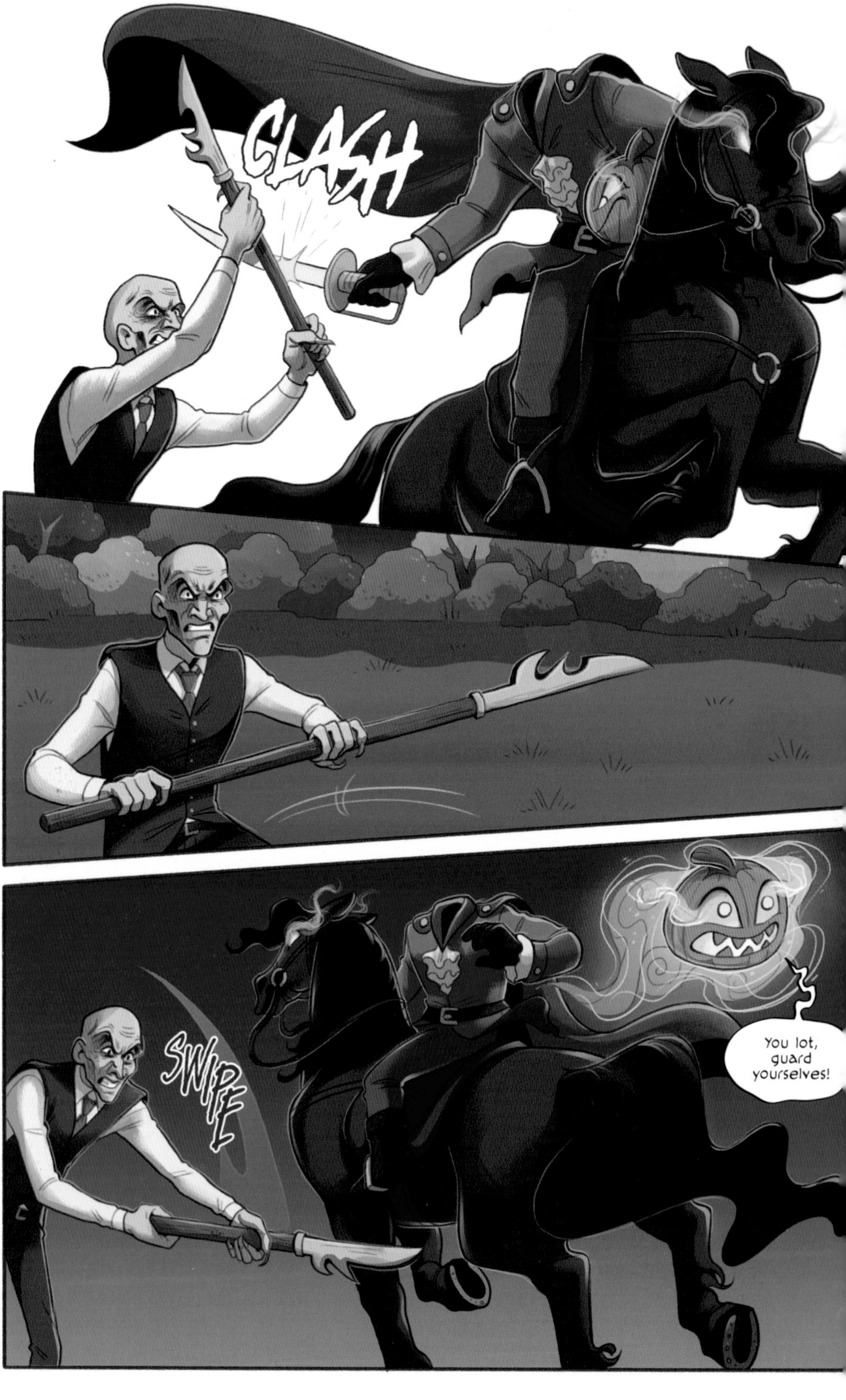
CLASH
SWIPE
You lot, guard yourselves!

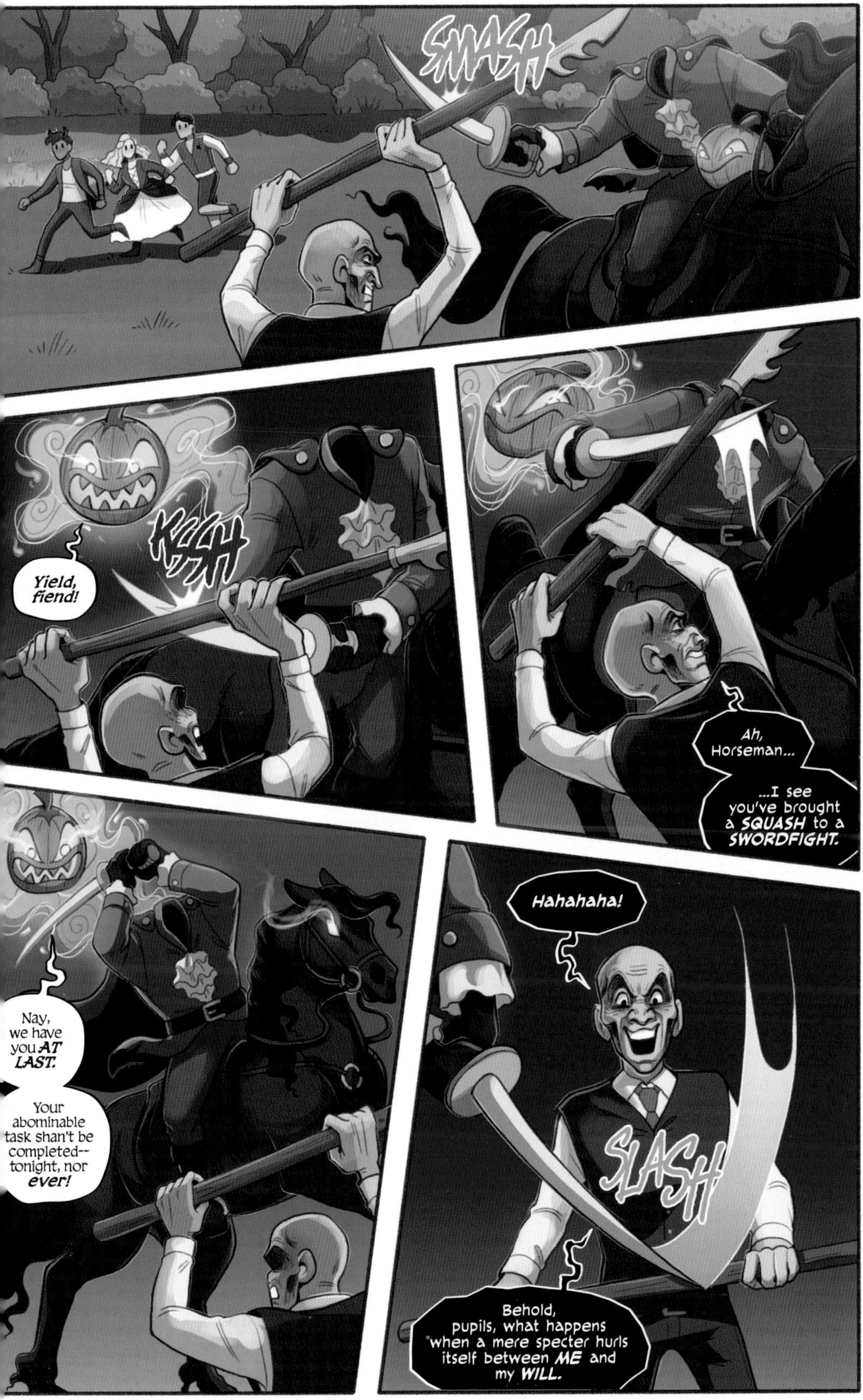
SMASH
KSSH
Yield, fiend!
Ah, Horseman...
...I see you've brought a SQUASH to a SWORDFIGHT.
Nay, we have you AT LAST.
Your abominable task shan't be completed-- tonight, nor ever!
Hahahaha!
SLASH
Behold, pupils, what happens when a mere specter hurls itself between ME and my WILL.

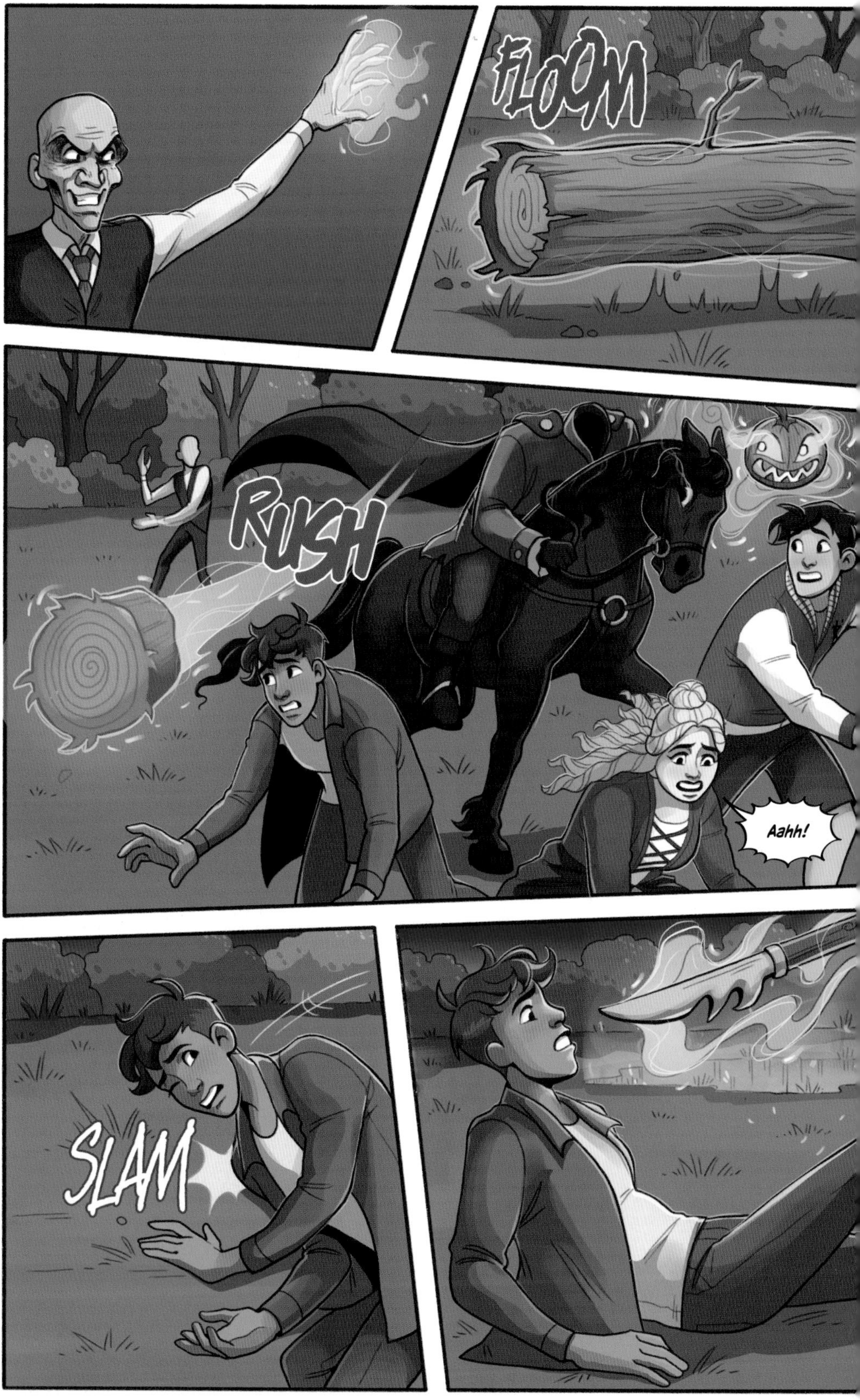
FLOOM
RUSH
Aahh!
SLAM

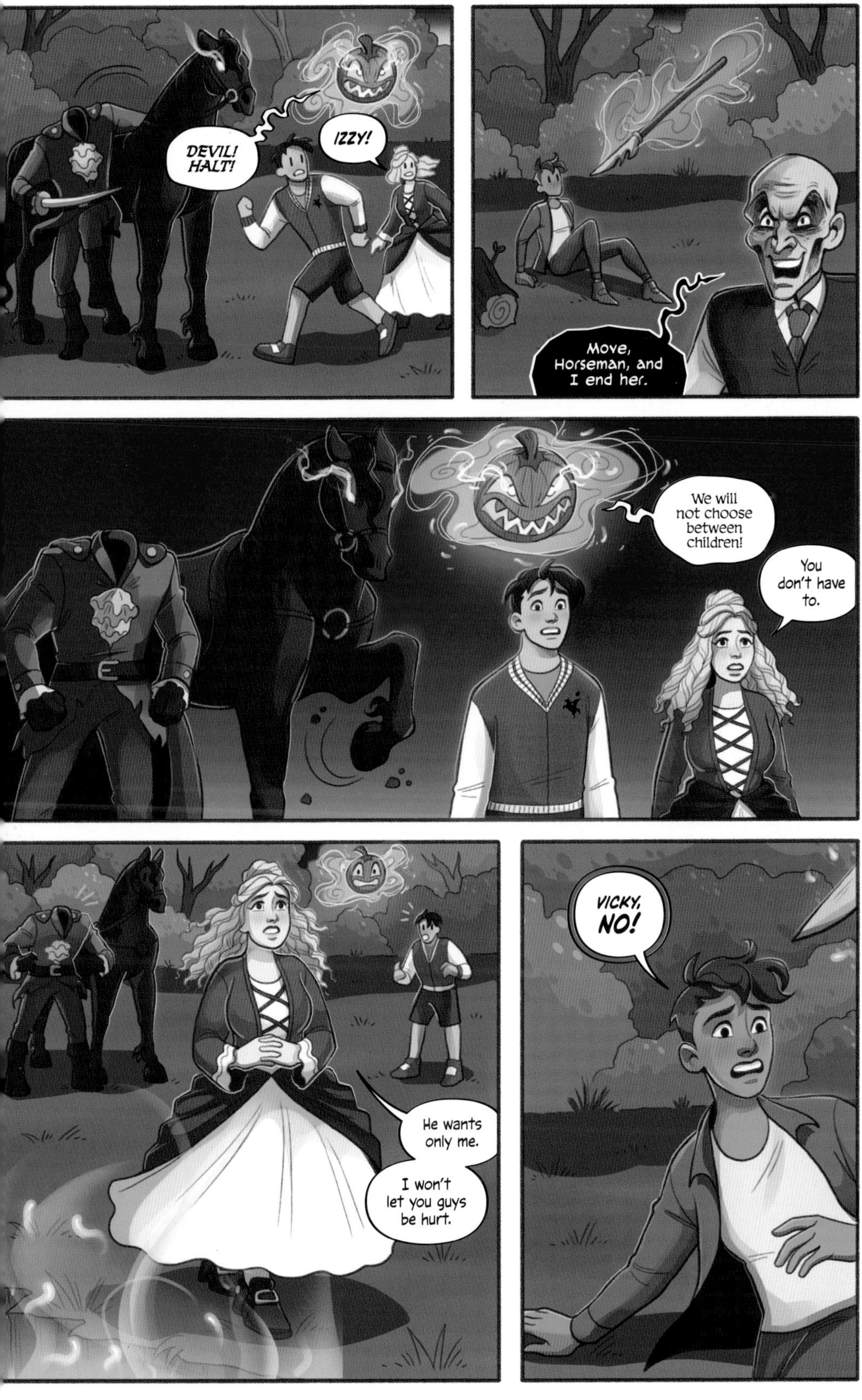
DEVIL! HALT!
IZZY!
Move, Horseman, and I end her.
We will not choose between children!
You don't have to.
He wants only me.
I won't let you guys be hurt.
VICKY, NO!

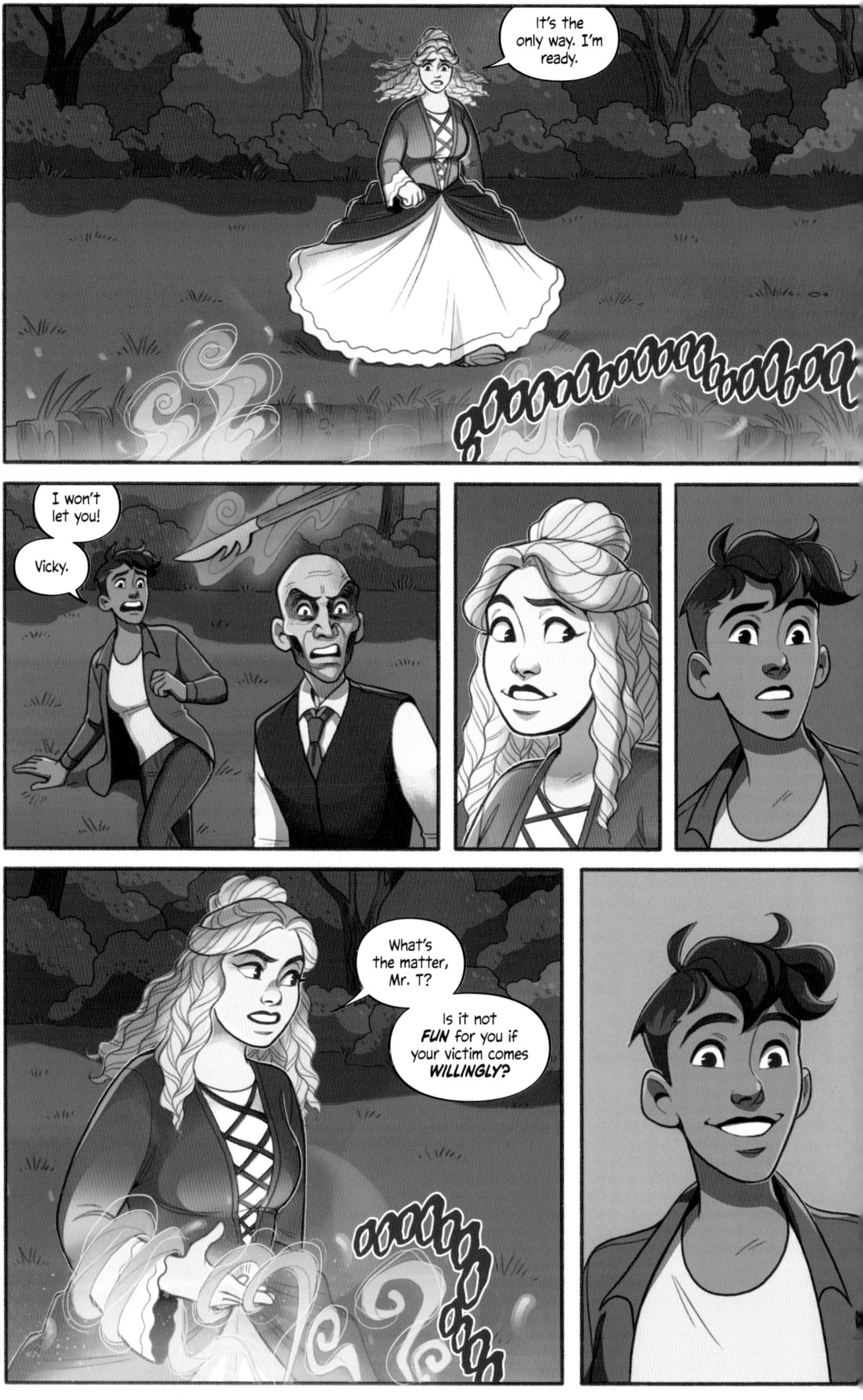

It's the only way. I'm ready.
gooooooooooooooooooooooooooooooq
I won't let you!
Vicky.
What's the matter, Mr. T?
Is it not FUN for you if your victim comes WILLINGLY?

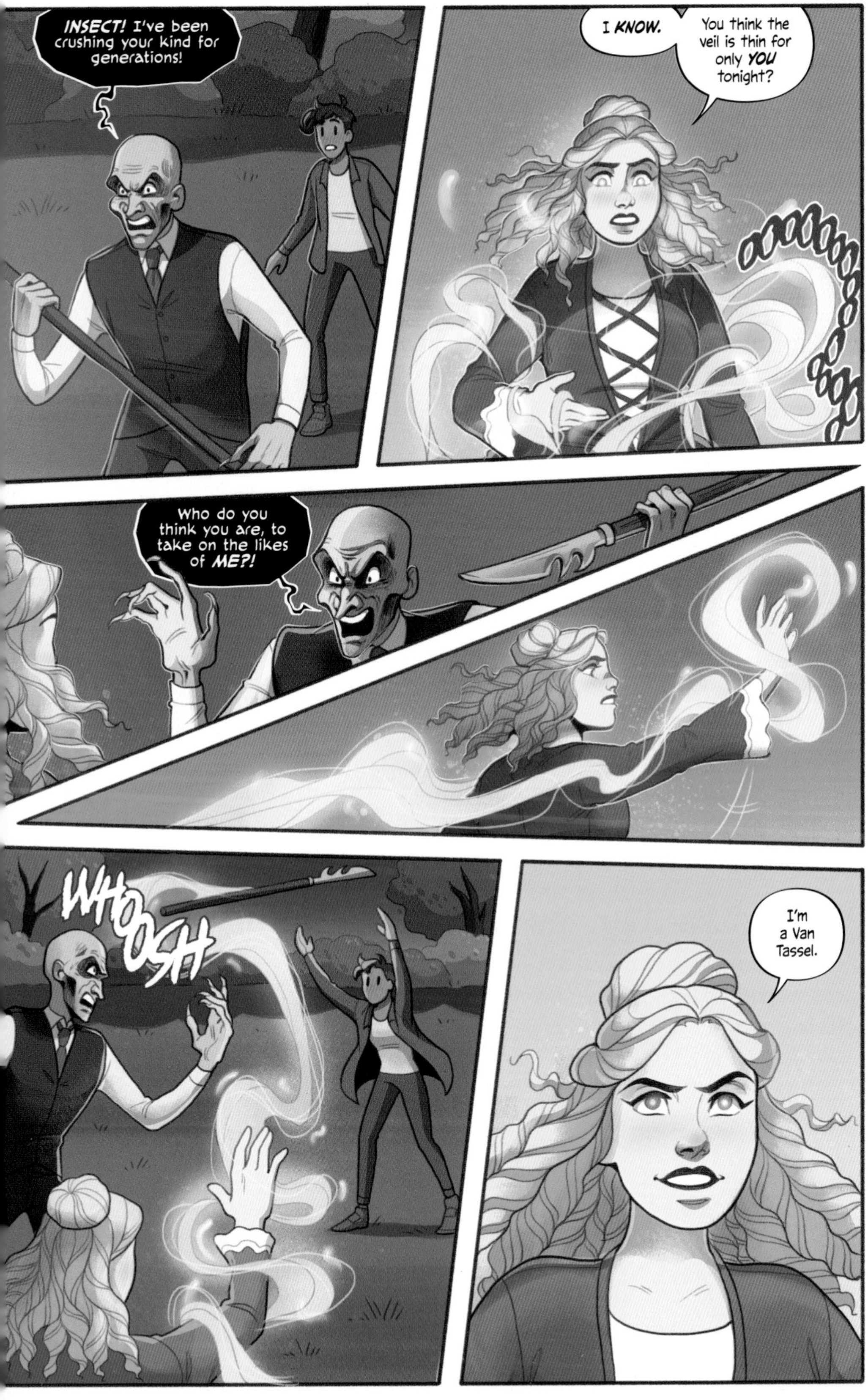

INSECT! I've been crushing your kind for generations!
I KNOW.
You think the veil is thin for only YOU tonight?
Who do you think you are, to take on the likes of ME?!
WHOOSH
I'm a Van Tassel.

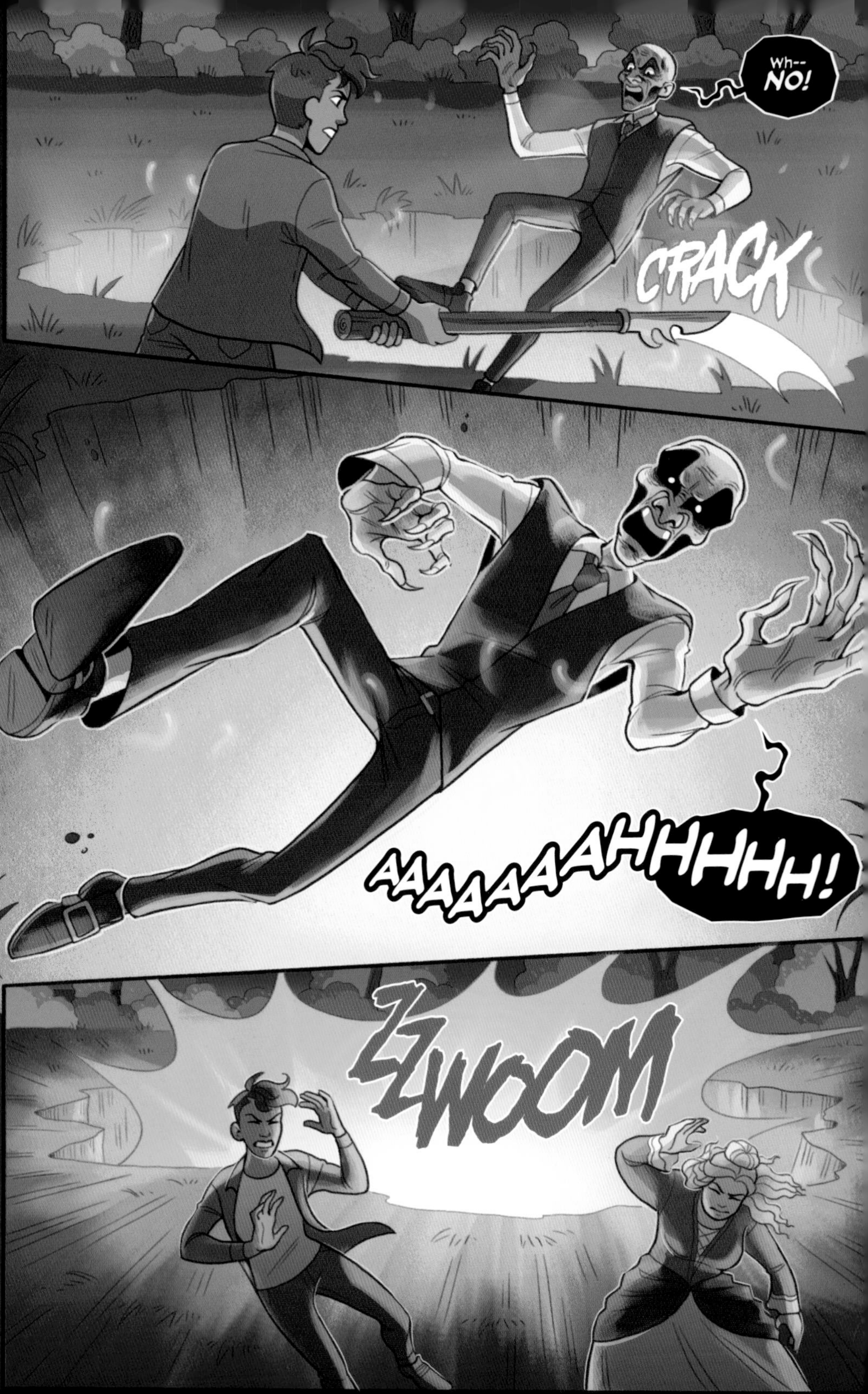
Wh--
NO!
CRACK
AAAAAAAHHHHH!
ZZWOOM

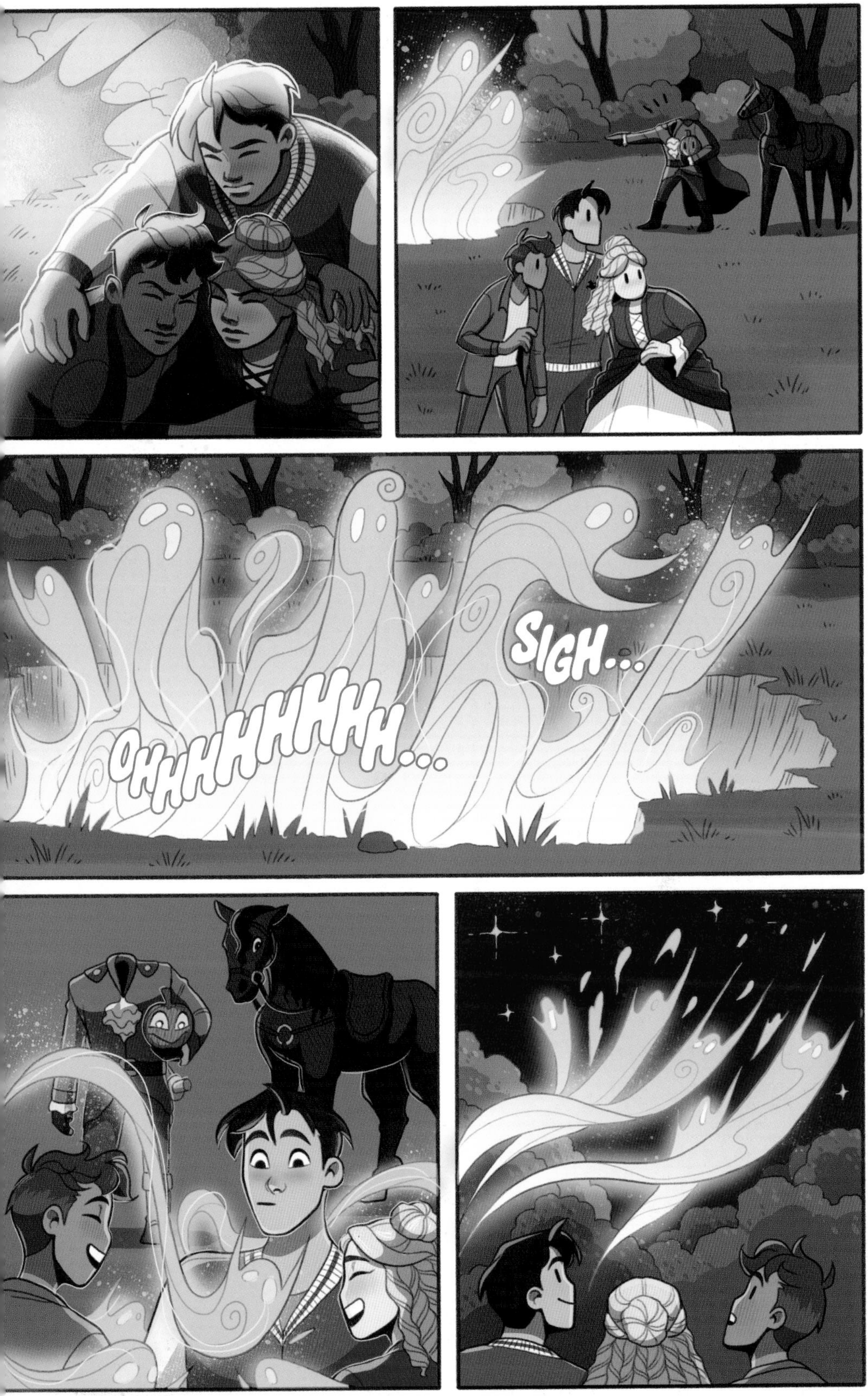
SIGH...
OHHHHHHHHH...

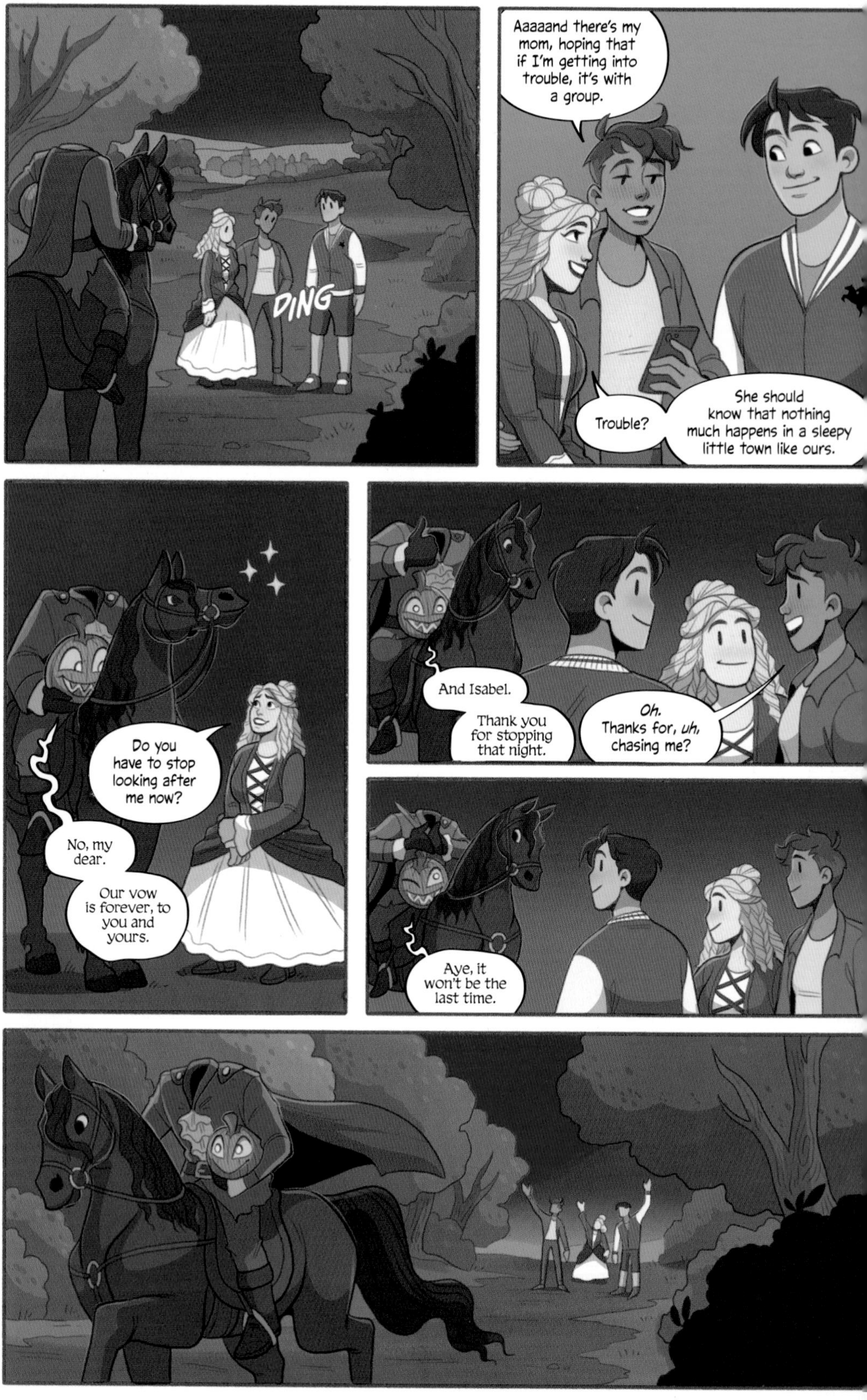
DING
Aaaaand there's my mom, hoping that if I'm getting into trouble, it's with a group.
Trouble?
She should know that nothing much happens in a sleepy little town like ours.
Do you have to stop looking after me now?
No, my dear.
Our vow is forever, to you and yours.
And Isabel.
Thank you for stopping that night.
Oh. Thanks for, *uh,* chasing me?
Aye, it won't be the last time.

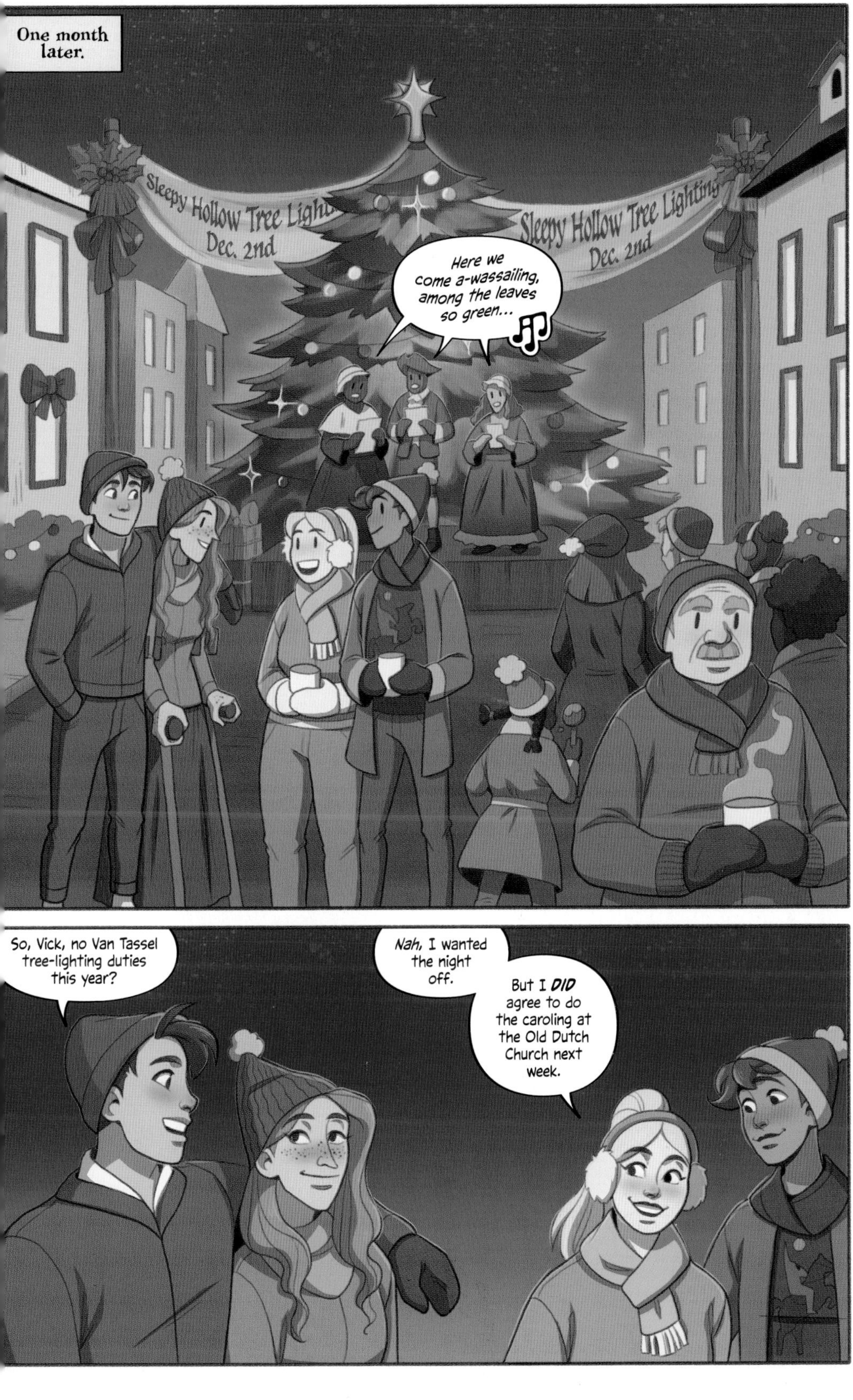
One month later.
Sleepy Hollow Tree Lighting Dec. 2nd
Sleepy Hollow Tree Lighting Dec. 2nd
Here we come a-wassailing, among the leaves so green...
So, Vick, no Van Tassel tree-lighting duties this year?
Nah, I wanted the night off.
But I DID agree to do the caroling at the Old Dutch Church next week.

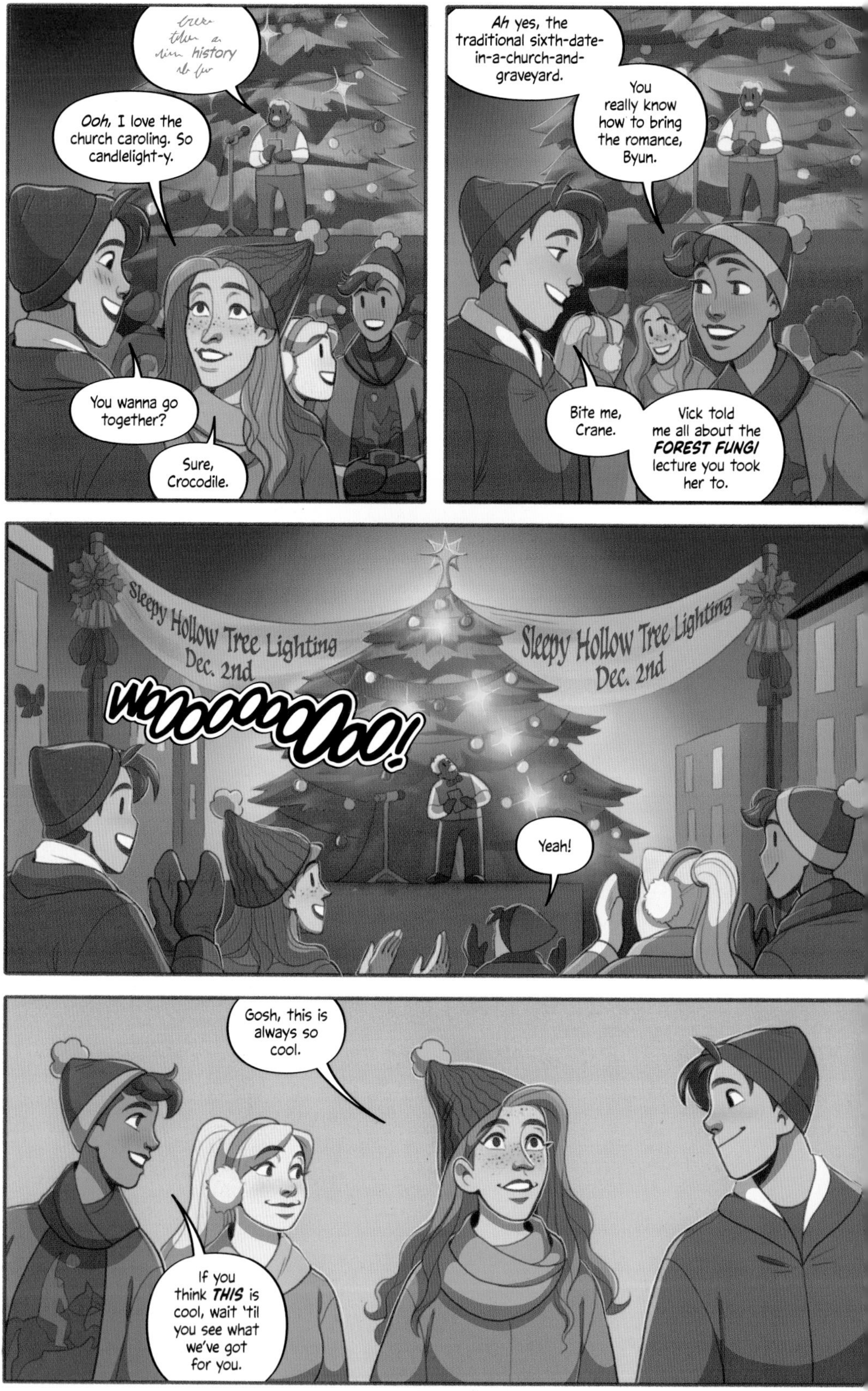
Ooh, I love the church caroling. So candlelight-y.
You wanna go together?
Sure, Crocodile.
Ah yes, the traditional sixth-date-in-a-church-and-graveyard.
You really know how to bring the romance, Byun.
Bite me, Crane.
Vick told me all about the FOREST FUNGI lecture you took her to.
Sleepy Hollow Tree Lighting Dec. 2nd
Sleepy Hollow Tree Lighting Dec. 2nd
WOOOOOOOOOOO!
Yeah!
Gosh, this is always so cool.
If you think THIS is cool, wait 'til you see what we've got for you.

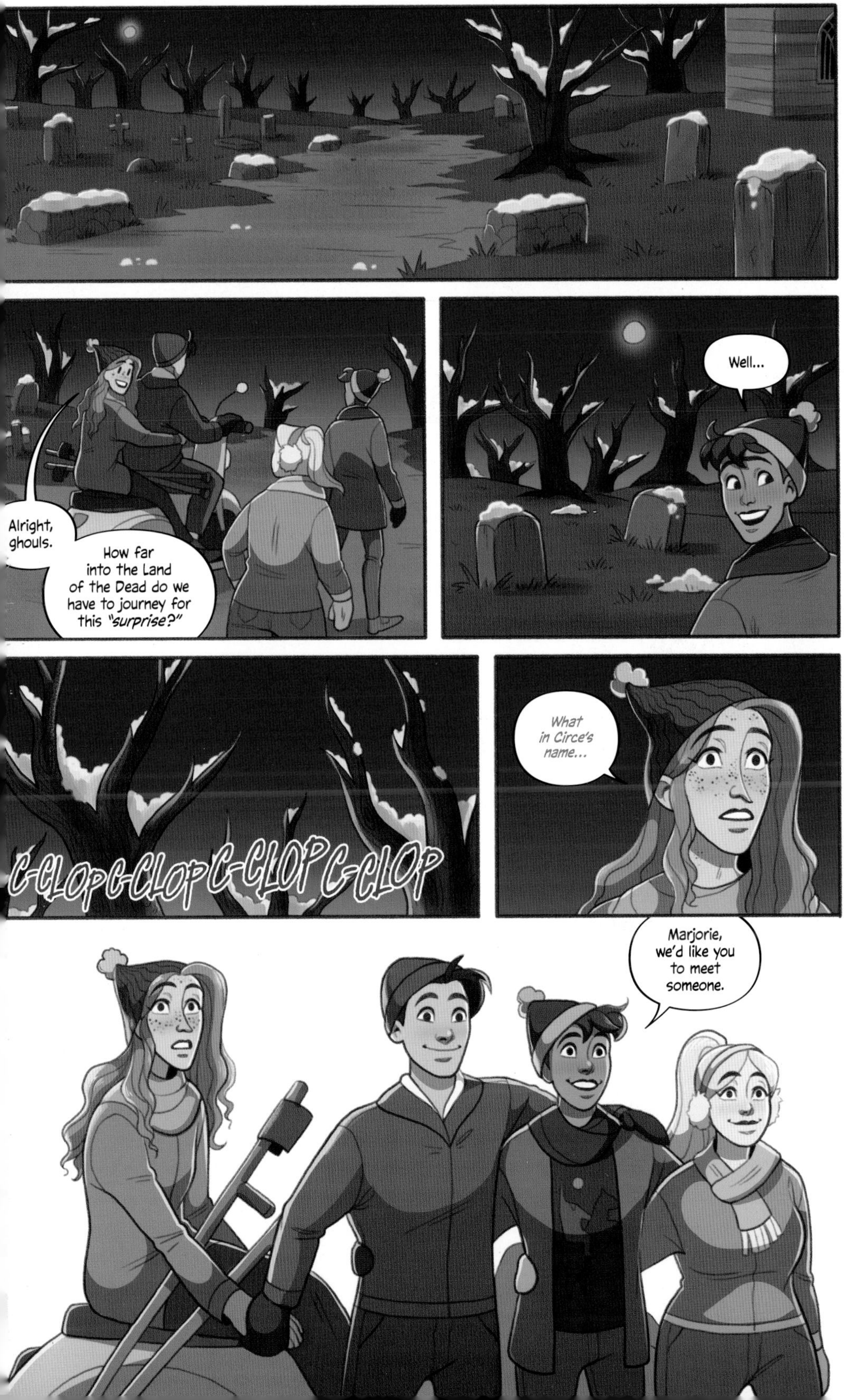
Alright, ghouls.
How far into the Land of the Dead do we have to journey for this "surprise?"
Well...
C-CLOP C-CLOP C-CLOP C-CLOP
What in Circe's name...
Marjorie, we'd like you to meet someone.

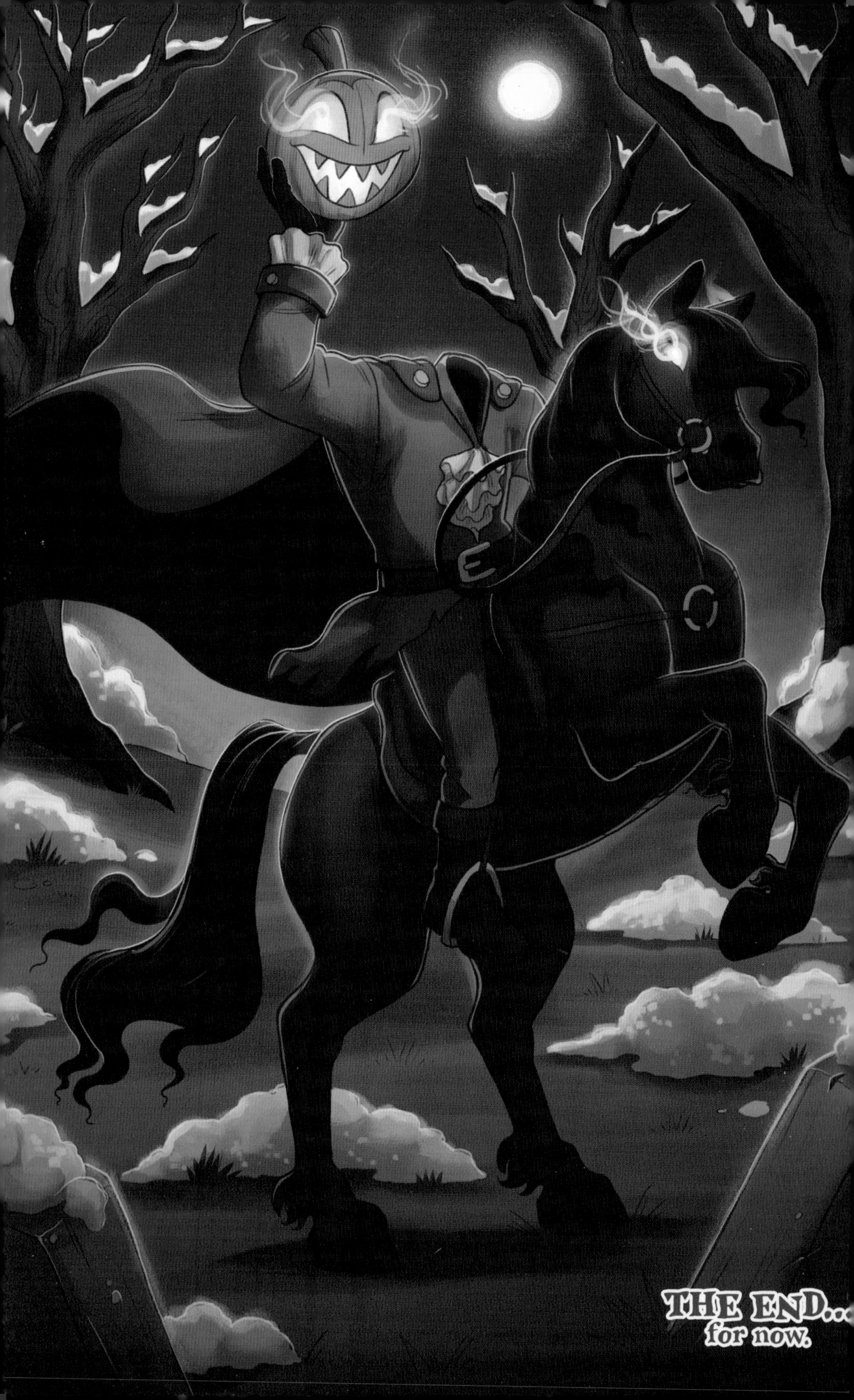
THE END...
for now.